THE BUTCHER

(A C. J. Cavanaugh Mystery)

Also by Michael R. Lane

<u>Mysteries</u>
The Gem Connection
Blue Sun
Six Weeks

<u>Fiction</u>
Emancipation
UFOs and God
The Family Stone
Long Way Home
Exchange Student

<u>Poetry</u>
A Drop of Midnight
Sandbox
Mortal Thoughts
Love & Sensuality
A Leap Year of Haiku

THE BUTCHER

(A C. J. Cavanaugh Mystery)

Michael R. Lane

BARE BONES PRESS
P.O. Box 9653, Seattle, WA 98109

Published by Bare Bones Press, Seattle, Washington.

The characters and events in this book are fictitious. Any similarity to real persons, living or dead is coincidental and not intended by the author.

Design: Bare Bones Press
Production: Bare Bones Press
Cover Art: Monika Younger

Bare Bones Press
P.O. Box 9653
Seattle, WA 98109

www.michaelrlane.com
www.barebonespress.com

Second Edition: September 2023

"Therefore rejoice, *ye* heavens, and ye that dwell in them. Woe to the inhabiters of the earth and of the sea! for the devil is come down unto you, having great wrath, because he knoweth that he hath but a short time." — Revelation 12:12

CHAPTER ONE

The award-winning London Grill, ensconced within the posh Benson Hotel in downtown Portland, is a place to enjoy the graceful décor and romantic lighting that creates a memorable and intimate dining experience. It is a restaurant that serves major celebrities and U.S. presidents. Yet on any given evening, it is characteristic to find this world-class dining establishment patronized by the wealthy to the common folk. With a menu that features traditional meals to elegant repast, and a wine list that is from a connoisseur's dream, it has no problem accommodating any culinary taste.

Bailey and Eva Singleton were celebrating their twentieth wedding anniversary at The Grill as the locals referred to it. A party of close family and friends had joined them on this momentous occasion. As was typical for The Grill, all was extraordinary. The ambience was sparkling but none more so than their table. Everyone in attendance at the party was enjoying themselves.

Bailey arrived in a wheelchair, surprising his guests that he was able to attend at all. Only a few weeks prior to their celebration Bailey had been involved in a car accident. Police and insurance accident investigators had cleared Bailey of any wrongdoing and placed the blame on the other driver who had run the stop sign. The accident saddled Bailey with a variety of physical injuries, the worst of which was the bruising of several vertebrae. His doctor prescribed bed rest until the vertebrae returned to normal. If Bailey had to be ambulatory, his doctor recommended he use a wheelchair to minimize the pressure he put on his back. Bailey was a trooper committed to participating in his anniversary celebration. The driver of the other car involved in that accident was not so lucky. He would not celebrate another moment of life.

***

The Liberated Wives Club was having their perennial monthly evening out. The day varied each month to accommodate their hectic schedules. Four women who had been friends since college had married, had children, and built successful careers, only to have divorce spoil their American dream. Kylie, Stephanie, Teri, and Michelle were all still beautiful women. They had aged gracefully into their mid-forties and had no signs of that changing as the years rapidly approached. Their self-respect suffered no damage from their divorces, although Teri and Michelle's bank accounts smarted somewhat from having to pay their ex-husbands sizeable alimonies. Kylie and Stephanie managed to break even. What they did on their cathartic evenings varied from quiet gatherings where they talked and enjoyed each other's camaraderie to unbridled events where anything went. The theme of this event involved the triple D's: dinner, drinks, and dancing.

Kylie Preston appeared the epitome of sophistication on this evening of frolic. It was a quality that came naturally to Kylie, a tall, fit, tan woman with shimmering brown eyes and an enchanting smile that could turn ice to water quicker than a blowtorch. Her hair was layered in golden brown waves framing her elegant face and flowing over her shoulders like soft moonlight without spoiling the view from the low neckline of her coral dress.

The Liberated Wives Club chose Fullman's as this month's place of honor. They had not been to Fullman's in close to a year, but it was much the same as they had remembered. The menu was diverse and delicious, the service exceptional, the crowd lively, and the wine list varied and affordable.

TLWC showed signs of a wild evening afoot. The women had arranged for a vacation day to follow in anticipation of tonight's events. Taking note of their wine intake, Kylie determined they would need that vacation day to recover rather than enjoy some leisure, as they had planned.

In spite of their negative experiences with their ex-husbands, the women still found men desirable. Any of them could find husbands in a heartbeat if that's what they wanted. For now, they found they were content savoring their independence. Even with the demands of work and raising a family, they still found "me" time. None of them were ready to relinquish that.

Kylie needed a night out. Lunsford Insurance is the Northwest's version of Lloyd's of London when it comes to insuring expensive items. As President of Acquisitions for Lunsford Insurance, Kylie had been struggling to convince the autonomous Lunsford family to join the corporate ranks. Her campaign was tanking. The Lunsford family was proud of their independence and the affordable, reliable service they provided clients from all rungs of the financial ladder. The family showed no signs of changing that stance. Their commitment was forged by generations of legitimacy, a position they could maintain due to the fact that they were the only shareholders that needed to be pleased. Since the Lunsfords were not greedy, that was not a daunting task. Kylie's waning attempts to get them salivating over fatter bottom lines if they joined the ranks was futile. Juxtaposed against their integrity and ethics, profits earned in a less than admirable manner was reprehensible, in their minds. It was a concept Kylie could not fathom. Profit was everything to her.

Besides losing that argument in the business arena, of late, Kylie was also having problems keeping her teenage son and daughter in line. Apparently, going rogue to them meant defying her authority at every opportunity. If the Lunsfords did not see things her way soon, Kylie feared serious trouble; but not with Lunsford Insurance. Aside from her recent underhanded attempts to coerce them into joining the insurance cartel, her work for Lunsford Insurance had been solid. For starters, Kylie could kiss goodbye the healthy stock options she would gain if Lunsford Insurance did not become a part of the corporate insurance conglomerate. The big problem Kylie foresaw was with the people she had been taking payoffs from for her efforts to sway the Lunsfords to join their cartel. If she did not show results soon, Kylie Preston had no idea how her unpardoning benefactors would respond. Her inability to deliver the multi-billion dollar insurance company into the hands of the insurance monopoly could produce serious negative consequences. If the fact got out that Kylie was taking money from corporate insurance despite the clever way they buried its source, it would not only mean the end of her career, but Kylie could face a number of criminal charges; the least of which would be bribery.

Kylie gulped her half-full glass of merlot to try to wash out of her mind the thought of going to prison.

"Slow down, Kylie," Stephanie said. "We've got all night to get hammered."

"You can't start too soon," Kylie said, refilling her wine glass from the open bottle of merlot left breathing on the table, hoping her merry smile fooled her girlfriends.

"I don't know about you," Teri said, "but I'm taking it slow and working my way up."

"Up to what?" Michelle asked.

"To dancing with a fine man, leading to — if he's lucky — a hot one night stand of OMG sex." TLWC laughed as if they had heard the funniest joke in the world, a reaction that would become common for them throughout the night.

"I'll drink to that," Michelle said. They all toasted the possibility of a single night of *amour*.

"Everyone have protection?" Teri asked. Michelle and Stephanie nodded in the affirmative.

"Check," Kylie said.

"Good. Let's all remember to behave like responsible adults," Teri remarked facetiously.

"Responsible adults who are ready to get their *freak on*," Teri said. The women cheered in agreement, toasting the sentiment with a sip of wine. The food arrived.

"Thank you." Michelle flashed a seductive smile to the tall brown waiter, probably twenty years her junior, who placed her meal before her.

"This looks delicious." The waiter nodded and walked away. Michelle watched him leave. "Nice butt," Michelle said. They all laughed.

"Why don't we eat before we start checking out guy's butts?" Kylie said.

"Good point," Stephanie said. "We're going to need our strength to squeeze 'em."

"And spank 'em a little." Michelle made the motion of spanking with her hands. TLWC laughed.

"Bad boy, bad boy," Teri sang. They all laughed again.

"Alright, then, it's settled," Kylie said. "Tonight, none of us goes home alone."

"Car keys, ladies," Michelle said. The women gave Michelle their car keys. Michelle called over the waiter with the cute butt. "What's your name, honey?" Michelle asked.

"Anthony, ma'am."

"Is there a policy here that employees can't socialize with customers who are attracted to them?"

"Only when we're on the clock, ma'am."

"What time do you get off, Anthony?"

"Eight."

"Would you like to meet me in the lounge when you do?"

"It would be my pleasure, ma'am."

"If you're lucky, it just might be."

"Yes, ma'am."

"One condition I'm going to insist on from the start," Michelle said.

"What condition is that, ma'am?"

"Stop calling me, ma'am."

"I'm afraid that's mandatory while I'm on the clock, ma'am. After eight…what should I call you?"

"You'll get that information in the lounge."

Anthony nodded with a smile, as if he had just received the most wonderful gift he could imagine. Michelle handed Anthony their car keys. "Could you see that these are put some place safe? We won't need them tonight."

"I know just the person to leave them with."

"Thank you, Anthony—may I call you Tony?"

"Yes, ma'am. When I'm off the clock, you can call me whatever you like."

Anthony left. The women celebrated Michelle's successful pick-up with high fives as The Liberated Wives Club settled down to enjoy their meals.

***

Bailey and Eva Singleton had taken out additional insurance policies on themselves to cover traumatic injuries not covered by their current auto and health insurance plans. That separate policy contained a four hundred thousand dollar payout upon meeting the stipulations of specific medical conditions. The sheer coincidence that all of Bailey's injuries happened to coincide with what was needed to fulfill policy conditions was somewhat suspicious to Carl Wheaton. The former Chief Investigator, now Investigative Coordinator for Lunsford Insurance, hired me to keep an eye on Bailey. What raised concerns about Bailey Singleton for Carl was not Bailey, but his doctor, Harry Boulder.

Dr. Boulder had been involved in a number of questionable insurance claims over the last few years. Each claim landed the good doctor sizeable fees from various insurance companies for treatments and meds the doctor prescribed for injuries and conditions that were difficult to pinpoint or disprove. Carl was convinced Dr. Boulder's patients believed the doctor's diagnoses. According to Carl's investigators, to their knowledge, none were faking their maladies. I saw no evidence up to this point that Bailey would alter that trend.

My junior partner Renita Harris and I had been tag teamed, following Bailey for three weeks. We saw no sign that his injuries were not genuine. Renita had taken the afternoon shift spying on Mr. Singleton, as planned. Renita would have gladly joined me for the night shift as well if it meant dinner at The Grill. I nixed that idea, explaining to Renita if Mr. or Mrs. Singleton saw us together, they might figure out we were watching. Renita claimed she could disguise herself so that wouldn't happen. I didn't buy it. I had seen Renita's attempts at disguises and they did more to make her stand out than blend in. Renita proved relentless in her attempt to sway me. As senior partner, I had no choice but to put my foot down. Tomorrow I hoped my junior partner would not still be pouting about my decision.

Bailey squirmed in his wheelchair from what appeared to be severe back discomfort. He had taken his prescription painkillers only a few moments earlier and was being wise about not drinking any alcohol. If Bailey were acting, then it would be on this evening he would tip his hand.

No one attending the anniversary celebration was aware that they had uninvited guests. Renita had insisted on giving her input before I went undercover. In the name of peace, I caved in to her demand. I played along as Renita looked me over like a drill sergeant, giving me a thorough inspection. Renita ordered me to stand erect, something that my six-four frame was already doing. Renita approved of my smooth brown face and head and gray herringbone designer suit, noting that she liked a well-groomed man. Renita remarked that wearing an open collar shirt was the right touch for a casual evening of dining out, and it didn't hurt that it helped to accentuate my fit body. We wrapped with Renita making comments that were even further beyond the pale, such as my boyish dimples, engaging brown eyes, and handsome square jaw, although, I had to confess, her compliments were appreciated.

I turned my attention to my lovely date. Destini Pendleton was striking in her steel-colored, form-fitting, off-the-shoulder dress. Her mocha skin was radiant. Her smile was something only her luminous hazel eyes outshined. In a place filled with elegance and beauty, Destini was the brightest jewel on the crown. I may be biased when it comes to the love of my life, but so what. When you love someone, no other opinion matters.

I had discovered plans for a Singleton wedding anniversary celebration at The Grill a week before, when I eavesdropped on a public cell phone conversation from Eva to finalize the arrangements. I asked Destini to join me in an undercover operation. Destini said she was glad to do it if I promised to make a night of it. My answer to her was an enthusiastic "Absolutely!" It was one of the things I loved about Destini. She could go with the flow. Pulling the double duty of being undercover and having a romantic dinner with me did not even raise one of her pretty eyebrows.

The Portland Police Bureau had called upon Destini, a decorated veteran homicide detective, to go undercover on a number of occasions. She was a seasoned professional who knew how to play the furtive game. I had a good view of Bailey from where I sat, able to look over Destini's shoulders at my suspect without concern of detection. My only distraction was the desire to plant a kiss on the silky bare shoulders of my covert partner.

***

A powerfully built man with blue eyes and blond hair was spying on The Liberated Wives Club from a table for two on the opposite side of the room. He, too, was enjoying the food and a delicate cabernet sauvignon that he sipped with his meal. It would be the only alcohol he would consume for the night.

Look at her, he thought with pure disdain. *She's having a great time, but at whose expense? I wonder how many lives she's ruined to pay for her expensive clothes and fancy hair and nails. How many people did she swindle to pay for her beautiful home and private schools for her kids? Did she ever stop to think of the people whose lives she destroyed in gluttonous pursuit of fulfilling her own ambitions of power and wealth? I'll bet she hasn't. I'll bet she doesn't miss a moment's sleep thinking about the people she betrayed to get to where she is; but she will. Before the night is over, she will.*

***

The party had ended by nine due to Bailey's worsening condition. His pain meds had made him drowsy and the people that cared about him showed mercy by ending the celebration early. Bailey had exhibited no signs of faking his injuries. By the time the Singleton party left the restaurant, I had rendered my final decision in favor of the claimant. Destini and I stayed. We had desert and coffee and off-the-clock conversation.

***

The Liberated Wives Club had made their way to the inviting lounge where dance music was blaring and drinks flowed. The lounge was large enough to be called a dance club in and of itself, with a long bar and a parquet dance floor surrounded by comfortable tables and chairs. The place was a quarter full, with no indication that this would change on a Tuesday night. The size of the crowd seemed insignificant. Those who were there showed they were there to party.

Kylie, Stephanie, Teri, and Michelle decided to set up camp at the bar. Michelle had been there for ten minutes when Tony showed up in street clothes.

"Would you like to dance?" Tony asked Michelle, tapping her on the shoulder from behind. Tony was even more dashing in his casual wear than he had been in his formal waiter's uniform, cute butt included.

"Absolutely," Michelle said, handing Teri her handbag and allowing Tony to lead her onto the dance floor. It wasn't long before Teri and Stephanie were out on the floor with dance partners, leaving Kylie watching their wine and bags.

"Would you like to dance?" a blue-eyed blonde stranger asked Kylie.

"No thanks," Kylie apologetically said.

The man glanced at the stack of handbags on the bar near Kylie. Kylie found his blonde mustache goatee combination bland. His hair hung to the middle of his neck, not the sort of thing that attracted her. Kylie was also turned off by his tattoos. He had one of a lightning bolt through a heart on the back of his left hand. Along the front of his neck Kylie saw what appeared to be the tail of a serpent coiling its way down his chest, slithering to who knows where. Kylie preferred the clean-cut executive types. She could tell he was in good shape even beneath his loose-fitting slacks and baggy dress shirt. There was something in the stranger's eyes that Kylie found unsettling but alluring. It was something dangerous that she couldn't quite put her finger on. That was a plus for the sort of man Kylie was looking for tonight.

"Pocketbook guard, huh?" he asked.

Kylie chuckled. "Handbag guard, actually."

"Would you like to dance when one of your friends relieves you of duty?" The man calmly stared at her, patiently awaiting her decision.

"Yes, I would."

"Mind if I keep you company until then?"

"Not at all."

The man took a seat at the bar next to Kylie. "My name's Harry."

"Harry, my name's Kylie." They shook hands. His grip was firm but gentle. Kylie liked that. It told her he was confident without feeling a need to be domineering.

"What's your last name?" Kylie asked.

"Does it matter?"

"That depends."

"On what?"

"Whether it's a funny name or not."

"Everyone just calls me Harry. You might persuade me to tell you my last name before the evening's done."

"Or I can put a stop to this conversation right now if you don't answer."

"You do have all of the power."

Kylie gave Harry a confident nod.

"I'm willing to gamble your curiosity will win out."

"You think?"

"Why don't I buy you a drink and let's talk about it."

"I already have a drink." Kylie picked up her glass of wine and took a sip.

"Then why don't I see if I can make you smile."

"And how do you propose to do that?"

Harry produced a quarter from his pocket. He showed it to Kylie. He let her examine it. Harry placed the coin on the bar and covered it with a cloth napkin. After waving his hand over the napkin a few times, Harry removed the napkin to reveal two quarters side by side. Kylie was mildly impressed, but rewarded Harry with a smile just the same. Harry raised his hand. He placed the napkin over the two quarters and waved his hand a couple of times over the napkin. This time when he removed the napkin, there were four quarters spread out. This time her smile was genuine. Kylie was amused.

"How did you do that?"

"It's magic," Harry said matter-of-factly.

"It's a trick, no more than sleight of hand."

"Isn't that what magic is, a good trick?"

"I don't know about that."

"It made you smile. That's all I care about."

Kylie thought about what Harry said for a moment, trying to decipher if he was being sincere or delivering a line. Then it dawned on her: did it matter?

"My last name's Boulder," Harry said. Kylie snickered.

"Harry Boulder," Kylie said. "I'll bet that name is a hit with the ladies."

Harry smiled. "Not so much. Guys find it funny, too."

Kylie laughed aloud. "I'm sorry," Kylie managed to say when her laughter withered. Harry raised his hand in understanding.

"No problem," Harry said. "I could have told you my last name in the first place to get that smile out of you."

"Your name is not funny."

"Oh, yes it is."

"No, it's not."

"Yes, it is."

"Really it's not; I'm just in a silly mood."

"Don't let me stop you."

"Do you want to know my last name?"

"I know all I need to know about you for the moment."

"Really."

"For the treasures I hope to discover, names are not necessary to reveal."

"Being a little forward aren't you?"

"Forward, backward, sideways, anyway you like it."

Kylie smiled. "Anyway I like it."

Harry smiled. "Anyway you like it."

Kylie found herself drawn to this man. A man she would not typically give a second glance. A man she knew only as Harry Boulder. He had a smoky, dangerous quality about him; a mysterious stare that made Kylie feel both vulnerable and alive. *Was she attracted to him like a moth to a flame?* Kylie asked herself. *Or was it more like unwary prey into a hunter's trap?*

Normally her instincts were dead on, with people. Kylie had honed them over years of working in a people-oriented business. She prided herself on being able to draw a summary judgment on someone within five minutes of meeting them. Harry eluded her initial instincts. Kylie blamed it on being tipsy and decided to relax and see what happened.

Before Kylie realized what was happening, Harry kissed her. She liked it. Michelle returned with Tony. Michelle and Tony were grinning at each other like giddy newlyweds. Michelle noticed a glow coming from Kylie, but kept quiet about it. Tony noticed it, too. It was easy to tell the stranger was its wattage source.

"My turn for handbag duty, sweetie," Michelle said with Tony hugging her. "Why don't you and your new friend...?"

"Harry," Harry said.

"Harry," Michelle repeated. "Why don't you and *Harry* have fun?"

"We will," Harry said, taking Kylie by the hand and leading her onto the dance floor.

***

Destini and I cruised west over the Burnside Bridge in my state of the art obsidian Mercedes-Benz Hybrid sedan with the soft sounds of smooth jazz emanating from my first-class sound system. It was not yet eleven and traffic was light; not abnormal for an uneventful Tuesday night in Portland. Destini had laid her head to rest on my shoulder, enjoying our moment of mutual bliss. Her tender side always amazed me. I had seen so much of her tough side from work that I'd forgotten her sensitive side existed.

"That's the first time we've been undercover together," Destini said.

"Was it as good for you as it was for me?"

"Better."

"So, are you ready to make me an honest man, Ms. Pendleton?"

"Are you asking me what I think you're asking?"

"You know your biological clock is ticking."

"I know maternal blackmail is not going to work. Women are having babies in their forties, these days. Not that I'm going to wait that long to have children."

"Will you marry me?"

Destini sighed. "Are you ready to accept what I do for a living?"

I took a moment to contemplate my answer. Destini being a homicide detective bothered me a great deal. Anything dealing with death bothered me. I had seen too much of it in my days as a DEA agent. As much as I could, I wanted to distance myself from it. Inviting someone into my personal space—even someone I cared for as much as Destini, who made her living dealing with murder—was something I could not overcome. I had to be honest. "I'm still working on that."

"It's better we not get married right now, anyway. I'm not ready to nest."

Driving along NE Sandy Boulevard, I cruised to a stop at the red light intersection of Sandy and NE 28th. I was disappointed in Destini refusing another of my marriage proposals and turned my head away from her to try to hide my frustration. Destini traced the scar under my chin with her finger. It was a keepsake I had from when I was in a bar fight in the service. Some have encouraged me to have the scar fixed with plastic surgery. Destini was not one of those people.

Destini gently cupped my face in her hands and turned my head to face her. Her eyes held mine for a moment. "When the time is right, it'll happen," she said. I nodded my assent. We kissed. Our kiss spanned the time it took the light to turn green.

"Mind if I come up for a nightcap?" Destini asked as I started through the intersection.

"I don't mind at all, if a nightcap's not all you're after."

***

A silver BMW i series sedan glided north along NE 28th Avenue through the same intersection where C. J. and Destini had shared a kiss. They were on the way to his place. Kylie was having second thoughts about Harry. He was a virtual stranger. Her carefree college days were well behind her. Kylie had been exaggerating to her girlfriends about the men she had been sleeping with for the past few years. Only a couple of the flings Kylie went on about happened. It had been a little more than a year since Kylie actually had a one-night stand. From what Kylie remembered, it had been physically gratifying, but left her empty in every other aspect. She couldn't even remember the man's name. All of the one-night stands of her life had occurred under specific circumstances when the time, place, and person coincided with her evaporated inhibitions from having imbibed too much alcohol. Kylie was on par with repeating that pattern tonight.

It wasn't due to Harry Boulder that Kylie was feeling apprehensive. Kylie found Harry to be charming and witty and better looking than she'd originally thought, although Kylie questioned how much the wine contributed to that last assessment. Kylie was having second thoughts about the whole idea of a one-night stand. Sex was sex; Kylie could handle that. Lately, Kylie had been craving male companionship of a more permanent nature. She wanted someone special in her life. Kylie was, quite frankly, starved for romance. The clever repartee between her and Harry had gone silent for a couple of minutes. When Kylie laid her head on Harry's strong shoulder, it was with the longing for romance in mind.

This is my final one night stand, Kylie thought. *After tonight, I won't settle for anything less than the real thing. I'm going to tell my girlfriends the truth about the men I haven't slept with. It's time to come clean. They'll understand.*

Emotionally, Kylie wasn't feeling up to sex. Kylie knew that if she wanted to back out, now would be the perfect time. Harry might get upset. Her read on Harry was that he would do the courteous thing in the end and take her home. For the moment, Kylie put her conundrum to rest and enjoyed the drive.

***

Kylie sat still on the casual beige living room sofa. The polyester queen sofa was cozy. It made her drowsy. It was approaching eleven, but felt like two in the morning to her. Kylie was nearing that time in her life when staying awake past midnight was becoming more of a challenge.

Harry's home was modest but tasteful and comfortable. Kylie noticed black-and-white photographs of people she assumed were family, and of Harry when he was a child. Family photographs made her uneasy these days. The divorce had made it so. The ones containing her ex-husband she relegated to a box in the basement. Kylie steered clear her gaze of the photographs.

Kylie did notice that every time she asked Harry personal questions about himself, he answered in a roundabout way. Kylie had found that to be the way of generally three types of people: those who were very private, those who were uncomfortable talking about themselves, or those who had something to hide. Maybe her host had suffered through a painful divorce, as well. Kylie was hoping that, instead, Harry fit into her first two category types.

Harry returned. "Don't worry, it's bottled," Harry said, handing Kylie a tall perspiring glass of water as he sat next to her on the sofa. Kylie graciously accepted the water with a smile. She had asked for a glass of wine. Harry had talked her out of drinking anymore and coaxed her into joining him for a glass of water as their nightcap.

Kylie had to admit that in some ways, she was as nervous as a teenager alone on her first big date. Kylie had expected to resolve her puzzle by the time they got to his place. She was still trying to reconcile having sex with Harry. Physically, she was still up to it, but her emotions had yet to come around. Kylie could still back out. Tell Harry she'd changed her mind and ask him to take her home. If Harry refused, Kylie would walk out and call an Uber or one of her girlfriends. If Harry tried to stop her, Kylie felt confident that her martial arts training would give her the advantage she would need to escape, even in her intoxicated state.

"If you're not feeling up to us, I understand," Harry said. It was as if he were reading her mind or, more precisely, her emotions. Kylie took a stiff drink of water. It was cool and refreshing. She took another drink.

"It's not you. It's..." Kylie couldn't finish her sentence. Saying "it's me" seemed too ridiculous to say, even though it was true.

"There's no need to explain. You don't owe me anything. I've enjoyed your company, and I hope we can see each other again—when we're both sober."

Kylie smiled and took another drink of water. "I don't remember you drinking much tonight," Kylie said.

"I knew I'd be driving." Kylie nodded and took another drink of water. Harry joined her.

"I can take you home now, or we can talk some more and I'll take you home later, your choice?"

Kylie felt the room spinning. She tried to answer Harry's question, but her words spilled out garbled, feeling like square marbles tumbling around in her mouth. Kylie assumed it was the wine catching up to her and the water flushing it through her system was creating the reaction. The spinning stopped and Kylie could not keep her eyes open no matter how hard she tried. Kylie stared at Harry, unable to move or speak.

"That must be the Ketamine taking effect," Harry said matter-of-factly. "In a few moments you'll be fast asleep."

Before Kylie could assess her situation any further, the room went black. Kylie fell back on the sofa. The glass slipped from her hand, crashing unbroken onto the floor. The water formed a dark stain on the carmine carpet. Harry casually took a sip of his water. He coolly watched Kylie's limp body. He knew he had put enough Ketamine into Kylie's water not only to make her unconscious, but to eventually stop her heart.

"I'll bet you have a hefty life insurance policy," Harry said. "Too bad."

Harry lifted Kylie from his sofa. Her flaccid body was light in his arms. "And now for the highlight of our evening," Harry said as he carried Kylie to her final destination.

CHAPTER TWO

It was a little past five a.m., pitch dark with a light rain adding to the void of night. Harry could not ask for more natural cover than if he were buried under a blanket of leaves. Harry drove the silver BMW with the headlights off. He prowled through a quiet northeast Portland neighborhood, searching for a place to park. This was one of the neighborhoods Harry had scouted for this express purpose. He was interested in neighborhoods with low theft and automobile break-ins. Nothing would be worse than to have some car thief spoil his plans. This calm middle-class neighborhood had very low incidents in that regard. It would be the perfect place to dump his cargo.

All of the street-legal parking places were taken. Harry hadn't planned on that. Each of the other nights he had scouted the area, there were four or five available parking spots. Harry parked in the deeper shadows in front of a private driveway. He had a good view of the entire street from there.

Harry killed the engine and glanced at his gloved left hand. He removed the glove and studied the fake tattoo of the heart with a lightning bolt cutting through it. Harry had done a good job, if he said so himself. He opened his coat and shirt and studied the fake serpent tattoo on his neck and chest. He had done an even better job on the serpent than he had on the lightning heart. *Maybe I should have tried my hand at art instead of what I do for a living*, he thought. Both fake tattoos had been symbolic gestures for him. The heart pierced by lightning represented the violent manner in which people he loved had been ripped from his life. The serpent marked his means of revenge.

A plump, middle-aged man wearing a security guard uniform exited a gray two-story house mid-block east of where Harry parked. Harry quickly buttoned his shirt and coat and slipped his glove back on. He watched the security guard get into his car and drive away in the opposite direction from where Harry parked. Harry wasted no time claiming the parking space.

Harry tossed the keys into the glove compartment and got out of the BMW, leaving it unlocked. He walked briskly west. He was unforgettable but indescribable, wearing a long black trench coat, dark sunglasses, black leather gloves, and a wool raven-colored toque hat with earflaps. Turning north at the next intersection, Harry walked one block and then turned west onto NW Pettygrove. Parked right where he had left it was his green Toyota Camry. He unlocked the car and jumped in.

He looked around to see who was about. The streets were clear. He removed his hat, gloves, and sunglasses. It was done. Harry was exhausted. The whole process had taken more out of him then he had expected. Fortunately for him, he hadn't made any appointments for the day, in anticipation of last night's big event. Harry Boulder wore a warm smile of weary satisfaction as he drove off into the night.

The morning sun was up with the promise of an overcast day. Harry retrieved the artificial electronic larynx from his coffee table and the cell phone next to it. The discovery had best happen in daylight for all to see. After testing the device by reciting the alphabet to make certain it was working, Harry pressed a speed dial option on the cell phone for the Portland Police Homicide Division. Three rings later, Detective Alvarez answered. Harry engaged the artificial larynx.

"Detective Alvarez," Harry said as if the two were dear friends, "there is a silver BMW, license plate ALPHADOC, parked on NW Overton Street, west of the intersection of Overton and 19th. The doors are open and the keys to the vehicle are inside the glove compartment. In the trunk of this vehicle, you will find four packages. Inside those packages are the remains of Kylie Preston. You should retrieve them immediately if you want them to be of any use for the greater good."

Harry hung up before Detective Alvarez could respond. He laid the artificial larynx and cell phone back on the coffee table. He would toss the cell phone down a storm sewer later. It was a disposable cell that Harry had paid cash for at some mom-and-pop sundry store outside of the city that he knew for a fact had no working video surveillance. *Good luck tracing it back to me*, Harry thought.

Harry stretched out on the sofa and pondered what would happen next. With terrorism being what it was, Harry expected the detectives would be concerned about the contents of the packages. That moment of choice could be critical. If the detectives decided to leave the packages where they were and let the bomb squad handle matters, it could ruin his plans. On the other hand, if the detectives elected to be proactive and do what they could to determine what was in the packages before the bomb squad arrived, all would be well. Harry was banking on the latter.

Harry yawned and stretched for a moment. He could hardly keep his eyes open. He contemplated going to bed. Harry never made it. He went to sleep right where he lay.

CHAPTER THREE

Rookie Homicide Detective Lauren McCaskill was in early, catching up on her paperwork. The Captain wasn't due in for another half-hour. The central precinct regular day shift wasn't scheduled to start for another hour and a half. Laurie, as she insisted on being called, was a five-eight, clear-blue-eyed Angelina Jolie lookalike with a sledgehammer attitude. Laurie kept her shoulder length dark blond hair pulled back in a tight ponytail while at work. She made it a habit to keep her body in top shape. The same could be said for her self-defense and weapons skills. That focused commitment to excellence for her job, while respected by most of her peers, did not bode well for her personal life. Most men found her intimidating, including some of her colleagues. The ones who didn't were often egomaniacal jerks. Compound that with the fact that Laurie wasn't nurturing and was attracted to artsy, sensitive men and Laurie was courting a formula for lifelong bachelorettehood. From her early thirties perspective, McCaskill could live with that. Her parents were another story.

The night shift detectives were out on call. Laurie was alone, and the place felt more like a tomb than a vibrant body of the justice department. McCaskill had transferred from the Vancouver, Washington police department where she was working Bunco. Laurie had wanted to move over into Homicide, but the likelihood of that was slim to none, since most of Vancouver's Homicide detectives were relatively young and there were no foreseeable plans to expand the department. McCaskill applied the old adage that if you want to move up, sometimes you have to move on.

Being one to keep her ear to the ground when it came to anything involving major northwest city police news along the northwest I-5 corridor, Laurie heard about a couple of Homicide detectives retiring from the Portland Police Bureau. McCaskill also heard that the bureau would be promoting in-house to fill their positions, but they would be searching for new blood to hire as rookie detectives. Laurie contacted Portland Homicide Captain Kelby Williamsen to let him know she was interested. Captain Williamsen agreed to put her name into the hat, but made certain she understood that his own officers would get first consideration.

Laurie tested number one in her group. Captain Williamsen could not allow a gem like her to get away and hired McCaskill for one of the available detective positions. Laurie was ecstatic. That was six months ago. Since then, McCaskill had been involved in twenty-one homicide investigations. The honeymoon was over. No one was treating Laurie like the new kid on the block anymore. Now she was just another homicide detective trying to catch up on her paperwork.

With a fresh start, McCaskill worked on keeping at bay her penchant for going off on her own. It was tough. Her stubborn spirit and active mind were not always willing to cooperate with what was best for the team. As a Bunco detective, her partner had accused her a number of times of doing her own thing. This earned her the unenviable reputation within the department of being a lone wolf. Laurie blamed her partner for being too slow to keep up. That didn't help matters any. Her more experienced senior partner, and thereby the lead detective, took offense. Laurie could not bring herself to apologize to him for what she regarded as the truth. It made for an abrasive relationship between them. They only spoke to each other on case matters. Aside from that, they had nothing to say to one another. Bunco was divided down the middle on whose side they were on. The more senior detectives sided with her partner. The younger detectives sided with Laurie. The Bunco Captain acted as their referee.

Captain Williamsen had gotten the straight skinny from McCaskill's Bunco Captain about Laurie's propensity for flying solo. Captain Williamsen warned McCaskill there would be none of that in his department. Laurie promised Captain Williamsen she would be a team player—and she meant it, at the time. What Laurie didn't realize was how difficult it would be for her to keep that promise. Her current partner was much swifter in all areas than her previous. Even so, there were times Laurie had to combat that nagging urge to sprint ahead on her own.

"How's it going?" Laurie had been so immersed in writing the homicide report that she hadn't noticed her partner come in. Laurie had been teamed with Homicide Detective First Class Angel Vasquez, whose real first name was Angelica. Vasquez was Laurie's brunette, brown-eyed, fifteen-year senior with more of a resemblance to Penelope Cruz. The happily married mother of two had found a way to balance her job commitment with her home life. While Angel did not exercise or train as much as Laurie, she did enough to maintain her figure and skills.

"It's going," Laurie said, stopping her flow. Detective Vasquez handed Laurie a cup of Starbucks coffee.

"Paperwork never stops being mundane," Angel said.

"That's encouraging."

"All jobs have their boring parts. It beats being shot at."

"I can't argue with that. How'd you know I was here?"

"Let's see: you're driven, dedicated, ambitious, and you have no social life to speak of. Pretty much a no-brainer."

Laurie and Angel were the sole female homicide team on the force. Laurie had taken some ribbing on that point, most of it good-natured, except for Detectives Whimple and Rockgarden (departmentally known as Schultz and Weasel). Laurie had no doubt Schultz and Weasel meant the mean-spirited, derogatory comments they had said behind their lying smiles and "just kidding" comment cover. Laurie knew she was going to have to put Whimple and Rockgarden in their place to get them off her back. When, she hadn't determined.

"Which case are you typing up?" Angel asked.

"Barry Hawton."

"Poor guy, he was in the wrong place at the wrong time."

"I don't call getting caught in the crossfire of two knuckleheads settling an argument over a fifty-dollar football bet with bullets as being in the wrong place at the wrong time."

"What would you call it?"

"Insane."

"If you keep thinking like that, you won't last long on this job."

"I need to become nonchalant about senseless death to survive?"

"You need to chalk some things up to karma, as flippant as that might sound. But whatever you do, don't lose sight of your humanity."

Laurie thought about how she considered some of her long-in-the-tooth Vancouver Homicide detective colleagues as being jaded about life. Angel, coming from that same place, made Laurie reassess her judgment.

"Yeah, well, karma's got a lot of explaining to do," Laurie said.

"When it comes to Portland homicides, that's our job. Do you need me to jump in?"

"Thanks, but I've got it. Is it my imagination, or is there more paper work in Homicide than there was in Bunco?"

"You'd know better than me."

"How do you stay on top of it?"

"I get done quickly and efficiently by staying focused on the facts. And when that doesn't work, I let my junior partner write most of the reports." Angel grinned. Laurie failed to see the humor.

Laurie knew the one thing Angel Vasquez had that Laurie disregarded was her reservoir of femininity. It was one of the greatest gifts Angel believed every woman had; just as she believed that masculinity was that same gift for men. Angel loved being a woman. She also loved being a cop. It took time, but she discovered she could be the cop she always wanted to be without sacrificing her femininity. It was a gift Angel occasionally used on her male colleagues to persuade them to go along with her way of thinking on a case. Laurie knew Angel had trained herself to keep it in reserve on the job, pulling it out when it was most beneficial to her. It was one of the weapons Angel was determined to teach Laurie how to utilize, for the same purpose.

Detective Alvarez took a seat behind her desk across from Detective McCaskill. Laurie remained focused on writing her report. Angel put her shoulder bag away in a deep desk drawer and was about to remove her black leather jacket when her telephone rang.

"Detective Alvarez, homicide."

Alvarez listened intently to the caller. McCaskill stopped what she was doing and took note of Alvarez's expression. It had turned from professional interest to intense. McCaskill knew that look. She knew Angel was fixated on ferreting the details from whatever it was the caller was saying.

"Hello? Hello?" Angel hung up.

"What was that all about?"

"I'll tell you on the way. Let's roll." Angel grabbed her coffee and headed for the door. Laurie did the same.

CHAPTER FOUR

I was still in my ivory Egyptian cotton terry bathrobe and chocolate hard sole wool slippers after having taken a shower. My morning run had been a good one, as had meditation beforehand. I was ready to start my day. I couldn't talk Destini into joining me for my run and the twin Terriers bailed on me to stay with Destini.

The love of my life saw to it that my tropical fish were fed and my zebra finches and terriers had fresh water and food. Destini had also used my time away to make us a breakfast of Greek omelets, toast lathered in strawberry jam, orange juice from frozen, and, for me, Earl Grey tea with a dollop of clover honey (for her, fresh-brewed coffee, straight).

It was just after seven, but seemed earlier to me. I was already having one of those days where I felt a step behind the rest of the world. Destini was dressed for work in a blue pants suit, gray blouse, and modest black flats. She was already wearing her shouldered-holstered weapon by the time we sat down at the kitchen table to eat. Destini and I had shared enough moments like this that I had a fair idea of what our married years would be like. Strike the job of homicide detective from the picture and that matrimonial preview would have been a done deal.

"I really have to update my sleepover wardrobe," Destini said over breakfast. "This suit is like four years old."

"No problem, bring over whatever you need," I said between chewing. "The master guest room is all yours. If it's any consolation, that suit still looks good on you."

"Thanks," Destini said with an appreciative smile.

"This is excellent, by the way," I said, pointing a fork at the food on my plate.

"The kitchen is my friend. Mind if I take your car to work?"

"That'll be the fifth time in three weeks."

"Do you mind?"

"Of course not, I'm simply curious as to why."

"It's more convenient. You live closer to my precinct than I do."

"Your house is just a few miles further from your precinct than mine."

"Not when you add up the time it takes for me to get home to get my car and drive back."

I nodded with a smile. "You like driving my new Mercedes, don't you?" I teased.

"What if I do?" Destini said with a smile. "It's better than my old Taurus."

"Why don't I buy you a new car? Go green."

"That's very generous of you, sweetheart, but a gift that expensive might be a little hard for an independent woman like me to accept from her man-friend-slash-lover. I'll go green when I can afford it."

"We could compromise."

"On the car or our relationship?"

"For now, the car."

"How so?"

"I'll make enough of a down payment on the car so that you can handle the monthly payments."

"I'll think about it. In the meantime, I have to get going." Destini wiped her mouth clean with her cloth napkin, got up, and gave me a quick kiss. I pulled Destini onto my lap before she could escape. Our breakfast kiss started a fire that Destini had to quench.

"You're a good man, C. J., who knows when to be bad."

"I'm feeling particularly bad at the moment."

"Hold that mood for later." Destini bounced off my lap and grabbed my car keys from the kitchen counter on her way to the front door. Booker, Andrew, and I followed her. Destini stopped at the front door and turned to face me, standing behind her.

"I would give you a lift to your office, but you're obviously not ready."

"Oh, I'm ready," I said, wrapping my arms around Destini's waist.

"I mean for work."

"Call it what you will." I kissed Destini. Destini licked her lips and smiled. She removed my arms from her waist as she returned my kiss.

"In case of emergencies," Destini said in a seductive whisper, "your car keys—"

"Will be in my desk drawer. I know."

"I love it when you do that."

"Do what?"

"Finish my sentences for me. It means we are of one mind."

"What am I thinking right now?"

"How am I going to get to work?"

"Not even close."

"That wasn't a one mind statement," Destini said. "I'm asking the question: how are you going to get to work?"

"I'll either ride my bike or take light rail."

"Good choices. Make sure you wear your reflective gear."

"It may draw a few stares on the light rail train."

"Very funny," Destini said as she opened the door.

"Are you free for lunch?" I asked.

"I have three cases we're tracking down leads on and a court testimony at eleven, but I might have time for a bite."

"Are you giving testimony on the Hagos case?"

"Yes."

"I thought that was a done deal?"

"Pretty much; it's just a matter of a second or third degree manslaughter conviction."

"Good luck."

"Thanks." After giving me a quick peck on the lips and saying goodbye to attention-starved Andrew and Booker, Destini left. I waved as I watched her pull away in my Mercedes. I thought she looked good driving my car. It made me smile. That thought was followed by the fact that Destini was going to work to track down murderers, and my smile disappeared.

I closed the door and returned to the kitchen. There I surveyed the breakfast mess left for me to clean up. Destini clearly didn't believe in the clean-as-you-go principal of cooking. I looked down at my terriers, seated on their hunches on either side of me.

"I don't suppose you two would like to help." Booker and Andrew looked up at me as if to say "not a chance," making a quick exit through the kitchen pet door to my enclosed backyard. "I didn't think so." I went to work, making my kitchen presentable again.

CHAPTER FIVE

"It's too early in the morning for crackpot duty," Laurie said as she and Angel arrived on the potential crime scene to investigate the anonymous tip left by Harry Boulder.

"I'm afraid that duty is twenty-four seven," Alvarez said as they approached the vehicle. As a precaution to the possible legitimacy of the caller's claim, Alvarez and McCaskill put on latex gloves. The location, color, make, and license plate number checked out. The detectives peered through the windshields. Everything looked normal. Detective Alvarez followed protocol. She had McCaskill radio uniforms to cordon off the area. Alvarez called in the Bomb Disposal Unit (or, as they preferred to be called, The Bomb Squad). The Bomb Squad arrived shortly before the detectives and checked the car for explosives using bomb-sniffing dogs. Satisfied with their initial findings, a bomb squad officer dressed to protect got inside the car, popped open the hood, and had a cautious look around. Once satisfied there, the same officer duplicated his efforts with the trunk. Inside the trunk were four neatly wrapped large brown paper packages bound with packing tape and twine. The bomb-sniffing dogs checked the packages. Once The Bomb Squad verified the packages were clear of booby traps, they gave Detective Alvarez the thumbs up.

In the trunk with the packages, Angel found a manila envelope addressed to the police. Angel carefully opened the clasp-only secured envelope. Inside was a laser printer letter addressed to "The Police." Alvarez read the letter aloud to McCaskill and anyone else within earshot: "In these packages are the remains of Kylie Preston. They are in good shape and useful for research and those in need. By now, you should have discovered Kylie Preston's personal effects inside of her purse beneath the passenger seat of this car. That is all."

"What a way to start the day," McCaskill said.

"No kiddin'," Alvarez said. "I'm banking our victim's not feeling too chipper, either."

"I didn't mean anything by it."

"I know, I know, I'm just busting your chops."

Since the case was shaping up to be a legitimate homicide and Detective Alvarez was senior officer on the scene, she took charge. Laurie watched and learned from a natural leader. Angel gave the go ahead for forensics to move in and check out the BMW and the packages without opening them. Alvarez and McCaskill rifled the car and examined the packages without getting in the way of forensics. The detectives were thorough and efficient. Alvarez found the purse mentioned in the letter stuffed underneath the front passenger seat. All of Kylie Preston's ID and personal effects appeared to be there, including a watch, earrings, and other jewelry the victim had most likely been wearing. The detectives finished their search for physical evidence before the more detailed forensics work was completed.

Alvarez had McCaskill run a check on the plate while Alvarez oversaw the rest of the operation. Once forensics were done, a police photographer/videographer was allowed to photograph and videotape the outside and inside of the car. The letter, in combination with the anonymous tip, had given Angel probable cause to haul the morbid packages, unopened, back to the medical examiner's office. Alvarez cleared the ME team to take away the packages. As the ME team carefully loaded the corpse cargo into their meat wagon, McCaskill returned with her report.

"I got a hit on the plate."

"That took longer than I expected."

"The car is registered to a Dr. Harry Boulder," McCaskill said. "I telephoned his house; that's why it took me so long."

"You telephoned the owner of the vehicle?"

"Yes," McCaskill said. "He wasn't home. According to Mrs. Boulder—the car owner's wife—her husband, Dr. Harry Boulder, is in Denver, Colorado attending a week-long medical convention."

"You don't say."

"Mrs. Boulder gave me the number where Dr. Boulder can be reached. His car is supposed to be parked at the airport parking garage because his wife hates driving to the airport."

Alvarez stared at Laurie with a look that seemed to mix disappointment with annoyance.

"Did I do something wrong?" Laurie said, dismayed. Alvarez kept an eye on her crime scene as the ME team finished loading the parcels and a police-contracted tow truck maneuvered into place to tow the BMW back to the crime lab.

"You telephoned the owner of this car?" Alvarez said in a voice that made it clear to Laurie that she was trying to maintain control.

"I spoke to his wife—"

"Car."

"Excuse me?"

"Get in the car *now*."

Alvarez marched toward their unmarked police car. Laurie was stunned. It took her a moment to catch up to Angel. The two of them got into the car. Laurie's mind raced, trying to determine how she may have screwed up. Laurie wasn't certain if it was her imagination, but it seemed to her that Angel's chest was rising and falling as if billowed by a blast furnace.

Angel stared straight ahead, as if the object of her displeasure were in front of their car rather than sitting beside her. When Angel Alvarez turned to face Laurie, her eyes bore into Laurie like a drill.

"Why did you call the owner of the BMW?" Angel spoke to Laurie in that same calm, piercing, accusatory manner she used to break down murder suspects. Laurie didn't like it, but the intensity radiating from her partner intimidated her to the point of silence on the matter.

"To get a jump on things," Laurie answered, operating from a personal code of honor taught to her by her father from the time she was a little girl. Her father had always told Laurie to be direct and truthful in all matters and she could never go wrong. Laurie wondered whether, if her dad were sitting in her place right now, would he still stand by that doctrine as Laurie continued to reflect on what she could have done to offend her homicide partner.

"Let's review the facts, shall we?" Angel's voice was low, her words tapered and measured. Laurie nodded. Angel invaded Laurie's personal space by scooting over close enough to be right in Laurie's face. There was an intensity in Angel's eyes that belied the sweet persona she could so easily project. Her face was tight with compressed anger. Laurie knew she was in trouble. She was waiting to hear why. "What do we know so far about this case?"

"A car belonging to a Dr. Harry Boulder has a dead body in the trunk."

"As a former Bunco detective, I didn't expect to have to tell you this; but apparently there are some things you need to be spoon fed. What we know is that this BMW belongs to a Dr. Harry Boulder. In the trunk was found the probable remains of a murder victim. We assume this because I received an anonymous tip that these things would be here, along with the letter we found that accompanied the packages. That is all we know. One thing we don't know is, for instance, who may be involved. Was it the person who made the phone call? Did the doctor make the call? Did he murder the person we found? If so, did he act alone? Was his wife somehow involved? Is someone framing the doctor? Do you get where I'm going with this?"

If Angel's words were fire, they would have melted the flesh from Laurie's bones. Each time before, when Laurie had made a mistake, Angel corrected her with calm patience as a teacher would a deserving pupil. At the moment, Laurie felt like a child being chastised by her mother for having neglected to do her homework. From where did this other person emerge? More importantly, Laurie thought with conviction, how could she keep her from surfacing again?

"Kind of," Laurie said, somehow managing to maintain control.

"Well *kind of* digest this fact. You don't do anything—*I mean absolutely nothing*—on any homicide investigation I'm in charge of without checking with me first. Are we clear?"

"Yes."

"Yes, what?"

"Yes, I'm clear on that point."

"I hope so. Because you only get so many passes with me. Use them up and you're out."

"It won't happen again."

Laurie had never seen this side of Detective Alvarez. It frightened her a little, especially since she had considered Angel to be a virtual softy when it came to her. Laurie knew Angel was tough. Angel wouldn't be where she was if she wasn't. But for Detective Alvarez to get nitty-gritty down and dirty dangerously bad—Laurie hadn't seen that coming.

"Let's pay Mrs. Boulder a visit," Detective Alvarez said without missing a beat. "I assume you have her address?"

"Right here," Laurie said, managing to keep the quiver in her belly out of her throat, pointing to the open notebook in her lap with her pen, both of which she had tight grips on without realizing it.

"You drive," Angel said. Angel scooted back over to the passenger side. Laurie put down her pen and notebook on the seat between them and started the car.

"Shouldn't we inform the victim's family about her death first?" Laurie found the courage to say.

"Who is the victim?"

"Kylie Preston."

"How do you know that?"

"We found evidence at the crime scene to confirm it." Laurie looked over at Angel, who was staring straight ahead.

"We found a purse at the crime scene with contents that belonged to Kylie Preston. We found packages in the trunk of a vehicle registered to a Dr. Harry Boulder. We don't know the presumed body belongs to Kylie Preston. Until we do, we do not put the family through any unnecessary trauma. Is that clear, Detective McCaskill?"

"Yes, detective."

"Good. We do, however, have a lead worth following. One that I would like to get to before the sun sets. So if it wouldn't be too much trouble, would you mind driving us there?"

Angel appeared stoic rather than angry. Laurie had seen her that way when she was wrapping her mind around a complicated case. Laurie waited a few heartbeats to see if Angel would acknowledge her.

"Now!" Angel yelled.

Laurie suppressed the urge to apologize again, and drove.

CHAPTER SIX

I entered the office to the smell of fresh ground coffee brewing. Renita deposited a delicious looking pumpkin scone on my desk.

"*Good morning, C. J.,*" Renita said with a chipper smile.

"Good morning," I said with a deliberate air of caution, bearing in mind the unpleasant conversation my junior partner and I'd had regarding last night's decision not to take her along. "I thought you said you would be in late today; something about you had something to take care of this morning." That mysterious something popped up after I snubbed my junior partner's persistent request to join me.

"It worked itself out." Renita stepped outside of my office and stood there with her hands folded comfortably in front of her. Renita was looking the part of a perky personal assistant. Two things I know about my junior partner is that she can be spiteful and she is subservient only when it suits her.

"We have a fair-sized caseload that needs our attention," Renita said with an obsequious grin, another clue that something was amiss.

"We're doing fine with our caseload." I made my way to my desk.

"You can never get too far ahead of the game," Renita cheerfully countered.

"Humph." I made myself comfortable behind my desk while trying to discern Renita's real intentions. "How was your evening?" I examined my pumpkin scone for any signs of tampering.

"*Great,* you know Ernest is an amazing man."

Ernest is Ernest Fullman, Renita's man-friend, a massive seven-three, near four hundred pounds of mostly muscle bouncer and half owner of Fullman's Restaurant. Ernest and Renita first met while we were working a very dangerous case some time ago. Ernest is a good man, honest and sincere. Ernest is in love with Renita. I'm not sure Renita feels the same, although she has a deep affection for Ernest that she denies when Ernest isn't around.

"I like Ernest and he likes me," Renita continued. "The bottom line is: we're friends."

Ernest knows how Renita feels about me and he doesn't like it one bit in spite of my repeated assurances that Renita is like my little sister. Ernest doesn't see it that way. He keeps a close eye on me when it comes to Renita. Like Destini, Ernest has tried to divorce our professional partnership. Ernest offered to bankroll Renita in her own private investigation firm. Renita isn't ready for that, but had she accepted his offer, I would have supported her one hundred percent.

For the time being Ernest saw me as a problem he would have to tolerate when it came to the woman he would like to marry someday. If Ernest believed I did anything to harm Renita, he would be on me like sugar on cane. If Ernest did anything to hurt Renita, I'd topple him like a lumberjack bringing down a northwest Sequoia. Implicitly, we had that understanding when it came to my junior partner.

"Glad to hear it," I said, satisfied my scone was tamper-free.

"Let me get you some hot tea to go with that." Renita rushed to the kitchen and returned in a flash with my favorite Song Dynasty Golden Peony porcelain tea mug.

"It's an organic blend of China white and Himalayan Oolong teas flavored with a touch of black currant and cherry," Renita said. "I bought it fresh this morning from that gourmet tea shop you like so much."

"You don't say." I breathed in the wonderful aroma of the freshly brewed tea.

"I didn't add your usual dollop of clover honey. When I tried it without the honey it seemed fine to me—but if you'd like, I'll put some honey in it for you." Renita stood by, waiting for me to taste it. I didn't. I busied myself with the paperwork on my desk. After a few moments, Renita grew impatient.

"Aren't you going to try it?"

"I'll get to it."

"*Oh for goodness sake.*" Renita grabbed the mug of tea and took a sip. "It isn't poisoned. I would never do that to you, or anyone, for that matter."

That was true. Renita might shoot you but she would never poison you.

"Sorry," I said. "I know how vindictive you can be."

"If you're talking about you not taking me to The Grill with you last night, I'm over that. Ernest helped me wash away the pain of your inconsideration."

"We both know you're not the catering type when it comes to work, so what's this kissing up all about?"

"Carl called."

"Did I miss turning back the clock an hour or something? Why is everybody on the move so early today?" Renita shrugged.

"Carl wasn't happy with our findings on the Singleton case and couldn't wait to tell us."

"Carl's never happy when his company has to shell out five figures or more." A big part of the reason I take on insurance investigation jobs is to help level the playing field. The people who hold up their end of the bargain and pay their premiums but fall prey to bad fate deserve to receive their due in both health care and compensation.

"Do you think they'll stop hiring us because we're not their lackeys?" Renita asked.

"Not as long as Carl's running the show and not Wall Street. Carl may gripe about doling out cash when it's due, but as long as it's fair, he can live with it."

"That could explain why he's given us another four cases he wants us to look into."

"Now, there you go. We'll split 'em up."

"I get first pick," Renita said.

"No, I get first and last pick. And why do I have the feeling you've already decided which ones you want?"

"Because I have," Renita said matter-of-factly.

"Let me guess: they involve some possible element of danger."

"All of our cases are *po-tentially* dangerous."

"Most of our cases are not dangerous," I said in earnest. "It's one of the reasons I enjoy this kind of work. You, on the other hand, seem to be getting bored with it."

"Is it too much to ask for a little more excitement around here than following people and mind-numbing stakeouts?" Renita wasn't ready for any dangerous cases, although she thought she was. I was still trying to teach her that stealth, not confrontation, was the best policy in handling undercover investigations.

"Remember the Bollinger case?" I asked.

"Oh, here we go again with the Bollinger case."

"I can use the Darcy, Teng, or Giza cases instead, if you'd like."

"So I got a little carried away. How many times are you going to keep throwing those up in my face?"

"You confronted each of them."

"*They were frauds.*"

"Something we were in the process of proving until you found it necessary to tell them about themselves."

"Somebody had to do it."

"It's not our job to pass judgment. It is our job to gather evidence. We then pass that information along to our clients. That is what we do and that is all we do."

"I have my rare outbursts under control." Renita tried playing it off as if it were ancient history. I wasn't about to let that happen.

"You pinned Miss Bollinger against a wall and tried to bad cop a confession out of her. We're damn lucky she didn't press assault charges against you."

"If she had, then she would have been exposed for the fraud she was," Renita said in an effort to justify her actions.

"We *did* expose her for the fraud she was. And why was that?"

"Because you went undercover and gathered incriminating evidence that she was faking her injuries," Renita answered like a reluctant teenager answering a stern question from her parent.

"Bailing you out in the process, which should serve as a reminder: that is what we are paid to do."

"I've learned my lesson. I know what to do now."

I believed Renita, in part. She had improved in both skill and temperament since the Bollinger incident. What she still needed work on was patience. There were times during the Singleton investigation when Renita was chomping at the bit to confront Bailey Singleton. Had I not talked her down, she might have done it. People who pay top dollar for our services frown upon behavior like that. I couldn't have Renita ruining our reputation even if she was one of my dearest friends.

"I'll look over the cases and decide which ones you can work solo."

Renita snatched the pumpkin scone from me as I was about to take a bite. "You need to watch your weight," she said. "I've noticed you've put on a couple of pounds around the middle. I'll be in my office doing paperwork on our mundane caseload if you need me."

Renita took a bite out of the scone as if it had insulted her and left in a huff. That was the spoiled Renita I had come to know and tolerate. I shook my head and took a sip of my tea. It was delicious. Renita stormed back into my office just as I set my tea mug down. She snatched the mug from my desk.

"Have you heard?" Renita asked, as if taking my tea from me was so common an occurrence it didn't merit notice.

"Heard what?" I leaned back in my chair.

"The Portland Police are seeking to question Dr. Harry Boulder as a person of interest in a murder."

"*Our Dr. Harry Boulder?*"

"Could there be two?"

"Yes, there could." I reached for my tea mug.

"Not in this case." Renita smacked my hand away.

"I thought he was at a medical convention in Denver."

"He is."

"But he's being accused of murder here in Portland?"

"According to reports, a body was found in his car. The police aren't releasing any specific details about the case except that Dr. Boulder is a person of interest in their investigation."

"Finding a corpse in your car will do that to a person. Did you hear anything else?"

"No. What we do is boring, C. J."

"We do what we're paid to do."

"Following people around to see if their claims are legitimate gets old."

"You want another *Gem Connection* or *Blue Sun* to liven things up?"

"Exactly," Renita said, the light shining bright in her dark brown eyes.

"You do recall we were almost killed."

"We were living on the edge."

"A razor's edge."

"At least we knew we were alive."

"I keep forgetting you're a bit of an adrenaline junkie."

"I just need some excitement for a change."

"Didn't you go hang gliding a couple of weeks ago?"

"And it was a blast," Renita said with zeal.

"Try skydiving, this weekend. That should feed your habit."

"Can't we do a little investigating on that murder case for the fun of it?"

"Only if we're hired as private consultants. This is not one of your computer games, Renita, where someone gets killed and they're back to life the next time you play. A human being is dead; dead because someone decided to extinguish their life. The people who care about that person are going to have to live with that grief. So don't make light of it."

"You're right, I know that, and I'm sorry." Renita snapped out of her momentary remorse. "But it would help keep our homicide investigating skills sharp."

"My skills are plenty sharp. Yours are still developing."

"Whatever." Renita sipped my tea. "This is superb."

"The police don't need our help." I ignored her gesture. "If they need any assistance, they'll turn to the FBI."

"We're better than they are."

"Have you been snorting the coffee grounds? Because your ego is way out of control."

"I'm just saying that we're good."

"So are a lot of other people and organizations. Show them the proper respect."

"Alright, already: settling down. It was just a thought."

"Where did you hear about all of this?"

"On the morning news. I can't believe you didn't hear about it?" Renita took another sip of my tea.

"It must have slipped by me."

"Wait a minute. You're usually telling me this stuff. This case has national attention. Every TV, radio, and internet news outlet in the Northwest has covered this story. How could you miss it?"

I shrugged. Renita wasn't satisfied.

"Let's see: the story wasn't in the morning paper because the body was only recently discovered, making it late-breaking news. You don't watch morning TV—or much TV at all for that matter—so you wouldn't have caught any news reports there. You typically listen to NPR driving into the office, who has been all over this story. *Oh my God*, Destini has your car again."

"You've got it. I took the light rail."

"I'm sure there was some buzz about it amongst light rail commuters. You'd have to be blind, deaf, and dumb not to catch a whiff of this murder."

Renita had me. I hadn't had a chance to look at my morning newspaper, and I don't watch morning television. I do plug into local and world events with my car radio on my way to work. I was floating on Cloud Nine due to the quality time spent with Destini, tuning out people with jazz through my earbuds during my entire commute. Love had sidelined my game.

"You are so whipped," Renita said with a chuckle.

"And that's a bad thing."

"It would be a good thing if it were me doing the whipping."

"Don't you have mundane caseload work awaiting you in your office?" I was not going to allow the conversation to meander down that path.

"Yes, I do. You owe me twenty bucks for this tea." Renita walked out of my office shaking her head with amusement, carrying my tea mug.

"Where are you going with my tea?"

"To my office."

"What about me?"

"Get your own damn tea!"

I got up and did just that.

CHAPTER SEVEN

Cloud cover dulled the bright autumn colors of Southwest Portland. "As much as possible, you want to conduct your interviews in person with anyone related to your case," Detective Alvarez said to McCaskill as they walked past the attached three-car garage along the paved path to the covered entrance of the Boulder's custom two-story, four bedroom house. Alvarez had lectured McCaskill numerous times during her ongoing training on multiple ways to conduct an interview. McCaskill had them all committed to memory. Alvarez knew that now would be a good time to reiterate this particular point after McCaskill's screwup of contacting a potential suspect by phone. "That way, you get a feel for when they are and are not telling the truth," Alvarez went on to say. Angel sounded as calm and friendly as she had before her dressing-down of McCaskill in the car. McCaskill nodded her understanding, not certain what to make of her mood swings.

"Chime in any time during the interview," Alvarez continued. "Since you've already spoken to Mrs. Boulder, she may feel she has a rapport with you, thereby feeling more comfortable opening up to you than me. If that happens, I will figuratively step back and allow you to take the lead." Alvarez rang the doorbell. She eyed McCaskill. The chip on her partner's shoulder was gone, but Alvarez had no doubt it would be back in no time. In the long haul, what Alvarez had done would be beneficial to a homicide detective she could envision as being in her position one day. McCaskill was that good. But for now, McCaskill needed to learn the ropes, and sometimes that climb had some broken glass embedded in the cord. "Don't worry, you'll be fine," Alvarez said to McCaskill for momentary reassurance.

A woman in about her late forties to early fifties answered the door. Alvarez took a quick physical inventory of the woman: slender,

Caucasian, probably Greek ancestry, about five-four or five-five, long wavy chestnut hair, expressive brown eyes, straight nose, thin eyebrows, clear skin, very little make-up, and well-groomed with expensive wardrobe, shoes, and jewelry.

"May I help you?" the woman said as if addressing a lower caste.

"Mrs. Boulder?" Alvarez asked.

"I'm Mrs. Boulder."

"Mrs. Ruth Boulder?" Alvarez asked.

"Yes."

"Mrs. Boulder, I'm Detective Alvarez and this is Detective McCaskill." The detectives showed Mrs. Boulder their badges. Alvarez noted her reaction to their introductions. Mrs. Boulder did not seem moved to distraction or shocked by their presence. That led Alvarez to believe Mrs. Boulder had not heard what happened, or she was one cool customer who was a part of it all.

"This is about my husband's stolen car, I take it?"

She hasn't heard about the body, Alvarez thought.

"In part," McCaskill said. Alvarez noted that either McCaskill was bouncing back faster than expected, or Laurie was showing her professional chops.

"What do you mean?"

"May we come in?" Alvarez said. "We'd like to ask you a few questions."

"Is that absolutely necessary?"

"Yes, it is, and it would be better if we did so inside," Alvarez said.

Mrs. Boulder let out a heavy sigh. She scanned her cul-de-sac. Alvarez and McCaskill knew she was concerned about the neighbors seeing any of this. Ruth Boulder stepped aside and reluctantly let the detectives enter.

Ruth Boulder quickly closed the door behind them before ushering the detectives into the formal living room. The house was as elegant and sophisticated inside as it was immaculate outside. Alvarez noticed a gilt-framed photograph on the mantel above the fireplace. A proud, happy portrait of a handsome twenty-something couple with two young children in the foreground. Alvarez recognized Ruth Boulder, and Dr. Boulder from his driver's license photo. It was no great deductive feat to determine the children belonged to the twenty-something couple.

"We would like to ask you a few questions," Alvarez repeated, matching the volume of the classical music softly playing in the background as they stood in the middle of the living room.

"What's this all about?"

"Mrs. Boulder, how certain are you that your husband is in Denver at a medical conference?" Alvarez asked.

"I didn't check up on him, if that's what you mean."

"We need to be certain of your husband's whereabouts, ma'am; say within the last twenty-four to forty-eight hours," McCaskill said.

"You're that young woman I spoke to on the phone earlier. You said you found my husband's stolen car abandoned on NW Overton?"

"Yes, ma'am, I did."

"You mentioned to my partner that your husband had left his car at the airport parking garage."

"I dread driving to the airport, and Harry is sweet enough to do it himself. The airport garage is a bit expensive, but Harry doesn't seem to mind."

"Do you have any idea how your husband's car wound up in northwest Portland?" McCaskill asked.

"Because it was stolen, of course. So much for airport security."

"That's the problem, ma'am: there was no sign of forced entry into the vehicle," Alvarez said.

"What do you mean?"

"Whoever was driving your husband's car probably had a key," McCaskill said.

"What in the world would Harry's car be doing there if it wasn't stolen?"

"That's what we're trying determine," Alvarez said.

"What are you suggesting? What's this all about?"

"Have you recently spoken to your husband?" McCaskill asked.

"I spoke to him yesterday."

"At about what time?" Alvarez asked.

"I spoke to Harry somewhere between eight and nine o'clock last night. Harry always checks up on me when he is away at one of these conventions to make certain I'm okay."

"Did he seem different to you in any way?" McCaskill asked.

"Different?"

"Did he sound different, for example?" Alvarez asked.

"No, and I don't like what you're inferring."

"Excuse me?" McCaskill said.

"My husband is a good man. We've had our problems in the past, but we've worked through those."

"And what might those problems have been that you've had to work through, Mrs. Boulder?" Alvarez asked.

"Harry had a little...," Mrs. Boulder paused as if what she was about to say was top secret and only to be shared with trusted sources. "Harry had a little infidelity problem in the past. But we've straightened out his wandering ways in therapy and he is more dedicated to our marriage than ever."

"Mrs. Boulder—"

"We're sure you have, Mrs. Boulder," Alvarez interrupted McCaskill. "We would like to know if there is any reason your husband may have come back to Portland within the last forty-eight hours—say, for a medical emergency regarding one of his patients, for example?"

"If anything like that had occurred, Harry would have let me know immediately what was going on and about when I could expect him home."

"Do you mind if we have a look around?" McCaskill asked.

Mrs. Boulder seemed taken aback by the question. "Why?"

"To see if we can eliminate your husband as a suspect," McCaskill said. It took all of Alvarez's willpower to prevent her from rolling her eyes at McCaskill's rookie mistake.

"*Suspect...in what?* What kind of detectives are you?"

"Homicide, ma'am," Alvarez responded.

"*Homicide?*"

"Yes, ma'am," Alvarez said.

"Is Harry all right?"

"As far as we know he's fine," Alvarez said.

"Mrs. Boulder, this is basic procedure for any investigation," McCaskill said. "We just need to clear certain hurdles before we can proceed to the finish line."

"You think my Harry murdered somebody? What did you find in my husband's car to ever make you believe such a horrible thing?"

"We're not free to divulge that information at this time, Mrs. Boulder," McCaskill said.

"Then I'm not free to discuss my husband with you any further," Ruth Boulder said.

Alvarez knew it was time to come clean. "We found something in the trunk of your husband's car," Alvarez said.

"It was the dismembered remains of a dead person," McCaskill added.

"Oh my God!"

Alvarez was again disappointed at her partner. All McCaskill had to say was they had found a dead body in the car. Informing Mrs. Boulder that the body had been "cut up" would only worsen any trauma Mrs. Boulder may have been feeling, creating more anxiety and lessening their chance of getting any more useful information from her. Mrs. Boulder looked as though she were about to pass out. Alvarez and McCaskill led her by her elbows to the sofa and sat her down.

"May I get you anything to drink?" Alvarez asked.

"No, no, I'll be fine. You found a cut-up body in the trunk of my husband's car?" Mrs. Boulder said with total disbelief.

"We're afraid so, ma'am," McCaskill said. "That's why we're here."

"Why you're here," Mrs. Boulder repeated to herself as if trying to comprehend the substance of that statement. *"You think my Harry had something to do with murder?"*

"We're not suggesting any such thing," Alvarez said, attempting to clean up her partner's slip. "We simply wanted to verify with you your husband's whereabouts, as matter of procedure."

"My husband is at a medical convention in Denver."

"Is there any way you can confirm that?" McCaskill asked.

"Why would I need to? He didn't do anything."

"We still need confirmation from another party about his whereabouts in the last twenty-four to forty-eight hours," Alvarez said.

"I'm sure he has hundreds of people who can vouch for him at the convention. He was one of their keynote speakers."

"That's the kind of confirmation that would clear him of suspicion," McCaskill said.

"My husband is a highly respected and successful man of medicine," Mrs. Boulder said. "He may have a few failings, as all human beings do, but a murderer he is not."

"Do you mind if we have a look around?" McCaskill asked.

"Why do you keep asking that?" Ruth Boulder said.

"As an additional hedge in proving your husband's innocence," McCaskill said.

"After all I've said, you still believe my Harry could have killed someone?"

Alvarez stepped in again to try to clean up another of her partner's missteps. "All we are doing is our jobs, Mrs. Boulder."

"You're not very good at it, if you ask me."

"Yes, ma'am, but we need to make certain all of the pieces of the puzzle fit," Alvarez said. "Part of that process is the process of elimination. By eliminating your husband, we can move on to find the real killer. Left to us, we would take your word for it and start looking for who *really* killed this person. But we have to answer to higher-ups, and they expect us to do things by the book."

"I don't know much about the law, but I do know this. To search our home, you need some kind of warrant. So the answer is no, you do not have permission to search my house for as much as a toothpick."

"Mrs. Boulder, this would be so much easier if you allowed us to do a quick search rather than make it official and bring in uniforms," Alvarez said. "Trust me. They will not be as gentle as we will with your beautiful home."

"I don't care. I want you to leave."

"If you would just let us have a look around," McCaskill said.

"Get out!" Mrs. Boulder's outrage cracked her distress.

"Yes, ma'am," Alvarez said, grabbing her partner around the shoulders and leading her toward the front door. Mrs. Boulder followed them. Alvarez and McCaskill stepped outside and turned to face Mrs. Boulder. They offered her their cards. Ruth Boulder slammed the door in their faces. Alvarez had a look of mild disgust on her face. McCaskill felt ill at ease.

"This has not been a red letter day for you, rookie," Alvarez said with exasperation, walking to the car. McCaskill followed in shamed silence.

CHAPTER EIGHT

After using another tea mug to make myself a fresh mug of Renita's wonderful tea blend, I set to work. At the Cavanaugh Investigation Agency, we are a first come, first serve agency. Money does not influence our policy. Unless a case comes our way that is of dire consequence, we adhere to that guiding principle. We had two outstanding jobs remaining that we needed to complete before proceeding on to our new cases. They involved extensive background checks for a Mr. Jack Carver and a Ms. Brittany Peters.

Jack Carver was the top candidate for a vice-president position with the Mercury Corporation. Their head of Human Resources contacted us to do a thorough background check on Jack Carver to make certain he was squeaky clean before offering him the job. Brittany Peters was the leading candidate for the regional manager position with Seamen's Bank, one of the largest banks in the northwest. Their head of HR contacted us to do a background check on their number one applicant to assure the same thing. When asked why they had chosen us, their answers were much the same. We came highly recommended by our previous clients. Our reputation was one of efficient, thorough, and dependable work. Clearly, they had done a comprehensive background check on us. I wondered what sources they used.

Background checks are simple. People would be amazed at how easy it is to obtain background information if you know where to look or who to ask. A great deal of the information can be found by phone or online. The legwork on these extensive background checks came when we interviewed the prospective employees' personal references. Checking out a potential employee's personal references are as much about the people he or she regards as friends—which are what personal references amount to—as it is about the candidate themselves. Here the 'birds of a feather will flock together' theory is employed. If you discover anything questionable in the character of their personal references that may reflect badly on the candidate, then that is something the investigator needs to take into consideration in their evaluation; but is not necessarily something that needs to be reported to the client. Other than that, you're pretty much looking at their credit history, criminal history, social behavior, affiliations, and any risky behavior that may affect their job performance or judgment such as drug abuse, gambling, or alcoholism. Physical and mental health histories are more challenging to come by and are illegal to use as a reason for denying anyone employment. For the latter reason, we refuse to consider looking into those areas for any employer.

I completed my background check on Jack Carver. After organizing my paperwork, I wrote up a favorable report on Carver and emailed it to the HR head of Mercury Corporation, carbon-copying Renita to keep her abreast of what was happening on my end.

I called Destini to see if she were free for lunch. "Give me one of your great massages after dinner and a hot bath at my place tonight?" Destini said, after she told me she couldn't make lunch.

"Consider it done," I said.

"I'll pick you up at about six."

"I can't wait."

"You'd better wait; I don't want you getting what I'm going to give you from anyone else." Destini was very professional. For her to talk that freely, she must have been somewhere private.

"Don't worry, I'll be patient."

"Most especially from Renita."

"I thought we were clear that situation was handled. Renita and I are friends and business partners."

"No fringe benefits?"

"You know me better than that."

"You, I trust. But I know homicide and women, and Renita is a very stubborn woman."

"I'm more obstinate than she is."

"We're all human."

"I could think the same about you and your partner," I said, referencing David Lieberman. A former Lewis & Clark College middle linebacker, David was six-three with a muscular build, short black curly hair, large dark eyes, a thick black beard, and a bountiful nose. Most women found him ruggedly handsome. Their favor increased when they discovered intelligence and sophistication prowled beneath that brawn. Destini was amongst that group of women. She thought highly of David, not only as her law enforcement partner, but also as a man.

"It has crossed my mind." Destini laughed after a brief moment of silence. "I'm just kidding."

"Make sure you are," I said, not joking in the least.

"I've got to get back to work."

"Be careful."

"Aren't I always?"

"Yes, you are. I love you." Telling Destini I loved her had become something I had grown comfortable doing, of late. Part of me questioned whether that was a good thing—the part indoctrinated by some to believe that a man telling a woman he loved her too much and too often was asking to be used. A song from Bill Withers came to mind: "If it feels this good being used then, baby, use me up."

"I love you too, gotta go." Destini hung up before I did.

CHAPTER NINE

After clearing our backlog, I dived headlong into the four new cases Carl Wheaton had sent over for consideration. Two of the cases I decided to let Renita do solo. The two cases Renita was not going to get were the gun nut and the psychologically unstable ex-boxer, although I was certain those were the two Renita wanted. People like them could be dangerous in the direst sense of the word. There was no way I was going to put my junior partner in that position. Renita would just have to be angry. I was about to inform Renita of my decision when my office phone rang.

"Cavanaugh Investigation Agency," I answered after the first ring.

"C. J., this is Shelly." Shelly Morton is the director of the Fremont Community Center. Destini introduced me to Shelly a few years back when I mentioned to her that I wanted to do some volunteer work. Shelly and I instantly hit it off. He was someone I considered a friend.

"Hey, Shelly, how are you?"

"I'm fine. How are you?"

"Good. If this is about that three-point shot I buried for the win on Saturday, I don't care what Monty says: my foot was behind the line," I said with levity. Shelly didn't bite.

"It's not about that." Shelly sounded concerned.

"What's going on?"

"Can you do me a favor?" Shelly didn't like to ask for favors. Whatever was troubling him had to be serious.

"I'll try."

"Some friends of mine think their teenagers have disappeared."

"What do you mean, disappeared?"

"The parents think their children have run away. They're worried out of their minds."

"Are they sure? Maybe they just forgot to tell them where they were going."

"Pretty sure."

"These parents aren't abusive, are they?"

"Not a chance I've known them since high school. I've known their kids all of their lives. They are excellent parents. If anything, I think they give their children too much leeway."

"Do you think their kids ran away?"

"They're your typical rebellious teenagers, so I'd have to say yes. I could see them doing something like that."

"Your friends should go to the police."

"They tried that, and it didn't work."

"I'm not following you on what you think I can do."

"Can you talk to them, C. J.? See if you can help."

"Finding runaway teenagers is not our forte."

"You've done it in the past."

"Under very special circumstances, and we were lucky then."

"They could use a little of that Cavanaugh luck right now. Will you talk to them?"

After giving it serious consideration, I said, "I'll talk to them but I can't promise anything."

"I really appreciate it," Shelly sounded uplifted. "I'll send them over."

"I can't wait," I said sarcastically.

"Thanks, C. J."

"You're welcome." We hung up. I wondered what I had gotten myself into. I walked into Renita's office. Renita was on the phone. I waited in the doorway.

"And how long did Ms. Peters work for you?" Renita listened and took notes.

"Un-huh, what was her position and responsibilities, if you don't mind my asking?" Renita listened and took more notes.

"I see. Thank you so much for your time. These are all the questions I have for now. Goodbye." Renita hung up.

"Brittany Peters checks out," Renita said, looking at her notes.

"Seamen's will be happy to hear that. I just got off the phone with Shelly."

"Shelly Morton?" Renita turned her full attention to me. Renita knew Shelly too, from her volunteer work at the center.

"A couple of his friends are worried about their teenagers. They believe their kids have disappeared."

"What do you mean 'disappeared'?"

"The parents think their kids ran away."

"Why don't the parents go to the police?"

"They did. For some reason, the police won't intervene. I told Shelly we'd look into it. The parents are on their way over."

"That's fine with me. I'll wrap this up. Do you want to have a look at it before I send it to Seamen's?"

"That won't be necessary. You've done enough background checks that you don't need me looking over your shoulder. Don't forget to cc me."

"No problem."

"Good job."

"Thanks. I wish *someone* showed as much confidence in me in other areas of our work as they do in background checks."

I ignored Renita's snide remark. Renita set to writing up Brittany Peters' official report.

"Did you get my cc on Jack Carver?"

"Yes."

"He's clean. That clears our docket for now."

"What about the four cases Carl sent over?"

"I looked them over."

"And?"

I knew Renita was anxious to know if I had decided to allow her to work at least one of the more dangerous cases on her own. The answer was no, but with a new situation brewing, now was not the time to tell her.

"We'll discuss them after we see what's going on with Shelly's friends."

Renita smiled. "That's sounding like a 'maybe' to me."

"Finish writing your report," I said, leaving for my office.

"*Yes sir.*" Renita needed to get in the last word.

CHAPTER TEN

Angel Alvarez could never get used to the stench of death, even masked in the sterile environment of the medical examiner's office. Laurie McCaskill wondered if she would ever become accustomed to it. The Chief Medical Examiner appeared oblivious.

Dr. Blake Saba had been with the Portland Police Bureau for twenty-seven years. He'd been recruited right out of medical school as a full time medical examiner by the late Colin Greene, founding father of the Portland Medical Examiner's office. The walnut-complexioned indigenous Klamath found that he preferred unlocking the causes of death to diagnosing the living. Blake had alert brown eyes and pitch black hair streaked with steel gray, which he wore in a ponytail held in place by an elastic black ponytail holder accented with a cracked eggshell bead. He stood five-nine and weighed in at a solid one hundred eighty pounds. Blake had a slight paunch not due to his lack of exercise, but for his love of rich cakes and pastries. The only jewelry Blake wore was a turquoise, red coral, and orange spiny oyster squash-blossom necklace made for him by his daughter when she was twelve. Blake kept his twenty-two-year-old gold wedding band, a symbol of love and commitment, in his pants pocket while he worked.

Dr. Saba moved with self-assured deliberateness and often spoke in the same manner in reference to his charges. That aspect of his personality—or lack thereof, according to some—had emerged over the years from a man who had seen all of the grotesque ways a human being can die. Blake had long ago gotten over the shock and depression that could accompany his job. Investing feelings in his work (he determined with help from his mentor Colin Greene) was a waste of time. How Dr. Saba could best serve the dead was through applying his intellect, medical education, and training towards aiding law enforcement in sorting out causes of death. That had become his professional purpose in life.

Blake appeared a natural in his crisp white lab coat and Kintpuash bolo tie as he waved his surgically gloved hands over the ghoulish jigsaw remains of Kylie Preston, assembled on a mobile dissection table.

"What's this?" McCaskill looked both disgusted and dismayed. She had never before seen a dismembered body. It made her squeamish to think that in our final days we are little more than what she saw.

"This is the body of one Kylie Preston—or what remains of her," Blake replied with an almost detached clinical fascination. "We were able to determine her identity based upon a number of distinguishing markers, including her fingerprints."

"You *found* her all cut up like this?" McCaskill was struggling to comprehend what she was looking at.

"Nothing gets by your partner." Blake gave McCaskill one of his lambent smiles that felt warm and caring even in jest. McCaskill could not resist smiling back at Blake, even with the knowledge that she was the object of his ridicule.

"She's doing all right." Alvarez came to the defense of her partner. Angel realized that this was the first intricate homicide case that Laurie McCaskill had the opportunity to work on. Angel Alvarez was trying to bear that in mind and be more patient with her. Laurie seemed to appreciate the gesture.

"Whoever killed Ms. Preston removed all of her major internal organs, including her heart; beheaded her; and severed her body at the joints—and it gets more bizarre."

"How's that possible?" Alvarez looked on in disbelief.

"Whoever did this went through a lot of trouble to preserve our victim."

"Preserve?" McCaskill said.

"They packed everything in coolers filled with ice."

"Where are her internal organs?"

"You can let me know when you find them, Detective Alvarez, because they weren't packaged with the rest of her."

"You're kidding?" Alvarez and Blake stared stone-faced at McCaskill in answer to her question for a moment before Alvarez asked, "Why would someone go through all of this trouble?"

"My thoughts exactly." Blake paused as if giving the question additional thought. "What I do know is that all of her missing internal organs can be used in transplants."

"I saw an organ donor card among the victim's personal effects. Think there might be a connection?" McCaskill's queasiness was giving way to her instinctual curiosity.

"It's possible," answered Alvarez.

Blake chimed in. "This could be an elaborate way to cover up what organ or organs they were really after."

"This sounds like black market organ harvesting taken to the extreme."

"Does organ harvesting go on here, doctor?" McCaskill asked.

"If by 'here', you mean the U.S., then not to my knowledge. The United States has some of the strictest laws, rules, and regulations in the world regarding the procurement and transplanting of human organs. And they are stringently enforced throughout the medical community."

"It's been my experience that when enough money is on the table, all laws, rules, and regulations go right out the window for some people." Everyone nodded in agreement to Angel's remark. "We'll look into it from the black market angle and will investigate possible matches to organ donors."

"It would be a bright spot to this grisly affair if her death benefitted others," McCaskill said.

"Kylie Preston didn't sacrifice herself. She was murdered. Knowing that their murdered mother's organs are part of someone who might be responsible for her death won't bring comfort to her children." Alvarez knew McCaskill was looking for the silver lining, but she was having none of it. The victim had her life ripped from her by a predator: a fact that Angel wanted her partner to embrace to her core—to hell with rationalizing the killer's motivation.

"Whoever did this knew what they were doing. From what I can tell from my preliminary examination, the arms, legs, and head were whacked clean off—probably using a meat cleaver."

"The same kind a butcher uses." McCaskill had overcome her queasiness. She had also shaken off Angel's rebuke to her attempt at optimism. She was in full homicide detective mode.

"Precisely, and they knew how and where to cut. Every hack appears to have been done with swift, accurate blows."

"He sounds strong."

"And possibly someone with experience in the meat industry," Alvarez added.

"Conceivably," Blake responded to Alvarez's comment. "The internal organs were surgically removed."

"Our killer is both a surgeon and a butcher?"

"Aren't they pretty much the same thing?" Blake smiled sympathetically at McCaskill's lame attempt at humor. Alvarez stared blankly at her partner. McCaskill cleared her throat and averted her eyes to Kylie Preston. "Is there any chance that more than one person was involved?" Angel glanced with pride at Laurie for her insightful question, returning her attention to Blake before Laurie noticed.

"Don't know. It's feasible. Whoever removed her internal organs had solid surgical skills. They used textbook mortuary incisions. I couldn't have done better myself."

"Butcher, surgeon, and/or mortician: what the hell is going on here?" Alvarez and Blake ignored McCaskill's query.

"They also knew how to pack the remains for optimum preservation. See that discoloration around the mouth and nose?" Blake pointed to the area on the guillotined head.

"Yes," McCaskill said.

"That suggests she ingested a fast-acting poison." McCaskill and Alvarez nodded.

"He put the blood he drained from her body into plastic jugs and packed the jugs in ice."

"Any guess as to why he went through all of this trouble?" Alvarez said.

"At first I thought it might be his twisted way of toying with us."

"That doesn't add up." McCaskill appeared to be studying the dismembered body parts rather than observing them.

"Why would you say that, detective?" Alvarez gave her partner the floor.

"Even the most arrogant homicidal socio—or psychopath wouldn't go through all of this trouble to play cat and mouse. Or to do something this horrible." McCaskill waved her hands over the remains of Kylie Preston much as a magician expecting her assistant to rise from the ashes of her death defying trick. "You have to be disturbed. Someone this meticulous, capable of going to this extreme, is looking to discourage discovery; not aid it."

Good, she's thinking in terms of profiles, Alvarez thought. *My little dressing-down hasn't put her off her game.*

"What's your guess about the killer?" Alvarez prodded. Blake looked on, observing Angel's training session in deductive reasoning in progress.

"Whatever motivated this person to kill," Laurie said, "didn't overshadow his humanity."

"Can you draw a conclusion from that?" Angel asked.

McCaskill was stumped, and it showed on her face. Alvarez and Blake realized Laurie had hit a brick wall in her rational. Blake took over.

"Right you are, Detective McCaskill. I believe whoever did this wanted to make use of every part of Kylie Preston to help others."

"Just like it said in the letter: a sort of human recycling thing," McCaskill said.

"More like a *humane* recycling thing," Alvarez retorted. "It's likely that in our killer's mind, his murder of Kylie Preston did society a favor."

"He is further contributing to society by preserving as much of her as possible. Every part of Ms. Preston has been conserved to the point that much of her can be donated to help those in remedial need—once all of the necessary medical tests are concluded and proper matches are found, of course."

"Except for her internal organs."

"I suspect our killer took the same cautionary care with her internal organs. If whoever did this was as careful and forward thinking as they were to preserve what you see before you, then they already had plans for the internal organs that are missing. They were probably also aware of the time frame for transplantable organs."

"What makes you say that?"

"The lungs and heart have to be delivered to the recipient within 6 hours maximum, although the heart valves can last up to 10 years under the right conditions. With the liver and pancreas, you have about 24 hours; the kidney 72; and corneas, 14 days. Bone and tissue like what you see here can last for up to 5 years."

"So what we see here can still be used even after the court trail once we catch this guy."

"We'll see to that."

"Corneas?" McCaskill stared at the decapitated head. Her eyelids were sewn shut. The victim's head had been shaved clean; the skull stapled back together in what made the top of her head appear as though she were wearing a grotesque skullcap. "He took her brain, too?"

"No, that was my doing, I'm afraid. I needed to examine the brain and we needed some tissue samples to analyze." Blake's statement seemed to calm McCaskill.

"There are over one hundred thousand people on a national waiting list for organ donations." Blake felt compelled to lecture on a subject he was passionate about. "More than a third of them will die before an organ can be found. The need for organ donors is increasing at a rate of around 1,000 people every month, with another name being added about every 10 minutes."

Compassion for victims beyond their assistance required a moment of silence before they were back on the case.

"Are you certain poison killed her?" Alvarez asked.

"We'll know for certain once the toxicology results come back from the lab. My professional guess would be yes. The tox report will also give us a head start on screening whether or not the tissue and bone matter the killer bequeathed is viable for transplant."

"Any sign she was forced to take the poison?"

"None."

"You think the killer knew our vic?" McCaskill asked Alvarez.

"If her consumption of the poison was voluntary, it suggests she at least felt comfortable enough with him to eat or drink whatever he gave her."

"Unless he was able to threaten her into taking the poison herself, like at gunpoint."

"That's also a possibility." Alvarez looked over the physical evidence. "I don't see any stomach contents."

"Alas, there are no gastric contents. The stomach and intestines were not included."

"Did you find any specific clues that could point us in the direction of her killer?" Alvarez asked with a hint of frustration.

"Nothing so far, but we've just gotten started. If there's any trace left of the killing agent, we'll find it." Blake took a moment to think before he spoke again. "Something strikes me as fascinating at the outset."

"What's that?" Alvarez asked.

"There's no evidence at any point during the dissection of this woman that the killer was angry. If anything, all indications seem to point to it being well-planned and methodical. Whoever butchered Ms. Preston did so without malice."

"That's interesting in a disturbing way."

"Thank you, Detective McCaskill," Blake said with a soft chuckle. "I'm glad you agree with my assessment."

"Why is that both interesting and disturbing?" Alvarez asked McCaskill.

"It just is."

"That's not an answer." Alvarez was hoping Laurie would draw upon her deductive reasoning and training. "Does that tell you anything?"

"Not really." Laurie appeared embarrassed.

"I believe the answers Detective Alvarez is searching for are that the murder was probably premeditated and that the victim was specifically targeted," Blake said with the empathetic tone of a teacher.

"Someone stalked this woman before killing her?"

"It's a strong possibility," Alvarez said.

"Any suspects, detectives?"

"One who coincidentally happens to be a doctor," McCaskill said. Angel concurred with a nod. "He may turn out to be the only suspect we need."

"One bad apple." Blake shook his head.

"I hear you." Alvarez gave the dismembered cadaver a final scan. "Keep us posted, Doc."

"Sure thing."

"Thank you."

"You're welcome, Detective McCaskill. Good hunting."

Alvarez and McCaskill left, buzzing with conversation surrounding recently discovered facts. Blake had already set aside ample blood, skin, and tissue samples for future lab analyses, if needed. The corpse evidence had been photographed. Cataloging those photos was still in progress. The Medical Examiner wasted no time draping the remains of Kylie Preston with a white cadaver cover and returning her to refrigeration. As an acting member of the Gift of Life Donor Program, Blake, along with a national network of coroners and medical examiners, were doing their best to ensure successful organ and tissue donations. Blake's office had done an exemplary job over the years of contributing to their success. This macabre offering would be no exception.

CHAPTER ELEVEN

Nick Jennings and Anna Foster arrived about an hour after I had spoken to Shelly. Anna, the mother of seventeen-year-old Eric, was in her mid-thirties, of average height, and chubby. Anna had a full round face and expressive clear blue eyes that seemed to question everything in their path. Nick, the father of sixteen-year-old Marie, was in his mid-thirties and about six feet, with a solid frame, square face, and narrow dark blue eyes. They both appeared haggard and desperate. They declined an offer of refreshment. They sat in the chairs across my office desk from Renita and me. Renita had wheeled in her office chair and sat beside me. The worried parents grasped hands not in the manner of people in love offering the other comfort, but as if they were trying to save the other from drowning in their own despair. Anna's eyes were red, as if she'd been crying. Nick's jaw muscles flexed. How distress had worked its grief so quickly on them astounded me.

A quick footnote to their story was that they were single parents. Nick became widowed when Marie was four. His wife died in a plane crash. Anna had Eric out of wedlock and she had lost track of Eric's deadbeat father by the time Eric was six.

"What makes you so certain your children ran away?" I asked both of them.

"Some of their clothes are missing," Nick answered.

"And each of them took a suitcase," Anna added.

"Did they leave a note or phone message?" Renita asked.

"No," Nick said.

"Nothing like that," Anna said.

"Shelly said you went to the police." I wanted to verify some of Shelly's information firsthand.

"*We did*," Anna said.

"The cops said they needed more to go on than a parent's intuition that their children had run away." Nick sounded irritated. An emotion Anna shared.

"Like we wouldn't know if something was wrong with our own kids," Anna added.

"How long have they been missing?"

"We figured it out yesterday evening, when they didn't come home from work," Anna said.

"We checked our kids' rooms and that's when we discovered some of their clothes were missing—"

"And they had each taken a suitcase," Anna interjected before Nick could finish.

"Did anything happen that the two of you can recall that might have precipitated their running away?" Renita asked.

"*Are you saying this is our fault?*" Anna sounded offended. Renita had the right idea, but she had gone about it all wrong. Renita needed to give them room to tell their story.

"Not in the least," I covered my partner's tracks. "But teenagers can be overly sensitive—or so I've heard."

"We take it neither of you have children?" Renita and I nodded our assent to Nick's question. "Sometimes they are a handful."

"But they're worth every minute of it and we want them back," Anna emphasized.

"Why do I get the feeling you know what this is about?" Nick and Anna looked at each other and then back at us.

"We had a fight," Nick said in a deflated voice.

"With your daughter?" I asked. Nick nodded.

"And me with my son."

"Regarding?"

"My son is very much in love with Marie." Anna sounded almost wistful about the idea.

Nick answered in more of the stern voice of a protective father. "And my daughter is crazy about Eric." His jaw muscles flexed.

Anna sighed, "They wanted to get married."

"They asked our permission and we refused."

"Here's some pictures of them," Anna said. Nick and Anna handed Renita and me two 5x7 photos of their teenagers. Renita and I soaked in the pictures. The strong resemblance to both parents was immediate, especially in the eyes. In both photos, Eric and Anna had their arms lovingly around each other, smiling as if the world were their jewel. The teenagers were clearly love-struck. It showed in their faces, smiles, and body language. You could see in their eyes a kind of blind devotion that encompassed their world and destroyed all logic and common sense. In a way, teenage love undermines all others. It may be reckless and consuming and even perilous, but no fire burns quite as bright as your first requited love.

"How recent are these pictures?" Renita asked.

"A couple of days," Nick said. "They're always taking pictures of themselves together."

"We printed them from their computers. Those are their latest screensavers."

"They're too young to marry in Oregon without our consent," Nick input. "We think they eloped to someplace where they won't need our permission to get married."

"The minimum age for marriage without parental consent in all U.S. territories is eighteen," I said.

"Then they must have figured out a way to get around it," I agreed with Nick.

"Did they take anything else?"

"Like what?" Nick asked.

"Like your car, for instance, or money or a credit card?" Renita said.

"No." Anna thought for a moment before continuing. "Just some clothes and a suitcase."

"They have their own cell phones," Nick added.

"What kids don't, these days?" My attempt to lighten the mood failed. Renita and I remained silent on the possibility of a smartphone tracking their children even if they had disabled their GPS. We would cross that bridge when we came to it.

"Do they have their own credit cards?" I asked.

"No. They have part-time jobs, though," Nick said. "Marie works for a sporting goods store."

"Eric works for a bookstore."

"I let Marie keep whatever money she earns—minus her cell phone bill."

"I do the same for Eric."

"Do you think they saved up enough money to run away?" Nick asked.

"We don't know," Renita said, but we both knew the answer was no. Part-time jobs don't pay enough to elope.

"They have something figured out," I said.

"Our bigger concern is that they might get hurt." Anna's face flooded with anxiety. "Or they may not come back to us after they get married."

"We're afraid they're afraid we might force them to get their marriage annulled." Nick's jaw muscles flexed again.

"Is that a valid concern on their part?" I asked.

"Maybe," Nick said with a shrug. "Right now, we can't say."

"All we want is our children home safe and sound."

"May we keep these?" I asked in reference to the photos.

"Sure," Nick replied.

"We'll see what we can do."

"We'll let you know as soon as we have something," Renita said.

"*Thank you,*" Nick said with the spirit of relief in his voice.

"*Thank you so much.*" Anna sounded the same.

"Don't thank us," Renita said. "We haven't done anything yet."

"Do you need anything else from us?" Nick asked.

"Not for the moment," I answered.

"How much do we owe you?" Anna asked.

"A twenty-dollar deposit will cover it for now."

"Twenty dollars—*that's all?*" Nick said.

"Ten dollars each should do it," Renita said.

"We'll bill you for any outstanding charges later—if any."

"Okay...alright, then." Anna managed to say. Both Anna and Nick appeared somewhat perplexed by our low fee as we all stood. That was understandable. Renita and I knew we wouldn't feel justified charging these parents for our help in finding their children. The worried parents unclasped hands and gave Renita ten dollars apiece.

"Right this way, and I'll write you a receipt," Renita said. The relieved parents thanked me with enthusiastic handshakes and some grateful words before following Renita into her office. I sat down and leaned back in my chair, clear on how to proceed with this case. Renita saw Nick and Anna out. Their gratitude seemed boundless; none of which we had earned as of yet. Renita joined me after they left.

"Are you thinking what I'm thinking?" I said to Renita as she stepped into my office.

"Probably," Renita said with a solemn look. I jumped up out of my seat.

"You take the airlines. I'll check the train station, bus terminal, and car rental places."

"I'm on it," Renita said as she went on the move. I followed her out and locked up behind us.

CHAPTER TWELVE

I had checked Union Station and the Greyhound bus station with no success. I was on my way to a local Avis when Renita phoned. Portland International Airport security was glad to help once Renita explained the situation to them. With the help of airport security, Renita had found a couple of airline employees who recognized Eric and Marie. I rushed to join Renita at PDX.

The passenger service agent who issued their boarding passes told us they had booked a one-way flight to Las Vegas. What better place to go for a quick nuptial? We also learned from the same service agent that the runaway teenagers had paid in advance using a credit card. The name on the credit card belonged to Eric Foster. From there, it became a simple matter of tracking their movements.

I telephoned Anna Foster to double check whether she had given her son his own credit card. Anna reaffirmed that she hadn't. The phony card had been supposedly issued by Seamen's Bank. I direct-dialed Seamen's central branch manager who knew Renita and me both professionally and socially. After explaining the situation to him, he, too, was glad to help. He gave me a breakdown on the credit card information, which they froze. The social security number attached to the credit card did not match Eric's social security number. Running a background check on the social security number, the bank was able to trace it to a Byron Sheff. Mr. Sheff had been dead for three years. It was a postmortem form of identity theft. That suggested Eric had somehow gotten his hands on a black market credit card. Fortunately for us, Eric had used the credit card to book a motel room and purchased a few items such as meals and novelty gifts, along with scheduling a quickie wedding ceremony for the next day.

These teenagers were not some fly-by-the-seat-of-your-pants runaways. They had planned this out. They had probably started around the time they realized they were never going to obtain their parents' consent.

To get married, even in Vegas, they had to show proof of age. That suggested they had forged documents such as driver's licenses and maybe even birth certificates to verify they were at least eighteen. I contacted the chief of police for Las Vegas, who I had dealings with back when I was a DEA agent, and he was a first-rate narcotics detective. I explained the situation to him and asked if he would do me a favor. Being the father of two teenagers, he could sympathize, and was glad to help.

A couple of hours later we were posted in the passenger arrival area outside the security checkpoint of Concourse C, watching the flow of passengers into the area. Anna and Nick were anxious. Renita and I stood behind the nervous parents who were keeping a sharp eye out for their teenagers. None of us knew what to expect. The Las Vegas Police Chief had kept his word and personally made certain the teenagers were on the next direct flight bound for Portland. The Chief also mentioned that he would bill me for the cost of the flight that he had paid for out of his own pocket.

Eric and Marie emerged into the arrival area, hugging each other and looking scared. Their tearful parents rushed to their children and engulfed them in their arms. This seemed to relax the teenager's fears. Renita and I were surprised at how forcefully the teenagers hugged their parents back. They were clearly overjoyed to be reunited with their parents. I don't know whether it was due to something the Vegas Police Chief had said, or if the kids were sorry they had hurt their parents, or a combination thereof, that precipitated the runaway's' emotional response. Whatever motivated their behavior, it was great to see.

Renita and I walked away with the warm satisfaction of a job well done. The kids may have been able to square things with their parents by coming home, but for other legal matters, it would not be that easy. We would do what we could to help Marie and Eric deal with any criminal charges levied against them for the black market credit card and forged documents. My guess was that if the families agreed to repay the bank debt on the credit card and they destroyed all forged documents, all would be forgiven; although with mandatory sentencing in place, one could never tell. Matters could get sticky if the bank or law enforcement decided to play hardball. My hope was that it wouldn't come to that.

"So, C. J., which of the four new Lunsford cases will I be working on solo?" Renita asked, killing my buzz.

***

Alvarez had informed Captain Kelby about their situation regarding the Kylie Preston case. The captain contacted the Denver PD and made arrangements to have Dr. Harry Boulder put on a non-stop flight to Portland. A uniformed Denver police officer accompanied Dr. Boulder as they exited Gate E6. Although the doctor was not handcuffed (nor did the Denver officer have a grip on Boulder), it was clear to any casual observer, from the close proximity and wary eye the Denver officer kept on the doctor as they walked, that Boulder was being escorted. With his muscular build (between five-eleven and six-one and about two hundred pounds), the blue-eyed, clean-shaven, thinning-grayish-blond-haired doctor appeared the GQ version of success, wearing a designer suit, shirt, tie, expensive shoes, and groomed as if ready for the magazine cover. Alvarez and McCaskill stepped up to greet Dr. Boulder and his escort.

"Detective Alvarez?" the Denver officer said. Alvarez and McCaskill flashed their badges and IDs. The officer took a cursory look at them.

"Dr. Harry Boulder, I presume," Alvarez said to the GQ man.

"I am. What's this all about, Detectives?" the doctor said with a haughty air. "This cop," Boulder gave a quick jerk of his head toward the Denver officer, "wouldn't tell me anything."

"We can take it from here," Alvarez said to the officer. The officer gave the detectives a curt nod. Alvarez and McCaskill shook the officer's hand. "Thanks for your help," Alvarez said to the officer.

Boulder did not appear to like being dismissed.

"My pleasure," the officer said to Alvarez's expression of gratitude. "I've never been to Portland. I like what I saw from the sky. I'll have to bring my family here on vacation sometime."

"Make it the summer," McCaskill said. "They'll love it."

"I'll remember that," he said to McCaskill. "Born here?"

"Born and bred in the northwest." The officer looked at Alvarez.

"I'm originally from San Diego."

"The land of sunshine. What brought you to the northwest?"

"Opportunity." Harry Boulder's patience was running thin. He remained quiet as he continued to try to sort out what these detectives wanted with him.

"I'm from Albuquerque myself," the officer said.

"I've never been there," Alvarez said, "but I hear it's nice."

"It is. I like Denver better." The officer checked his watch. "I'd better get going. My return flight leaves in thirty-four minutes. Which way to Gate D4?"

"That way," McCaskill pointed due west.

"Thanks. Good luck." The officer marched toward Terminal D.

"Now that you've dispensed with the pleasantries," Boulder said, sounding perturbed, "again I ask: what's this all about, Detectives?" Alvarez stood on one side of Boulder, McCaskill the other.

"We need to ask you a few questions, Doctor," Alvarez said.

"Regarding what?—And why was it so important to cut my conference short and force me on a plane home?" Then, as if struck by the worst possible scenario for such a necessity, Harry asked, *"Is my wife okay?"*

Alvarez noted Boulder's concern for his wife as legitimate. Unless Boulder was a much better actor than she gave him credit, Alvarez also believed the doctor was in the dark about why they wanted to question him. Alvarez would let the evidence speak for itself. Her gut instinct told her that Boulder was probably guilty of a number of other sins, but he had nothing to do with the murder of Kylie Preston.

"Your wife is fine," McCaskill said in answer to his question.

"My children — nothing's happened to my children, has it?"

"No," McCaskill said.

"All of your questions will be answered downtown, Dr. Boulder," Alvarez said. "As will ours. Now, come along."

"Questions, *downtown*? I demand to know what this is all about."

"All in good time," Alvarez said. Alvarez grabbed Boulder by one wrist; McCaskill the other. Boulder seemed surprised by their strength. "Let's go, Doctor."

"Let go of me," Boulder protested as he tried to free himself. Alvarez and McCaskill applied simultaneous wristlocks on Boulder, straightening his arms behind him and forcing Boulder to bend forward at the waist. Boulder stopped struggling, grunting with more discomfort than pain.

"Either come along quietly or we'll put you in cuffs and drag you," Alvarez said with calm confidence. Dr. Boulder looked from Alvarez to McCaskill back to Alvarez before deciding.

"I can walk on my own. I don't need you two handling me as if I were a common criminal."

"Common is not a word I would use to describe you, Doctor," McCaskill said.

"*What?*" Boulder said.

The detectives released their holds. "Come along, Doctor," Alvarez said. The detectives escorted Dr. Harry Boulder back to their car without another word from him.

CHAPTER THIRTEEN

Alvarez and McCaskill had been interrogating Dr. Harry Boulder about the murder of Kylie Preston and deflecting the skillful legal interventions of his top shelf criminal attorney for over three hours, with more to show for the suspect's innocence than guilt. The doctor was mortified by the accusation and shaken to his core by the grisly coroner photos of Kylie Preston shown to him by the detectives. The detectives had no choice but to release the doctor with a stern warning to remain available to them for further questioning. Alvarez knew more than ever that he wasn't the killer, after their intense grilling. Protocol required she follow through to the end on their only lead.

It had been an exhausting day. The detectives knew many more days like these were ahead before they captured the killer. The eight other murder cases they were working had been ignored. Angel knew they would hear about that from the Captain in the morning.

Angel collected the printout of her daily report from the department laser printer and placed it in her partner's in-basket for Laurie to review. McCaskill acknowledged Alvarez with a nod, maintaining focus on piecing together her daily report.

Alvarez locked her service weapon in her desk. She hip-holstered her off-duty thirty-two revolver, then grabbed her purse from her desk drawer and fished out her car keys. "Leave your report in my in basket when you're done," Angel said. "I'll review it before we hand them in to the Captain in the morning."

McCaskill nodded as she continued typing. "Quite a day, huh?" Alvarez said, slipping her shoulder bag over her left shoulder.

"One I won't forget." Laurie continued to type.

Alvarez took a moment to gather her thoughts before she spoke. "I may have overreacted a little at the crime scene earlier today. I apologize—"

"It was my fault," Laurie interrupted, surrendering her full attention to Angel.

"May I finish?" Alvarez more ordered than requested. Laurie nodded. "I can get a little intense when it comes to my cases. While I applaud your initiative, I abhor—yes, I said abhor—when it is born of ignorance. I can't accept that. Whenever you venture into unique territory, then ask first. There is no such thing as a stupid question; only stupid answers and actions, alright?"

"Yes, I'm—"

"Don't say you're sorry again. Being sorry once is always enough between partners."

"Right." Laurie nodded.

"Go out and socialize tonight," Alvarez said. "Blow off some steam, but don't drink too much or have unprotected sex."

"Detective, partner, and substitute mom," Laurie said.

"I can live with that." Alvarez meant it. "Dancing works for me. That and sex. Being married to a great guy, I get the best of both worlds."

"Rub it in, why don't you."

"Good night, detective." Laurie found herself smiling at Angel having called her detective. She always enjoyed the sound of the title, especially coming from her partner.

"Good night, Detective," Laurie said.

"And, just for the record, I thought Mrs. Boulder's toothpick line was pretty good," Alvarez said as she was leaving.

"Me too," Laurie said as she returned to writing her daily report.

CHAPTER FOURTEEN

Renita came into the office the next day at one-seventeen in the afternoon, presumably her way of protesting not landing one of the cases she had wanted to investigate. Renita was wearing a black ruffled wool and cashmere wrap draped over a sophisticated navy blue V-neck cashmere sweater dress with a matching cardigan, and elegant metallic pumps. She held a cloud-silver pleated flap clutch. Her shoulder length curly black hair was impeccable. Sparse makeup brought forth a soft glow to her lovely features. Renita looked as if she were ready to attend an upscale event or was returning from an all-night party session with Ernest. Nothing about Renita made me think that she was not refreshed. Her eyes were clear and her body language strong, good indicators that Renita was well rested. If Renita had dressed up for the office, her reasoning escaped me on how that part of her plan fit into torturing me. Even looking as stunning as she was, Renita had to know I had become impervious to any of her attempts at seduction.

"Good afternoon," I said to Renita as she attempted to walk past my office to her own without as much as a glance. Renita stopped. She turned and stared at me as if I were a bother as she removed her wrap.

"Good afternoon, boss." Renita stepped into my doorway.

"You're a little overdressed for the office." Renita shrugged off my comment.

"I felt like wearing something nice," Renita flippantly said. "It helps me deal with my most recent disappointment."

"It would have been *nice* of you to call to let me know that you were going to be late."

"Were you concerned?" Renita asked, toying with me.

"Yes."

"Sorry, boss, it must have slipped my mind."

"Try not to let it happen again."

"I'll do my best," Renita said, still sounding flippant.

"You'd better do more than try." I kept my tone sober. "Because as much as I care about you, I will fire you if you cannot behave professionally."

"If I were doing the work I deserved, professionalism would not be a problem." Her tone switched from flippant to defensive.

"You are doing work comparable to your skill level. When you're deserving of more responsibility, you'll get it."

"And how is a person supposed to prove themselves when one is not being given a chance?"

"One earns additional opportunities by doing their assigned jobs well."

"Whatever." Renita was losing patience with our debate. One thing I thought Renita would be aware of about me, by now, was that I am not stubborn unless I have good reason to be. My concern for her well-being will always outlast her attitude.

"Take it or leave it," I said. Renita appeared stunned by my nonchalance. I hadn't meant to state it that way. I didn't mean that; I hadn't meant what I said. Renita stepped up to my desk, dropping her wrap and clutch on my paperwork.

"They arrested that doctor for the murder of Kylie Preston," Renita said, not only changing the subject but sounding more like the investigative partner I enjoyed working with. That compromise was as close as I was going to get to an apology or a declaration of cooperation, for the moment. It was good enough for me.

"They haven't arrested Dr. Harry Boulder," I said. "They questioned him."

"What he did to that poor woman: butchered her like she was some kind of animal."

"His cutting was more precise than that, from what I've read. The killer apparently harvested her organs and even preserved her head in ice."

"That's horrible!"

"Yes, it is," I said matter-of-factly.

"What is this world coming to, C. J.?"

"The kind of world you're anxious to jump into with both feet."

Renita turned her head from me with a slight huff.

"NPR said they had to let Dr. Boulder go due to a lack of evidence. The police still see him as a person of interest."

"Do you think he did it?" Renita turned her head to look at me.

"I have no idea. I'd have to see the evidence and interview Boulder before I could even form an opinion. As you know, you can tell a lot about a person from a face-to-face meeting."

"That's true. From what I've seen of Dr. Boulder during my time following Singleton, I would never have suspected him capable of something like that."

"Looks can be deceiving. All sorts of people are capable of anything," I said with somber reflection. A DEA flashback was creeping into my consciousness; one that reminded me of the case we were discussing. I tried fighting it off.

"What do you mean?" Renita noticed my shifting frame of mind. We had been together long enough that we were receptive to each other's moods. I didn't want to burden Renita with one of my dark memories. Those were something I wished to shield Renita from for as long as possible.

"I hope you're spared the dark side of life like the person who killed Kylie Preston probably lives in. There's nothing there for anyone but suffering and regret."

The words slipped out. I had meant to change the subject. Renita could see I was slipping into one of my rare broodings. She knew it usually related to my DEA days, a past I rarely revealed much about to her. Renita had even asked Destini about it, only to discover Destini was as blind about that part of my life as Renita was.

I don't share my coarser experiences of my time with the Agency with anyone aside from my ex-colleagues. As with soldiers of war, they are the ones who understand those battles best. Destini was content to leave it alone, at least for now. Renita did not possess that kind of patience. There was a constant gnawing in her gut to get at the facts. That was what made her a good investigator. Controlling that gnawing and not having it control you was an area she still needed to work on. I knew that one day, Renita would hone her investigative skills to the point that she would pry into my past and discover some of my sordid secrets. When she does, Renita will want to talk to me about them. I don't know how I'm going to handle it when that time comes. For now, I needed to pull it together.

"Do you like my new dress?" Renita modeled it for me. I knew what she was doing. It was working.

"It's lovely, but inappropriate for the business of the day, don't you think?"

"I wasn't planning on wearing it on my stakeout."

"Good," I said. "You'd stand out like a Nordstrom model at the Goodwill in that outfit."

"All right; then I guess I'll take it off." Renita started slipping out of her dress.

"Not in my office, young lady," I said, pointing toward my open front door. "*Out.*"

"Picky, picky, picky," Renita grabbed her wrap and clutch. "And, just for the record, Ernest took me to lunch at Park Kitchen. I wanted to look extra special for him." Renita exited with a playful smile. I watched her go, shaking my head in amusement. Renita was attempting to distract me from the brink. *That kid sure knows how to get a rise out of me*, I thought for a moment before a nefarious flashback of my DEA past found its way into my porous consciousness.

CHAPTER FIFTEEN

It was an upper-middle-class neighborhood in Bible belt America at mid-Spring. At 1:23 p.m., most people were at work. Some homemakers were at home. Our interest focused on an inconspicuous house where the owner worked out of his home at a time when that was rarely feasible. We were a raiding party of six DEA agents. The drug dealer we were about to take down was a middle-management narcotics dealer. He was also a known killer. That was his street rep. Local homicide believed he was responsible for at least a dozen murders. They had yet to find anything that would stick.

We scurried to the drug dealer's house from our vehicles, parked around the corner out of sight. We managed to make it to his front door undetected. We pinned ourselves, three against the walls, on either side of the door. The lieutenant dispatched a team of two agents to circle around to the back of the house. The rest of us waited, remaining quiet and focused.

I had been with the DEA for almost a year. It was my second raid. Most of my work up until that point had been surveillance and office work. While my military training and combat experience had prepared me for open warfare, urban combat was a whole other matter. I was in good hands. The agents I was with were all raid veterans.

The two agents radioed the lieutenant that they were in position. "Stay on my hip and do exactly as I tell you," the lieutenant whispered to me. I nodded my assent. Locked and loaded, everyone readied themselves.

The agent with the battering ram stood in front of the door awaiting the lieutenant's signal. The lieutenant raised his hand. We held our collective breaths. The lieutenant dropped his hand in a chopping motion.

The agent with the battering ram broke open the front door. "Go! Go! Go!" the lieutenant yelled at us and into the radio as we bolted inside.

We went in prepared for anything. We moved with precision, ready to respond to any type of resistance. There was none. Searching the house, we found the person we were after eating a mixing bowl full of cereal with milk while reading the morning newspaper. The dealer was covered in blood. The six of us trained our weapons on him. He did not budge. He did not even look at us. It was as though he was unaware of our presence.

The lieutenant quoted the man his Miranda rights. The dealer did not respond. The lieutenant ordered the two agents who had entered by the back door to search the upstairs. Me, he ordered to take a look at the cardboard boxes we had swept past in the living room on our way to the kitchen.

I opened a few of the cartons stacked eight across and five deep, and looked inside. The cartons I opened contained PCP, Ecstasy, Crystal Meth, LSD, and heroin; all ready for distribution. Since the unopened cartons appeared identical, it was safe to assume their contents were the same. As I returned to the dining room to report my findings, the two agents the lieutenant had sent to check the upstairs ran by me outside. I hurried to the dining room to find the other DEA agents had not moved. Neither had the dealer. I reported to the lieutenant what was in the boxes. There were smiles all around. We later learned it was a twenty million dollar bust: a regular red feather in our caps day.

The two agents who had bolted outside returned, apologizing for their reaction. They told us there were bodies in the bathroom. The agents appeared nauseous. Most of the color had drained from their faces. They had rushed outside to vomit, not wanting to contaminate the crime scene. The dealer turned the page of his newspaper, leaving bloody fingerprints where he had touched it as he continued to read as though we were not there.

The blood on his person had begun to congeal. The dealer shouted out four names to come and eat. The lieutenant grabbed the dealer by the arm, attempting to pull him to his feet. The dealer shoved the lieutenant away, his free arm liberating his captured arm from the lieutenant's vice-like grip with a twist. The lieutenant fell. The dealer scowled at us, finally acknowledging our presence.

Another agent and I attempted to restrain the man. The dealer went berserk. We were losing the slippery battle against the man steeped in blood. He was not a big man, but he was incredible strong. Two other agents joined the fray. Even after breaking the dealer's arm while trying to cuff him, he continued to fight. The dealer seemed oblivious to pain. We later learned he was high on PCP. Even after we secured him in the patrol wagon, shackled, beaten, broken, battered, and bruised, he continued to throw violent tantrums.

After the lieutenant called it in, the four of us who had entered through the front door reentered to check the rest of the house. The lieutenant ordered the two DEA agents who had recovered from their bout with nausea to stand guard at the front and back entrances to make certain no one came in or out.

What we found repulsed even my veteran colleagues. It was a tragedy that will haunt me for the rest of my life. Had I not seen the splattered remains of bodies due to explosives in the service, I would have gotten ill. Blood spatter painted the walls. In the bathtub were piled the butchered remains of a woman and three young children, pooled in their own blood. One agent found the hammer that had been used to bludgeon them. Another agent found the power saw used to slaughterer them. According to forensics, the woman and children—while probably unconscious due to repeated hammer blows to the head—were still alive when they were butchered. The ME confirmed that. We later learned that they were the dealer's wife and their three children. The deranged dealer had done that to his family...to people he presumably loved and who had loved him. All of us stared at the horrific sight in heartrending silence, trying to grasp the incomprehensible.

The drug dealer tearfully confessed to the murders of his family once he came down from his PCP high, although he couldn't remember anything about it. No one involved in the case doubted the authenticity of his remorse. Multiple psychologists agreed that the reason we found the drug dealer in a stupor was due to a combination of shock and PCP, working in concert to protect his conscious mind from the horrible acts he had committed. The temporary insanity plea kept him off death row. He is still serving a life sentence in a maximum-security prison with no chance for parole.

CHAPTER SIXTEEN

Me, Monty, and three teenagers named Jamaal, Preston, and Duane (who was nicknamed 'D') were playing four teenagers and Ernest in a mid-morning full court basketball game at the Fremont Community Center. Jamaal pushed the ball up-court. The opposing point guard stepped up to defend Jamaal. Jamaal waved off a pick I wanted to set for him. Preston and I fanned out to the wings. Jamaal maneuvered the ball across mid-court with his defender draped all over him. Monty and D took turns diving toward the basket.

Monty was a short, powerful man with aubergine skin and an incredible smile who sometimes told prison stories as though they were nostalgia. Monty and Ernest Fullman were partners in Fullman's Restaurant. They were also volunteers and mentors at the Center.

Jamaal passed me the ball. I dribbled hard to the basket before my defender, with Ernest backing him, forced me toward the top of the key. Jamaal set up on the wing. I bounced passed the ball to D, who had faded to the three-point line in the left corner. I stayed put near the foul line. D dribbled hard down the line toward the basket before his defender cut him off, with Ernest sliding over to support him. D bounce passed the ball to Monty, who had shaken his defender by coming hard from the weak side. Ernest slid over to stop Monty, assisted by both Jamaal's defender and mine. Monty passed the ball to Jamaal. Jamaal faked out his defender, who had recovered with a hard jab step to his right, driving to his left. Ernest cut off Jamaal. Jamaal kicked the ball out to me, still floating around the foul line. My defender moved in tight, respecting my jumper. I bounce passed the ball to D, who was making his home on the strong side of the court. D passed the ball to Preston. Preston no look bounced passed the ball to Monty. Monty went up for the layup. Ernest slid over to stop him. Monty floated past Ernest to the other side of the hoop, making a reverse layup tight to the rim before Ernest had a chance to block his shot. Monty gave Preston and me a high five as we hustled down-court on defense. We were still down eleven to fifteen in a game played to sixteen.

On the next possession, the teenager with the Jay-Z cut in his hair finished us off with a twelve-foot jumper: an open shot made possible by a great pick set by Ernest, on me. After suffering my third straight defeat with three different lineups, I declined an offer from the next challengers to run with them. Monty accepted in my place. The winners took a brief bathroom and water break before stepping back onto the court to defend their reign.

At seven-three and nearly four hundred pounds, Ernest was by far the biggest man out there. It didn't help that he was agile and athletic. To attempt to instill some sense of fairness to the games, Ernest volunteered to operate no closer than ten feet from the basket on the offensive end. The problem with that strategy was that Ernest had good range from the three-point line in, and he was an excellent passer. The big man was the primary reason his team kept winning.

Ernest was about to collect his fourth consecutive victory from the sidelines when Shelly Morton blindsided me as I was discussing with Jamaal, Preston, and D their possible career choices after they graduated high school. Shelly sauntered up to me wearing white sweat socks, black leather sandals, baggy basketball shorts, and a loose-fitting T-shirt that read "Yes You Can." His chubby face and chubby body made the tan skinned man appear lovable. One look into his intense brown eyes dispelled any hint that he was a pushover. Those same brown eyes turned reassuring in a deserving person's time of need. Every kid at the Center knew that Shelly meant business. Those same children also knew they could come to him in confidence with any concern. The man with Shelly, I had never seen before.

"How's it going, C. J.?" Shelly said.

"Don't ask. I haven't won once today."

"What's the matter? Your three-point shot not working?" Shelly said with his winning smile, another misleading characteristic that he might be a softy. The teenagers said hi to Shelly, then excused themselves to join some of their friends after we agreed we'd talk later.

"More like too much Ernest," I said. "He's crushing everybody." As if on cue, Ernest palmed a twelve-foot jumper attempt by a teenager and fed a perfect outlet pass to his point guard for a fast break that led to a score.

"Cheer up," the stranger said in a baritone voice, "there's always next time."

"C. J. Cavanaugh, this is Richard Weston."

Richard Weston and I shook hands. He had a powerful grip. It didn't surprise me. He appeared to be someone who worked out a lot. Weston stood about five-nine and was clean-shaven, with straight brown hair and a nose slightly bent to the left, possibly the result of a fight. His clothes and shoes were bargain basement but his grooming was tight. His blue eyes rested on me like a warm blanket. "Nice to meet you."

"Likewise. Everyone calls me Wes."

"I wonder why." Shelly and Wes smiled.

"Are you the same person who saved Eric and Marie from making a terrible mistake?" Wes asked.

"I doubt if they'd agree it was a mistake, terrible or otherwise, but my partner and I may have had a little something to do with stopping their wedding."

"Your partner?"

"Renita Harris, Wes," Shelly said. "C. J. and Renita are the best private investigators in the city—the best in the northwest, for my money."

"That's very high praise," Wes said.

"So says the man who has yet to pay for any of our services."

"And I'd like to keep it that way."

"I know who I'll be coming to first if I need any detective work." I considered correcting Wes on the difference between being a detective and an investigator but decided to pass.

"Wes is a family and relationship counselor. He's counseling the Jennings and Fosters through their teenage love crisis."

"I wouldn't call it a crisis. They're just a couple of young people who are in love, and for them nothing else matters."

"How's that coming?" I said to Wes.

"Good, the families have a few hurdles to clear but overall they're on course to resolving them."

"Let me guess: you're getting the parents to respect their children's feelings toward one another, while getting the children to appreciate their parent's concerns," I said.

"That's it in a nutshell. Have you ever thought about being a counselor?"

"In an unofficial capacity, he already is. That's a big part of what C. J. does for some of these young people."

"I'm glad to hear things are working out for those families. They're good people."

"That they are," Shelly said. "Thanks for putting in a solid for the kids with the bank and the police." Working with young people most of the time, some of their jargon had rubbed off on Shelly without him even realizing it. I always found it amusing.

"No problem," I said. "You're not balling?" I asked Shelly.

"I twisted my ankle a couple of days ago. It still needs time to heal."

"What about you, Wes? You play?"

"Maybe next time. I have to get going. I have a session in less than an hour. Nice meeting you, Mr. Cavanaugh."

"Call me C. J."

"C. J.," Wes said as we shook hands again. "Shelly, I'll talk to you later." Wes lightly patted Shelly on the back. Shelly nodded. Wes left.

"I haven't seen him around before," I said.

"Wes is new to the area, from Oklahoma. He has a modest practice in the Bannock Building over on Willamette Boulevard."

"I considered opening my office over there: more office space for your money, easy access, and plenty of parking."

"Yet you chose downtown."

"What can I say. I love downtown."

"Wes stopped in around the time Marie and Eric ran away and asked if he could do some volunteer work."

"Of course you said no."

"Not in this lifetime. He does a group therapy session for our most troubled teens every other week. The kids really like him."

"Cool."

"Next!" the teenager with Jay Z in his scalp said after swishing a winning fifteen-footer.

"I'm back in, Coach," I said to Shelly.

"Go get 'em."

I joined my four new teenage teammates, hopeful of dethroning the champs. Monty decided it was time to sit one out.

CHAPTER SEVENTEEN

Two months had passed since the gruesome murder of Kylie Preston. I had flown home to Pittsburgh to see my family for a few days over Thanksgiving. I returned to Pittsburgh over the Christmas through New Year's holidays to celebrate Christmas, Kwanzaa, and New Years with the people I loved most. Destini had gone to Atlanta to do the same, that week. Renita stayed put. She was already home.

Our family's New Year's celebration is always extra special. We gather at a nondenominational church for Night Watch Services on New Year's Eve. This tradition can be traced back to December 31, 1862, in the African American community. It was then known as Freedom's Eve. On that night, African Americans came together in churches and homes all across the nation, awaiting news that the Emancipation Proclamation had become law. At the stroke of midnight on January 1, 1863, all slaves in the Confederate States were declared free. When the news was received, there were prayers, shouts, and songs of joy as people fell to their knees and thanked God. African Americans have gathered in churches on New Year's Eve ever since, praising God for bringing us safely through another year.

Dr. Harry Boulder had been cleared of any involvement in the death of the woman found cut to pieces in the trunk of his car. Some people held onto the belief that Dr. Boulder had done it. They blamed the system, his money, and wealthy connections as one (or all) of the reasons why justice was denied. Anyone with inside access to the case knew Boulder was innocent. The valid downside to that realization meant that the real killer was still at large.

Something criminal had come out of the thorough investigation of Dr. Harry Boulder. Due to the necessary scrutiny into his life as a result of homicide suspicion, his practice of gouging Medicaid, Medicare, and private insurance companies on medical costs had come to light. The victimized had lined up to prosecute Dr. Boulder. Lunsford was near the top of that list.

Renita and I had settled into a steady work rhythm both independently and as a team. We kept each other posted on the daily progress of our individual cases and bounced ideas off each other about the best ways to proceed. Initially, Renita was unhappy with the case divide; but once our investigations were underway, she matured into the labor without so much as a huff.

Renita had wrapped up the Sessions' case in favor of Lunsford. I had done the same with the Grassley case. We were discussing the two remaining Lunsford cases in Renita's office when Carl Wheaton paid us an unexpected visit. I had only seen Carl a couple of times since the murder of one of his colleagues. I had offered my condolences the first time. Carl didn't seem to want to talk about it. I left it alone.

Carl walked in wearing his trademark three-piece suit; this one a navy blue pinstripe. His black double-breasted trench coat was open and his black leather shoes were spit-shined to a high gloss. Carl stood about a head shorter than my six-four frame. His body was lean and strong from his love of running and tolerance for weight lifting. Carl scraped his clean-shaven baby face a year ago for a full reddish-brown beard. The change made him look both rustic and a bit menacing. When Carl removed his black fedora, it exposed his faded hairstyle. With the beard, it made him look ten years older than his mid-forties. Carl thought that growing a beard had done him good despite only his lackeys agreeing with his testament.

Renita and I exchanged pleasantries with Carl and then, as was his custom, we got down to business. The three of us made ourselves comfortable in my office, all of us drinking cold water we had helped ourselves to from the filtered water in the kitchen. Carl was typically professional, but with an upbeat edge. Today that edge was dull.

"I want to hire you to investigate Kylie Preston's murder," he said, his uneven brown eyes appearing a bit distant. "I've already spoken to Alan Lunsford on the matter and he's all for it. Whatever it takes to find her killer, he's more than happy to help."

"Carl, that's not what we do," I said.

"You've done it in the past."

Here we go again, I thought, *another special request.* I felt as though I should have been spinning records rather than running a specialized investigation agency.

"Those were unusual circumstances," Renita said.

"You know we don't normally get involved in homicide investigations," I added. "You have a team of investigators at your disposal. Why not use them?"

"If I thought we could deliver, I would. The truth is: we don't have any homicide investigators on our staff. We lack the expertise."

"You mean, like the homicide detectives employed by the Portland Police Bureau already working the case," I said.

"I know Angel Alvarez is good, and that she's been all over this case. Angel probably has another dozen cases that require her attention. I need to know that someone topnotch is focused on solving this crime."

"C. J.'s right, Carl. If you want more hands on deck then maybe you should make use of the abundance of investigative resources already at your disposal."

"The police are still your best bet," I said. "At some point the FBI may become involved if they need help. You can't ask for more law enforcement than that."

"It would mean a lot to me if you two would take the case. The Lunsford family would be grateful if you did, as well. I'll quadruple your normal rate."

Renita's eyebrows went up.

"It's not about the money," I said.

"Then what's it about?"

"How many times do I have to say it? The police can do a better job of investigating Kylie Preston's murder than we can."

"I know no one will try harder to find Kylie's killer than you two."

Renita gave a slight twist of her head. "He's right about that, C. J."

"Do it as a personal favor to me."

I let out a heavy sigh, prepared to give it some thought.

"*We'll do it,*" Renita blurted out. I looked at my partner, who shrugged and gave a beseeching smile.

"What do you say, C. J.?" I did not see how I could turn Carl down, especially after my partner had already committed.

"We'll look into it. If we think we can help, we're on board."

Carl became ecstatic. He jumped up and uncharacteristically gave Renita and me a hug. *"Thank you; thank you so much."*

"There are no guarantees," I said.

"I'm confident we'll get to the bottom of this." I looked at my partner with furrowed brows. Renita had been caught up in the moment. To make that kind of statement under those circumstances is akin to a promise. A promise there was no way we were certain we could deliver on. Renita realized she had said too much. "I meant to say: we'll do our best," Renita amended, trying to reel in her mistake.

"I know how it works," Carl said. We all returned to our seats.

After a moment of solemn contemplation I said, "Tell us everything you can about Kylie Preston."

Carl let out a heavy sigh of relief. He took a moment to compose himself before he spoke. "I started at Lunsford's as a salesman."

"You, a salesman," I said with amusement. "I can't believe that." Renita agreed. Carl was a natural investigator, but I couldn't see him selling bottled water to a thirsty billionaire on a scorching summer's day.

"Believe it. I sold life, auto, theft, renters, flood, and fire insurance. I sucked at it. Kylie was my manager. She took me under her wing and taught me the people skills I lacked. Before I knew it, I'd worked my way from the bottom to the middle of the pack. Kylie didn't stop there. She showed me how to handle office politics and make them work for me. At some point, Kylie must have realized I'd peaked as a salesman, because she suggested I consider other careers within the insurance business. I don't know how she knew, but Kylie talked me into trying out being a fraudulent claims investigator, and I loved it.

"When Kylie was promoted to Regional Manager, she took me along as part of her team. Before I knew it, Kylie promoted me to lead investigator. As Kylie moved up the company ladder, she dragged me along with her. Before I knew it, I was Head Investigator for Lunsford Insurance. I discovered I'd acquired the position in large part due to a glowing recommendation Kylie had written for me. I got the promotion because Kylie Preston believed in me. Maybe she was grooming me for a leadership position all along; I don't know. What I do know is she saw something in me that I didn't know existed, and helped bring it to the surface. I owe her my career."

"Are you sure there wasn't something more between the two of you?" I asked.

"If you're asking if we were lovers, the answer is no; not that I wouldn't have leaped at the chance. Kylie was a dear friend and mentor. I learned everything worth knowing about the insurance business from her."

"I read in the newspaper that she was President of Acquisitions," Renita said.

"That's right."

"Someone in her position must have made enemies along the way," I said.

"Of course."

"Any of them want to see her dead?" My question appeared to give Carl pause while he considered the possibility.

"None I can think of that would follow through on it, especially in such a gruesome fashion. What would cause someone to do something that ghastly?"

"I wish I knew," Renita said.

"No, you don't." Renita and Carl stared at me as if expecting something more on the topic. "Can you find out what insurance policies Ms. Preston was involved in during her tenure?"

"It may take some digging, but sure. She was with the company for over twenty years."

"Send us what you can," Renita said.

"Anything else?"

"That'll do for a start," I said after Renita and I had given Carl's question some thought.

"What are you going to do in the meantime?" Carl asked.

"We'll keep you posted on our investigation with regular reports," I said.

"The same way we normally do when we investigate your insurance claims," Renita added.

"This is not an insurance claim."

"We realize that," Renita said, "but there's no reason the procedure needs to change."

"Fair enough. Thanks again for taking the case."

"Our sincere condolences on the loss of your friend," I said.

"We're really sorry, Carl," Renita said. Carl gave us a faint smile that vanished as quickly as it appeared.

"You know my mom died of cancer," Carl said.

"Yeah," I said.

"My dad and grandparents were devastated. My grandfather did what he could, but he wasn't good with emotions. My sister was in denial. Kylie was there for me every step of the way. She was my shoulder to lean on. She didn't need to be. Kylie was a good person."

Renita and I responded with slight nods. There was nothing to say and we all knew it.

"I'd better get going," Carl said in a voice resigned to that fact. "Kylie was divorced. She has a couple of teenagers from that marriage."

"We know," I said.

"We read about it in the paper," Renita said.

"Their dad flew in from Philadelphia as soon as he heard. He's been staying with them at Kylie's house. He's going to take his kids back to Philly when the school year is up. I'm going to stop by and see if there's anything I can do. Mind if I get started on that research tomorrow?"

"Not a problem," I said. "Get it to us whenever you can. We'll get on it as soon as we clear our docket."

"Send to me all of the outstanding Lunsford cases you have, and I'll have some of my investigators take it from there."

"Consider it done," I said.

"Are you working any other cases for anyone else?"

"That's it for the moment," Renita answered.

"If you don't mind, I'd like for you to exclusively work on Kylie Preston's murder."

"Sure," I said.

Carl and I shook on it. Renita and Carl shook on it.

"If there's anything we can do, Carl, let us know," Renita said.

"Just find the person who did this." Renita and I nodded. Carl showed himself out, looking somber.

"I think he was in love with Kylie Preston," Renita said after the front door snapped shut.

"I believe you're right."

"I wonder if his wife knows."

"That's a very good question."

I had an unsettling sense there was something besides the obvious that Carl wasn't telling us about his involvement with Kylie Preston. My gut also told me I wasn't going to like what I found.

CHAPTER EIGHTEEN

Destini took me to dinner at Jimmy Mak's to celebrate justice. Destini and Liederman had been working on the Kasparova case for a little more than a year. The leads were difficult to unearth. As they peeled back layer upon layer of the murder victim's life, suspects emerged and vanished on a wave of palpable alibis. A month ago, Destini and Liederman uncovered a tiny clue that led them right to the doorstep of the murderer. It had been something they had overlooked, like a comma in a sentence. They had arrested the killer this morning on a mountain of solid evidence they had unwittingly been accumulating all of this time. Destini was as giddy with excitement about closing the case as a scientist discovering the cure for cancer. I enjoyed seeing my love that way. The source of her exuberance made me uneasy, although I had learned to mask it well.

The Mel Brown Quartet was taking a break from a great jazz set. Destini was enjoying a chocolate spoon cake for dessert. I was doing the same with a sinfully delicious slice of New York style cheesecake that I knew I would regret eating during my morning run. After an hour of a jubilant, play by play breakdown on the trail of evidence that led to the miraculous arrest, our conversation had steered from her recent victory to flit around our lives in general. The conversation was wading in that general pool when I mentioned, "Carl hired my agency to work on the Kylie Preston murder."

Destini stopped eating and looked at me with mild disbelief. "You're kidding?"

"No, I'm not."

The amused glow in Destini's hazel eyes deepened and sharpened to a penetrating stare. "Why?"

"The murder victim was a dear friend of Carl's."

"Were they close?"

"Close enough."

Destini's stare softened. "I'm sorry to hear that. Give Carl my condolences."

"I will. I know Angel is working the case."

"She and Laurie McCaskill."

"Angel is solid. What's McCaskill like?"

"Smart, serious, focused, driven."

"Sounds like someone I know."

"If you're referring to me, I'd say you're right."

"Is she married? Does she have any children?"

"No and no."

"Again, sounds like someone else I know."

"Are you trying to tell me something?"

"I'm simply pointing out some interesting similarities between you and—"

"The modern working woman," Destini said, completing my sentence more to her liking.

"—between you and Detective McCaskill. Any extrapolation otherwise is your doing."

"I'd stop right there before you venture onto thin ice."

"Message received."

"How's McCaskill working out?"

"So far, no complaints. Why are you so interested in Detective McCaskill?"

"Just curious."

"Curious as to how she's going to react to you treading on her terrain?"

"Yes." Destini chuckled. "What's so funny?"

"This should be interesting."

"It shouldn't be a problem. We'll make sure to walk gently with our investigation so not to crack any eggs."

"And how do you plan on doing that?"

"That's how we roll."

"The nature of this murder makes it a high-profile case. Flying low and slow is not going to keep you off the radar."

"Angel knows us."

"McCaskill doesn't. All detectives are territorial. I would've thought you knew that by now. Angel may tolerate your working on her case, but

McCaskill is trying to establish herself. She's not going to appreciate you snooping around her homicide, particularly one that is garnering national attention."

"You're saying I should stay clear of the investigating detectives?"

"I'm simply warning you not to expect to be welcomed with open arms—at least by McCaskill."

"Are I ever?"

Destini smiled. "I suppose not."

Destini returned to enjoying her spoon cake. "I can't say I'm surprised," Destini said after swallowing a spoonful of cake.

"What aren't you surprised about?"

"Carl has a lot of well-deserved confidence in you after all of the quality work you've done for Lunsford. That and the fact that you've managed to solve a few tough murder cases on your own. And if you tell anyone I said that, I'll deny it."

"Your secret's safe with me. I didn't solve those cases on my own. I had help from people like you and Renita."

"You were the one who put the pieces together. Have you ever considered becoming a homicide detective?"

"Me a homicide detective, that's a laugh."

"With your background and proven track record, you'd be a shoe-in to join the force. I might even be able to pull some strings and get you assigned as my partner."

"Working with you does sound tempting."

Destini knew how I felt about death. Yet, she was serious about her suggestion. Perhaps her underlying motivation was to get me to see what her work meant to her. If I saw the world through her lens, maybe I'd change my mind, or, more importantly, have a change of heart about her job.

Murder was the main issue, here. I had seen too much needless slaughter in my life to make resolving it by apprehending its culprits my daily profession. Every homicide inquiry I had ever been involved in as a private investigator, I had been dragged into; the Kylie Preston case being no exception. A dreadful memory was seeping into my mind from my DEA past that I deflected in order not to flash back. Destini must have realized something was happening. She called off her full court press.

"It was just a thought."

"Liederman would love being replaced as your partner," I said, lightening the mood. "He might want to take me out back to discuss it."

"Dave will live. As you well know, our relationship is strictly professional."

"You're friends."

"Friends who are both involved with other people."

"Has Dave asked Lillian to marry him yet?"

I knew Lillian. I'd had opportunities to chat with David's woman-friend at special events and functions we attended as couples together. Lillian was charming, intelligent, beautiful, and determined. All personality traits of Destini, exposing me to the fact that Dave and I had similar tastes in women. Lillian was in love with Dave. I did not get the vibe from Dave that he felt the same about her. I knew I was being irrational. Destini was the kind of woman to confess if she had strong feelings for anyone else. It was silly of me to think that Destini would cheat on me. Jealousy is an irrational beast that can take you for a bucking bronco ride only to toss you like a rag doll when done, leaving you face down in the dirt whining about your life. So be it. I was on that wild ride until I tamed it or it threw me.

"Dave hasn't worked up to it yet, but it's coming," Destini said.

So is interplanetary space travel, I thought, *but I don't expect to be here when it happens.* "You and Dave are friends as well as professional partners," I said.

"Meaning?"

"Your situation is no different than mine with Renita."

"You left out one major detail."

I already knew where Destini was headed. Since I'd taken matters this far, I'd might as well finish the race. "What's that?" I said in response to Destini's comment.

"My partner's not in love with me the way Renita is in love with you."

The playful debate of Dave versus Renita had turned serious. I could see it in Destini's eyes and heard it in her voice. It was time to shut it down.

"Thanks, but no thanks," I said.

"About what?"

"Your homicide detective offer. I like being my own boss. Having you as the boss in my personal life is quite enough."

"If only that were true, my love." Destini wiped her berry lips with her white cloth napkin. "When the doctor didn't pan out for the murder, it made sense that Carl would turn to someone he trusted to pick up the ball."

"The Lunsford family wanted me to become involved as well."

"Really," Destini said, sounding pleased and surprised. "Now I'm really impressed."

"Portland Homicide is great at solving murders," I said with conviction. "I tell everyone who is willing to listen."

"We know it, but the public doesn't seem to get the message. Have you told Angel you're going to be working her case?"

"Not yet."

"I'd like to be there for that."

"It shouldn't be a problem. Angel and I have worked together before. We get along well."

"You've exchanged information on mutual persons of interest in regards to different cases you were working. You've never worked together on the same homicide investigation."

"I'll clear it with Angel tomorrow. Everything should be fine."

"Maybe. Make certain you keep the Captain in the loop."

"I will. I'll let you know how it goes with Angel."

"Please do, I'm always in the mood for a good laugh."

"Not always, but I'll tell you anyway."

"How's Renita going to fit into all of this?"

"I'm not certain. Renita doesn't get that investigating a homicide can put you in the crosshairs of a killer."

"I know, that's why I'm asking. She's going to want to be in the mix."

"Renita doesn't do any field work on this case without me."

"Good luck with that plan." Destini sounded amused.

"Right now my plan is to keep an eye on her," I said. "The trick is doing so without her realizing it."

"That might work, unless something comes up when you need to split up to get the job done. Dave and I go through that all of the time. All detective partnerships do."

"I know, I know; Renita and I have been through that too."

I didn't want to give much thought as to how I was going to keep Renita in check during the Preston murder investigation. With my willful partner, I knew it was going to be a challenge that would have to be addressed on an incident-by-incident basis.

"I don't want to see any harm come to Renita either," Destini said. "Sooner or later you're going to have to let that woman fly."

"You've certainly changed your tune about Renita. There was a time all you wanted me to do was fire her."

"I'm still all for that. But you're obstinate and she's your partner. The more accomplished she is, the more valuable she is to you. And the safer you'll be."

"It's me you're worried about, not Renita."

"I'm always worried about you. Your job can be dangerous, too. Renita gets more of my 'general caring about human beings overall' kind of concern. The concern I have for you runs much deeper than that."

"I'll always be there for you."

"You'd better be, because after I break you down to accept my profession, we have a life to build together."

I was speechless as we looked into each other's eyes. What I had witnessed was a back door acceptance to my marriage proposal and we both knew it. Destini took a sip of her coffee. I did the same with my hot tea. The Mel Brown Quartet began their next set.

"You remember to be safe for the both of us," Destini said with genuine anxiety. I was a bit shaken by her tone. I had worked dangerous cases before. Destini always showed concern; but never to this extent. She was afraid for me.

"I'm always careful," I said. "I love you."

"That goes without saying," Destini said, her indomitable spirit returning. "I love you, too."

And the band played on.

CHAPTER NINETEEN

Brian Dixon was a doughy, balding, middle-aged man who had stopped wearing contact lenses due to a vision condition known as presbyopia. His new reading glasses did not compliment his ruddy, puffy face. This did not stop him from wearing them all of the time, even though he did not need to. Brian had been a licensed public accountant and investment counselor for thirty years. He took great pride in his work. He loved unraveling what seemed to most to be the mysteries of accounting and personal and business investing. Brian also enjoyed swindling his most lucrative clients out of a sizeable share of their money. He was very good at it. So good, in fact, that most never realized what he was up to until it was too late. The few that had the courage to take Brian to court, lost. Brian was excellent at bending the law without breaking it. It wasn't his fault if they were ignorant of how money works. As far as Brian was concerned, he was doing them a favor. Maybe next time they wouldn't be so gullible.

His wife left him over his despicable business practices and his infidelity. She took their children and returned to Maine. There she married a marine biologist whom she often called 'honey' and Brian's children called 'Dad'. Brian's children called him 'Brian'.

His past caught up to him (or karma, as his ex-wife would say). Because of his seedy reputation, clients were becoming more difficult to obtain. His current crop of steady small-potato bookkeeping jobs weren't worth cheating. Like so many others, Brian had lost most of his money due to squalid economic times. All of his investment strategies tanked. His savings had eroded to the point where he was scrambling to keep up with the third mortgage he had taken out on his house.

His doorbell rang at 8:27 a.m. It was Sunday, and Brian was expecting a potential client at nine. While Brian found it unusual for someone to desire to conduct business on a Sunday, opportunity had no boundaries. Brian grabbed his thirty-eight. Doing so had become a habit over the years. There were remnants of threats made by irate clients who had threatened to kill him. A couple of his previous suckers had attacked him. Brian wasn't a fighter. In each incident, Brian lost the fistfights but won in court. His assailants were still in prison. Since Brian had coerced the Johnny-come-latelies into giving him power of attorney over their finances prior to their discoveries, Brian legally cleaned them out, much to the chagrin of their families, who were helpless to stop him.

Brian took a cautious peek through the peephole. He didn't recognize the face. "*Who is it?*" Brian said, readying himself for the possibility of a physical attack.

"Russell Keegan! We spoke on the phone a couple of days ago!"

Russell Keegan owned a number of coin operated laundromats in northeast Portland. Russell was about to expand into a citywide chain. Based on their conversation, Mr. Keegan was on the verge of procuring the capital he needed for expansion. Russell Keegan was looking for a trustworthy accountant to surrender his bookkeeping to so that he could concentrate on overseeing his business. Brian had asked Russell a few cloaked questions to ascertain how much Keegan knew about accounting. Not much, was Brian's conclusion. The same type of questions revealed that Russell knew even less about investing. Brian almost salivated over this golden goose being served with naive stuffing.

"Just a minute!" Brian said. Brian scrambled to put away his thirty-eight. He checked his appearance in the fireplace mirror. Brian resembled a dumpy early Roman Catholic monk with a tonsure hairstyle in a dark business suit and tie. Genetics had provided him the perfect disguise for fleecing souls. Brian smiled all the way to the front door at that revelation.

"Mr. Keegan," Brian said with a well-rehearsed warm greeting. "Please come in."

A brown haired, brown-eyed, well-dressed man in a two-piece designer suit and tie stepped inside as if he owned the place. Brian took particular notice of the expensive leather briefcase Keegan was carrying. Brian imagined it filled with money. It made his smile broaden.

"I apologize for keeping you waiting, but I was in the middle of some confidential paperwork. I had to lock it away before we met. You understand."

"Yes, I do." Russell Keegan shook the hand Brian offered him.

"Right this way, sir." Brian led the way to his windowless office. If nothing else, Brian kept a clean and tidy house. Cleanliness was next to faultless details and strong organization, according to Brian. Key elements that he believed kept him out of prison.

"Please have a seat," Brian said.

"I prefer to stand."

Possible eccentric, Brian thought. Brian had no problem with that. With the money Brian could see making from Russell Keegan, both legitimate and through swindling, Keegan could dance around the office naked and Brian would be okay with it.

"Can I offer you something to drink?"

"I'm fine. Let's get down to business."

"Let's."

Brian took a seat behind his desk. Russell placed his briefcase on his Brian's desk and opened it. He removed an accordion file from the briefcase and handed it to Brian.

"These are my accounting records for the last three years for the eight coin-operated laundromats I own," Keegan said. Brian removed the paperwork from the folder and began leafing through it. The bookkeeping at first glance was organized and efficient. *This is going to be easier than I thought*, Brian mused.

Russell pulled out a manila folder from his briefcase and handed it to Brian. "Here is my business proposal for the twelve new coin-operated laundromats I plan to open citywide."

Brian cut short his cursory review of Russell's current business holdings and refocused to where he knew the big money would emerge. Brian opened the folder as if he were unlocking a treasure trove. Brian sought out the bottom line. He spotted the figure right away on the last page of the proposal, five million dollars. Brian could hardly stop himself from jumping up and doing cartwheels around the room. Russell stepped around the desk to stand beside Brian.

"I want you to review my numbers," Russell said, tapping the proposal with his left forefinger, "to make certain I haven't missed anything."

"Do you foresee any problems procuring the loan?"

"None at all. I'm in good standing with the bank. My real concern will be the conditions of the loan. Of course, I want to get the lowest possible interest rate with a realistic repayment plan."

"Of course."

"Having a pair of fiscally savvy eyes like yours giving me a second opinion would help me go into negotiations with a great deal more confidence."

"I understand."

"For example," Russell leaned in close, lightly placing his right hand on the back of Brian's chair. Leafing through the proposal with his left hand, Russell pointed at a section of the proposal he wanted to elaborate on. Brian gave his complete attention to where Russell was pointing.

"As you can see, my annual projections from my first quarter are modest."

Brian nodded as he began crunching the numbers in his head. Russell reached into his jacket pocket with his right hand and uncapped a hypodermic syringe.

"I based my first quarter projections on sixty percent—" In one swift motion, Russell extracted the syringe from his pocket, plunged it into the back of Brian's neck, and injected the solution. Brian reacted with shock and dismay. He reached a hand behind his neck after Russell had extracted the syringe.

"What did you do?" Brian slurred before his body slumped face down upon the desk, dislodging but not breaking his reading glasses.

***

Russell had been inside Brian's home before. He had broken into Brian's place to case it. Once Russell saw the lay of the land, he knew how he would transport his comatose victim.

Russell left the office to close all of the downstairs winter curtains. He returned to the office and checked Brian's pulse. Calm and steady. He had injected Dixon with enough Ketamine to assure he would remain unconscious. Russell returned to the living room and cleared an area of everything except the large Egyptian area rug. Russell carried Brian from his chair and placed him near one edge of the area rug. He would roll Brian up in the rug and loosely secure the roll with twine to allow for air circulation when he returned. Russell gathered up everything he had brought with him, taking care to wipe the place clean of his fingerprints before he left.

Russell Keegan drove his green Toyota Camry from Brian Dixon's place to the Fred Meyer parking lot not far from where Dixon lived.

Russell parked his car next to a carpet cleaning van parked farthest from the store. Russell Keegan got out of his car and slipped into the back of the van. Inside the van, Russell changed out of his suit and into a pair of nondescript work coveralls. He replaced his designer dress shoes with a pair of work boots. Russell continued to wear the brown wig and contacts, but added a mustache that matched his wig. After putting on a pair of dark sunglasses and exchanging his briefcase for a pair of work gloves, Russell moved from the back of the van to the driver's seat and drove the van to Brian's home.

He backed the van into Brian's driveway and swung open the back doors once he parked. Russell went to the front door and rang the doorbell. After waiting a moment, Russell opened the door he had left unlocked and pretended to talk to Brian as if he had answered the door. After a moment of make believe conversation, Russell stepped inside, closing the door behind him.

Dixon lay where he left him, in a deep slumber. Russell rolled Dixon in the carpet and secured him as planned. He loaded the carpet roll into the van without any trouble. He faked another bogus conversation with Brian before closing and locking the front door. Without further delay, Russell drove away.

At his home, Russell opened the garage door using his automatic garage door opener. He backed the van partway into the garage, leaving enough room to unload the carpet roll (soon to be corpse). Russell took the carpet into the house through the connecting door and down into the basement. He unrolled the carpet, leaving Dixon stretched out and still fast asleep. He drove the van back to the Fred Meyer's parking lot, where he changed back into his original disguise, got into his Toyota, and returned home. Let the police discover the stolen van in the Fred Meyer parking lot. Russell was confident that whatever clues they might find would not lead them back to him.

CHAPTER TWENTY

Desk Officer Alan Healy was on duty as he had been for the last twenty-two years. I've known the once-Sergeant, now-Lieutenant, for as long as I've known Destini. Al had a commanding voice and an official bearing: qualities that made him perfect for the position. I had no doubt he would make Desk Captain one day. While I wouldn't call us friends, we were on friendly terms.

"Well, well, well; if it isn't Mr. Cavanaugh come to pay us working folks a visit," Al said with a wry grin. "I haven't seen you since the department Christmas party."

"How are you, Al?" I said as we shook hands.

"As well as can be expected with this slipped disk."

"When did that happen?"

"Playing football with my kids," Al said, "I skidded on some wet grass and fell on my ass. The next thing I know, my wife's driving me to the emergency room because I can barely walk."

"How are you feeling now?"

"Better, thanks; the doctor says my back is fine, but I should take it easy for a couple of months. Can you imagine me taking it easy for that long?"

Too be honest, I didn't know Al well enough to answer that question, but I played along. "No, I can't. Should you be standing?"

"Standing is fine; I have to minimize any sudden movements. The up side is I get to delegate a lot of my normal house duties to my teenagers," Al said in a conspiratorial tone. "And I'm milking that well dry." Al gave me a wink.

"I guess every dark cloud has a silver lining."

"That it does, my friend," Al said. "That it does. So what can I do for you, C. J.?"

"I'm here to see Captain Williamsen."

"Is he expecting you?"

"No."

"What's it's about?"

"The Kylie Preston murder case."

Al let out a low whistle. "You mean that poor girl who got hacked to pieces?"

"I'm afraid so."

"You have some information on the case?"

"You could say that." Al had tried prying information from me in the past, without success. By now, he knew that if I wasn't forthcoming with it, he should let it pass. With his inside connections, Al knew he would discover soon enough whatever it was I was being evasive about.

Al picked up the phone and called Captain Williamsen. After a brief conversation with the Captain, Al sent me to Homicide, making me promise not to allow so much time to pass before I saw him again. I said that I wouldn't, having no idea whether I'd be able to keep that promise, as we shook hands again before parting company.

CHAPTER TWENTY-ONE

On my way to Homicide, I spotted Angel and her new partner. "Detective Alvarez," I called out to the woman wearing a dark linen suit and sensible black shoes.

"C. J.," Angel said with a pleasant smile. We hugged. "How are you?"

"I'm good. You're looking good."

"I'd better keep it tight if I want to hold onto my man."

"Luis will love you thick or thin. You're his heart and you know it."

"I'm not taking any chances," Angel said. "C. J. Cavanaugh, I don't believe you've met my new partner, Laurie McCaskill."

"Nice to meet you, Laurie."

"Likewise," Laurie said as we shook hands.

"If you're looking for Destini, she and Liederman are out in the field," Angel said.

"I was hoping to talk to you."

"About what?"

"I hear you landed the Kylie Preston investigation."

"Yes, we did," McCaskill said. She too was wearing a dark suit and sensible shoes. Laurie pulled back her unbuttoned blazer to display her gold detective shield clipped to her belt. "Do you have something you want to share about the case?"

"In good time."

"You're Destini's boyfriend," McCaskill said.

"Guilty."

"I've heard about you," McCaskill said as if speaking to a delinquent child she was keeping an eye on.

"People do talk."

"They say you're one hell of a private detective."

"Tell *them* I said thanks; and it's private *investigator*."

"Excuse me?"

"You're a detective. I'm a private investigator."

"I don't recall requesting any civilian assistance on this case," McCaskill said.

"I was hired by the head of Lunsford Insurance to look into the matter."

"Carl Wheaton hired you? Why?" Up until then, Angel had been standing back, enjoying the back-and-forth. I answered with a refrain I knew I was going to have to become accustomed to using.

"The victim was a dear friend of Carl's. He wanted as many effective minds on the case as he could muster."

"And that would be you," McCaskill said with dry sarcasm.

"Myself and my partner Renita Harris."

"Where is Renita?" Alvarez asked, trying to loosen the tension.

"Minding the store."

"That's where you should be," McCaskill said, as if issuing a command.

McCaskill's bush league attempt at intimidation was more entertaining than threatening. Normally I would toy with a person like McCaskill for a while for my own personal amusement. Time was of the essence. It had been months since Kylie Preston was murdered. The trail could be ice cold by now. It was time to get to the gist of the matter.

"Detective McCaskill," I said, "you're new here, so let me educate you on a few matters. I have the ear of the mayor, the D.A., and your police chief. I have worked well with all of them, aiding the police department in resolving some of the city's most challenging crimes. Now we can quibble about territorial rights, or I can and will go over your head and gain the clearance I need to have access to all of the information you gather on this case. The advantage for your cooperation with me is that I'll share with you everything I uncover. You don't, and I won't. And there is nothing you can do about it. Your move."

McCaskill thought about what I said for a moment, looking me up and down as if sizing me up for a fistfight. "Just stay out of my way," McCaskill said before she turned on her heels and made a beeline for the Homicide Department.

"That went well," Angel said.

"I wouldn't be surprised if she's paying the Captain a little visit about now."

"I doubt it. She's not the type to go running to the Captain every time she has a problem. You do know how to make a memorable first impression. I'll talk to her. She'll be on board. Just don't expect her to be happy about it."

"How do you feel about me working the case?"

"Does it matter?"

"It does to me."

"Your investigative skills are excellent. You've done right by the police department. I'm cool with it, but don't tell anyone I said that."

"I wouldn't dream of it."

"I have to find my partner and try to put some water on that fire you started. Headed my way?"

"I am."

As Angel and I talked as we walked to the Homicide squad room, I rehashed in the back of my mind my first meeting with Laurie McCaskill. I found it both interesting and disturbing that McCaskill warned me to stay out of her way and not *their* way, meaning her and Detective Alvarez. That was a bad sign. McCaskill could be a maverick. If McCaskill were dead set on marking her terrain, she could do the case more harm than good. I would keep a close eye on McCaskill to make certain she didn't put her ego first, and undermine or sabotage Renita and my efforts in order to make herself look better. It wouldn't be the first time professional rivalry lead to career sabotage. More than anything, I was concerned about Alvarez. Mavericks have a tendency of getting their partners hurt; or worse yet, killed.

CHAPTER TWENTY-TWO

When I walked into the Homicide squad room, I took a moment to trade barbs with some of the detectives I knew. Angel left me in search of McCaskill. The few detectives who didn't know me gave me hard, curious stares as I walked unescorted through their territory. On the way to the Captain's office, I noticed Angel and McCaskill had disappeared.

Captain Kelby Williamsen's door was open. I looked in. He was focused on the paperwork before him on his desk. I knocked on the door. The hefty blond, blue-eyed second generation Norwegian looked up over his reading glasses.

"C. J., it's good to see you," Captain Williamsen said as he maneuvered himself from behind his desk to greet me with a firm and hearty handshake.

"Good to see you too, Kelby. I wish it were under happier circumstances."

The Captain closed the door as he offered me a seat. "I agree, but what are you going to do?"

The Captain made himself comfortable behind his desk of organized clutter. "Al tells me this is about the Kylie Preston murder?"

"I've been hired by Lunsford Insurance to investigate."

Kelby's face became stern as he thought for a moment. "That's highly unusual, C. J. Any particular reason they think we're not doing a good enough job of handling the Preston murder?"

"Not at all, Captain. Kylie Preston was one of their own. People close to a murder victim have a tendency to get a little antsy when they don't get immediate results. This is their way of keeping from feeling helpless." While my explanation was both honest and manipulative, Kelby knew what I was saying to be true. I was using that mutual knowledge to soften my involvement and as a show of respect.

"I understand that, but private citizens meddling—even an investigator as professional as you—mucking around on one of my cases is disconcerting."

"I'll make you a deal, Captain. Whatever worthwhile information I manage to dredge up, I'll turn it over to your detectives pronto."

"That goes without saying."

"So we have a deal?"

"If I said no, would it make any difference?"

"I'm afraid not."

The Captain thought about it. My guess was that he was less concerned about me working the case than he was about how his detectives would take it.

"My interest is in helping your department to apprehend this criminal in any way that I can. We both know how thorough Angel is, and if anyone can solve this murder, she can. Look at it this way, Captain: it's a whole lot easier when you have someone concentrating on solving a single murder on the department's behalf rather than a dozen."

"Try a couple of dozen," Kelby said. I nodded. "Welcome aboard." The Captain reached over his desk with a smile and an open hand. As we shook on it, Alvarez and McCaskill reappeared.

"Normally I'd be upset about anyone setting foot into one of our cases, but seeing as it's you, I don't have a problem with it. Think you'll be able to work some of that Cavanaugh magic on this one?"

"I'll do my best."

"That's all I ask of anyone; might as well get this over with."

The Captain got up, opened his door, and popped his head out to call Alvarez and McCaskill into his office. I stood to greet them. The Captain shut the door, closed the blinds, and then took his seat. The rest of us remained standing.

"What's going on, Captain?" Alvarez asked.

"For starters," the Captain said to McCaskill, "from all accounts you're doing a great job. Keep it up."

McCaskill was all smiles. "Along with the attagirl," the Captain said, "you can expect a three percent raise."

"Congratulations," Angel said, patting McCaskill on the back as the Captain shook her hand. I echoed Angel's sentiments to McCaskill.

"I was hoping for five," McCaskill said.

"I was hoping for six-pack abs," Kelby said, "but that's not going to happen, either. Take the three. In today's economy, it's what I could get, and it didn't come easy. The raise is retroactive to the beginning of this month. You'll see the adjustment in this pay period."

"Thank you, Captain," McCaskill said, shaking the Captain's hand again.

"Don't thank me. You're going to earn every red cent."

"I thought I already had."

The Captain paused for a second as if to allow McCaskill to savor the moment. "That's part of the good news. Now for the rest. C. J. is going to be working on the Kylie Preston case with you."

"We know. He told us," Alvarez said.

"*What?* Am I the last to know?"

"*Are you kidding?*" McCaskill said to the Captain. Her joy turned to disbelief.

"Not in the least," the Captain said. "He was hired by Lunsford Insurance to look into Kylie Preston's murder. C. J. is going to investigate the Preston case with or without us. I think it's best for everyone concerned if we work together on this. C. J. already has a good rep with the top brass, so clearing it with them shouldn't be a problem."

"We don't need investigative help from civilians," McCaskill said.

"McCaskill, you're new here, so let me educate you a little about this man. C. J. Cavanaugh has worked with us on a number of murder cases of which we may not have caught the killers had it not been for him. Detective Alvarez will attest that Mr. Cavanaugh has one of the best investigative minds around—"

"So I've heard. I cannot believe you're sanctioning this—"

"And he will be adding his skills and experience to your team in an effort to assist in the capture of this demented killer. Now, how is that a problem?" The question was rhetorical. McCaskill didn't get that.

"I don't care if he's Sherlock Holmes. It's *my* case," McCaskill said. Alvarez and I flinched. Alvarez gave McCaskill an admonishing stare. My look was more sympathetic. The Captain's face drew in on itself like a crab retracting into its shell. His stare penetrated McCaskill. The Captain stood, placing his hands palms down on his desk and glaring at McCaskill.

"Then how's this, Detective," the Captain said with a hiss. "You'll do it because I said so. Since that case you just referenced falls under *my* jurisdiction, this conversation is over. Are we clear?" McCaskill nodded, realizing her mistake of challenging the Captain's authority.

"Yes sir," Alvarez said.

"I wasn't talking to you, Detective Alvarez. I didn't hear you, McCaskill. Are we clear?" The Captain's eyes bored into McCaskill's face. McCaskill, to her credit, didn't flinch.

"Yes sir."

"Good," the Captain said, taking his seat. "Now, Angel, you're still the lead, of course, so you'll call the shots."

"Right, Captain."

"Is that all right with you, C. J.?" I knew that Kelby was not asking for my permission but confirming what he had decided.

"That's fine with me, Captain."

"I want you to show C. J. everything you have on the Kylie Preston murder," Kelby said to Angel.

"Yes sir," Alvarez said.

"That means *everything*," the Captain said as he glared at McCaskill.

"Yes sir," McCaskill said.

Captain Kelby Williamsen put on his reading glasses and returned to tackling the paperwork before him, a sure fire signal that there was nothing left to discuss. "That'll be all," Kelby said, not looking up. McCaskill opened the door and stormed out. Alvarez sauntered out after her. I followed.

CHAPTER TWENTY-THREE

We ended up standing around Angel and McCaskill's desks with each of them standing behind their own desks and me floating near the middle. Angel opened a file drawer, yanked out a case file, and dropped it in front of me with a thud. The label read 'Kylie Preston'. I picked up the report and began reading.

"So the car was stolen from the airport long-term parking garage," I said, trying to break the ice as I read.

"If that's what the file says," McCaskill said, not masking her irritation.

"Security cameras didn't get a good look at him—"

"Because he avoided the cameras as much as possible and wore a hat and sunglasses. We know; we wrote the report."

"Any identifying marks on the car thief?"

"If there were, they'd be in the report."

"What about the way he walked?"

"Are you kidding?"

"No, are you?"

"Look, buddy," McCaskill said as she stepped up to me. I looked down at McCaskill. Other detectives stopped what they were doing to watch. "Everything we have is in the report. If you don't see it written down in there, then we didn't consider it important enough to note."

"You're certain the man who took the car from the airport long-term parking garage was not Dr. Harry Boulder?" I asked Angel, bypassing McCaskill's outburst.

"We're certain," Angel said.

"I don't appreciate your ignoring me when I'm talking to you," McCaskill said.

"Settle, Detective," Angel said. "We're under orders to cooperate and that is what we're going to do."

"I'll bet you were a real terror on the playground," I said to McCaskill.

"*Excuse me?*" McCaskill said.

"When you had to wait your turn to use the playground equipment. I'll bet you were chomping at the bit to shove those other kids out of the way."

"What is this nonsense?" McCaskill said.

"But the grown-ups wouldn't let you. You had to wait your turn." I ignored McCaskill's flare-up and pushed forward.

"What the hell are you talking about?"

"When you didn't get your way, you pouted about it," I said with calm reassurance. McCaskill was getting edgy. I knew I had hit pay dirt on her personality. So did McCaskill, shifting the source of her anger from offensive to defensive.

"You're not a Homicide detective."

"You don't know what I am or what I can bring to this case. All you know is that I'm tramping around in your playground and you don't like it."

"First of all, it's not a playground; it is very, very real. And you're right, I don't like it." McCaskill jabbed me in the chest with her forefinger.

"Tough; life is full of compromises. Grow up and get over it."

Angel snickered, as did every detective within earshot. I could see in McCaskill's eyes that she wanted to take a swing at me. I was waiting to see if she was that foolish, as was everyone else. McCaskill backed off and headed for the bathroom. Angel draped her jacket over the back of her chair. I returned to reading the file as if the conversation with McCaskill had never happened, committing the information to memory. The show was over. Everyone else returned to work.

"Is Renita working this one with you?" Angel asked.

"Yep," I said, continuing to read.

"That should be interesting. Renita's greener than McCaskill when it comes to murder investigations."

"Tell me about it, with twice the attitude."

McCaskill returned, not appearing any calmer than when she left. McCaskill draped her jacket over the back of her chair once she noticed Angel had done so.

"How's Pete?" I asked Angel. Peter Joaquin was Angel's ex-partner. He recently retired after forty years on the force. He and Angel were close. Some said too close.

"He's doing good. He's still trying to figure out what to do with all of his free time. He's driving Judy crazy." Judy was Pete's third wife.

"He'll settle in. Before you know it, he'll be sending you postcards from some tropical island paradise."

"I don't doubt it."

"Are you done with our report?" McCaskill said. Laurie did not like Angel and I making nice.

"You'll know when I'm done." I continued to pour over the report. McCaskill plopped down in her chair. I could not resist the urge to pour a little salt into McCaskill's open emotional wound. "Do you miss Pete?" I asked Angel. I watched McCaskill from the corners of my eyes. If looks were bullets, McCaskill would have killed me. Angel shook her head at me, walked away, and got herself a cup of coffee before setting to work sifting through her current caseload.

The ME report detailed the condition of Kylie Preston's dissected body and the type of poison used to kill her. Her cause of death was attributed to an overdose of Ketamine, a general anesthetic used in human and veterinary medicine. Other facts emerged that news agencies had reported on in general, but were more explicitly detailed. Some details were news to me. McCaskill tried to work, but spent most of her time glowering at me. When I was done, I handed the file back to Angel.

"See anything interesting?" Angel asked.

"Yes, all of it."

"She meant: did you see anything that we might have overlooked?"

"No." The truth was, I was starting to formulate a profile on the killer from what I had read. Some people and information in the report required further investigation on my part. Until I saw where that led, there was nothing to share.

The Captain marched out of his office and headed straight for us. Kelby handed Angel a piece of paper with something handwritten on it. "I just got a call about a homicide at that address. From what I've been told, the preliminary M.O. matches Kylie Preston's."

"We're on it, Captain." Angel jumped up and grabbed her jacket. McCaskill followed suit.

"Mind if I tag along?" I asked.

"Yes, we do," McCaskill said, as if that were the final word. The Captain looked from McCaskill to Angel. Angel looked to the Captain for his input.

"Your case, your call," the Captain said to Angel, returning to his office.

Angel looked at me for a drawn-out moment. "Don't get in our way." McCaskill's jaw dropped.

"I know the drill."

"Let's go," Angel said. "Use your own wheels, C. J."

"What's the address?" Alvarez showed me the address written on the paper. "I'll meet you at the crime scene."

"We can't wait." McCaskill traded in her acrimony for bitter sarcasm. I followed the two detectives out, trying not to speculate on what lay ahead.

CHAPTER TWENTY-FOUR

Jeffrey Whimple was on his way back to his desk when Angel Alvarez's phone rang. Like a fool, Whimple stopped his pot-bellied body instead of walking by, pretending not to hear it. If a detective's telephone rang and the detective or their partner was not available, then the nearest detective answered it. In the past, it had been a courtesy. The Captain had made it a mandate. Whimple took a quick glance at the sign-out board. Both Alvarez and McCaskill were marked 'out'. Whimple was nobody's secretary. Especially for a couple of chicks he believed didn't belong there in the first place. Whimple took a quick glance at the Captain's office as the telephone continued to ring. The Captain was in conference with C. J. Cavanaugh. Whimple knew the Captain was watching him out of the corners of his eyes. The Captain was always watching his department out of the corners of his eyes.

"Detective Alvarez's phone, Detective Whimple speaking," Whimple answered in his naturally husky voice.

"Is Detective Alvarez available?" The man formally disguised as Russell Keegan asked.

If she were here, I wouldn't be answering her damn phone, Whimple thought. "No, she isn't," Whimple said with detachment. "May I take a message?"

"Listen carefully, Detective Whimple, because I will not repeat myself," the mysterious voice said.

"I'm listening." Whimple positioned a writing pad on Alvarez's desk and grabbed a pen from her pencil holder, not missing the fact that the caller was using some sort of electronic device to disguise his voice.

"The remains of Brian Dixon can be found at his home," the voice said. "The body is in four brown paper packages."

Whimple started to write, but stopped. "Are you saying you killed someone?"

"I am."

"And you did it in the same way Kylie Preston was murdered."

"Precisely. The sooner you get there, the better chance Brian can be of use for people in need of human parts."

Whimple listened carefully to the electronically altered voice, trying to pinpoint anything distinctive about it as the caller elaborated on preserved bodies and time being of the essence. Whimple waved over his partner, Leonard Rockgarden, to listen in right before the killer gave Whimple the late Brian Dixon's address. A slender man of about six feet, with dark brown hair, blue eyes, and a pitted face that didn't take kindly to shaving, rushed over to listen in.

"How do we know you ain't some nut job wasting our time?" Whimple asked.

"That's why they pay you the big bucks, genius," the voice said. "Investigate, Detective. Goodbye."

The alias Russell hung up. Whimple hung up, trying not to appear stunned. His heavy-jawed face did not pull it off.

"What was that all about?" Rockgarden asked.

Whimple's murky blue eyes darted back and forth for a moment. He took a quick glance at the Captain. The Captain was still in conference with Cavanaugh. Whimple grabbed Rockgarden by the arm and led him out of the squad room. The two of them walked around the corner and down the hall that led to the property room. The hall was empty. Whimple ran a meaty hand over his thinning grayish-blond hair as he took one last look around to verify they were alone.

"I think we got another one of those Kylie Preston-type murders on our hands," Whimple said.

"Then we should turn it over to Alvarez and McCaskill," Rockgarden said. "Let them worry about it."

"And miss this opportunity."

"I don't follow."

"Let's check it out first. Make sure it's not a prank."

"And if it isn't?"

"Then we've got ourselves a homicide to solve."

"What about Alvarez and McCaskill?"

"What are you, a member of their cheerleading squad? Screw them. Do you see them going out of their way to help us?"

"We've never asked them to."

"That's beside the point," Whimple said. "If we grab a high-profile collar like this one, it could mean promotions for both of us."

"Promotions mean raises. I could go for that."

"So could I. I'm tired of being passed over for less qualified wannabes because top brass has a hard-on for this affirmative action bullshit."

"Me, too."

"If we bring in this bastard, they'll have to give us promotions—or at the very least, commendations. There won't be any way around it."

"But its Alvarez and McCaskill's case," Rockgarden said. "If this tip checks out, they're going to find out about it. Alvarez will hit the roof and McCaskill will be right there with her. What's going to stop the Captain from handing us our asses?"

"Isn't the Captain always saying he doesn't play favoritism?" Whimple said.

"Yeah, so?"

"If he tries to pull us off the case," Whimple said, "we make a stink that he's favoring his female detectives. The Captain's a tough SOB, but he wants to be chief of police someday. That could be a problem, with a discrimination accusation in his jacket."

"Oh, I get it, we play the reverse discrimination card," Rockgarden said.

"Now you're catching on."

"What are we waiting for? Let's go check it out." Whimple agreed with a crooked smile.

CHAPTER TWENTY-FIVE

I arrived at the crime scene shortly after Angel and McCaskill. The three of us approached together. We were surprised to find Whimple and Rockgarden coordinating the investigation. Whimple and Rockgarden were quietly known as Schultz and Weasel within Homicide. Schultz because Rockgarden was said to somewhat resemble the dimwitted German Sergeant from the television show Hogan's Heroes. In actuality, Whimple looked more like an over-the-hill Dennis the Menace. It was his Nazi attitude and shallow reasoning that more closely resembled the character.

Rockgarden drew his nickname from a different source of inspiration. He was rumored to be on the local syndicate boss's payroll. There were a couple of unsolved murders of key witnesses against Portland crime bosses that Weasel was believed to have had a hand in. Unfortunately, proof and suspicion are worlds apart. Angel wasted no time getting to the bottom of the situation at hand.

"What are you two doing here?" Angel addressed Whimple and Rockgarden.

"Didn't the Captain tell you?" Whimple said. "We're the ones that called it in."

"And how did you get wind of this homicide?" Angel said.

"We received a call," Whimple said.

"Let me guess: a man with an electronically altered voice told you where to find the body," Angel said.

"That's right. What the hell is he doing here?" Whimple asked with contempt in reference to me.

"Captain's orders," Angel said.

"He's been given detective privileges by executive decree," McCaskill said with disdain.

Get a grip, McCaskill, I thought.

"Son-of-a-bitch," Whimple said.

"Good to see you, too."

"How the hell did that happen?" Rockgarden said.

"It's a long story," Angel said.

"The short of it is, I'm assisting on the case."

"Now, that is a crime," Rockgarden said.

"You would know," I said, implicating Rockgarden's reputation for being on the take. Rockgarden scowled at me. I stared back.

"We will anyway," Whimple said. "We checked out the tip, and low and behold if it ain't like the Preston murder."

"What have you got?" Angel asked.

"The assumed vic's name is Brian Dixon, a 46-year-old white male, divorced accountant who lived here alone," Whimple said. "We found four brown paper packages in the living room when we arrived. The similarities to the Preston case became apparent. We assumed the packages contained what was left of Brian Dixon. From the looks of the place, the vic may have been killed inside, but he wasn't butchered here."

"So the killer took the body someplace else to chop it up and package it, and then brought it back to the house," Angel said.

"Looks that way," Rockgarden added.

"How did he transport the body?" Angel said.

"We don't know," Whimple said. "Forensics is still checking the house for clues. The meat wagon's already taken the packages back to the morgue."

"Whoever this maniac is, he's got a huge set of balls to pull this shit off," Rockgarden said.

"Thanks for following up, we'll take it from here," Angel said. Whimple and Rockgarden looked at each other, smirked, and then looked back at Angel.

"We're going to work this case," Whimple said.

"It's our case," Angel said.

"The Preston case was yours," Rockgarden said. "This one's ours."

"Both murders have the same M.O. That means that, by default, this case belongs to us."

"You haven't solved the Preston murder," Whimple said.

"What's your point?" McCaskill asked.

"Maybe what's needed is a fresh pair of eyes," Rockgarden interjected.

"Are you saying you're better cops than us?" Angel said.

"I'm not suggesting anything like that." Whimple said with a grin. "All I know is: we're not giving up this case."

"We'll see what the Captain has to say about that," Angel said.

"Yes, we will," Whimple said. "Although I do find it interesting the Captain felt you two needed help solving the Preston murder." Whimple tilted his head in my direction.

"We don't need his help, and we don't need yours," McCaskill said. I was bored with the sparring match, and much more interested in what I could learn from the crime scene. I walked toward the house.

"Where do you think you're going?" Whimple said.

"To investigate while the four of you work out your territorial dispute."

"This isn't over," I heard Angel say before she and McCaskill scurried to join me. I glanced back at Whimple and Rockgarden. They were walking to their car with satisfied expressions.

CHAPTER TWENTY-SIX

The forensic team had found blood, saliva, and hair they believed belonged to the victim on his office desk and the large Egyptian area rug in the living room. Forensics had also uncovered a number of good sets of fingerprints about the house. The detectives and I would have to await results from the lab for identification before anyone involved in the case knew whose they were. Our own investigation throughout the house proved fruitless. I parted ways with my colleagues when we left the crime scene. Angel said she would keep me posted on what developed. I thanked her. McCaskill had nothing to say.

When I returned to the office, I was surprised not to find Renita there. I called Renita on her cell. She didn't pick up. I became concerned. It wasn't like Renita not to answer her cell. I considered going to look for Renita when Destini's words came to mind: "You're going to have to let her fly sometime."

Allowing her to fly solo on a murder investigation still didn't feel right. I swallowed my concern and went to my office to write up my daily report on what I had learned about Kylie Preston, and a separate new report on the Brian Dixon murder case I had stumbled upon. As with all of my cases, I kept detailed records. I would include a verbatim record of the police report I had seen on Kylie Preston's, recalling it right down to the last period. My findings on the Brian Dixon case would go unreported to Carl. Only the police, Destini, and Renita would have access to that information.

Renita walked in with a chipper smile as I was writing up the preliminary report on the Brian Dixon case.

"Where the hell have you been?" I could not believe how upset I was. "I've been trying to reach you." It was as if my teenage daughter, possessing only a learner's permit, had taken my car out for a spin without my permission.

"Sorry; my cell was being blocked." Renita appeared startled by my attitude.

"Blocked how?" I asked, not changing my tone.

"In the airport security office. They don't allow cell phone usage there."

"And what were you doing there?"

"Well, *Dad*, I was kind of on a date," Renita said with an attitude of her own.

"With Ernest?"

"No, *Dad*, I was out on a pseudo-date with Aron."

"Who the hell is Aron?"

"He's an airport security guard. I met him on the teenage runaway case we worked a few months back."

"So you're cheating on Ernest?" I asked in amazement.

"Try and follow me, C. J."

"I'm listening."

"First of all, you need to calm down," Renita said, dropping her attitude.

"I *am* calm."

"No, you're not. You're upset. I can hear it in your voice and it shows all through your face and body language."

I took a moment to compose myself. I closed my eyes and took a couple of deep breaths. It helped. My annoyance subsided to displeasure. When I opened my eyes, Renita was smiling.

"That's better. You always get like this when we work a murder case."

"Like what?"

"Overprotective and paranoid about where I am and what I'm doing."

"Murder cases make me jumpy."

"Who do you think you're talking to? We've worked together too long for me not to know you almost as well as you know me. Murder cases do not make you jumpy. If anything, you become keener and more alert. You're like a jungle cat stalking its prey. It's quite a turn-on to watch."

"What's your point, Renita?"

"My point is, there are times when I'm going to go my own way on investigations. And you're going to have to trust me when I do."

"Have you been talking to Destini?"

"*What?*"

"Nothing. We've had this discussion before and I told you what I'd do if you went off on your own during a murder investigation."

"Then you are going to have to fire me, because I'm not going to stop."

We were at an impasse I had hoped would never come. The question I had to answer for myself was who was correct. Me, for believing Renita was still not ready to work a dangerous case on her own, or were Renita and Destini correct in that it was time to let Renita fly? I felt like a father being forced to let his daughter grow up faster than he wanted. The answer came quick.

"Here's the deal: you check in with me before you do whatever it is you're planning on doing."

"*Yes.*" Renita pumped her fist.

"There's more."

"Right, of course," Renita settled down. "I'm listening."

"If I say no, then you *don't* do it. If I stipulate we do it together, then you wait for me and we'll do it *together.* If you're working alone, I expect you to call me when you arrive on the scene and call or text me every five minutes afterwards."

"*Call or text every five minutes.*"

"That's the deal. At least that way, I'll know you're safe."

Renita sighed. "Deal." I stuck out my open hand to shake on it. Renita pulled me to her and gave me a warm hug. I hugged her back like a father who did not want to let go of his child. "Thank you for this opportunity," Renita whispered into my ear. "You won't regret it."

My stomach was churning. I was already regretting my decision. "You're welcome." Renita kissed me on the cheek. We released our grips on each other.

"Why were you at the airport?"

"I knew Dr. Harry Boulder's car was stolen from the long-term airport parking garage."

"How did you know that?"

"News reports."

She's paying attention to detail, I thought. *We're off to a good start.*

"I figured if we could get a look at the security footage from the time the car was stolen, maybe we could spot something that airport security or the police missed."

"You went to see this Aron to find out if he could help."

"Aron hit on me when I was seeking airport security's help on those teenage runaways. Like any smart woman, I left the door open in his mind that someday there might be a possibility for us."

"You seduced him."

"No, seduction is something I do to Ernest and attempt on you. Aron, I flirted with getting him on a hook, so to speak. I never knew when I might need his help again. So what if I gave him the impression that we *might* go out on a date sometime?"

"How do you suggest a date?"

"I never said that I would go out on a date with him. If he interpreted anything I said or did to mean that I would, then that's not my fault, now, is it?"

"What did you say when he asked if you had a boyfriend?"

"I changed the subject."

"You were coy and that worked?"

"He was so busy checking out my body, it wasn't difficult."

I nodded.

"This may come as a shock to you, C. J., but I am very persuasive when it comes to the opposite sex."

"Gender."

"Pardon?"

"The word is gender. The word sex is often misused when referencing a person's gender."

"Whatever."

"Don't make it a habit to use your seductive qualities. It's unprofessional and in most cases unnecessary; not to mention it could land you into more trouble than you know."

"I'll remember that," Renita flippantly said. (Translation: it's going in one ear and out of the other.)

"The bottom line is, I have the security footage." Renita produced a flash drive from her pants pocket. "Let's see what we will see." She waved the flash drive in front of my face.

We didn't see anything on the security footage not written up in the official police report. Three things became clear from watching the car thief: he was taller than Dr. Boulder, he moved like a younger man, and he appeared to be in good shape. One thing gnawed at me as I watched the car thief-slash-possible-killer walk away from us toward the car. I felt like I had seen him before; but for the life of me, I couldn't pinpoint where. I was running through recent memories in my head when my office phone rang. It was Angel calling to inform me that the ME had verified the identity of the vic as Brian Dixon.

CHAPTER TWENTY-SEVEN

The next day came and went without any new developments from our end on either murder case. Angel telephoned to fill us in on the latest on the Harry Dixon investigation. When I mentioned to Angel that she didn't have to keep us posted on the Dixon case because we were only given express permission by the Captain to work the Kylie Preston murder, Angel acknowledged she was aware of that. Since the Captain refused to remove Whimple and Rockgarden from the Harry Dixon investigation, Angel was more than happy to pass along any information she believed might help show them up.

The police computer lab had pulled up Brian Dixon's appointment calendar from his laptop. The morning of his death showed a scheduled Sunday meeting with Russell Keegan. Angel and McCaskill had beaten Whimple and Rockgarden to the punch and interviewed Keegan at his home. While the Captain did not take Whimple and Rockgarden off the case, he also had no problem with Angel and McCaskill working it, as well, as long as it did not interfere with their outstanding caseload.

The owner of a number of northeast Portland coin operated laundromats denied knowing Brian Dixon. Keegan also disavowed any knowledge of a scheduled meeting with the deceased accountant. Keegan had a rock solid alibi to support his claim. Keegan had attended Sunday morning Mass at Saint Rose Catholic Church, a staple for him and his family. After Mass, Keegan taught Sunday school to a class of twenty-three children.

That was the second time the killer had masqueraded as someone who could easily prove his innocence. That suggested to me that he only used their identities to get close to his victims. The killer had no desire to see an innocent person punished for his crimes.

All of the fingerprints from the Dixon residence were accounted for. Most of them belonged to the vic. From the interviews Angel and McCaskill conducted, all of Harry Dixon's current and previous clients had verifiable alibis during the time of Dixon's murder. Although Angel mentioned clients who were dissatisfied with Dixon's business practices and who were delighted to hear of his death. I asked Angel if she had anything new on the Preston murder. She didn't.

I took Destini dancing at "Been There, Done That." It was one of our favorite nightclubs. They played music oldies ranging from the sixties through the nineties.

"Why are Schultz and Weasel still working the case?" I asked Destini as we slow danced to a Peabo Bryson classic.

"It's a matter of priorities. They were first on the scene. It could appear the Captain was playing favoritism if he were to reassign the case to Angel and McCaskill."

"Even if the assigned detectives are incompetent morons? And the case has the same M.O. as a case other detectives are working?"

"I agree that the case should be assigned to Angel and McCaskill, given the circumstances. Until the Captain says otherwise, Schultz and Weasel will continue to be the primaries on the Dixon case. What's the matter, baby? Are you afraid of the big bad racist cops?" Destini said in a motherly tone.

"Schultz is racist. Weasel is just dirty. My concern is that I may hurt one of those boneheads."

"You're going to have to lock horns with them at some point."

"Hopefully it won't be until I bring in the murderer."

"That confident, are we?"

"My chances are a lot better than Schultz and Weasel."

"What about Angel and McCaskill? They're still working the Dixon case."

"Angel is legitimate competition. McCaskill hasn't proven herself yet."

"Be careful, Rockgarden and Whimple still have the power of the badge, and they know how to abuse it."

"I'm always careful when working a murder case."

"I'm not talking about the investigation. You know those jerks have a jones for you. They'll be looking for any reason to bring you down."

"Give me some credit; I've dealt with people like them my entire life."

"Whatever you do, don't let one of them bait you into hitting them again. I was able to pull some strings to get you off the last time. I don't know if we'll be so lucky again. Besides, I can't be seen fraternizing with a known felon. It wouldn't be good for my career," Destini teased.

"I'll be careful, honey."

"You promise?" I pretended to consider Destini's question for a moment.

"Promise me, C. J."

"I promise not to punch them out."

"I'll take what I can get."

"What can you tell me about the investigations?"

"Oh no, you don't: they are not my cases and you are not going to get me mixed up in this mess."

"I was testing you." I only half meant it.

"Sure you were."

"Maybe this will convince you." I pulled Destini closer for a kiss.

CHAPTER TWENTY-EIGHT

With Angel and McCaskill at a dead end and Schultz and Weasel in the mix, it was time for Renita and me to step up our game.

"I can't believe Destini wouldn't give you the scoop on any of the Preston or Dixon cases," Renita said as I drove us to the neighborhood of Dr. Harry Boulder.

"Destini's right not to get mixed up in our investigation. Too be honest, it wasn't fair of me to ask. They're not her cases so she probably knows less than we do about them."

"You're her man. If she wanted to find out, she could."

"Destini never mixes her personal feelings with work."

"If you were my man, I'd give you anything you wanted, when you wanted it, and how you wanted it."

"Aren't you with Ernest?"

"So? I'd drop him like a hot potato for you, baby."

"I thought we were past that."

"I'm still working on it."

"Try harder."

"I don't know that I'll ever get over you." I made a right into the cul-de-sac where the Boulders resided.

"Yes, you can, and you will. It's not that difficult. Other women have tried and succeeded before you. I can give you their phone numbers so they can talk you through it, if you like. "

"So you say. So...you...say, and why do you still have your ex-girlfriends' phone numbers? Does Destini know about this?"

"Let's focus on the task at hand, shall we?"

"How are we going to get police information without an inside source?"

"We investigate for ourselves."

I found a parking space. My plan was to knock on a few of Harry Boulder's neighbors' doors to find out what they might have seen or heard around the time Kylie Preston was murdered. Maybe time had brought something worthwhile to mind that hadn't surfaced when the investigating officers interviewed them.

"You want to split up?" Renita said. "We can cover more ground faster that way."

"No need, there are only a few houses. It won't take long."

The neighbors who were at home were of no help. They hadn't seen or heard anything out of the ordinary. Last stop, Dr. Harry Boulder.

CHAPTER TWENTY-NINE

We identified ourselves as private investigators looking into the Kylie Preston murder for a concerned client. When asked who, we pleaded client confidentiality. We made it clear to Dr. Boulder that he was not a suspect. We simply wanted to ask him a few questions about that fatal day. The doctor did not know our history. He was unaware that we had spied on one of his patients, Bailey Singleton, for Lunsford Insurance to make certain he had a legitimate claim. There was no reason for the doctor to know otherwise. Our work had nothing to do with the fraudulent medical claims lawsuits filed against Boulder by the federal government and a number of private insurance companies that included Lunsford. Once we cleared the final hurdle of convincing Boulder that we were not reporters masquerading as detectives, he let us in.

Dr. Boulder maintained his arrogance even though he was on trial for his medical license and freedom. We saw Ruth Boulder briefly, when the doctor allowed us in to ask our questions. The stress on their crumbling lives had taken a toll on his wife. It was early afternoon and she was still in her bathrobe. She looked pale and drawn. Ruth Boulder offered us something to drink in speech that was a bit slurred. Renita and I thanked her, but declined. Ruth Boulder gave us a weak smile and disappeared somewhere upstairs with a full glass of red wine in hand. We took the seat on the sofa offered us by Dr. Boulder. He sat cross-legged in a reading chair to the right of us.

"Thank you for seeing us, Doctor," I said.

"Anything I can do to help."

"As I said before, we're here to try to find out who murdered Kylie Preston."

"That poor girl." My read on Harry Boulder was that his sympathy was sincere.

"I agree," Renita said. "Can you tell us anything that might help?"

"I was in Denver at a medical convention, as I'm certain you're aware. The next thing I know, I was being escorted back to Portland to answer dreadful questions about the dissected remains of a woman left in my car. And that's all I know."

"We realize you had nothing to do with her murder," I said. "We believe it was committed by someone pretending to be you."

"The police said that too. Why?"

"That's what we're trying to determine," Renita said. "Can you give us any reason why someone might want to frame you in this way?"

"Not even my worst enemies would murder, dissect, and package a human being like a slaughtered animal and have the wherewithal to leave them in my car to get back at me. That kind of sadistic behavior goes beyond revenge for anything I could have possibly done to anyone."

I couldn't agree with the doctor more. "The person who did this stole your car from the airport parking garage," I said.

"That's correct. I still don't understand why they chose me?"

"The why we can only speculate on, but one thing seems clear. The fact that they stole your car suggests to us that Kylie Preston's murder was premeditated. Unfortunately, your stolen car and identity are the only common links we have to go on. That's why we were hoping you could tell us something that could lead us to a viable suspect."

"I don't even know anyone who knows how to steal a car."

"No one comes to mind on both counts, then?" Renita asked.

"Not a soul." Boulder appeared to be exhausted for the first time. "The police asked me the same sorts of questions and I couldn't help them, either. If I knew something remotely helpful, believe me, I would tell you."

I did believe him. "Thank you for your help, Doctor." I rose from the couch with Renita joining me. The doctor chaperoned us to the front door.

"The bastard who did this destroyed more than one life, you know," Boulder said. It wasn't my place to mention that the murderer did not cause the doctor to defraud the government and insurance companies: that was his own doing. Instead, I said I understood, as did Renita. We shook his hand, thanked Dr. Harry Boulder for his time, and left.

CHAPTER THIRTY

Michelle Griffin was shaking as we questioned her about her friend's gruesome death. Michelle was the sole member of The Liberated Wives Club who had seen Kylie's butchered remains. Even though she was not family, Michelle had insisted upon it as a prelude to her full cooperation. What Michelle saw made her both violently ill and racked with remorse: the kind of common remorse the living have toward a beloved deceased who they falsely believed they could have had a hand in saving. Michelle confessed to us that she was having trouble sleeping because she continued to have nightmares about what she saw. She was also having trouble eating. That truth showed itself in her sagging clothes, the bags under her eyes, and the pallor of her skin.

Michelle was willing to help us with our investigation. She invited us into her office to answer any questions we might have. What Michelle remembered about the man who had introduced himself to them as Dr. Harry Boulder was that he was blonde and muscular with a tattoo of a serpent on his chest and another of a dagger through a heart on the back of his left hand. The fake doctor was charming, according to Michelle, with a hint of modesty that made him seem almost shy at times. Michelle thought long and hard about our questions, trying to weed out any telling details about this imposter, but she couldn't recall anything more about his physical appearance or distinguish any uniqueness about his speech or mannerisms. Michelle blamed herself for having had too much to drink that night and not noticing. We reassured her that a sober witness would not have remembered much more than she did, and that was the truth.

"He seemed like a decent choice for a one-night stand." Michelle fretfully puffed on a cigarette. "If I'd suspected that son-of-a-bitch was some sort of crazed murderer, I would've moved the bastard along from the start."

"No one could have known," Renita sympathized.

"This sort of tragedy is unpredictable," I added.

I don't think Michelle believed us, even though what we said was true.

Renita and I interviewed the other members of The Liberated Wives Club, all of whom were eager to help. The rest of the interviews could be summarized in the following manner: all of the women were still shaken by what had happened to their friend. While their recollections varied about the possible assailant's physical appearance and personality, they all remembered that the suspected killer identified himself as Dr. Harry Boulder, albeit not the same Dr. Harry Boulder they had been asked to identify in a police lineup. Unfortunately for us, they had nothing new to add to the information they had already given the police. The clear conclusion remained that someone had used Dr. Harry Boulder as an alias. The question was why. In parting, the surviving members of The Liberated Wives Club all wished us luck in finding Kylie Preston's killer, emphasizing that if there was anything they could do to help, for us not to hesitate to please let them know.

Michelle had been forthcoming about what she had done the rest of that "dreadful night," as she described it. We tracked down the waiter from Fullman's Restaurant with whom Michelle had sex. He had nothing more to add to The Liberated Wives Club testimony. While we were at Fullman's Restaurant, we had a gratis meal compliments of Renita's man-friend, Ernest.

CHAPTER THIRTY-ONE

I called Nicholas Evans to set up a time when we could meet to discuss the murder of his ex-wife. He was a tough sell as to why he should cooperate with us when he had already told the police everything he knew. I pushed our independent angle and he bought it. Since I saw no reason to involve his children, I suggested a time when they would be at school. Evans agreed. Renita and I arrived at his ex-wife's house at 10:00 a.m. the following morning.

Nicholas Evans was neither blonde nor muscular. While he was about six-five, his body could best be described as lanky, with a potbelly. His thick black hair was streaked with silver gray. His squared-jawed, clean-shaven face put one in mind of a middle-aged Rock Hudson before the onslaught of AIDS.

Evans invited us in. His attitude seemed more congenial from when we'd spoken last. He led us into the kitchen where he offered us coffee and a bagel. Renita accepted his offer. I declined.

The three of us sat down at the kitchen table like new friends. Evans was sipping his coffee from a cup that read "World's Greatest Dad." In the washed-out mid-morning light, the undergraduate professor of Modern World History at Villanova University appeared both regal and austere. I wondered how much of the latter had to do with his ex-wife's murder.

"You never told me who hired you to find Kylie's killer." Evans stare was resolute. His northeastern accent was a product of his Philadelphia upbringing. Being from Pittsburgh, I immediately picked up on it.

"I'm sorry," I answered, "but that information's still confidential."

"Confidential information even from the father of her children?"

"Lunsford Insurance hired us," I said after a moment's thought. "They want to do everything in their power to capture the person that did this to a member of their insurance family."

Evans nodded as if he understood. "Carl Wheaton didn't have anything to do with this, did he?"

The question took us by surprise. I could see Renita in my peripheral vision, looking at me reacting to what Evans had said. I continued to stare at Evans, my expression unchanged. My poker face was in play. Evans had noticed Renita's reaction to his question. He looked back and forth between us. Renita remained quiet. I pushed forward with the conversation. To do otherwise would alert Evans that Carl was involved. Until we knew what his specific interest was in Carl, it would be best to play dumb. "Carl who?" I said.

"Carl Wheaton. He's the Chief Investigator for Lunsford Insurance."

"As I said, Mr. Evans, Lunsford Insurance hired us," I said, trying to avoid the direct lie.

"Because if that bastard had anything to do with this, the three of you can go straight to hell." A flash of anger burned in his clear brown eyes.

"I see." Renita was dumbfounded. She took a bite out of her bagel. "If you don't mind my asking, where were you on the night your ex-wife was murdered?"

"That's a helluva question."

"It's a helluva circumstance."

"I was grading assignments early that morning and teaching classes later in the day. When I wasn't doing those things, I was with my girlfriend and a handful of other university professors and their significant others, all of whom can vouch for me. Have you not spoken to Detectives Alvarez or McCaskill? They took my statement. I'm sure it's a matter of police record by now."

Renita had read the police report I had transcribed from memory on the Kylie Preston murder. We were both aware of Evans' alibi. Normally I would press a potential suspect to see if their live testimony accorded with their previous story. In Evans' case, I felt no need. I believed him. We moved on.

"We've read the police report, but thank you for verifying it," I said.

"Why you?"

"Why us what?"

"Why did Lunsford decide to hire you two?"

"Because we are very good at what we do." My statement was seasoned with a genuine hint of modesty.

"Are you better than the police?"

"Let's just say we don't have their caseload to worry about."

"We can concentrate on one crime at a time," Renita chimed in, having regained her composure.

Evans looked down at his coffee as if something called to him in the depths of the hot black liquid. "How can I help?" His voice was laced with woeful resignation.

"Do you know of anyone who wanted to harm your wife—in that way?" I asked.

"By *that way*, I'm assuming you mean slaughtering Kylie like a farm animal." Evans sounded like a person resigned to a dire inevitability.

"I'm afraid that's exactly what I mean."

"No." Fatigue had set in, and it showed in his body and the sound of his voice.

"Had she received any death threats that you're aware of?" Renita asked.

"None that I'm aware of, but we didn't talk about those sorts of things."

"What did you talk about?" I asked.

"Mostly the kids and alimony payments." Evans voice trailed off, as if referencing the last part with regret.

"You mean the alimony she was paying you?" Renita said.

"Yes."

"Were you satisfied with the amount you were getting?" I asked.

"It was more than enough. Before you travel down that road of suspicion, know this. I wanted Kylie to stop paying me anything at all, but she refused."

"Why did you want her to stop?" Renita asked.

"What I wanted were our children, not her money. Since the courts— justifiably so, I might add—granted her custody, the alimony was more like a vindictive act to get back at her."

"Back at her," Renita said, "about what?"

"What she did."

I was confused. One glance at Renita proved she was, as well. "You're going to have to fill us in, Mr. Evans."

"Kylie and I divorced because she was having an affair. That's why she refused to stop paying me alimony. Kylie felt she owed me for what she had done."

"Can you tell us who she was having an affair with?" I asked.

"Is that important?"

"He could be a person of interest," Renita said.

"I was teaching at Portland State University at the time. I came home for lunch, which was something I rarely did. Kylie was changing the sheets on our bed. A whiff of sex was still in the air. Kylie wouldn't tell me who she was with. I pressed her for weeks about it, but she wouldn't give up a name. Kylie was tough, that way. The more you pushed, the more she pushed back twice as hard. I admired that quality about her. All Kylie would tell me was that she had made a mistake, and that it would never happen again. We both knew that was a lie. Intellectually and from a personality standpoint, Kylie and I were very compatible. Our sex life was never great. We never quite clicked on a physical level. For physical satisfaction, Kylie found what she needed from other men."

"You still haven't told us who *he* is," I said.

"He's a member of the Lunsford Insurance family."

Without looking at Renita, I knew she was drawing the same conclusion. "Who, Mr. Evans?" I pressed.

"Carl Wheaton."

Renita gasped. Evans stared at her. Renita took a sip of coffee.

"Carl Wheaton," I repeated, to give Renita an opportunity to compose herself.

"You know him."

"The same Carl Wheaton you mentioned earlier?" I tried to move the conversation along in the hope Evans did not piece together our relationship with Carl.

"He's the one." Evans stared off into the distance.

"Why do you think Carl Wheaton was having an affair with your wife?" Renita asked.

"Because they were always attracted to each other. You could see it any time they were in the same room. The way Carl would look at Kylie when he thought no one else was watching. The way Kylie would look at Carl when she thought no one noticed. They had a thing for each other. Anyone with eyes could see that. Anyone with a pulse could sense it."

"You said your wife never told you who she had an affair with," I said.

"No, she didn't. Kylie wouldn't crack; not even during the divorce. That was one of the most troubling parts of the whole nasty business. I'm sure Kylie kept quiet not in an effort to save our marriage, but his. Do you know Carl Wheaton?"

Renita and I looked at each other before I answered. "Yes, we do."

"We've done work for him in the past," Renita added.

"He hired you, didn't he?"

"Yes, he did," I said.

"Did he tell you about the affair? Or his fondness for my wife?"

"No sir, he didn't," I said, feeling embarrassed.

"This conversation is over."

"We just have a few more questions," I said.

"I want you out of my house."

"Don't you want to help us catch your wife's murderer?" Renita said.

"*Ex-wife*, and yes, I do. But as far as I'm concerned, that bastard had as much to do with Kylie's death as anyone."

"How so?" I asked.

"If he didn't have an affair with Kylie, we'd still be together and she wouldn't have been trolling for sex at some damn nightclub."

"Was Carl Wheaton the only man your wife had an affair with?"

"Their infidelity was the only one that was incessant. All the rest came and went."

"How can you be so sure?"

"I'm not going to tell you that. I know, and the rest is none of your damn business."

"Just a couple of more questions," Renita said.

"Leave my house."

"No matter what happened, she is still the mother of your children. That has to count for something," I said.

"Get out!" Evans yelled, standing and pointing toward the front door.

In leaving, we apologized to Nicholas Evans for upsetting him. We gave Evans our cards, asking him to contact us if he had any information that might help solve the murder of his ex-wife. He slammed the door in our faces.

"Carl should have warned us about the affair," Renita said as we walked to my car.

"Yes, he should have."

"I can't believe Carl would cheat on his wife. I wonder what else he's been keeping a secret."

"Whatever else Carl has going on in his personal life, I could care less about. He withheld vital information from us that had a direct bearing on our investigation."

"Are we going to have a talk with him about it?"

"Damn right we are."

CHAPTER THIRTY-TWO

We baited Carl Wheaton to our office under the pretense of having urgent news regarding Kylie Preston. For whatever reason, Carl never questioned why we needed to share our urgent intelligence in person. Carl marched into our office in eager anticipation of the breaking news, wearing a gray herringbone three-piece suit, his black trench coat draped over his arm. His black fedora was in hand, and his shoes were their usual spit-shined. The beard was gone, and with it his menacing, rugged appearance. Instead, he looked ten years younger. After Renita and I made Carl comfortable with coffee in my office, the interrogation began.

"Why didn't you tell us about your affair with Kylie Preston?" I asked. Carl looked at me, then Renita, who was sitting next to me. There was a blip of an expression on his face that was a dead giveaway. That didn't seem to matter to Carl for the moment. He composed himself and delivered his phony renunciation.

"That's nonsense. We weren't having an affair." His voice did not waver. His lying face was good. If I didn't believe Nicholas Evans, I might have believed Carl.

"Her ex-husband seems to think so," Renita said.

"A long-running affair, at that," I added.

"Nick always believed Kylie was fooling around on him." Carl tried to sound dismissive.

"Maybe because she was." Renita raised an eyebrow at Carl.

"Nick is a great guy who loved Kylie—maybe too much. Sometimes his imagination took him over the edge when it came to Kylie and other men. She was a very attractive woman. Who could blame him? Kylie and I were dear friends and nothing more."

"It's good you have such a high opinion of Nick, because he thinks you're a bastard," Renita said.

"He told you that?"

"More specifically: a bastard that he holds partially responsible for Kylie's death," I added.

"You can't be serious." Renita and I stared stoically at Carl as he looked back and forth between us. "Nick and I have had our quarrels, but I never thought he would ever take it this far." Carl appeared stunned by our offering.

"Quarrels about what?" Renita said. Carl realized he had slipped, and righted himself.

"Nothing worth talking about."

I was growing weary of Carl's charade. It was time to hog-tie this bull. "Either come clean about the affair with Kylie Preston or we're dropping the case."

"There's nothing to come clean about."

"Why did you hire us to find Kylie Preston's killer?"

"Because I'm confident you can."

"If you believe us so capable of finding a psycho killer that the police have yet to apprehend, how long do you think it will take for us to dredge up proof of your infidelity with Kylie Preston?"

Carl was still hesitant about being forthcoming. He needed more of a push.

"We've done a lot of work for you over the years on a wide variety of investigations. You should know by now that uncovering the details on your illicit affair with Ms. Preston will be child's play for us no matter how well you think you've covered your tracks."

Renita nodded in agreement. Carl was shaken to the core. I knew him well enough to know he was wrestling with anger and despair.

"Whatever you tell us, Carl, is confidential," I said. "None of it will ever make it back to your family."

If nothing else, Carl knew he could trust us. He began with a heavy sigh.

"Kylie and I became lovers before we were married, back when I started out. Since she was my boss, we kept it a secret for obvious reasons. Back then, it was an on-and-off-again thing that neither of us expected to last. Kylie met Nick and we drifted apart. Shortly thereafter, I met Andrea. A few years back, Kylie invited me to dinner. Kylie said she wanted to talk shop about something very important. We got together for dinner and the next thing I knew, instead of talking shop, we were talking about the good old days. At the time, I was going through a rough patch with Andrea. Kylie was having problems with Nick. One thing led to another and the next thing I knew, we were rekindling our passions in a hotel room."

"Did Kylie ever mention what this very important thing was she wanted to talk to you about?" I asked.

"No, like I said: she changed her mind. From that point on, Kylie and I met a couple of times a month."

"By 'met,' you mean having sex?" Renita said.

"Yes," Carl said with shame.

"Go on," Renita prompted.

"Kylie told me she was ready to leave Nick. She asked me to leave Andrea for her."

"A proposition that you rejected," Renita said.

"I did. I couldn't leave Andrea. I love her and the kids too much."

"Not enough not to screw around," Renita said.

"Renita, chill," I said.

"She's right. By the time Kylie was killed, it had been over between us for a year."

"The Evans' divorce was just over three years ago," I said.

"I know."

"You carried on with Kylie Preston for another two years after her divorce," Renita said.

"Off and on, yes," Carl said, resigned to his indignation.

"Now that that's all out in the open," I said, "where were you on the night Kylie Preston was murdered?"

"You can't possibly believe I had anything to do with her murder?"

"You've lied to us about the affair," Renita said. "There's no telling what else you've been hiding."

"I lied about the affair for good reason: to protect my family. The prime suspect looks nothing like me."

"You said it, Carl: the man who picked up Kylie Preston is a suspect," Renita said. "We don't know that he did it."

"If the man who picked up Kylie didn't do it, then why doesn't he come forward and clear himself?" I couldn't help Renita out with that bit of solid reasoning from Carl.

"Maybe he's dead, too," Renita said. "Maybe you killed him."

"That's your crackpot theory: that I hired someone to impersonate Dr. Harry Boulder and have him pick up Kylie so that I could murder her and cut up her body. And to cover my tracks, I killed the phony Harry Boulder."

"Anything's possible," Renita said.

"I'm seriously having second thoughts about hiring this agency to find Kylie's murderer."

Renita was way off base. I needed to bring some sanity back into the inquiry.

"Where were you when Kylie Preston was being butchered, Carl?"

"You can't be serious, C. J.?"

"Could be you had a motive," Renita said.

"What motive?"

"Kylie Preston could have threatened to expose your affair," I said.

"If Kylie had threatened to expose our affair, she would have been too late."

"Meaning?" I said.

"Andrea already knew about our affair. She'd known all along. She was willing to let me off the hook if I ended the affair once and for all. I did."

Where was your wife on the night Kylie Preston was murdered? I thought. I could have kicked myself for thinking that. Years of dealing with crime, most especially during my DEA days, and I would at times still expect the worst of people. It was a question I dared not ask Carl; at least not until I gathered enough evidence to justify such an accusation.

"You have an alibi, I take it," I said.

"I can't believe you're interrogating me."

"Just doing our job," Renita said.

"The job I hired you for, remember? A decision I'm having serious second thoughts about."

"Where were you, Carl?" I asked.

Carl's jaw dropped. He stared at us as if we were utter strangers asking him intimate questions. After closing his mouth, Carl told us he was at home with Andrea and their children when Kylie was killed.

"We believe you," Renita said, and we did.

"I can't believe you would think I was capable of butchering a human being—most especially someone I love."

"We didn't," I said. "Like Renita said, we're just doing our job. Narrowing the field of suspects helps us hone in on the killer. In this case, eliminating you happens to be part of the process; nothing personal."

"Me, a suspect."

"Everyone in the life of the victim is a suspect," I said. "Most murderers aren't murderers until they kill."

"That's bullshit: what happened to Kylie was cold-blooded premeditated murder. Not some violent emotional outburst."

"We agree," I said.

"And you think I'm capable of that?"

"No, we don't," Renita said.

"It doesn't mean we'll stop asking questions," I said.

"What happens next?"

"We keep looking. That is, if we haven't been fired."

"Not yet; I heard the Brian Dixon murder went down the same way."

"It would appear so."

"So you're working the Dixon case, too?"

"Not officially, but we'll be keeping an ear and an eye out for anything that might help in solving Kylie Preston's murder."

"Keep me posted, will you?"

"We will. Thanks for coming in. I hope we weren't too hard on you."

"I'll live." Carl grimaced almost as soon as he uttered those words. I assumed he felt it an inappropriate pun, considering what we were discussing.

We walked Carl out. Carl left, appearing to be a man bent, but not broken.

CHAPTER THIRTY-THREE

"How's your family?" I asked Dr. Blake Saba as we shook hands after entering his office. The Chief Medical Examiner and I go back a few years. I met him through Destini at the Portland Police Bureau's annual summer picnic. Blake and I found we had a mutual passion for Native American history. Blake and I got together for casual dinners to educate each other on what we knew on the subject. Without being conscious of it, we were carrying on an oral tradition that the First People and Black Africans share.

"Everybody's doing well," Blake said. "My wife keeps asking me when you're going to marry Destini. According to her, it's fate."

"We're working on it."

"Don't let her get away."

"I'll do my best."

"Do whatever it takes." I nodded. "You just missed Angel and McCaskill."

"I'm not sure that's not a bad thing."

"I heard you received carte blanche from the Chief."

"The detectives didn't tell you to hold back any information from me, did they?" I half-jokingly asked.

"Portland's finest would never do any such thing," Blake sarcastically responded.

"Because they know that you wouldn't."

"Precisely."

"I thought Rockgarden and Whimple were working the Dixon case."

"They are, but Angel and McCaskill are free to snoop around as much as they like."

"That should make for some interesting crime-fighting moments in the squad room."

"Oh, yeah."

"Blake, you remember Renita," I said, giving my partner a fatherly touch on her shoulder. Renita had been quietly standing by. That was not like her. Normally Renita would have introduced herself into the conversation a lot sooner. Her lack of assertiveness suggested to me that she was nervous.

"How could I forget?" Blake said as Renita and Blake shook hands. "You're even lovelier than I remember."

"Thank you," Renita said.

"I don't recall your ever setting foot inside my office before."

"This is my first time."

"Your first time with me, or your first time ever being in a medical examiner's office?"

"Both."

"Then I'll try to make your first time as painless as possible," Blake said with a considerate smile.

"I'm sure I'll be okay."

"You're both here to view the remains of Brian Dixon, I take it?"

"We are," I said.

"Renita, have you ever been to a slaughterhouse?" Blake asked.

"No."

"Then, to be honest, I'm not certain you want to make this your first time," Blake said. I was in agreement with Blake, but Renita had been insistent. Another part of me wanted Renita to see the actual corpse of a murder victim. Maybe that would dull her morbid desire to become involved in homicide cases.

"Don't worry about me. I'll be okay." Blake and I looked at each other. I could tell Blake agreed with me that this was a bad idea to allow Renita to see Brian Dixon. If Blake wanted to stop her, he could. He had the authority.

"Are you sure you're up to this?" I asked Renita.

"Not a problem," Renita said with confidence. "Let's do it."

"Right this way." Blake led us into the autopsy area. Aside from an occasional nod from the people we passed, no one in the room seemed to make much of our presence. They were all preoccupied in their own world of discovery.

"Here we are." Blake opened the door of the tomb labeled 'Brian Dixon'. He pulled out the stainless steel slab. A white cadaver cover concealed Brian Dixon. Blake pulled back the cover, exposing his dismembered remains. The stench of death was minimal. I had smelled much worse. Renita almost vomited. While well-preserved, his body was sapped of the color that lifeblood provides.

"Are you okay?" Blake asked Renita.

"Fine," Renita said, all of the confidence drained from her face and voice.

"Our toxicology report determined that Brian Dixon was killed by a lethal injection of—"

"Where's the bathroom?" Renita managed to say before her stomach contents almost rocketed out of her mouth.

"Down the hall to your left," Blake answered. Renita took off running.

"I hope she makes it."

"She'll make it to the bathroom. I hope she's going to be okay otherwise."

"Dixon was killed by a lethal injection of Ketamine. The anesthetic was delivered into the brain at the base of the neck."

Blake picked up the severed head to show me the injection point. Brian Dixon's eyes had been removed from their sockets and his eyelids sewn shut.

I nodded. "Quick and painless."

"Exactly." Blake reverently placed the head back in its place.

"His internal organs were removed but were not included with his remains. The body was drained of blood, probably after organ extractions. What you see here are the detached parts, laid out. The killer had strong surgical skills and went to great lengths to preserve bone and tissue. The victim's blood is in cold storage."

"*Everything* was preserved?"

"As much as possible, packaged and packed in ice."

"It's easy to see why Dr. Boulder was a prime suspect. His brain appears to be intact." I pointed at the skull.

"The killer did the same with Kylie Preston. That's a good thing. There's no better container for the human brain that the human skull."

"Is that why you think he didn't remove it?"

"That would be my guess. I'm going to have to breach that container in order to examine his brain for clues and extract some tissue samples for the lab. To reiterate: whoever did this had both experience in dismembering bodies as well as medical training. They knew what they were doing. Like I told Angel, there was no evidence of malice in what this killer did. It was cold, calculated, surgical science."

"Anything else?"

"I wish. We couldn't find a print or fiber or hair sample in the whole lot."

"Thorough and detached. What's his motivation?"

"I wish I knew, but that's why you're here."

"Why don't I ever get the easy cases?"

"We save those for ourselves."

"Was there a letter?" I asked.

"You mean like in the Kylie Preston murder?"

"Yes."

"There was. Except for the personal information relating to Brian Dixon, the rest read the same. He wanted us to donate as much of the victim as we could to those in need."

"That's considerate."

"Waste not, want not. Mentioning the letter brings to mind something else. You know the remains were wrapped like packages, correct?"

"Yes."

"I was talking to Pat over at forensics, and she said that the twine and packing tape used in both of the killings turned out to be common items you could buy almost anywhere. But the wrapping paper was brown butcher paper."

"Butcher paper."

Blake nodded.

"That's odd; why do you suppose he used butcher paper?"

"When you find out, we'll both know. It wasn't the easiest way to go. When's the last time you saw butcher paper on sale at your local convenience store?"

I was not surprised that fact had been omitted from the forensics report I had read. Neither Angel nor McCaskill had mentioned it, either. That made me assume the investigative authorities had discarded the use of butcher paper as an insignificant detail.

"What happened to Kylie Preston's body?" I asked, assuming Blake's last question to be a rhetorical one.

"After we gathered all of the data we could, her family allowed us to donate her remains to a bone and tissue transplant center. We received permission from Brian Dixon's family to do the same. Once all departments are satisfied they've gotten everything they can from his remains, and the necessary medical tests are concluded to clear the harvested materials, then we'll make the donations."

Hence, the proverbial silver lining, I thought. "May I see the note?"

"Forensics has it."

Blake pulled the cadaver cover back over the remains of Brian Dixon and closed the tomb. We returned to Blake's office. On the way, I knocked on the women's restroom door and called to Renita. Renita said she was fine, just before she retched.

Blake and I veered off from the discussion of murder to the Modoc story of how and why Kumokums created the world and everything in it. It was a story that was as ancient as man, and could have very well been a precursor to those of mainstream religions. The similarities between Kumokums's story and those of, say, Genesis were striking. We touched at how such a coincidence could occur from peoples separated by such great distances, and speculated on the possibilities of how that shared vision could have happened.

Renita joined us in Blake's office, looking like death warmed over.

"How are you feeling?" I asked.

"I've been better," Renita confessed.

"The first time is always the worst," Blake reassured.

"It gets easier?"

"No it doesn't," Blake said. "You become accustomed to it."

"Any leads?" Renita asked.

"I'll fill you in on the way back to the office. Thanks for your time, Blake." Dr. Saba and I shook hands.

"You're more than welcome."

"Yes, thank you," Renita said as she shook Blake's hand.

"You might want to take it easy for awhile," Blake said. "Vomiting dehydrates the body and robs it of nourishment."

"I'll keep that in mind." Renita was embarrassed.

"Let's do dinner soon, Blake. I'll cook."

"I'd like that."

"Dinner...excuse me," Renita said as she darted from the room, holding her stomach and covering her mouth.

"Was it something I said?" I smiled.

"Not nice, C. J." Blake shook his head and smiled back.

CHAPTER THIRTY-FOUR

I sent Renita home to recover from her first bout with a homicide corpse. It being Friday, Renita would also have the weekend to recuperate. I spent what was left of the workday typing up a detailed report and mapping out our investigative strategy on Brian Dixon. The latter was what I was in the process of doing when in burst Detective Laurie McCaskill. Detective McCaskill spotted me behind my desk and marched into my office. Judging by her expression and body language, McCaskill wasn't here to invite me out for drinks.

"So you're working the Dixon case." McCaskill said, still brimming with negative attitude.

"I am, and you confirmed this how?" I nonchalantly said.

"The Chief ME," McCaskill said. McCaskill watched me. She was trying to get a read on me. I gave her nothing.

"Blake told you that?"

"You know the ME?"

"For a lot longer than you. I hear you and Angel have been investigating the Dixon homicide."

"That's none of your concern."

"Isn't that Whimple and Rockgarden's case? Do they know you're snooping around on their case behind their backs?"

"It should be ours."

"The Captain doesn't see it that way."

"The Captain," McCaskill snorted. "For some reason he thinks you're God's gift to detective work."

"Did the Captain say that?"

"Of course not."

"Then why would you assume the Captain feels that way?"

"His actions speak louder than his words."

"I don't deny Captain Williamsen's a man of action, but I know for a fact that he regards me as an asset to be utilized on specific homicide investigations. No different than when I help out Bunco or Narcotics."

"You're just a little Suzie Lawmaker aren't you?"

"I'm more like Larry Lawmaker. Look, McCaskill, if you can't handle the competition, maybe you should scurry on back to Vancouver Bunco where you apparently didn't have any."

McCaskill drew in a heavy breath. "I can handle anything you can dish out."

"I can see that. That's why you're standing here whining about me playing in your sandbox."

"What is with you and playground metaphors?"

"It harkens to the fact that you need to grow up."

"I don't appreciate your going behind our backs to interview Nicholas Evans. If you wanted to know anything about Evans, you should have come to us."

"We have clearance to investigate wherever, whenever, and whomever we see fit. While your cooperation is appreciated, your approval is not required."

"We're the lead detectives on the Preston case."

"Angel is the lead detective on the Preston case. We report to her."

"You know that the widower called the chief complaining about you."

"Do tell."

"Mr. Evans said that you led him to believe that you were working for us when in fact you're working for Carl Wheaton. Apparently he and Carl Wheaton have a bit of friction between them regarding his deceased wife."

"And?"

"Did you?"

"Did I what?"

"Misrepresent yourself to Mr. Evans?" McCaskill grinned as if she had just turned the tables in our little chess match.

"Mr. Nicholas Evans is not a widower. They were divorced. Kylie Preston—maiden name restored—was single when she died. We did not misrepresent ourselves to Mr. Evans. Nicholas Evans has a long-standing beef with Carl Wheaton that had nothing to do with our murder investigation. You believe Mr. Evans because you want to, not because his accusation is bound in evidence."

"So you say."

"Why wasn't Carl Wheaton mentioned in your report?"

"He was never a viable suspect."

"You know this how?"

"I checked him out. That is what good detectives do: investigate all possible suspects."

"Good detectives also include such findings—or lack thereof—in their reports. Judging by your 'I' admission, Angel allowed you to go solo on the Carl Wheaton follow-up. You reported back to her that there was nothing to it. Angel probably trusted you to include that information in your written report. I suppose you were having a bad day and forgot. But that's pure conjecture on my part. I'm sure you read about our meeting with Nicholas Evans from the written report I emailed Angel."

The grin vanished from McCaskill's face. "What's your angle, Cavanaugh?" *Spoken like a veteran Bunco detective*, I thought.

"Angle? What are you talking about?"

"I mean, are you after the glory? 'Private investigator trumps police by apprehending psycho killer.'" McCaskill waved her hands as if she were displaying a banner headline.

"My motivation is the same as yours: to capture this murderer; nothing more, nothing less."

"Just remember the Preston case is ours. Stay out of our way."

"Where's Detective Alvarez?"

"None of your business." McCaskill was attempting to skirt the question. Her doing so verified what I suspected. McCaskill was here on her own volition. That suggested to me that Angel had no problem with how we were proceeding on the Preston case. I decided to press McCaskill on the absence of her partner.

"Does Angel feel the same as you do about me being involved in the Preston case?"

"Yes, she does."

"That's interesting. I've known Angel a lot longer than you have, and I have never known her to need anyone to speak on her behalf; especially a rookie partner."

McCaskill's jaw flexed. Her glare narrowed to laser points. At that moment, I believed McCaskill wanted me dead.

"Stay out of our way or, with or without the Captain's blessing, I will bring you down."

My father had taught me that mental toughness was far superior to physical toughness. That same principal had been reinforced throughout my military and DEA training. If McCaskill wanted a test of wills, she had chosen the wrong person to duel. I didn't doubt that McCaskill had truckloads of guts. McCaskill would not have made it this far without it. The will to fight and survive during my DEA days had given me barges of fortitude. I had experienced things that would have given McCaskill nightmares. Still, my motivation to stay the course was not personal, but professional. I had made a commitment and I was going to see it through. If McCaskill followed Angel's lead, McCaskill would see that and try to work with Renita and me rather than bucking for a fight. In time, McCaskill would learn that lesson. For the moment, it appeared that message for McCaskill would come the hard way.

"I've heard your threat; now hear mine. If you ever burst into my office unannounced again, I will file an official complaint against you for harassment."

"You would do that?"

"In a heartbeat."

McCaskill looked into my eyes. I knew she was trying to determine if I were bluffing. Turf wars between law enforcement colleagues occurred all of the time, even if I was no longer officially recognized as one. Judging by her recent behavior, McCaskill was going to have enough civilian complaints to contend with in the not-so-distant future before she got the message. If she asked around the office about me ever filing a complaint against a detective, McCaskill would discover I had done so on more than one occasion, against Whimple and Rockgarden. Who would have thought that Schultz and Weasel would one day be my ace in the hole? I wouldn't file a complaint against McCaskill because I didn't feel she deserved that in her jacket for standing up for what she believed. She didn't know that. McCaskill nodded as if to say she was standing down.

"Now, is there anything else, Detective? Because I have work to do."

McCaskill glared at me for a moment longer before she stormed out. Her accusation of me being a glory hound troubled me, not because it spoke to a truth in me, but because I knew better. The last thing I ever wanted was to work a murder case. Her glory hound accusation may have applied to the speaker. My read on McCaskill was that she was a loose cannon. McCaskill was new to the force. A high-profile collar like the Preston or Dixon case would look great in her jacket. The problem with that sort of thinking is that it often causes one to take their eye off the ball. That momentary lapse in focus could cause physical or professional harm to herself, her partner, or anyone else involved in the case. It made me concerned for Angel. I would take care of Renita.

CHAPTER THIRTY-FIVE

About a half-hour after Detective Laurie McCaskill left my office, in strolled dogged veteran crime reporter for the *Willamette Times* Shawn Calloway. His colleagues called him "Scoop" because he had an uncanny way of uncovering stories that no other reporter in town could. I thought of the slender, carrot-topped, freckled-faced journalist more as a barracuda. Because he came at me, head on. That approach emerged after Shawn discovered that his shrewd tactics didn't work on Renita or me. I had an educated guess as to why Shawn was paying me a visit.

"One of my PPB inside sources tells me that you're working the Dixon murder," Shawn said.

What Shawn said was believable. He had sources everywhere. Since he had covered the Preston murder for his paper, it made sense that he would be covering the Dixon murder as well. Whoever his source was on that particular topic had not informed Shawn that we were working the Preston homicide. It didn't matter. There was no need to let Shawn in on our truth, in either case.

"You don't have any PPB inside sources," I said in jest.

"You'd be surprised," Shawn said with a smile. "Is it official? Has The Butcher struck again?" Shawn was trying to get the real story. His smile disappeared, but there was a gleam in his green eyes. The PPB had not released an official statement on the status of the Brian Dixon homicide. If Shawn could find a reliable source to quote that the same killer was responsible for both the Preston and Dixon murders, he would have scooped the local and national press again.

"*The Butcher*," I said.

"That's what I'm calling the maniac who's chopping up people. Kinda catchy, huh?"

"No, and it's not the least bit original."

"You can't deny it's accurate," Shawn said, gathering up his red ponytail with his right hand and flipping it.

"You need to talk to the detectives in charge of the case."

"I have. They aren't saying one way or the other."

That came as no surprise. Whimple and Rockgarden didn't like the press, and they hated Shawn Calloway. Shawn had been the loudest voice trying to have them booted off the force due to numerous complaints filed against the detectives for alleged police brutality. Shawn had also been looking into Rockgarden's involvement with local organized crime. Like much of the local press, Calloway was unsuccessful in his campaign against the heavy-handed detectives, and he had yet to prove anything against the slippery Rockgarden.

"I've got nothing for you, Shawn."

"That's what so many say before I wear them down."

"Wear away, oh mighty river of the press."

"Are you working on the Brian Dixon murder investigation for the PPB?"

"No."

"Then why were you spotted coming out of the city morgue earlier today?"

"I was visiting a friend."

"And who might this friend be?"

"Didn't your informant tell you?" If Shawn knew any more, he would tip his hand, here.

"Might that friend's name be Dr. Blake Saba?"

"There are a lot of people who work at the city morgue," I said, not taking the bait. "A number of them I am acquainted with; some I regard as friends. You tell me. Who was I there to see?"

"Why was Renita with you while you visited this alleged friend?"

"Why not?" Shawn was fishing. I was guessing that whatever snitch was feeding Shawn his information had seen Renita and me come and go from the building and little more.

"Is Renita a friend of this friend of yours?" I had to chuckle at the absurdity of the question.

"Renita is an acquaintance of this friend of mine."

"Renita didn't know this friend of yours before making his acquaintance?"

"I didn't say that."

"You implied that Renita didn't know this friend of yours before then."

"Did I? I don't recall doing any such thing." I leaned back in my chair with a smile, placing my hands behind my head. This was turning out to be more fun than I could have anticipated.

"Humph, I can see you're being particularly stubborn today."

"Stubborn as a rock."

"So you're holding out on me." Shawn's cell rang. He stepped into the outer office to take the call. It only took a moment before he was back.

"In answer to your question, I'm always holding out on you, Shawn. You're a reporter. That's the way it is."

"You know you can tell me anything," Shawn said as if he were my shrink. "I'll simply quote you as a confidential source."

"I'll bear that in mind."

Shawn nodded. He had at least verified what he had come for: that was Renita and I were somehow involved in the Dixon murder investigation. Next, Shawn would look for some way to rope us in so that he could use us to help make his story.

"I'll be going—"

"To do some *real* investigative reporting," I interrupted.

"I have a dinner date to get ready for, which reminds me. What's Renita's favorite restaurant?"

Shawn had been hinting at his romantic interest in Renita for some time. Whether Calloway's suggestion of inviting Renita to dinner was for that cause or a means for him to land an inside source, I couldn't be certain. I was sure if I asked Calloway about it, he would deny such ulterior motives.

"You're asking because?" I said in answer to Shawn's question.

"I'd like to take her there sometime."

"I doubt Renita's interested."

"How do you know?"

"Because she's seeing someone, and he's not you."

"*Touché*. First thing tomorrow, I'm all over this story. And I won't stop until I get it."

"Good for you."

"See you soon, Cavanaugh. Tell Renita I said hello."

"No chance of that."

Shawn left with a sly smile. Unlike McCaskill, Shawn Calloway was a formidable opponent. He was quick and resourceful and had patience and guile. In combination, those qualities were difficult to misdirect. I decided to deal with Shawn if and when the situation required it. I took a moment to clear my mind. Then I returned to outlining how to proceed with the Brian Dixon murder investigation.

CHAPTER THIRTY-SIX

For the next week, Renita and I tore into Brian Dixon's life. We split the research right down the middle. All of the legwork, we did together. Renita had changed since her trip to the morgue. Her vibrant personality was still there, but tempered at the appropriate times with a serious edge when it came to our investigation work. That serious edge was something Renita had lacked far too often in the past. She almost never flirted any more. Our teamwork had gone from good to great. I began to see in her what I always believed she had the potential to become: a Grade-A investigator.

What we learned about Brian Dixon was unflattering, to say the least. Dixon was divorced. His parents were deceased. He frequented strip clubs and prostitutes. His two children did not seem to care that "Brian"—as they referred to their father—was dead. His younger brother, who lived in South Dakota and who hadn't spoken to Brian in years, showed more remorse. Aside from mourning Brian's passing as much as one might a pet gerbil, the younger sibling did not seem to care about the circumstances surrounding his brother's demise. Dixon's few current clients found him to be okay as a person and an accountant. From the list of swindled ex-clients who hated Dixon, none had the skill, knowledge, or restraint it would take to do what had been done to him. Add to that, that no one in Dixon's life had any connection to Kylie Preston, and we had reached a dead end.

After we went as far as we could on the Brian Dixon investigation, we paid a visit to Whimple and Rockgarden. Much to their chagrin, the Captain made Weasel and Schultz hand over copies of their police report to Renita and I. The report contained nothing we didn't already know. If anything, we could have informed the detectives in charge about a few things they had missed. Considering Whimple and Rockgarden's condescending attitudes toward us, we opted not to do so.

CHAPTER THIRTY-SEVEN

Before I worked for Lunsford Insurance, I did what I normally do: I did a thorough background check on the company. I was impressed by what I found.

Bradford Lunsford managed a salt mine in the hot desert valley of Camp Verde, Arizona. His brother Abbott saw to the day-to-day operations and their brother Thorpe managed the local lodgings. There wasn't much to do but eat, sleep, and work, so the men saved their money. Once they saved enough, they decided to leave the dessert and head to what they had heard was the cool lush green of the great northwest. When they arrived in Oregon, they were not the least bit disappointed.

The Lunsford brothers stopped in Roseburg, planning to rest up for a couple of days before venturing further north. A local dining house that also served as a watering hole for the locals was where they decided to eat. The brothers overheard some men talking about a local sawmill that was shutting down because of outdated equipment and poor management. The brothers, being astute businessmen, smelled an opportunity and decided to look into it.

The sawmill was located on the banks of the North Umpqua River near the speck of a town called Glide. It was just as the men in the bar had said: rundown and in need of solid management. The brothers bought the mill and set about doing something different. The Lunsford brothers did their research and discovered that Oregon already had over 170 operating sawmills and counting. What was missing was a paper mill. The transcontinental railroad had already been established. That not only meant more accessibility to the state of Oregon, but to the rest of the expanding territories. If the brothers played their cards right, they could get a strong foothold on the paper industry in the northwest.

Lunsford paper established itself as the finest paper mill west of the Mississippi. The Lunsford brothers were conscientious men who had a deep, abiding respect for nature. They were the only logging business who employed ecologists. The Lunsford brothers made certain they, or those they did business with, did not do anything that would have disastrous ecological impacts on Oregon's pristine forests.

The Lunsford brothers felt equally responsible for their employees. The brothers made certain all of their equipment was maintained to the highest levels. They also allowed the workers to establish their own safety guidelines that the brothers implemented to the letter.

Because of the dangerous nature of working in a paper mill, the brothers had trouble finding reliable, affordable health insurance for their employees. Rather than continue to wrangle with insurance companies over the issue, the Lunsford brothers established a fund that allowed their workers to contribute a certain percentage of their salaries, which the brothers would match. This fund would not only cover all medical costs that might incur due to a job-related injury, but it would also pay the injured party a percentage of their wages until they could get back on their feet. When the Lunsford brothers sold the paper mill for a king's ransom to the largest paper manufacturer in the country some years later, at the bequest of their former employees, the Lunsford brothers continued to offer them health coverage in the form of insurance minus their personal contributions, with the new owner's blessings.

Word spread about the Lunsford health insurance plan, and other people wanted to join. Before the Lunsford brothers knew it, they were insuring homes, businesses, ranches, and farms. The brothers branched out from there into life and disaster insurance. From there, they kept expanding until, one day, they looked around and discovered they were the number one insurer in the state of Oregon.

Word about Lunsford Insurance spread throughout the northwest like an unchecked wildfire. Within a few short years Lunsford Insurance became the most respected and trustworthy insurance company in the entire northwest.

The Lunsford brothers have since passed on. Their descendants have continued their legacy. The Lunsford family did more than run a very profitable business. They maintained the integrity forged in the mission statement of its founders. To continue to do so necessitated they remain free of the insurance cartel whose sole objective was profit over people.

While Lunsford continued to treat its clients with dignity, that didn't mean that Lunsford Insurance was a soft target for swindlers and con artists. They checked and triple checked suspicious claims. If your claim was legitimate, they were only too happy to give you what you deserved. If you proved to be fraudulent, they would come down on you like a mighty Oregon redwood.

That integrity made them number one in my book. While I will continue to work for insurers who belong to the cartel, I will not allow them to dictate the outcome of my investigations. If they choose to drop me for not being their puppet, so be it. My veracity means more to me than their payoff. In that regard, Lunsford and I are in complete agreement.

CHAPTER THIRTY-EIGHT

"We should have the Brian Dixon murder case, Captain," McCaskill said.

Captain Kelby Williamsen looked across his cluttered desk at Detective Laurie McCaskill. *She looks young enough to be my oldest daughter*, Kelby thought. They had been going back and forth over this issue for the last five minutes. The Captain was determined to convince his bright new detective why turning over the Dixon case to her and Angel would not be a good idea. The Captain offered McCaskill a donut. McCaskill passed on the offer with a polite "No thank you, sir."

"I'm sorry, Detective, but there's nothing I can do. It's protocol. Whimple and Rockgarden landed the case and unless they choose to hand it over to you and Angel, it's theirs."

"But the Dixon homicide has the exact same M.O. as the Preston murder."

"You get no argument from me there, but protocol is protocol. What if the situation were reversed? What if Whimple and Rockgarden had been working on the Preston murder and you and Angel landed the Dixon case? Would you want me to force you to hand over your case to Whimple and Rockgarden because they were working a case with the same M.O.?"

"No, I wouldn't," McCaskill reluctantly agreed. "But Captain," McCaskill lowered her voice to a whisper, even though the Captain's door was closed and Whimple and Rockgarden were out of the office, "I haven't been here that long and even I know that Whimple and Rockgarden are the worst homicide detectives in this office."

The Captain gave a slight jerk of his head. There was no way Captain Williamsen was going to confide in a subordinate his opinion regarding the capabilities of anyone under his command. He knew it would be foolish, not to mention professional suicide, if word ever got out that he had done so.

"While you're entitled to your opinion, Detective, that's for me to decide."

"What about Cavanaugh, sir?"

"What about him?"

"He's just going to get in the way, Captain."

"Cavanaugh will not get in your way, I can assure you. He's far too good an investigator for that."

"And his partner?"

"Renita Harris? She's not bad either, but I'm sure Cavanaugh will be keeping her on a short leash. The same way Angel is doing with you."

McCaskill let out a barely audible "Humph." Captain Williamsen realized he had struck a nerve. That was his intention. *Maybe now McCaskill will realize what it feels like to be on the sharp end of a prodding stick, and will back off,* Kelby thought.

The Captain's telephone rang. "Excuse me for a moment, Detective. Captain Williamsen, Homicide." McCaskill started to leave to give the Captain privacy. Captain Williamsen signaled for McCaskill to remain in her seat. "I see," the Captain said, writing down a name and address that McCaskill could read upside down. "I'll send someone over right away. Just sit tight and don't touch anything." The Captain hung up. Captain Williamsen's face was grim with thought.

"What was that about, sir?"

"It could have been a crackpot or a crank, but my gut tells me different. That was a Mr. James Caulfield. Mr. Caulfield said someone left suspicious-looking brown paper packages bound in twine on his doorstep. He also said his wife has been missing for a couple of days and he's afraid she might be in those packages."

"The Butcher," McCaskill said with a gasp.

"So, my detectives are calling him that, too."

"Yes sir, we are."

"I can't say it's not appropriate." Captain Williamsen ripped the piece of paper from his writing pad and handed it to McCaskill. "Look into it."

"I'm on it, sir."

"I?" The Captain said, giving McCaskill an inquisitive stare.

"I mean we; Angel and I."

"Never forget that, Detective. Teamwork is what gets the job done around here. Now grab your partner and check it out."

"Yes, sir," McCaskill said, rushing out to find Angel.

CHAPTER THIRTY-NINE

I had a Motown collection CD playing. The song "Just My Imagination" by The Temptations filled my office with a gentle spritz of sound. I had picked up a lunch of succulent meatloaf, crisp green beans, and real mashed potatoes. I was in the process of carving up my meatloaf when the front door opened. Shawn Calloway walked in.

"That looks good," Shawn said, walking into my office as if it were his own. "Where'd you score that?"

"Lazzarani's; it's one of today's lunch specials." Shawn eyed my lunch like a man who hadn't eaten for days.

"I know where I'm going for lunch and what I'll be having."

"Well, you won't be having any of mine. What can I do for you, Shawn?"

"Where's your smoking-hot partner?"

"None of your business."

"Is she still seeing that bouncer over at The Lair?"

"Does it matter? Either way, it's not you, and that bouncer owns half of Fullman's. A fact you seem to keep forgetting."

"One day Renita will be mine."

"So you say. Again, what can I do for you, Shawn?"

"I hear you were hired to track down The Butcher?"

"You're sticking with that name."

"Why not? It's catching on."

I recalled a hit man known as The Butcher who worked for high-end criminals to eliminate problems and send a searing message to any would-be competitors. That Butcher would chop up his victims and wrap their remains in butcher paper. That Butcher was also a cannibal. He would cook a portion of his victim, such as their kidneys, liver, or brains, and eat it. I knew for a fact that the Butcher was dead. Killed in a shootout with the FBI. The Temptations "Ain't Too Proud to Beg" changed the spritz.

"I'm sure it'll make your top twenty all-time serial killer nicknames."

"Maybe; maybe not." Shawn gathered up his ponytail and flipped it back. "So what can you tell me about this madman?"

"Nothing," I said, enjoying a slice of meatloaf.

"Nothing as in you're not talking; or nothing, as in you don't know anything?"

"I mean nothing as in I don't know anything," I said after swallowing. "And it's none of your business what I do or do not know."

"Same old bull-headed C. J. You might as well spill. In the end, I always get my story."

"There's nothing to *spill*, and killing two people does not make someone a serial killer."

"Haven't you heard?"

I laid down my utensils and looked at Calloway as if he had just asked me about UFOs. "What are you talking about?"

"They found another body cut up, packaged, and left on the doorstep of a James Caulfield over in Grant Park."

"You've got to be kidding," I said, astonished I hadn't been informed by Angel about that new development.

"It's all over the AP wire service. The Police haven't officially ID'd the body yet, but there's speculation that it's Caulfield's wife because she's nowhere to be found. Early indicators are that it's The Butcher's handiwork. I gather you don't know anything about it, by your reaction."

Shawn reached for a green bean. I slapped his hand away.

"It's the first I've heard of it."

"Looks like someone's out of the loop. Maybe your girlfriend will be more helpful?"

"If, by my girlfriend, you mean Detective Pendleton, then you already know that she's not working the case."

"I'm aware of that. Alvarez and McCaskill are. Speaking of working it, what can you tell me about McCaskill? She's hot."

"Ask her out sometime and find out for yourself," I said, believing McCaskill would ream Shawn a new one for doing so.

"I'll do that. I just thought your girlfriend—Detective Pendleton— might have shared some insight on this case with you. Detectives talk amongst themselves about these things. Maybe Destini dropped some of that shop talk in your lap."

"I would tell you this why?"

"Because we're friends," Shawn said with an unconvincing smile.

"And you always exploit your friends?"

"I do what I have to in pursuit of a hot story. You scratch my back and I'll scratch yours. You keep me in the loop about what's happening on your end, and I'll pass along anything—or anyone—I come across. Deal?" Shawn extended his hand for a handshake. I didn't shake.

"No." I picked up my utensils and took a mouthful of tender, juicy meatloaf. The Temptations' "Ball of Confusion" changed the spritz to a throb.

"How's the food?"

I nodded as I was chewing. "That's good," I said after swallowing.

"Well, it's clear you're out of the loop, and the only thing you're doing is making me hungry."

"You'd better get yours before it's gone. They sell out of this special in a hurry."

"If you find out anything about this case, give me a call."

"Nope."

"Thanks. Tell Renita I stopped by."

"Nope."

"See yah!"

Shawn left as quickly as he came. I tried to enjoy my lunch, but I couldn't. Shawn's news had spoiled my appetite. I couldn't stop thinking about the possible third victim and the fact that Angel had not bothered to call me about it. McCaskill, Rockgarden, and Weasel I would have expected that from, but not Angel. I didn't mind saying I was disappointed. I picked up the telephone to call Angel and then decided against it. This was a face-to-face matter. I dropped my lunch into the kitchen compost bin and headed over to Central Precinct.

CHAPTER FORTY

I marched into Central Precinct. The Desk Officer said "Hi" as I strode past him with a quick wave. I walked into Homicide and right up to Angel and McCaskill's desks. They weren't there. I asked one of the detectives if he knew where they were. He answered they were in Interrogation Room 3. I burst into IR 3. Angel and McCaskill were interviewing a worried and disheveled-looking white male who appeared to have been crying.

"What the hell are you doing in here? Get out," McCaskill yelled.

"C. J., we're in the middle of something," Angel said, more annoyed than upset.

"Why didn't you call me?" I asked Angel. Angel grabbed me by the arm and escorted me out of IR 3, closing the door behind her.

"What is your problem? You never bust in on a detective conducting an interview, especially when they're about to break a case."

"He's the killer?" I asked, looking at McCaskill and the disheveled, red-eyed man through the two-way mirror. McCaskill was back at putting the squeeze on him.

"Yes, he is," Angel said.

"He's The Butcher?"

"The Butcher? That guy, no."

"What?"

"That's James Caulfield. His wife was Sarah Caulfield. The dead woman we found cut to pieces and stuffed in coolers and left on his doorstep."

"Sounds like the same M.O."

"That's what he thought, too. What you have in there is a copycat killer."

"Are you sure?"

"Positive. Blake had a quick look at his work and could tell right away that the same person did not kill Sarah Caulfield. It was nowhere near as precise, neat, or clean as The Butcher's. That woman had been carved up by someone who had no idea what the hell they were doing. McCaskill and I suspected Caulfield was a fraud when we first saw the parcels. The killer used twine to wrap the packages, but not butcher paper, and he hadn't properly stored her remains for possible donation. The damn things were leaking all over the place.

"James and Sarah Caulfield were in the middle of a vicious divorce. Sarah Caulfield had filed on grounds of chronic infidelity, extreme emotional distress, and physical and verbal abuse. She had plenty of solid evidence on her husband to back up her claims. James Caulfield was on the verge of losing everything. He decided to murder his soon-to-be-rich-on-his-money ex-wife and make it look like The Butcher had done it in order to stop his slide over the cliff. We were this close to wringing a confession out of him when you barged in." Angel demonstrated how close with her thumb and forefinger they had been. You couldn't have fit a dime between the two. "Now we're back at square one."

"I wouldn't go that far," I said, attempting to lighten the mood. "Maybe more like square three or four."

Angel wasn't amused. I felt like a fool. Angel picked up on my vibe.

"Feeling rather stupid, huh?" Angel said.

"It shows?"

"It does, and you should. I'm going back in there and help my partner finish nailing this sick bastard. You're going to leave with your tail between your legs. Later, when I call you, you're going to have a great way of making it up to us for your rude and untimely interruption. I'm not saying what that apology may involve, but you might want to think along the lines of concert tickets for me and McCaskill to see Beyoncé. As you may know, she's appearing at the Rose Garden. I hear her performance is amazing."

"The last I heard, Beyoncé was sold out."

"She is, but I'm certain you'll find a way to get us tickets. We'll only need two. My husband has no interest in going and I'm sure I can convince McCaskill not to bring a date."

"I might be able to work something out."

"If you want back in our good graces, you will."

"I didn't realize I had ever been in McCaskill's good graces."

"I'm working on her. Floor seats would be preferable, but center seats will be acceptable."

"Floor seats," I repeated in a shameful daze.

"Or center, no more than ten rows deep."

"Center, no more than ten rows deep," I echoed.

"And dinner. I'll let you choose the restaurant. From what Destini tells me, you have excellent taste in restaurants."

"I think I can swing that."

"See that you do."

"I'm leaving now."

"You know the way out." Angel had a smug grin on her face that would not let go. I turned tail and left as my friend had suggested. I could feel her amusing stare eyeing my every step. That was one of those embarrassing moments I would hear about from a variety of sources for the rest of my life; Renita and Destini being at the forefront of that line. I wondered how much it would cost to buy Angel and McCaskill's silence.

CHAPTER FORTY-ONE

Reacting as I had to the news of a possible third Butcher victim on my watch made me aware I was more invested in his capture than I had realized. James Caulfield confessed to the murder of his wife. Through a Rose Quarter connection, I was able to land Angel and McCaskill a couple of front row, floor seats at the Beyoncé concert. Dinner at The Gilt Club was a lot easier to come by, since I have a standing reservation at that upscale restaurant. Driving and parking was not an issue for the Detectives' night out. I threw in limousine service as an added measure to convey the sincerity of my apology. Except for the ribbing that had already ensued, all's well that ends well.

Carl had offered to pre-screen Kylie Preston's client information if I informed him what to look for. I told Carl I appreciated his offer, but that it wasn't necessary. We wanted to see everything. What a mistake that was. We were ill prepared for the volume of information Carl provided to us on Kylie Preston.

Carl delivered Kylie Preston's personnel files to us on a flash drive. Carl apologized for the delay. The Lunsford family had to give their approval before any of Kylie Preston's information could be released, which they did. No electronic files existed on much of Ms. Preston's earlier work. The Lunsford family viewed it as an opportunity to transfer that paperwork to electronic medium. This, of course, required scanning a mountain of paperwork.

The documents were placed in file folders in chronological order spanning Ms. Preston's first to last year of employment with Lunsford Insurance. I had Renita copy the files onto our on-site and offsite backup storage drives before doing anything with them. Once the files were secured, we began the arduous process of weeding out valuable information one folder at a time.

Kylie Preston had been involved, in one manner or another, in the issuance of thousands of insurance policies and claims throughout her career. I would have preferred to print everything out. Reading something on paper works better for me than reading it on a screen. There is something about the tactile experience of paper that makes me feel connected to the information in a way that the detached experience of reading on a screen does not. Not to mention, I feel more mobile with paper than I do with a computer. All you need is light by which to see, not electricity by which to exist. Had we printed out in full the amount of material Carl provided us with, it would have filled boxes. Even I couldn't justify what a waste that would have been.

Our review of Kylie Preston's electronic paper trail gave us clear insight to the path of a stellar career. Kylie Preston's rise to V.P. of Acquisitions for Lunsford Insurance began as a door-to-door policy salesperson more than two decades earlier. Ms. Preston appeared to be a natural in that department, as she always exceeded her quota. Her acquiring her own sales force seemed a foregone conclusion. As a sales manager, Kylie Preston spent her time approving or rejecting policies her sales force brought in, although she occasioned a sale during that period in an effort to more than likely to keep her skills sharp. Also included in her duties, for a time, was the acceptance or rejection of policy claims. That was commonplace for Lunsford in the early days before they developed a department to handle that specific area.

Kylie Preston climbed the promotion ladder by at first expanding her own sales force and then by taking over other offices, ultimately becoming V.P. of Sales and Marketing for the region. Lunsford was not a company to rest on their laurels. They had for some time been investing in other profitable commodities to hedge their bet against an expanding and changing business climate. When the company committed to diversifying, Kylie Preston seemed a natural fit to head up the venture. Ms. Preston was promoted to V.P. rather than president because only a Lunsford family member could ever be president.

Renita and I set ourselves to the arduous tasks of pouring over volumes of information in search of the proverbial needle in a haystack that would garner us a hot lead. Renita and I went through it and siphoned out the deceased and those who were satisfied by their treatment and settlements. That left us with those who were disgruntled for one reason or another. We focused on those people. We compiled their information in the same manner we would for a background check. Once we amassed all of their information, we went to work in search of viable suspects. That entire process took us eight business days. We didn't work the weekend. We spent that quality time with our significant others.

CHAPTER FORTY-TWO

The modest single-story log cabin home I purchased a few miles east of Oakridge next door to the Willamette National Forest was in immaculate shape. The elderly couple who had retired to it discovered they missed their family more with each passing year. After eight years of rustic life, the couple decided it was time to move back home. Their eldest son, who lived in their home town of Billings, Montana with his wife and two children, were only too glad to take them in. While the couple admitted they would miss the cabin, they were also looking forward to being near their children and grandchildren.

Spring was in full bloom, and with it came the vibrant pulse of life. I talked Destini into allowing me to whisk her away for a weekend getaway. What I didn't tell Destini was that I had bought a cabin. It was a secret I had kept even from Renita. I had managed to slip away for a couple of weekends under the guise of visiting friends in California. What I did during that time was redecorate the cabin and redo the landscaping to my own style. That included getting rid of the vegetable garden that I liked but knew I would not be around to maintain.

After Destini proclaimed how much she loved the place was when I broke the news that I had bought the cabin. Destini was thrilled by my confession. Once Destini settled down, she began making suggestions on how to improve "our" cabin getaway.

Destini and I talked as I cooked, and she kept me company. Our conversation jumped around from shop talk to politics, family, religion, art, music, friends, and then some. No subject was taboo. When I interjected a topic that had been on my subconscious mind, it rather took us both by surprise.

"When did you get over your lone wolf syndrome?" I asked as I mashed the potatoes.

"About eight months into my rookie year. Why do you ask?"

"Just curious."

"Ted Wiley was my partner—you never met Ted. He had been on the force for thirty years; twenty-two of those as a homicide detective. We had this quadruple homicide, a family of four. The guy had used a hatchet to murder them. It was literally a bloody mess. I set my sights on nailing the perp. I, of course, knew everything, having been a homicide detective for all of eight months. I charged ahead. Ted tried to rein me in, but I wasn't having it. The next thing I knew, I was knee deep in a situation that I wasn't ready for. Ted pulled me out of the fire. From that point on, it's been teamwork for me. I'm still possessive about my cases, but I'm open to cooperation from any source that can help solve them within the boundaries of the law."

"What was the situation he saved you from?"

"Maybe I'll tell you when we're retired with grandchildren, but not before." I smiled at her comment.

"I was always more team-oriented. I played basketball, football, and some soccer in high school. In the military, it's a way of life. In the DEA, most of the people I worked with were acclimated toward that way of thinking, as well. Maybe it was because we knew teamwork was the best way to defeat the forces we were up against."

"When you went undercover, you were flying solo."

"That's different; you're only responsible for yourself."

"I don't follow."

"It's different when your actions can affect the livelihood or safety of others."

"Is this about McCaskill?" Destini asked, zeroing in on where our conversation was headed.

"More like Angel."

"What are you getting at, C. J.?"

"I think McCaskill is a loose cannon. She's so fired up to prove how good a homicide detective she is that she could wind up endangering her partner."

"Aren't you being a little melodramatic?" I told Destini about McCaskill's visit to my office. "I see," Destini said in response. "She has had a hair up her butt about the Preston and Dixon cases. I'll pass your concerns along to Angel."

"Thanks."

"You can thank me later."

"I'm all for that." Destini gave me a hug from behind as I squeezed fresh garlic into the smooth and creamy mashed potatoes.

We had a modest dinner of grilled salmon, green beans, and garlic mashed potatoes that we enjoyed with a light Pinot Noir. Completing our meal with a hot dessert tea and cheesecake made us perfect candidates for the front porch swing.

The western slope of the Cascade Range was our front yard. We sat there snuggling in awe of what we saw around us. Sunlight flowed down from an azure sky. Majestic Oregon sequoias reigned over a wealth of pristine nature. The mood was perfect to purpose marriage to Destini yet again. Instead, I chose a different course.

"Can I share something confidential with you?" I asked as we gently swung back and forth on the front porch swing.

"Oh my goodness; it has something to do with the case you're working on, doesn't it?"

"How can you tell?"

"Your tone of voice. You always sound *extra* professional when you want to have a work conversation."

"I didn't know that, but you're right. It's about Kylie Preston's murder."

"I thought we were here to forget about work."

"It'll only take a moment to brainstorm this with you."

"Let's get it over with," Destini said with a sigh.

"Something showed up during the examination of Kylie Preston's files."

"What was it?"

"It appeared to both Renita and me that a number of claims that she rejected were legitimate. Of course, there's no way of knowing for certain without doing a personal investigation into each suspect case. But from what I've read, and what my instincts are telling me, Ms. Preston denied claims that should have been paid in full."

"How the plot thickens. Now you know what I go through on a regular basis with my homicide cases."

"The victim isn't often the only victim."

"Exactly."

"We're guessing that's how Kylie Preston kept her fat bottom lines. She was obviously greedy. All indicators point to that. Whenever and however she could make a buck, she leapt at the opportunity."

"Do you think Carl knew about Preston, or the Lunsford family?"

"Carl was still selling insurance during that time. His name wasn't mentioned in any of the suspicious claims. As far as the Lunsford family is concerned, I'm leaning toward no. They don't get involved in the day-to-day operations. And there's more."

"Really?" Try as she might, Destini could not resist a good mystery.

"I ran across some information in Kylie Preston's records that I believe was put there by mistake."

"What makes you say that?"

"She was pressing the Lunsford family to band with other large insurance companies."

"Preston was trying to get Lunsford to become part of what you call the insurance cartel?"

"Yes."

"How was that going?"

"Not well. The Lunsford family kept turning her down."

"That's good news, because I've heard horror stories about how some of these big insurance companies operate. I know how first-rate I have it with Lunsford at PPB."

"Kylie Preston kept trying to convince the Lunsford family how much more profit they could generate if they joined—or at least adopted—the practices of the cartel, with no success. According to in-house investigative reports, the Lunsford family was suspicious that Kylie Preston was plotting with the insurance cartel to take over their insurance company."

"Real life corporate espionage." Destini was intrigued. "Are you thinking the Lunsford family had something to do with knocking off Kylie Preston?"

"Who's to say? When that much money's on the table, anything's possible."

"Not to mention the Lunsford family name."

"True; they'd been keeping an eye on her for more than a year."

"I don't know, C. J., Preston would have to have been both greedy *and* stupid to try something like that. From what I've heard, the Lunsford family is as sharp as they come when it comes to business. Who did the in-house investigation?"

"More than one person was involved. There are reports from Preston's personal assistant, her accountant, and numerous other people she had contact with, both within and outside of the company. Her office and private conference room were bugged. So was her home phone and cell. She was also being followed. There were reports of her taking clandestine meetings with top level officials from the insurance cartel."

"So you're thinking the Lunsford family *did* have something to do with Kylie Preston's murder."

"It gets worse."

"How?"

"Carl Wheaton coordinated the entire in-house investigation."

Destini let out a low whistle. "Carl spied on a woman he loves for the company he loves. That puts a whole other spin on loyalty. You and I both know Carl would never go so far as to commit or orchestrate a murder."

"From what I've seen in my law enforcement career, no one is above suspicion."

"Does that include me?"

"No, it doesn't, but I thought we were talking about Carl."

"Continue."

"I don't believe Carl did it, but he may know who was involved."

"Why have her murdered in so gruesome a fashion? Why not your standard run-of-the-mill hit or staged accident or suicide?"

"All good questions."

"Why hire you to find Preston's murderer if he had something to hide?"

"That's my strongest reason for not dogging Carl on what I've stumbled upon. With PPB homicide coming up empty, it wouldn't make sense for him to involve Cavanaugh Investigations if he was involved. And, according to Carl, the Lunsford family wants to find Kylie Preston's murderer as much as anyone."

"I take it Renita doesn't know anything about this?"

"How did you surmise that?"

"Your use of the first person when you referenced the cartel information."

"Very sharp, Detective," I said with pride.

"I have my moments," Destini said with a knowing smile.

"We divided the research. It happened to be amongst the information I was going through. I decided to keep my mouth shut about it for the time being."

"Wise choice. What are you going to do next?"

"Continue to investigate, see where it takes us."

"And if it leads back to Carl, and/or the Lunsford family, then what?"

"Do I need to answer that?"

"Remember how you're always telling me to be careful about my work?"

"Of course."

"Now it's my turn. Be careful where you tread on this case, C. J. Money and power still operate above the law."

"You don't have to remind me."

"It takes a cold hand to order a murder like Kylie Preston's—if that's what it was."

"As cold and as ruthless as an essential business decision."

"How does Brian Dixon fit into all of this?" Destini asked.

"He doesn't, as far as I can see. If he fits in at all, it could be as a red herring."

"If Carl and/or the Lunsford family are involved, and they feel threatened by you, they may decide to take action." The deep concern in Destini's voice shook me to the core. I didn't want to cause her any reason for concern.

"I'll be careful."

"You'd better make certain you have the goods on these people before you breathe a word of this to anybody."

"If it comes to that, I'll be certain to make sure I have all of my ducks in a row," I said with a smirk.

"I'm serious, C. J."

"I know you are," I said, matching Destini's resolve.

"If these people are capable of ordering a hit like the one they did on Kylie Preston, to do that to one of their own to protect their interests, then they're capable of anything."

"Don't I know it, which is another reason I'm keeping Renita in the dark for the time being. The less she knows, the less chance anything will happen to her."

"Good luck with that reasoning. I can't believe I'm saying this, but telling Renita the whole story may be her best defense."

"How do you mean?"

"If you tell Renita everything about the Preston case, then she can decide for herself how deeply she wants to become involved."

"You know Renita will stay the course, come hell or high water."

"Then she'll know what she's in for. It may make her more alert and more focused of her own safety as well as yours, instead of you having to feel as though you have to babysit."

"This is all about that 'letting Renita fly' sort of thing, isn't it?"

"Something like that. Renita is an adult. One day she'll probably have her own detective—"

"Investigation," I said, interrupting Destini.

"Investigation Agency. Are you going to hold her hand then, too?"

"I guess not." The thought of Renita starting her own investigation agency felt like watching a child leave home. I knew it would happen one day. I just never imagined the very real possibility that day would come so soon. I couldn't imagine the Cavanaugh Investigation Agency without her.

"The bottom line here, C. J., is that you and Renita need to be careful."

Destini looked deep into my eyes. It's not often I see the love of my life so vulnerable. Destini touched my face for a moment, then kissed me. My Love squeezed me tighter and rested her head on my chest. For the first time, I was frightened; not for myself, because neither death nor wealth worried me. It was because I realized that if anything happened to me, how that would affect Destini and the people I loved. It was a heavy burden that I was, for the moment, not certain I could bear. I took a deep breath. Destini did not budge. We sat locked in that still frame for a time, our silence our only form of communication, as we gazed out from the porch swing at a mighty forest range of listless nature.

CHAPTER FORTY-THREE

McCaskill had just relieved herself in the second stall of the woman's bathroom of the PPB homicide department. She was washing her hands when Destini Pendleton walked in. They were alone.

"We need to talk," Destini said, stepping up next to McCaskill as she lathered up over the bathroom sink.

"About what?" McCaskill had had brief conversations with Detective Pendleton. She found Pendleton to be helpful and encouraging. Those two elements were vacant from Pendleton's personality at the moment. They appeared replaced by a searing toughness for which Pendleton was known.

"You're working a case with C. J. Cavanaugh," Destini said. McCaskill rinsed her hands and shook excess water from them into the basin.

"That's right, the Preston murder." McCaskill dried her hands with a succession of two paper towels.

"Word is, you have a problem with it."

McCaskill balled up and tossed the last of the used paper towels into the trash bin. Destini blocked her way as McCaskill started for the door. The two women eyed each other. McCaskill was tough. From what she'd seen from the senior detective, Pendleton was tougher. Everyone knew that Destini and Cavanaugh were an item. McCaskill hadn't given any thought to the matter. She hadn't considered how her attitude toward Cavanaugh might play out with PPB's star homicide detective.

"I have a problem with anyone else working any of *my* cases."

"Your cases. Last I heard, you were a junior homicide detective and Angel was the prime. That would make them Angel's cases."

"I meant *our* cases." McCaskill was embarrassed about having overstepped her bounds once again.

"Sure you did. Listen, C. J. Cavanaugh is one of the finest investigators around."

"Are you sure you're not biased?"

"Positive. If you drop the attitude and open your mind, you might learn a thing or two."

"And if I maintain my attitude?"

"Then you'll have to deal with me. And I can and will make things very unpleasant for you around here."

"I'll think about it."

"I won't."

McCaskill managed to restrain her trembling until Pendleton left. McCaskill was not easily intimidated, but Pendleton had just opened that door. Pendleton had threatened her. She could go to the Captain with a complaint. How that would play out would not bode well for her career over the long haul. At the very least, McCaskill considered mentioning it to Angel.

McCaskill took a moment to gather herself. Her Captain and Angel both had high regard for Cavanaugh. In fact, the only people McCaskill had encountered who'd had anything negative to say about Cavanaugh's investigative skills were Whimple and Rockgarden. McCaskill knew their opinions couldn't be trusted. Whimple and Rockgarden slandered the reputations of everyone they disliked from the mayor on down to the people who emptied their trashcans, including her and Angel in their mix. There was nothing to be gained by McCaskill defying Pendleton, even if it was in her nature to resist. Logic trumped fear and obstinacy for the moment. She would play nice.

CHAPTER FORTY-FOUR

Renita and I had set aside a short stack to follow up on from the thousands of Kylie Preston documents we reviewed in the hope they could lead us to something worthwhile. Another tedious but necessary aspect of the investigation process got underway when we interviewed each person we believed to be a possible suspect. A number of them no longer resided in the northwest. Those interviews we conducted by phone. None of them was a hit.

Renita wanted to split up the bulk of the remainder of potential suspects so that we could go through the interviews faster. I was uncomfortable with that approach. Renita doing fieldwork on a murder investigation alone was still unfathomable to me. What made me most uneasy was that I still believed that Renita did not recognize the scope of what we were up against. Making matters more troubling was that I hadn't shared with her the possible implications that Carl and/or the Lunsford family could be involved. We might be chasing a professional killer.

Although this particular murderer had specific targets in mind, that didn't mean that he would not be averse to eliminating anyone who got in his way. We could find ourselves in his path. If so, based upon clear evidence of his willingness to kill and butcher, he would have no problem eliminating us. In war, there are often unintended casualties of the best-laid plans. We were at war. Renita only had a vague ideal what that was like.

My partner and I debated the issue of whether or not she should be allowed to conduct independent inquiries. Renita and I offered our pros and cons. My big selling point was that working together in these interviews would be better for both of us, pulling out the 'two heads are better than one' philosophy. That didn't work. Destini's advice kept nipping at me the entire time I was trying to convince Renita about working together. After I had played all of my cards and came up empty, I decided it was time to open that door.

"Renita, there's something I have to tell you." Renita looked at me, grasping the seriousness of the moment. She waited. I let out a heavy sigh before I could continue. I told Renita about the information I had run across in the files Carl had given us. Renita listened, taking in every word.

"Do you believe the Lunsfords had anything to do with Kylie Preston's murder?" Renita sounded stunned.

"To protect their life's work, let's just say anything's possible."

"Do we talk to them—the Lunsfords, I mean?"

"Not yet, we'll keep digging. We're going to need a lot of concrete evidence in our pockets before we approach heavy hitters like the Lunsfords."

"Not to mention, we don't want to piss off our number one client."

"It's not only that. Even if we gather enough evidence against them for murder, we'd better make certain it's airtight. If they were behind any of these killings and they got wind that we suspected them, let's just say they might seek to remedy the situation."

"You're saying they might kill us, too?"

"That wouldn't be necessary. They could make certain all parties involved in the previous killings cooperated in absolving them from being implicated one way or another."

"It still sounds to me like you're talking about someone being taken out, any way you look at it."

"As a last resort."

"How does Carl fit into all of this, C. J.?"

"My guess is he's not involved. I doubt that he would be foolish enough to hire us if he was."

"Couldn't the same be said about the Lunsfords? I mean, they want us involved as well."

"You're right. Which is why I believe that—for now—they are not likely candidates, but—"

"I know, I know, we need to keep an open mind."

"Exactly."

Renita thought for a moment before she said anything more. "We'll do the interviews together this time; not because I can't take care of myself, but I want to be there to watch your back."

I accepted Renita's conclusion with a double nod.

Means, motive, and opportunity were what we grilled our short list of 124 possible suspects on regarding the murder of Kylie Preston. All of our candidates had two things in common: they had threatened Kylie Preston for having denied their claims, and they had medical training. While we encountered some interesting characters during our interviews, some who were even "glad that swindling witch was dead" (to quote one of them), no one stood out as our potential murderer. Most had rock solid alibis. The few who didn't were physically disabled to the point of being incapable of dismembering or dissecting a human being.

A month's worth of diligent investigative work had passed, and we were back at square one. On the up side, throughout the entire process Renita was a professional team player. Not once did she flirt or revisit the debate about investigating on her own. Destini was right. Renita was ready to fly. I was the one reluctant to let her go.

CHAPTER FORTY-FIVE

Renita and I were eating our takeout lunches at Pioneer Courthouse Square in the heart of downtown Portland. We had claimed a seat on the curved brick steps in Portland's living room. We were part of an enthusiastic crowd enjoying good jazz in a venue arranged like an amphitheater. The weather was warm with a hint of spring rain in the air. Winston and Smoky were playing a permit-sanctioned jazz concert to a packed house. The seasoned veterans had recruited three talented young jazz musicians to accompany them on drums, bass, and saxophone. Smoky switched between a three-piston trumpet and an arch-top hollow-body electric guitar with F-holes, dependent on what the song required. Winston played a digital 88-Key Roland V-Piano. All instruments sounded incredible in the hands of their masters. The young bloods blended in well with the jazz virtuosos.

Smoky's real name is Holland Jenkins. The Marylhurst music grad and self-taught philosopher wore his trademark baseball cap bill straight ahead. He was a mocha-skinned man with a groomed white beard who played the piano as effortlessly as the healthy breathed. His distinctive style of musicianship was smooth and lilting, which was how Smoky obtained his nickname. His power runs on the keyboard were just as impressive, delivering his brilliant episodic flourishes with equal tour de force.

Winston Davis was a self-taught musical genius and decorated Korean War veteran. His deadpan expression and fervid eyes masked his passion and sensitivity even as he laid down some monster riffs on the guitar or trumpet.

There was not an instrument Winston and Smoky could not play well. Winston and Smoky occasionally performed street corner concerts near Pioneer Courthouse Square. Large crowds always formed, forcing the police to break up their extemporaneous performances. This was their first scheduled show in years. They had used a large can or an instrument case for donations during their Courthouse Square concerts, the proceeds of which they turned over to the Rescue Mission on Burnside Avenue. Today, the open guitar case at the foot of the stage served that purpose.

They called themselves The Music Makers, a name they threw together for the purposes of having something to put on the permit application. Even a casual jazz listener would recognize most of the pieces they played. My favorite compositions from their performance were "Elegant Flower" and "Blue Train." Renita preferred the jazz staples "Birdland" and "Take Five."

Renita and I hung back after the performance until the admirers and generous patrons thinned out. Winston introduced Renita and me to their young ensemble. Smoky joined Renita and me while their band mates assisted the roadies breaking down the stage, instruments, and equipment.

It had been a month since I had seen my friends. For Renita, it had been a little longer. We spent most of our chat catching up on what we missed. Except for the advent of the new musicians, nothing had much changed for Winston and Smoky. They hadn't decided whether to make The Music Makers a permanent thing. If they did, they knew they were going to have to come up with a more authentic name. At this stage in their development, they saw themselves as mentors, since neither Smoky nor Winston had any desire to rejoin the music business.

They teased me about Destini. They teased Renita about Ernest. We got on them about their love lives, which weren't doing half bad.

"How's that Kylie Preston murder investigation coming?" Winston asked.

"Or, should we say, The Butcher," Smoky added.

Renita and I were taken by surprise. I levelled my eyes on the front men for The Music Makers. "How'd you know about that?"

"The Butcher?" Smoky shrugged. "That maniac's all over the news."

"You do read the newspaper," Winston said. "Don't you?"

"Don't be snarky."

Smoky chuckled. "Snarky, I like that."

"Better than smug, jackass, or jerk." Winston grinned.

"Depending on the company and circumstance."

"True."

"Ahem! Back on point, if you wisenheimers don't mind."

"Wisenheimers?" Renita looked at me in astonishment.

"It means smart aleck."

"I know what it means, C. J. I thought they retired that word centuries ago, along with the horseless carriage and bloomers."

Everyone had a good laugh at my expense, including me.

"Mind we not," Smoky said before the laughter perished.

"Huh?" I was stymied. Renita and I gave Smoky the same baffled look. Winston appeared tickled.

"To quote you, C. J.: 'If you wisenheimers don't mind.' Mind we not."

"Clever." Winston continued the jest.

"More like humorous, but that's apples and oranges."

"I prefer tangerines and apricots."

"Are we going to get a straight answer out of you two today?" Renita's eyes widened in agreement with my question.

The two musicians appeared to sober. "You must forgive us," Smoky said with a note of delight still dancing in his voice.

"We're still juiced from our performance." Winston mimicked his friend.

"We hear all sorts of things." Smoky adjusted his cap so that the bill shaded his eyes even more. "You two should know that by now."

Both men gave us impish smiles.

"The trail's so cold on our investigation, it ended in a freezer."

"You still haven't said: who told you we were working the case?" Renita asked.

A couple of excited fans interrupted to ask Smoky and Winston for their autographs and a quick photo op. The jazz masters obliged and encouraged their fans to ask the same of the rest of the band. They did not.

"We ran into Angel at "Been There, Done That" a couple of weeks back," Smoky said.

"She was there with her husband."

"The topics of Kylie Preston and The Butcher just kind of slipped into our casual—"

"— and up to that point, pleasant," Winston interjected.

Smoky nodded, "—conversation."

"I believe Angel mentioned something about C. J. working the case, Winston."

"I believe you are correct, Smoky."

"Only C. J. – she didn't mention me?"

Winston turned on the charm. "You were implied, my dear."

Smoky followed, as suave as a Wynton Marsalis Quartet. "You and C. J. are a dynamic duo."

"Like Smoky and myself, modestly speaking, of course."

"Everyone knows that."

"Including Destiny."

Renita pursed her lips. "You had to go there, Smoky."

"A riff in the C. J. and Renita groove." Winston answered for his musical brother.

Charisma from the right source could work on my partner. Her smile and pleasant tone confirmed that it was. "It's a little late for you two to be out shaking a leg. Isn't that past your bedtimes?"

Winston and Smoky smiled at each other, then at us. "The kid's got geriatric jokes." Winston winked at Smoky.

"Age bashing. So beneath you, Renita." Smoky wagged a well-manicured finger at Renita. "We don't shake a leg, honey. We were dancing with our ladies all night long."

Winston demonstrated what his colleague meant by pretend slow dancing while holding a lady in his arms. "Your generation wouldn't know much about this, would they? They're too busy keeping it *nasty*."

"That's keeping it real," Renita retorted.

Smoky feigned concession. "Sorry...*real nasty*."

"You can still do that? Dance, that is," Renita smirked.

"Young lady, there are a lot of things we can still do." Winston answered in stride.

"Some of which exude pleasures of which you may never experience in your lifetime," Smoky added.

Renita put up her hands in mock surrender. "We're heading down the road of too much information." We all laughed.

"Have you gentlemen heard anything about the Preston or Dixon murders?"

Smoky gave a slow shake of his head to my question. "Unfortunately, the answer is no."

"There's nothing on the vine about who killed those unfortunate people," Winston added.

"If you hear anything, please pass it on."

"You know, C. J., Angel said the same thing to us when we were out dancing past our curfew."

"Except that she didn't disparage us about our age, like some people." Smoky rolled his eyes in Renita's direction.

"Comments like that could discourage one from coming forward with any information, valuable or otherwise, that one might stumble upon. Wouldn't you say so, Smoky? With our failing memories and all."

"Don't forget our diminishing eyesight and hearing," Smoky added. "And if I recall correctly, Angel even complimented us on our dancing."

Winston placed a gentle hand on his friend's shoulder. "That she did, my brother. That she did." The tables had been turned like a Joshua Redman saxophone counterpoint. Renita took the hint.

"I'm sorry. I apologize. Please let us know if you hear anything." Renita raised her voice as if speaking to the hearing impaired. "Do I need to write that down, or did you hear me okay?"

Winston and Smoky grinned their approval of Renita's witty retort. Winston's hand fell back to his side.

Smoky responded, "It wouldn't matter if you wrote it down, with our failing eyesight and all."

"You can count on us to pass along anything that comes our way." In syncopated rhythm, Winston shifted the mood from jovial to serious. We stood in grave silence for a few beats.

"We appreciate it," I said.

Smoky looked in the direction of the stage. "We'd better lend a hand to speed this up," Smoky said in reference to packing it in.

Winston looked to the sky. "It feels like rain. And you know how that wreaks havoc on our brittle arthritic bones."

Renita shook her head and smiled. We hugged our friends and left them to what needed to be done. We were off to do the same.

CHAPTER FORTY-SIX

Any minute now, Mitch Baker was expecting a reporter to pay him a visit. Mitch was surprised to learn that anyone would be interested in doing a story on him. It had been years since he had been involved in the thick of Multnomah County development. Now retired, widowed, and childless, Mitch was rarely a blimp on anyone's radar. It would be nice to have an opportunity to talk about his achievements; to reminisce about a life that had passed by much too fast.

Mitch had decided to wear a suit for the occasion, open collar with no tie. He wanted to appear casual but professional without seeming desperate. Mitch still had his hair cut once a week; hair that was no longer thick, dirty blond but white and thin enough to see through to his scalp. His blue eyes had dimmed from bright to dull over the years, accentuated only by a distant passion or pleasant memory. Mitch remained slender because he ate lean meals. He didn't crave meat anymore; a dip that had occurred years before as a dire consequence of the sudden death of his beloved wife.

Mitch was a wine lover who at one time wanted to become a connoisseur. A sommelier convention at King Estate Winery in Southern Oregon was too good an opportunity to pass up taking steps toward that goal. Even with the enticement of a weekend away in the quiet scenic wine country, his wife refused to join him because she found the topic of wine dreadfully boring. How could a convention on such said topic not be more of the same?

Mitch came home bursting with fascinating information to share with his indifferent wife about his weekend adventure, only to find her dead on the kitchen floor. She had been preparing herself a sirloin steak when it happened. The ME said the stroke was so massive, it paralyzed her. She never had a chance to dial 9-1-1.

The only woman he had ever loved was gone from his life forever. Mitch blamed himself. Had he been there, he believed he could have saved her. He could have been the one to make the call. The crippling memory of his wife lying dead on the kitchen floor haunted Mitch. He could still see her wearing the pink bunny slippers Mitch had gotten her for her birthday that she never seemed to take off. The doorbell startled Mitch. He took a moment to compose himself before he answered.

"Mr. Baker?" the man with the red ponytail asked when Mitch opened the door. Mitch noticed the press ID dangling from his neck like a laminated medallion. A picture of the man with a red ponytail, his name, and the publication he represented were on it.

"That's me," Mitch said.

"I'm Shawn Calloway from the *Willamette Week*," the man said. "We spoke on the phone earlier about a newspaper interview."

Mitch had never seen Shawn Calloway in person. He had seen his picture in the *WW* and on occasion television appearances as a person of interest on news broadcasts. Mitch was an avid reader of the *Willamette Week*. Shawn Calloway was a good reporter who handled hard news. Mitch was guarded but curious about what interest the *WW* reporter had in him.

"Of course," Mitch said as if the appointment had slipped his mind. "Come in."

Shawn Calloway walked in. "I appreciate your taking the time for an interview."

"Not a problem," Mitch said. "Right this way." Mitch led Shawn into the upscale, formal, old English-styled living room. "May I offer you some refreshment?"

"I'm fine. It's a real honor to meet you, Mr. Baker."

"Oh, why's that?" Mitch said, leery of the compliment.

"Because you have done so much for this city—this state, for that matter."

"Thank you."

"You're a perfect example of what is best about the private sector when placed in the hands of a conscientious, dedicated man of the people. Some of your forward thinking on neighborhood development and public transportation was light years ahead of anyone else during your time. Now almost every state utilizes some of your ideas in one fashion or another to help shape their city's progress. You have changed the course of history and added to the greater good in the process."

"I appreciate you saying so, young man."

"I'm sorry if I'm behaving like a rabid fan, but I enjoy meeting people who have made positive contributions to our nation through the private sector. It's not something that receives enough attention. They are the real heroes in our society."

Mitch did not trust reporters. It had been his experience that they were in it for personal gain; at least, the ones he had encountered were. Whom they hurt in the process was of little concern to them. His read on Calloway was that he seemed impressed by him; even enamored. Mitch was willing to give Calloway some leeway to see where it led.

Mitch positioned himself in front of his reading chair. Shawn stood before the sofa. "Have a seat, Mr. Calloway."

"Please, call me Shawn, and thank you." Shawn sat. Mitch waited until Calloway was seated before sitting himself.

"And you can call me Mitch."

"Do you mind if I record our interview? It's always better for me than taking notes."

"Not a problem."

Shawn pulled out a digital voice recorder from his shirt pocket. "For the record, Mr. Baker, you are consenting to recording this interview."

"I had no idea interviews had become so formal."

"I know it's a little ridiculous. The newspaper requires official consent, these days." Shawn pointed the high tech device at Mitch.

"For the record, I consent to recording this interview."

"Thank you." Shawn pointed the recorder back at himself.

"What would you like to know first, Shawn?" Shawn pointed the recorder at Mitch just before he spoke. It would be something Shawn would do throughout the interview.

"I am here speaking to Mitchell Donovan Baker. Mr. Baker, you served as Director of the Association for Oregon Progress, is that correct?"

"That's correct."

"In actuality, you started the organization."

"Yes, I did, back in 1978," Mitch said with pride.

"And part of your organization's mandate was to keep Oregon moving forward through economic progress and development; is that not also correct?"

"That's also correct, yes."

"Is there any truth to the rumor that your association bribed government and mortgage brokerage and loan officials?" Shawn asked, not changing his demeanor or tone.

"There is no truth to those vicious lies and rumors," Mitch calmly replied. "Everything we did was above board."

"As a major developer, you had much to do with what some might regard as the gentrification of portions of Multnomah County."

"What I and the association did was for the betterment of Multnomah County—and Oregon—as a whole."

Mitch was not surprised by Shawn's accusations. He had addressed them numerous times during his tenure and even for some years afterwards. They had no proof then, and he was confident Shawn Calloway had no proof now, even though the accusations were true.

"Then how do you explain the hundreds of people forced from their homes due to heightened mortgage interests rates they could not pay?"

"Mortgage interest rates are established by the Federal Trade Commission and the state. That's not my doing."

"We both know there are ways around FTC and state mortgage lending rate regulations. Even more so, if you have high-priced attorneys leading you down the path."

"That being said, I still had no control one way or another over such practices. Those issues you would have to take up with mortgage brokers, banks, and mortgage lenders. I had nothing to do with their policies or interest rates."

"You made a lot of money during that time."

"I can't complain; nor do I apologize. It's the American way."

"Some might describe it as more of the robber baron's way."

"There was nothing unscrupulous in how we conducted business. Those who had a beef with our practices could have taken us to court."

"That would have been expensive. I doubt the people who were cheated could afford to hold out long enough to combat a wealthy organization like yours."

"Justice at any price is worth fighting for. If our critics believed they were in the right, then they should have shown the fortitude to fight for their beliefs," Mitch said with a wily grin.

"I suppose that's true."

"Of course it is."

"Forced foreclosures allowed you and members of your association, who had first dibs on so many of those foreclosed properties, to swoop in and gobble them up for pennies on the dollar."

"Taking advantage of a golden opportunity is also the American way." Mitch showed no sign of guilt or remorse.

"Even if that golden opportunity was manufactured by illegal means?"

"I have no knowledge of any such wrongdoings, as I've said before."

"You and your business associates turned those communities into exclusive residential and business properties."

"Again, the American way."

"The stars aligned themselves for you, is that it?"

"I had no hand in how those circumstances played out."

"You have to admit they are rather fortuitous occurrences."

"So was Columbus discovering America, but I had nothing to do with that, either."

"But much like Columbus's discovery of the New World, many indigenous people were massacred and displaced."

"Nothing of which has any direct relationship to me."

"Some would beg to differ."

"Are we discussing my time as a developer, or the founding of this nation?" Mitch had to admit it had been a long time since he had a worthy sparring partner. He was enjoying this as much as Calloway appeared to be.

"I ventured off course, although you did bring up the Columbus analogy."

"In order to reference how ridiculous the argument is that I had anything to do with circumstances beyond my control."

"Did you have the ear of decision-makers in office that could aid you in your vision?"

"To a certain degree, of course: the association's input was regarded as valuable. They listened, then made decisions based upon what they deemed best for the continuing progress of the county."

"Some would see you having such access as collusion."

"Do I need to draw upon another analogy to exhibit how ridiculous that conclusion is?" The two men smiled at each other. Shawn turned off the recorder.

"I'm sorry about rehashing old complaints. It's something that needed to be addressed in the minds of readers in order for them to accept all of the good you've done for the community."

"I see," Mitch said; and he did. "You're laying the foundation for a buildup."

"Now that we've gotten that aspect of the interview out of the way, let's move on to how you helped make Multnomah County, and most notably Portland, one of the best places to live in the country."

"You flatter me."

"With the facts. May we continue?"

"By all means." Shawn turned on the recorder.

"I'm here with the esteemed Mitchell Donovan Baker, perhaps the most prominent developer in the history of the northwest. How are you feeling today, Mr. Baker?"

"Great; and you can call me Mitch."

"Mitch, let's start with some basic background information to give our readers some prospective on whom you are as a person...discover more about the man behind the legend."

"Shoot."

"Can you tell me a little about your formative years? What were your parents like, for example?"

"*Marvelous*. My dad was a stonemason. My mom was a homemaker, which was common for a woman of that era."

"So I've heard." They both smiled.

"My parents were simple, loving, hardworking, God-fearing people who raised their children to be the same."

"You have one brother and two sisters. Is that correct?"

"Yes. I am the second youngest. My sister Kathy was the oldest. She passed away a few years ago."

"I'm sorry to hear that."

"I appreciate your sympathies. My brother Bernie and sister Amie are doing just fine."

"You were married."

"Yes, my wife passed away a number of years ago. She was an amazing woman who I miss very much." Mitch toyed with the gold wedding band that he still wore in memory of his wife.

"I'm sure she was." Shawn sounded sincere. "The two of you didn't have any children."

"No, we didn't."

"May I ask why?"

"I guess it wasn't in the cards for us." Mitch could not quell his sadness at the thought. Mitch found out a few years into their marriage that he was incapable of fathering children. His sperm analysis revealed he was infertile. None of the recommended treatments he tried corrected the problem. The prospect of not having children seemed to trouble him a lot more than it did his wife. In time, he came around to her way of thinking and accepted their fate.

"Did it bother you to be part of a childless marriage?" Shawn asked, as if reading his mind.

"We didn't need children to fulfill our commitment to one another. Our love was more than enough."

"Does any of your family live nearby?"

"No, Bernie lives in Texas. Amie lives in Nebraska."

"You grew up in Kentucky, if I'm not mistaken?"

"That's right."

"What brought you to Oregon?"

"I was adventurous in my youth. I wanted to see the world. Figured I'd start with my own country and branch out from there. So I headed west."

"Straight for Oregon. Most people would pick California," Shawn said with a grin.

"It wasn't my intention to settle here. I made my way across the country from state to state, picking up work here and there and spending some time with locals while I earned enough money to move on. A few years later I found myself in Washington State just shy of the Canadian border."

"That's quite a journey."

"I can't complain. Of all the places I'd been in my travels, Oregon seemed to suit me best. I returned and stayed."

"Did that experience in any way lead you into becoming a land developer?"

"You're a pretty sharp fellow. I'm going to have to keep my eye on you," Mitch chided.

"Thanks," Shawn graciously accepted the compliment.

"Meeting so many people from so many different walks of life is what helped me find my calling in life."

"I don't know if most Americans would regard being a land developer as a calling, but a sentence."

Mitch laughed. "I suppose it's all in how you look at it. For me (and I might add, my colleagues), helping build a better tomorrow was an opportunity to do the greatest amount of good for people."

"Crooks and thieves notwithstanding."

Mitch grimaced. "There's always a little bad mixed in with the good in every profession. The bad stuff gets the headlines."

"If it bleeds, it leads."

Mitch nodded.

"It sounds to me like you weren't in it for the money."

"That's right; I set my sights on an area I felt I would do the most good. I had a strong business sense. I understand how infrastructures work, and I was good with people. For me, it seemed like a natural fit. It didn't hurt that my dad was a stonemason."

"It's in your blood."

"I think so."

"Did you ever consider running for any other office?"

"I had thoughts about becoming mayor a couple of times. But once I saw what the mayor had to deal with on a regular basis, I let that idea fly right out of the window." Mitch and Shawn both smiled.

"Did you have any memorable experiences you'd like to share—either good or bad?"

"I've had a number of experiences both ways, but I'd rather keep those to myself."

Shawn nodded. Shawn's cell phone vibrated. Shawn turned off the recorder and checked his caller ID. Mitch was feeling good about how the interview was progressing, but he was aggravated by the interruption.

"Excuse me, I have to take this." Shawn stepped outside of the living room, still within easy earshot of Mitch.

"Why are you calling me while I'm in the middle of an interview?" Shawn sounded irritated.

Good, Mitch thought. *The interview must be going well, for him to be annoyed. If it wasn't, he would have welcomed the interruption as an opportunity to blow me off.*

"Can't it wait?" Shawn said, and then listened.

"I know it's a front page story. I wrote it."

"At least give me another half hour to finish the interview."

"*Alright, already.* I'm on my way." Shawn terminated the call. He returned, looking flustered. "That was my editor. I have to get back to the office to do a rewrite so my piece can make it to print in a couple of hours."

"Front page story, huh?"

"Yeah, I've been lucky," Shawn nonchalantly said. "I get a number of those."

Mitch liked the idea of having his story told on the front page of a major local newspaper.

"Can we finish this later?" Shawn asked.

"Of course."

"If there's enough interest from the article, and I believe there will be, how would you feel about doing a biography on your life?"

"Are you kidding? I'm not that interesting."

"Based on what I've heard so far, I beg to differ."

"I don't know. I'll have to think about it."

"Let's have dinner tonight. We can finish the interview and bat around the idea of writing your life story."

Mitch had nothing else going on. At the very least, he might get a good meal out of it.

"Why not."

Shawn wrote down his address and cell number on the back of one of his business cards and handed it to Mitch. "Around seven good for you?"

"Seven's fine."

"Good. I'll see you then." Shawn gave Mitch a quick handshake and rushed off just as his cell phone vibrated again. Mitch slipped Shawn's business card into his wallet, and then tried to decide what to do with the rest of his day.

CHAPTER FORTY-SEVEN

Renita and I decided to take a stab at something we should have done a lot sooner to see if it bore fruit. Call it a last ditch effort. Call it a desperate attempt at resurrecting an investigation that had gone into cardiac arrest. We arrived at The Lair during happy hour. The place was brimming with patrons from both sides of the legal tracks, as was typical for The Lair. Renita and I spotted Monty Halbrook laying down some lines that were working on an attractive woman with peach skin and big brown eyes who was sitting on a bar stool at the south end of the bar. The smooth-shaven, aubergine-skinned man with a perfect smile wore a designer suit that looked tailor made for him. Monty had set his derby on the bar. His bald head gleamed in the warm light.

We waded through the crowd to get to Monty. I tapped Monty on the shoulder. He turned and rolled his eyes when he saw me.

"Will you excuse me for a minute, sugar?" Monty said as he ground out his cigarette. "I have business to discuss."

"Hurry back," the woman said with a sultry smile before taking a drag on a cigarette of her own. The Lair had obtained a special exemption from the statewide smoking ban. How? I didn't ask and Monty wasn't telling.

"Oh, I will." Monty kissed her hand. The woman exhaled smoke out of the side of her mouth to an empty space behind the bar. "Keep an eye on my hat for me, baby."

The woman put on Monty's derby. I had to admit it looked good on her. They kissed. Absentmindedness set in with Monty after the kiss as they became lost in each other's eyes. I tapped Monty on the shoulder again.

"In my office," Monty said as his tone shifted from sweet to irritated. Renita and I followed Monty into his office. Monty shut the door behind us and unbuttoned his suit jacket. Even beneath his expensive shirt, you could tell his stomach was as flat as an ironing board. Being in fighting shape was an occupational necessity when many of your clients were of a criminal bent. If I didn't know Monty better, I'd swear he was about to get physical.

"What is it?" Monty said, posting himself behind his desk. All of us remained standing.

"Why all the hostility?" I said, ready for a fight in case I was wrong.

"Because I'm looking to close the deal on Ms. Sweet Thang out there and you two are blocking my action. I've been working on that woman for close to a year now and the time is near."

Renita and I tried to hide our amusement. Monty was normally as cool as freezer mist. Seeing him annoyed was something we weren't accustomed to. That, in and of itself, was funny. The fact that this player cared enough about Miss Peach Skin to be cross told us that he was fond of that woman. That added another layer to our delight.

"We'll make this brief," I said. "What can you tell us about the person who murdered Kylie Preston and possibly Brian Dixon?"

"*That wacko who chopped up those people?*"

"One and the same," Renita said.

"*Are you kidding me?*" Monty sounded exasperated. "Why in the world would you think I knew anything about that sick bastard?"

"We were hoping you might have heard something," Renita said.

"If I had, I would have turned it over to Angel pronto."

"Angel was here?" I said.

"Of course," Monty said. "About a week after the first murder happened. You know how it is. Any time something serious goes down, this is one of the first places reporters and law enforcement come for information. I'm surprised it took you two this long. With you seeing Ernest and all," Monty said to Renita.

"Ernest and I don't like to mix business with pleasure."

"Wise philosophy."

"Were Rockgarden and Whimple here?" I asked.

"Yep, Schultz and Weasel showed up asking about Brian Dixon. They tried pulling that good cop, bad cop bullshit on me to pressure me into telling them something I might not without duress. They even threatened to shut down my place for violating smoking laws. Jackasses; I've got that covered in a blanket and hog-tied to a stump. I almost laughed in their faces."

Again, the unasked question of how Monty managed to skirt around state and federal public smoking ordinances came to mind. Monty felt the same way I did about Rockgarden and Whimple. They were a waste of detective badges, as far as we were concerned.

"What'd you tell 'em?" Renita said.

"Just what I heard."

"That being?" Renita said.

"Dixon was a regular. He was into swindling people out of their hard-earned cash and he liked hookers. That's all I knew about the guy."

"What about Kylie Preston? Do you remember seeing her in The Lair at all?" I asked.

"A couple of times, her and her girlfriends. They mostly frequented downstairs."

"Did Kylie Preston connect with anybody when she was up here?" Renita asked.

"Nah, a few tried, but none succeeded."

I asked, "Was Angel alone when she stopped by?"

"All by her lonesome." I was surprised Angel hadn't introduced McCaskill to the value of The Lair. Perhaps Angel didn't think her partner was ready to take that step.

"Did Angel stop back to ask about the Dixon case?" I asked.

"Nope, why?"

"Just curious." Angel not stopping through to ask about Brian Dixon suggested to me that Angel was keeping it low-key that she was snooping around Whimple and Rockgarden's case. From what McCaskill had told me when she stormed into my office the other day, Angel had forgotten to drive home the message for her partner to do the same.

"While we do have a code of silence in The Lair," Monty said, "we draw the line at psycho killers."

"That's good to know," I said.

"Is that it?"

"That's it," I said, "unless Renita has any other questions?"

"I'm good."

"Then you won't mind if I return to that beautiful lady at the bar," Monty said with a broad smile.

"Be our guest," Renita said. "Don't let our little murder investigation stand in the way of you having sex."

"If I had anything—*anything at all*—on that crazy son-of-a-bitch, I would have said something. Believe me when I tell you that even the worst person out there would do the same."

Renita nodded. I read Monty. Monty was not beyond lying if it suited his purposes. He had done his time for his crimes. Murder was never his thing. Ratting on murderers; well, let's just say it depended on who the victim was. Nothing about Monty spoke to me that he wasn't telling the truth.

"You'd better hurry," I said. "I think I saw someone making a move on your conquest as soon as you turned your back on her."

"Funny," Monty said. He opened the door. We walked out. Monty followed us out and locked his office.

"You two know your way out. Unless you intend on sticking around to enjoy the ambience?" We could see the doe-eyed woman talking to a good-looking man in an expensive designer suit. She had removed Monty's derby and placed it on the bar.

"Looks like another shark is swimming in your waters," I said.

Monty glared at me. For an instant, I could see a fury in his eyes that comes from doing hard time. Monty buttoned the top button on his suit jacket and put on his game face.

"This ought to be interesting," Renita said.

"Oh yeah," I said. Renita laughed. I smiled. "My money's on Monty."

"I'll take that bet," Renita said. We found a table near the action and ordered pot stickers. To drink, I ordered a ginger ale, since I was driving. Renita opted to do the same as we watched the drama unfold.

CHAPTER FORTY-EIGHT

Mitchell Baker arrived at a few minutes after seven. He intended to be early, but Mitch had trouble finding Calloway's place. Had Mitch written down Shawn's verbal directions, it would not have happened. Mitch thought about calling Shawn to inform him he was lost. His male ego would not allow him to make the call. He was determined to find Calloway's place on his own. Mitch backtracked all of the way to his home to regain his bearings. Once he did that, he did an internet search on his smartphone. The directions led him right to Calloway's front door.

Thick green hedges, that parted at a concrete path leading to a sweeping wooden front porch, walled in the humble city bungalow. A gravel driveway led to the garage from the street. The enclosed two-car garage appeared to be a recent addition. It was connected to the house at the far side of the backyard. Mitch had been instructed by Shawn to park his car in front of the garage. Although it was a safe neighborhood, Shawn cautioned Mitch that doing so would insure no one would vandalize or steal his car.

In the back of Calloway's home was a long wide swath of well-groomed, uninterrupted lawn: a wealth of land one would not expect to find in the city, but in areas that were more rustic. Mitch saw windows, but no patio or back door to the house. He assumed that meant you could only enter the house from the back, through the garage. Mitch thought about knocking on a window, but decided against it. That would be impolite.

As Mitch walked to the front of the house along the gravel driveway, he noticed Calloway had a fair amount of unoccupied land all around his home. That was interesting for a neighborhood where land was at a premium and most houses were nestled up snug to one another. Mitch assumed that meant that Calloway owned it. It was one way to explain developers not cashing in on prime real estate such as this. To make what Shawn had to happen in this neighborhood would require money or inheritance. Mitch would see what he could learn about his host's private life during dinner.

The banks of casement windows on either side of the front door were darkened from within by blackout drapes.

"You made it," Shawn said upon opening the front door after the first ring. "Come in."

Mitch stepped into the warmth of the foyer. Shawn closed the door behind him.

"Sorry I'm late."

"An hour is late. A few minutes aren't worth mentioning."

"This is for you," Mitch said, handing Shawn a bottle of Adelsheim 2015 pinot blanc, "a little something from my modest wine cellar."

"You didn't have to." Shawn politely accepted the offering.

"I would have felt remiss if I hadn't."

"Right this way." Shawn led Mitch into his living room. The house was more spacious inside than it appeared capable from the outside.

"Whatever you're cooking smells delicious."

"I can promise you, it's like no other lasagna you've ever tasted."

Mitch could have kicked himself. He should have asked Shawn what he planned to serve so that he could better match the wine with the food.

"*Lasagna*," Mitch said. "Had I know that's what you were serving, I would have brought a Chianti or Cabernet Sauvignon."

"No problem, it's not like I'd know the difference."

Mitch had thought as much. That's why he'd brought one of his lower-end bottles of wine. "I love lasagna."

"It's meatless lasagna. I'm not much of a meat eater."

"Neither am I."

"It has a couple of unique ingredients that give it a distinctive flavor. It was my mother's secret recipe."

"She must be proud to have her son carry on the tradition," Mitch smiled.

"She passed away when I was young; hence the word 'was.'"

"I'm sorry for your loss; my condolences."

"Thank you."

A moment of awkward silence seemed to suck the life right out of the room. For an instant, Mitch could have sworn he saw a flash of searing rage in Shawn's green eyes.

"I've given some serious thought to your idea about writing my biography." Mitch's comment restored some of the previous vitality.

"And what have you decided?"

"Let's go for it."

"*Fantastic.*" Shawn patted Mitch on the shoulder. "We can work out some of the details over dinner. Why don't you have a seat and I'll go check on our supper."

"Is there anything I can do to help?"

"You're my guest, just relax."

"I can do that."

On the far side of a couple of minutes, Shawn returned with two wine glasses filled with pinot blanc. "I hope you don't mind. I took the liberty of opening your gift before dinner. I thought it might be an appropriate way to celebrate our writing partnership."

"The wine was yours to do with as you chose."

"Here's to doing justice to the story of a great man."

"I wouldn't go that far."

"Let history be the judge." Shawn and Mitch clinked glass. Both men drank deep.

"That's delicious," Shawn said. Mitch had to agree.

"I can't wait to taste your cooking."

"I hope you'll find it as good as this wine." Shawn took another drink.

"I'm sure it's even better," Mitch said, doing the same.

"Once I toss the salad and warm the bread, we'll be ready to eat. Can I get you anything else while you wait?"

"I'm fine, thanks."

"In the meantime, have a seat and make yourself comfortable and I'll show you into the dining room as soon as I'm ready to serve." Shawn darted off before Mitch could respond. Mitch did as Shawn suggested. He made himself comfortable on the beige living room polyester queen sofa. The wine helped Mitch relax.

Mitch surveyed the living room, study, and the part of the dining room that was visible through the entranceway as he drank his wine. He noticed photographs of people he assumed were some sort of relations to Shawn, although Mitch failed to see any resemblance. The photo of a woman and man with a young boy seated between them on a sofa much like the one Mitch was sitting on struck home. Mitch assumed the adults in the photo were the parents of the child. He also assumed the boy between them was Shawn. He was partly correct. Mitch did not keep any pictures of his wife in plain sight. Any prolonged memory of her could send him into a deep depression. He'd almost committed suicide the last time he strolled down memory lane.

Mitch had to confess he was unimpressed. Shawn's home was meek, by Mitch's estimation. Mitch had heard that reporters didn't make much money. The furnishings he saw reminded him of poor residents he was forced to visit to keep up appearances during his political career. While typically clean, the impoverished residences were cheaply furnished due to the fact the tenants couldn't afford better. *It wasn't his problem then, and it's not his problem now*, Mitch thought.

If this book deal worked out with Calloway, then maybe Mitch would make enough money to buy a small vineyard. Mitch had dreamed for some time of developing his own label. This could be his ticket into that arena. The ideal swirled around in his head as he finished his glass of wine. Mitch put the empty wine glass down on the coffee table. The fact there weren't any coasters around wasn't his problem, either.

Mitch became drowsy. He was surprised at how swiftly the wine had gone to his head. He blamed it on the fact he'd drank too quickly rather than taking his time and enjoying each sip as he normally would. When his head fell back against the sofa cushions, Mitch didn't fight the sensation. *If he just rested for a moment, he would be fine.* That was all he needed to clear his head. Mitch closed his eyes and spiraled into a deep slumber from which he would never awake.

Shawn reentered the living room to find what he expected: Mitch passed out on his sofa. The Ketamine cocktail had worked. Even asleep, Shawn despised the man he blamed for much of his heartache. What he was about to do to Mitch was something Shawn would thoroughly enjoy.

Shawn entered his garage from the house. Mitch was right: the only way you could enter the house from the back was through the garage. Shawn pulled Mitch's car into the blind safety of his garage before he returned to his third victim.

CHAPTER FORTY-NINE

Lilting instrumental jazz filled Fullman's Restaurant with soothing background noise. As was usual, the food and service were first-rate. The restaurant was brimming with vibrant diners who would attest to as much. Renita and Ernest were amongst them.

"I thought we were going to keep business separate from our personal lives," Renita said.

"This case is different," Ernest said.

"How?"

"You're investigating a sick asshole, that's how. What if this psycho comes after you?" Ernest took a sip of his 7up on the rocks. He was still on duty as manager and security head of the restaurant. Being an equal partner in both The Lair and Fullman's Restaurant allowed him to take prolonged breaks whenever he wanted.

"It doesn't work that way, honey." Renita touched his hand. "We're the hunters."

"This is not a game, Renita. This crazy S-O-B can shoot back."

"You are sounding more like C. J. every day."

"C. J.'s right. We both are. Murder is no joke."

"You don't have to tell me that." Renita took a sip of her chardonnay. "The Butcher didn't shoot any of his victims, just for the record."

"I don't like it."

"Don't worry. I'll protect you, sugar." Renita rubbed his hand.

"Very funny."

"I thought so." Renita leaned over and kissed Ernest on the cheek.

"I don't understand why C. J. is even allowing you to take part in stalking this psycho."

"As much as this may pain you, sweetheart, I am a partner in The Cavanaugh Investigation Agency. Murder cases are going to keep coming.

I'm going to keep working them every opportunity I get, when they do. I am a private investigator. I want to be a good private investigator."

"You're already a good private investigator."

"I want to be one of the best; how better to achieve that goal than to work with the best?"

"How is chasing after lunatic killers going to improve your learning curve?"

"A big part of why I got into investigative work was to solve mysteries. Can you think of any criminal mystery greater than catching a killer; specially one who is as unstable as this guy?" Renita regretted mentioning the unstable part as soon as it passed her lips. She wanted to defuse Ernest's concern, not ignite it.

"Humph," Ernest grunted, then took another sip of his 7up. "I could use something stronger."

"You're working; don't be silly."

"Don't you think I know that?" Ernest snapped. His outburst caught the attention of nearby diners. Renita let it go. Renita knew Ernest was upset. Picking at him about his tone, attitude, or objection would only make matters worse. Nothing more was said between them until the concerned diners withdrew their attention.

"Why not just become a cop?" Ernest winced after mentioning it. Renita noticed his reaction. She knew Ernest regretted making the suggestion. He probably realized that would be like her going from the frying pan into the fire. Renita did like Ernest. His feelings mattered a great deal to her. She was touched by his honest concern over her safety.

"I'd thought about becoming a cop, but it's not the life for me."

"You mean, you'd have trouble abiding by the law instead of bending them like you sometimes do working with C. J.," Ernest said with a slight smile. Renita liked his smile. It altered his demeanor from menacing to teenage cute.

"Something like that." Renita smiled back. "And those uniforms are just plain ugly."

"No, they're not."

"Those drab colors do not work well with my skin tone."

"You may have a point there. Fashion is important when fighting crime. Where would Wonder Woman be without it?" They both chuckled.

Their dinners arrived. Renita and Ernest thanked the server and dug in.

"Do you mind if I stop by your place tonight?" Ernest asked after they had enjoyed a couple of mouthfuls of their meals.

"Not at all. I'll probably be asleep, so use the key I gave you."

"You do realize sleeping is not what I have in mind," Ernest quipped.

Renita played along. "What did you have in mind?"

"It's better if I show you. Otherwise, it might get lost in translation."

"I can't wait for the show to begin."

"Don't get started without me."

"Oh, I won't, sweetheart." Ernest and Renita kissed, then stared into each other's eyes. Renita could see love bubbling up from Ernest's soul. Renita looked away first. She was afraid Ernest would see that she didn't love him; at least, not yet. Renita stabbed a sautéed mushroom and ate it. Ernest cut a piece of well-done porterhouse steak and did the same. In spite of occasional interruptions that drew Ernest back to work demands, Renita and Ernest spent the rest of their time together at Fullman's, enjoying their meal and making playful lover's conversation.

CHAPTER FIFTY

Mitchell Donovan Baker was dead. The Ketamine mixed in with his wine had done the job. The man posing as Shawn Calloway removed his green-tinted contacts and red human hair wig with a satisfying grin. He had planned his ruse with the belief that Baker had never met Shawn Calloway; a fact he realized when Baker failed to expose him as an imposter. He chose to masquerade as the talented and respected reporter to appeal to Baker's vanity. It worked. He was also intrigued that Calloway had dubbed him "The Butcher." Calloway did not realize how close he was to the truth. He stuffed his disguise into a large brown paper bag. He would incinerate them soon. He set the bag on the floor next to the polyester queen sofa before he tossed Baker over his shoulder like a side of beef and carried him into the basement.

He laid Baker on an ambulance gurney, adjusted to waist high. He placed the artificial ventilation mask over Baker's nose and secured the mask in place just as he had done with his previous victims. He turned on the portable medical ventilator. It was important to keep an oxygen flow to the bloodstream in order to maximize the viability of transplantable organs. That was why he did not immediately kill Brian Dixon. He needed his respiratory and circulation systems working to preserve the donor organs. Once he wheeled Dixon into the theater, then he finished the job. The ventilator also staved off the onset of rigor mortis and tissue decay.

After double-checking to make certain the artificial ventilator was working, he returned upstairs to retrieve the brown paper bag. Wearing latex exam gloves, he rifled Baker's pockets and removed all of his personal belongings, including his platinum watch and gold wedding band. Everything he found, he put into a 9x12 manila clasp envelope addressed to the police, except for his smartphone which he would burn along with his disguise. Already inside the envelope was his standard laser-generated letter for "The Police." A letter personalized enough to account for Mitchell Baker. He secured the contents by fastening the clasp. He stripped Baker clean, putting his clothes and shoes into a dark green plastic garbage bag that he would night drop at a Salvation Army donation center. Baker's underwear and socks were added to his incineration bag.

He secured Baker to the gurney with the patient retention straps across his legs and chest. There was chrome wire shelving that fronted a good portion of the north wall, which he used to store miscellaneous items. The north wall was the wall nearest the garage, which he had built himself. He unlocked the swivel casters and wheeled the wire shelving away from the wall. The shelves rolled silently across the clean concrete floor. Once the shelves were out of the way, he pulled out an automatic garage door opener from his pants pocket, pointed it at the north wall, and pressed the button. A low hum from motors started up. A door noiselessly and smoothly swung open and automatically stopped once the door became perpendicular to the west wall. He reached inside the opening and turned on the lights.

A room, twice as large as the garage above, filled with light. The years of labor and expense it took for him to construct this place was worth it. There was no paper trail, since he had paid cash for everything. You could see the fake north wall from its flank. He had cut concrete blocks thick enough to maintain a solid-looking face and mortared them together to appear the same as the rest of the basement walls. Then he had secured the much lighter wall to drywall attached to a stud wall. Onto the stud wall he had connected two screw-driven automatic garage door openers that acted like top and bottom hinges. From inside the basement, it was undetectable. He placed his incineration bag and the manila envelope on Baker's person and wheeled Baker, along with the portable medical ventilator, into the room. After he and Baker were inside, he closed the false wall behind him with a press of the button from the automatic garage door opener.

They had entered his cathedral of vengeance; a place where he exacted revenge from the worst sinners in his life. Here they would receive penance—his penance—and, if their God willed it, forgiveness: something he was incapable of granting to people he despised.

Mounted high on the west wall, he had a framed, faded black and white wedding photograph of his parents. It was taken before their only son was summoned into their lives. Richard and Anne Bell were a handsome young couple. Their youthful faces were alight with the implicit promises of wonderful tomorrows to come. Little did they realize that their lives were destined to take a different path. How could life promise so much and deliver on so little?

His father was a primitive hunter. He killed his prey with a longbow and arrow. His dad was shot and killed during a hunting accident by a man with a deer rifle. Shortly thereafter, an unscrupulous accountant by the name of Brian Dixon cleaned out his dad's lucrative dry cleaning business. Dixon cooked the books to make it appear that his father's dry cleaning business had gone bankrupt. In reality, Dixon had embezzled the money. The courts proved useless in helping his mother retrieve any of their assets. Dixon had complete control over the paper trail. There was nothing his mother could do to dispute it.

Lunsford Insurance refused to make good on his father's quarter-million dollar life insurance policy. Kylie Preston was the person in charge of approving the claim. According to Kylie, his father's death was due to his own negligence. Preston claimed his father had not been wearing proper safety gear during the time of his unfortunate death. In part, that was true. It was a warm, humid day on the day his father was shot. His father's hunting buddies confirmed that his father had removed his blazing orange vest and hat in order to change his sweat-drenched shirt. The person who shot him was taking aim at a buck. He missed the buck and killed his father.

Lunsford Insurance made a pity offering to his mother of ten thousand dollars. His mother was outraged they would even consider bargaining over her husband's life as if he were a used car. Lunsford's refusal to pay held up in court thanks to strong testimony by Kylie Preston. Her victory forced their family to rely on whatever work a widowed homemaker could find.

The man who killed his father accepted full responsibility for his actions. His grief and remorse were genuine. The shooter confessed he had been drinking heavily the night before and that his vision was blurred when he took the fatal shot. He was convicted of involuntary manslaughter. He had atoned for his sin. Others complicit in the destruction of his family had not. "Why?" was the question he believed he kept seeing in his mother's eyes right up until the day she died.

The cathedral was as sanitized as any modern hospital operating room. He pocketed the device and wheeled Baker over near his creation of a state-of-the-art surgical tent; a tent large enough for him to operate comfortably on his murder victims. Everything was ready. He had seen to it after his bogus interview with Baker. All of his surgical equipment, including his meat cleaver, were sterilized and placed inside a large stainless steel instrument tray within easy reach of the autopsy table inside the tent. All other items that needed sterilization had been done so on site, or purchased that way. The morgue freezer unit outside of the tent was primed, as was the smaller one inside of the tent. The ice machine had been running for hours and was filled with its self-perpetuating ice cubes.

Two of the sinners had been served justice. Now, add to that a third. The Association for Oregon Progress had swooped into their working class neighborhood a couple of years after his father's death and bought up as much property as they could by offering everyone ten percent above market value. Some sold; but not all, as AOP had hoped. Mitch Baker had plans to gentrify the blue-collar neighborhood. In order to do that, Baker needed all of their properties.

All they had was their home, when his father died. For him and his mother, it had sentimental value. A number of others in the neighborhood had similar sentimental attachments to their homes. With Baker at the helm, banks, mortgage lenders, and brokers hiked their rates by as much as twenty percent, in some cases, in order to force them out. The good-faith loans were not restricted from such exorbitant rate hikes by state, local, or federal laws. Most sold quickly. A very few held out. His mother was one of them. His mother, who had already been working two jobs in order for them to survive and hold onto their home, added a third. Even working three jobs was not enough. She was forced to sell for pennies on the dollar; a costly penalty for having stood in the way of AOP.

He smiled to himself as he prepped for surgery, musing about how simple it had been to talk a conniving unethical blowhard like Baker into believing he was worthy of history. Looking the part of a surgeon in his hunter-green surgical scrub suit, hood, mask and safety goggles, he lifted Baker like a sleeping child from the gurney and placed him onto the autopsy table.

Mitch Baker lay as still as a stone. "You would have liked my mom's lasagna," he said as he stood over Baker. "But then, why should I waste her delicious recipe on one of the people responsible for ruining her life? You're about to meet your long-overdue fate. Maybe you'll be reunited with your wife; although I doubt you'll be joining her if she was a good woman. Was she a good woman, Mitch? Or was she a greedy, soulless slime like you? Either way, it's out of my hands. I'm not even certain you have a soul worthy of Hell."

He preferred classical music when he operated, and popular music when he cleaned. He turned on his iPod. Under Bach, he chose "Suite No. 1 in G Major," the first of "The Six Unaccompanied Cello Suites." The surgical tent filled with the full deep sound of the cello. The mastery of the artist led him into his first incision.

You bleed because your heart pumps blood through your body. If you cut a corpse and turn it over, the blood may drain out; but it's not likely due to the blood congealing and clotting. The imposter inserted a catheter into a large vein in Baker's right leg. Based on the principle of a hemodialysis machine, his scaled-down version used a blood pump and a heparin pump in combination with a saline solution to prevent blood clotting, for when the blood would be pumped out of Baker's body and into sterilized half-gallon plastic jugs. When the time was right, he would turn on his custom-built device. The pump would shut off once the jug was filled due to a signal from a flow control switch that the imposter had installed. A mild beep would sound, also one of his unique design touches, to let him know it was time for another jug. He would pinch closed the outflow tube, pull it from the full jug, and shove it into the next. Then he would cap the full jug. The process would continue until all of the blood was drained from the victim's body. At such time, he would place the lid on the cooler and transfer it to the morgue freezer unit outside of the surgical tent. Three jugs were set in coolers and packed in ice, in the end.

He had learned a great deal about dissecting the human body from his time in the Army. He had served as both a field doctor and a medical examiner. When he left the military, he had no desire to pursue a career in the medical profession. He instead found himself working in a beef slaughterhouse, and then as a butcher. As a butcher, he felt right at home. It was during his time as a butcher that he first considered revenge on behalf of his parents.

The procedures had become clinical and routine at this point. He was very careful as he mined each internal transplantable organ; not because he cared any for the deceased, but due to an almost reverent concern he held for the possible recipient. Time was critical. The faster he could extract the organs and cold store them, the better chance they would be of use. As he removed each internal organ, he placed it into a sterilized plastic bag. He would then place the organ in the lab freezer unit inside the surgical tent.

With swift precision, he removed his victim's healthy kidneys, liver, pancreas and small intestine. The surgery went even faster than with his two previous unwitting donors, and he packaged each organ with tender care as he went. He turned off the medical ventilator before cutting through the breastbone with his sternum saw. The Butcher switched on his customized blood transfusion machine. With the chest cavity laid bare, a healthy heart and lungs were easy prey.

Once all of the transplantable internal organs, along with the corneas, had been removed, packaged, and stored for preservation, he set about extracting the remaining (to his knowledge) non-transplantable organs such as the stomach, large intestines, and gallbladder. These he would stuff into sterilized plastic bags, as well, and place them in the morgue freezer unit outside of the surgical tent. His sole purpose for removing the non-transplantable entrails was to liberate the torso from decaying properties. He wanted to gut the torso in order to better preserve it.

The last surgical procedure he performed was to chop off his victim's feet, legs, thighs, hands, forearms, and arms, and decapitate his head, in that order. He was an expert at locating the exact place to strike with his razor-sharp meat cleaver for a clean cut. Most times, the part would be neatly severed with one mighty blow. At the hip joints, it took at least two. His time of working in a slaughterhouse and as a butcher had trained him for that. He had become accustomed to being efficient and precise when it came to dissecting meat for the market. He would wrap the limbs and head in plastic wrap and place them in the morgue freezer unit outside of the surgical tent. He would then sew up the torso and place it in a large cooler with a bed of ice, fill it with ice, and place the large cooler in the morgue freezer unit.

He partially filled a cooler with ice and nestled the transplantable internal organs from the lab freezer unit into the cooler before covering them in ice and placing the cooler in the morgue freezer unit. He continued the process until all of the harvested organs, head, and limbs were placed in ice-filled coolers and stored in the morgue freezer unit along with the blood-filled jugs.

It was imperative that he got the internal organs to his connection as quickly as possible. He stripped off his surgical scrub suit, hood, and mask and shoved them into the incinerator bag. The goggles, long johns, and wool socks he wore beneath his scrubs, he would wash. He put on a pair of insulated long-sleeved coveralls, a clean pair of wool socks and insulated work boots, and slipped on a pair of cotton chore gloves before reclaiming the coolers containing the transplantable and non-transplantable organs from the morgue freezer and carrying them upstairs.

From his disposable cell, he texted Mod734: "Dinner is served." Within seconds came a reply: "Good, we're famished."

He had sent an earlier text to Mod734 on the same disposable phone before he operated, as he had done with all of his victims. "Just got home with the ingredients for tonight's meal. I'll let you know when it's time to eat." He called it his "pre-op appetizer." Within a minute of that text came the response: "We'll be ready."

He turned off his porch and living room light. When he opened his front door, he was confident no one could see or hear him or what he was about to do. He slipped out onto the front porch, placed the coolers side by side in the far west corner, and returned inside. In less than five minutes, he received a text from Mod734: "Everything looks delicious." The packages had been delivered.

Returning to his cathedral, he put on some popular music. He chose a play list that had a variety of R&B, reggae, rock and roll, country and pop. He set to the process of giving his cathedral a thorough cleaning, something that he had become efficient at. When everything was cleaned to his satisfaction, he went upstairs to shower and dress in dark jeans, a black T-shirt, and black loafer deck shoes.

The Dark Web had supplied him with everything he needed to deliver his donations in a timely manner. He was astounded to discover what was available. After surfing transplantable organ dark net sites and social networks for years, he uncovered what he sought.

There was a secret, underground organization who called themselves Curantis, which is Latin for 'caregiver.' Curantis was comprised of a small group of medical professionals ranging from medical record keepers to paramedics to nurses, physicians, and surgeons. All banned together with one primary purpose. That was a deep, abiding commitment to saving lives through organ donations. How they differed from the norm was that they placed no moral or legal restrictions on how those life-saving gifts were obtained. Curantis was a no-questions-asked institution. How their mandate conflicted with the Hippocratic Oath and differed from black market organ harvesting was not The Butcher's to question. He could only pray they were used for the greater good after the organs were out of his hands, since there was no way he could follow up on their claims. Satisfaction may have brought back the curious cat, but he would not be trapped in that inquisitive web.

The Butcher feasted on his mother's lasagna. Afterwards, he took a well-deserved nap. When he awakened, he would parcel the remaining coolers in brown butcher paper held together by packing tape and twine. Then he would load his humane gifts into his victim's car and leave the car somewhere for the police to find.

CHAPTER FIFTY-ONE

Renita was in her office, sitting at her computer, when I walked in. I stepped into her doorway. "What's up?" I asked.

"Nothing." Renita sounded bored. "Just checking my emails." There wasn't much to do, with our investigations into the murders of Kylie Preston and Brian Dixon at a standstill and having no other cases to keep us occupied.

"Want to go to lunch? I'm buying," Renita said with a smirk. "I won a little extra cash yesterday on a sucker bet."

I gave Renita a bogus smile. Renita was referring to the bet I'd made with her regarding Monty and the peach-skinned woman at The Lair. The other guy managed to steal her from Monty. You might think that a man like Monty would have roughed up his competition or had Ernest toss him out. Monty was interesting in that way, when it came to women. He always allowed them to make their own choices. When they did, he respected their decision. Monty wouldn't stand in their way. Maybe it had something to do with the unfailing respect he had for his mother. I don't know. I'm not sure Monty does, either.

"I'm game. Anything interesting?" I said in reference to Renita's emails.

"One of my college girlfriends had a baby boy, ten pounds, four ounces."

"That's a big baby."

"Her husband's a big man."

"That's something to think about if you and Ernest have children."

"Who said anything about me and Ernest having children?"

"You two haven't talked about having kids?"

"We haven't even gotten to the subject of marriage."

"Ernest would marry you in a heartbeat."

"So would a number of men," Renita nonchalantly said. "That doesn't mean I'm going to walk down the aisle because the opportunities are available."

I nodded.

"I was thinking about what sort of congratulatory gift to send them," Renita said.

"That's out of my area of expertise."

"I've finally found something you're not good at."

"Keep digging, there's more."

"For instance?"

"Like I said, keep digging. Information like that is best peeled off one layer at a time." Renita smiled.

"And I'm just the woman for the job," Renita said with calm resolve.

"Yes, you are." The information metaphor gave me an idea. I went to our storage closet and wheeled out our reversible dry-erase whiteboard. After I dusted it off with paper towels, I set it up in our waiting area.

"What are you doing with that relic?" Renita asked when she saw me wheeling the whiteboard past her office.

"Let's do a profile of our murderer." Renita stepped out of her office to join me.

"Haven't we done that already?"

"We haven't put all of the pieces together, yet."

"That's because we don't have any pieces to put together."

"Let's try to deduce, rather than think."

"Meaning?"

"Let's summarize what we do have."

Renita's interest was piqued. I could see it in her eyes and body language. "Where do we start?"

Since I had more experience at profiling than Renita, I suggested that she go first.

"Kylie Preston was drugged and butchered," Renita said.

"Let's break down her murder. Kylie Preston ingested a fatal dose of Ketamine." I wrote down "delivery system Ketamine."

"Ketamine is used for general anesthesia in both human and veterinarian medicine and is easily obtained," I said.

"The same thing happened to Brian Dixon."

"Except, in Brian Dixon's case, he received an injection of Ketamine at the base of his neck."

"So?"

"That suggests the killer is knowledgeable in more than how to concoct a deadly brew. He knew where and how to administer it. That could mean medical training."

"That's assumed, from the way he dissected the bodies."

I wrote down "probable medical and surgical training?"

"The killer packed the bodies in ice," I said.

"In order to preserve them."

I wrote down "preserved bodies."

"What happened to the internal organs?" Renita asked.

"Good question. Dr. Saba believes the victims' internal organs were treated with equal care. Let's go with his supposition." I wrote down "preserved internal organs."

"Why?"

"Based on the short shelf life of transplantable internal organs, Angel and McCaskill checked all transplant centers in the northwest, only to come up empty on any donors or transplant operations that needed to be performed within the critical timeframe of the murders."

"Does that mean the killer removed the organs for some other purpose?"

"Or the transplant operations could have been executed at an illegal facility." Renita nodded. I wrote down "organ transplants?" as a sidebar for the moment.

"The killer wrapped the coolers in brown wrapping paper," Renita said.

"Not brown wrapping paper; brown butcher paper."

"What's the difference?"

"Good question; why use butcher paper rather than regular wrapping paper? The butcher paper was waxed. So he was going the extra mile."

"Where did you pick up that tidbit?"

"It was in the coroner's report."

"Butcher paper helps keep meat cold longer. Since he's interested in preserving his victims for as long as possible, that would make sense."

"I don't know if butcher paper helps keep things cold longer. It does hold up better against moisture than regular wrapping paper. If his choice of wrapping paper fed into that assertion, then why didn't he use waxed paper, or put the items in plastic lawn or garbage bags?"

"Good questions," Renita said.

I wrote down "brown waxed butcher paper."

"Our killer could have been a butcher at one time," I said.

"That's a stretch."

"It is, but let's go with it." I wrote down "may have worked as a butcher."

Renita nodded. "He was trying to preserve whatever he could for transplants," Renita said. "He mentioned that in his letters."

"Right, the letters were another interesting touch. They also lend more credence to the theory he was doing the same for the internal organs." I moved "organ transplants?" from the sidebar and into the main flowchart of information without the question mark.

"True," Renita said. "It was as if he didn't want the police wasting too much time identifying the victim. Why?"

"He wants to help people in need even after he's taken a life. The less time the police spend on the basics, the greater chance the victim's remains could be used for the greater good."

"Who does that?"

"Outside of people in the medical field, I don't know."

"He could have been a doctor. Or maybe he still is."

"Good point." I wrote down "possible deranged doctor."

"Does the color of the wrapping paper have any significance?" Renita asked.

"It might. Butcher paper does come in white, too."

Renita nodded, but offered no comment. I moved our profiling along.

"Each of the bodies was discovered in stolen, abandoned vehicles," I said.

"Right; what does that mean?"

"Besides being a killer, he's also a car thief."

"Maybe he has a criminal record."

I wrote down "car thief, possible record."

"This killer is a chameleon," I said.

"A chameleon?"

"Someone who is good at impersonating someone else."

"He did pose as Dr. Boulder, to seduce Kylie Preston," Renita said.

"And the laundromat chain owner Russell Keegan, as well as a carpet repair guy that the neighbors saw." I wrote down "chameleon."

"What does that tell us?"

"These are not crimes of opportunity. This guy has a plan."

"You make it sound like he's fishing."

"More like hunting. I'm not a professional profiler, but I'm willing to bet this guy fits the psychological profile of a major predator. He's using these disguises to lure his victims."

"Whoa, you're suggesting criminal mastermind stuff."

"This guy is bold and decisive and talented enough to convince people that he's who he says he is. Once he does, he kills them, butchers them, and tells the police where to find the remains that he's preserved. I'd say that fits the bill."

I wrote down "high IQ."

"If he's a con man, then he might have a criminal record."

I wrote down "possible con man." 'Criminal record' had been covered.

"There's something more to the story," I said. "A good con man always knows enough about his mark to have the confidence to work his scam."

"Are you saying the murder victims knew their killer?"

"More like the killer knew the murder victims. A good con man doesn't reveal himself to his mark until he's ready to work them; or in this case, murder them."

"We're talking about a person who is calculating enough to manipulate his victims into a vulnerable position in order to take their lives, and twisted enough to cut them into pieces."

"Yep." I wrote down "killer had prior knowledge of victims."

"What's his motivation?" Renita asked.

"It could be a number of things: revenge, revolt, haphazard terror, the thrill of fulfilling some perverse psychological need—at this point, I couldn't say for sure." I wrote down "motivation?"

"Why haven't we or the police been able to uncover a connection between this person and his victims?" Renita said.

"Because he's probably living under a fictitious or stolen identity."

"What makes you think so?"

"Both a hunch and an educated guess."

"That makes sense. It would prove easier to approach his murder victims."

"Especially if the murder victims haven't seen him for a long time."

"You mean, like since he was a child?" Renita said.

"It's a possibility."

"So, is plastic surgery on the table?"

"I haven't ruled it out." I wrote down "false identity" and "plastic surgery."

"He's been able to disguise himself, murder, butcher, steal, and dump," I said. "This requires a home base, considering the time, equipment, space, and facilities you would need to dismantle and package a human being."

"A centralized place of operation," Renita said.

I wrote down "central place of operation."

"I'm convinced our killer lives somewhere within Multnomah County; quite possibly Portland. I also believe he is someone who has a history in this city and a connection to each of our murder victims."

"You base that speculation on what?"

"All of the victims have been dumped in Portland. He knew when and where to deposit the vehicles without arousing suspicion. A stranger doesn't go into neighborhoods with that kind of information."

I added "somewhere in Multnomah County, possibly Portland" onto my last note.

"Do any of those criteria correspond with anyone we interviewed?" Renita asked.

"No."

"Then what's this all about?"

"It gives us clues; indicators of what to be on the lookout for when we're interviewing people."

"How do we know we haven't already interviewed the killer?"

"We don't. Breaking through the façade of a person this clever won't be easy."

"In summary, we're looking for someone familiar with Portland," Renita said. "A chameleon, con man, or car thief with a false identity who may have been a butcher and who has a medical and surgical background and a history with his victims. Unless he's just a total nut job, in which case most of our theories go right down the drain."

"Pretty much."

"And how is this helping?"

"We're weaving together facts, theories, and speculations. Somewhere within that net of information is where we'll find the clues to catch our killer."

"I don't see it."

"In time, it'll all add up. Sooner or later, it always does."

"It's the later part that worries me most."

CHAPTER FIFTY-TWO

Renita and I met with Angel and McCaskill to compare notes on our parallel investigations regarding the Preston homicide. The unfortunate thing was that both investigative teams were spinning their wheels. We had run into dead end after dead end with not a light in sight. One bright spot came out of our meeting. The Captain had been piling new homicide cases onto Whimple and Rockgarden. Since the veteran detectives had struck a brick wall regarding the Dixon case anyway, they grudgingly turned over the case to Angel and McCaskill to lighten their caseload. That was a smart maneuver by Captain Williamson to maintain morale without appearing to play favoritism.

McCaskill had calmed down since our last meeting. She was not only cooperative, but also downright cordial. Recalling her previous visit to my office to warn me about treading on her territory, I wondered what had happened to change her outlook toward Renita and myself. I was still concerned about McCaskill's gung ho maverick attitude being a detriment to Angel. McCaskill was still hungry to prove herself. What better way to do that than by solving a big homicide case? The fire in her belly was still there. I could see it in her eyes when she didn't think anyone was watching.

On the way out, I ran into Destini. She was free for lunch. I invited Renita along, sweetening the offer of my treat as a show of appreciation for all of the hard work Renita had done. Renita asked for a raincheck because she had already made plans to meet Ernest for lunch. Destini was glad to hear Renita would not be joining us. Destini at least had the courtesy to wait until Renita was out of sight before saying so.

***

We chose a Greek restaurant not far from the police station. Destini began telling me about the latest news regarding her detective partner and friend David Liederman after we ordered.

"Dave has a new girlfriend."

"So soon," I said. "He just broke it off with Marla a couple of weeks ago."

"It turns out his new girlfriend is the reason he broke it off with Marla."

"Dave is a player now?"

"Hardly; he met Nora about a month ago."

"Nora's his new girlfriend?"

Destini nodded. "Nora Doucette. He said he thinks she's the one."

"Whoa, that is serious. Have you met her?"

"Not yet. I told Dave the four of us should get together for dinner sometime."

"So you can check her out; or did you leave that part out?"

"I simply want to meet the woman who's captured my partner's heart."

"That's a partial truth. The other part is: you want to give her a good interrogation."

"Why would I do that?"

"To make sure she's good enough for Liederman."

"Dave is capable of choosing the right woman on his own."

"*Please*, you've been trying to fix Dave up since I met you."

"What's wrong with that? He's a good man. A good man needs a good woman."

"No argument here; so why are we together?"

"I don't know how to take that. Are you implying you or I are the bad one in this relationship?"

"I'll let you be the judge." Destini smiled.

It was good to have some playful banter with Destini. We had gotten into a constant mode of shoptalk, of late. Neither of us seemed to mind that we were violating our implicit rule of not allowing work into our personal lives. Even though her partner David Liederman still somewhat fell into the shoptalk category, the personal nature of the conversation made it excusable.

"You and Renita seem to be getting along."

"What do you mean? Renita and I always get along."

"I mean, the two of you seem to be getting along in a professional way. Not in the 'she's a hoochie after my man' sort of way. What's changed?"

I responded, annoyed, "Renita is far from a hoochie."

"That struck a nerve." Destini smiled. I moved the conversation along.

"I had a talk with Renita about her professionalism that must have set her straight."

"You've had those talks with Renita before."

"My powers of persuasion finally kicked in."

"You're persuasive, no doubt about that. Those persuasive powers have not been successful with Renita in the past. Why now?"

"Renita has changed since our visit to the ME."

"There's nothing like seeing your first murder victim on a slab to knock the nonsense out of you."

"Especially if that corpse has been mutilated."

"I heard Renita was as sick as a dog." Destini was enjoying the news.

"And then some. The poor kid vomited her guts out. I had to send her home to recover."

Destini laughed. "I would have paid to see that."

"You are relishing her humiliation way too much."

"I am, aren't I?" Destini continued laughing.

"Since then, Renita's has not only been more focused, but she's respected our professional boundaries, as well."

"If I'd known that was all it took to keep Renita from chasing after you, I would have taken her to the morgue a long time ago."

"Eat your lamb and let's change the subject," I kidded. "This morbid conversation is getting out of hand."

"You never said how your meeting with Angel and McCaskill went. Any breakthroughs on the murder investigation?"

"I'm afraid not. Angel and McCaskill got their hands on the Dixon case."

"It should have been theirs all along."

I nodded. "Nonetheless, there are no new leads. For that matter, there are no leads of any kind."

"Something will turn up; keep at it."

"Thanks for the encouragement. What about you? Weren't you supposed to arrest someone today for the Bozeman murder?"

"Larry Maloof," Destini said. "We picked him up this morning on his way into work. We grabbed him in the employee parking lot. Maloof took a swing at me, believe it or not. How stupid was that?"

"He did what?" As hard as I tried not to, I always got upset when anyone attacked Destini. She was one of a handful of people I would kill for.

"He didn't connect," Destini reassured me. I took a good look at her face to make certain she was telling the truth. Destini noticed what I was doing and sighed.

"I can take care of myself, you know."

"I know," I said, which I did. It didn't stop me from feeling a need to protect her. Call me chauvinist if you want, but that's just the way it is with me.

"I ducked the punch and was about to catch him with an uppercut to the ribs when Dave spun him around and slammed him against Maloof's pickup. I slapped the cuffs on him and it was over."

"Are you telling me Maloof didn't struggle?"

"He did at first, but then a hard punch to the solar plexus took the fight right out of him."

"You or Dave?"

"Guilty," Destini confessed with a grin. Destini's smartphone vibrated on her hip. She took a long look at the message and sighed.

"C. J., I'm sorry. They moved the Yocum arraignment up to one. It wasn't supposed to happen until three. Dave and I need to be there. I'm going to have to cut short our lunch."

"No problem, I understand."

Destini stood to leave. I stood with her.

"Do you want me to box up the rest of your lunch for some other time?" I asked.

"That's very considerate of you, sweetheart, but that's okay. You can box it up and give to someone who needs it."

"I'll do that." Destini gave me a quick kiss on the lips then took off. I was sorry to see her leave, but I watched her go with pride.

***

The imposter made himself comfortable on his sofa. He removed the disposable cell phone from its packaging and laid it next to the artificial electronic larynx on the coffee table. He cleared his throat. He turned on the artificial larynx. He called Detective Angela Alvarez.

"Homicide Detective Alvarez," Angel answered on the second ring.

The imposter engaged the artificial larynx before he spoke: "Detective Alvarez, so good to hear your voice. I so much prefer speaking to you than Detective Whimple. His telephone manners leave a lot to be desired."

"Who is this?"

"Come now, don't tell me you've forgotten me so soon. Or are you attempting to trace this call?"

"I'm just trying to find out who I'm talking to."

"You are speaking to the man who will give you the directions on where to find my latest kill."

"I'm listening."

"There is a black Cadillac Escalade SUV, Oregon vanity plate B-I-L-D-I-T, parked on Level 2, Section 1020 of the Lloyd Center Mall parking garage. Hurry now, before he spoils."

"Can we expect to find the usual?" He could hear the uneasy tension in her voice.

"Sealed and delivered."

"I didn't catch all of the information. I'm a slow writer. Can you repeat it?"

The imposter knew Detective Alvarez was stalling. Just as he knew she didn't have enough time to trace his call.

"Then I hope you have a good memory," he said, terminating the call. He removed the device from his larynx, switched it off, and then turned off the cell phone. He had parked the car at the location he gave Detective Alvarez a couple of hours earlier. That time his disguise was a simple false beard, baseball cap, and glasses. The imposter would dispose of the cell phone in his usual manner by tossing it down a storm sewer.

***

I finished my lunch and headed back to the office, handing off what remained of Destini's lunch and five dollars to a homeless couple panhandling for change. Renita was not in the office when I arrived. I assumed she was still at lunch with Ernest. I used the time to summarize, in a written report, what had transpired on the Kylie Preston murder up until that time.

I (Cedric J. Cavanaugh), Renita Harris, along with Portland Police Detectives Angela Alvarez and Laurie McCaskill are working in a cooperative effort on the homicide investigation of Kylie Preston. Ms. Preston was murdered and butchered after being last seen by a man posing as Dr. Harry Boulder. Every possible lead was exhausted to apprehend the imposter and probable killer, without success.

During the course of our Preston investigation, Brian Dixon was murdered and butchered in the same fashion as Kylie Preston. The murder victims had no relationship of either a professional or a personal nature that we are aware. The Dixon murder has led us down the same path of non-discovery. At this point, Renita and I will review the short list of suspects we compiled from the Lunsford Insurance complaints aimed at Kylie Preston over the years, concentrating on those of a more vociferous nature.

I was thinking of what else I could add to the report when my telephone rang. I answered on the first ring.

"Cavanaugh Investigation Agency."

"C. J., its Angel. We've got another one."

CHAPTER FIFTY-THREE

I had telephoned Renita to tell her another body had been found. Renita was driving back to the office when I reached her. I gave Renita the reported location of the third victim and agreed to meet her there.

A third body was discovered in a black Escalade in the Lloyd Center parking garage. I stood by with a couple of uniforms and mall security who were assigned crowd control. I picked the brains of the mall security guards in the outside chance they might have information about the Escalade or the dumpsite that the rest of us didn't. The effort proved to be useless.

Angel, McCaskill, and forensics surveyed the dumpsite and the Escalade. Renita arrived a few minutes after me. We greeted each other with curt nods. I filled Renita in on what I knew up to that point, which was very little. I waited off to the side of the dumpsite with Renita for a signal from Angel as to when it would be clear for us to have our shot at examining the crime scene.

Angel and McCaskill made a good team. They communicated well as they examined the Escalade and the surrounding area, pointing out areas deserving closer scrutiny as they went along. The more I watched the detectives, the more I questioned my earlier assessment of McCaskill. Maybe I was wrong about her. Maybe McCaskill was a team player.

The detectives saved the worst for last. When they opened the back of the Escalade, there were the all too familiar neatly wrapped four brown paper packages. I found myself taking a deep breath even though I expected to see them. Renita shook her head in sad disbelief. The detectives and forensics searched in and around the packages for any clues, without touching them. They hadn't found any, judging from their expressions. When forensics and the detectives finished their initial investigations, Angel took a few minutes to compare notes with forensics and McCaskill before she waved us over.

I had reviewed with Renita, over the last few weeks, how to conduct herself at a crime scene. I took Renita on simulated field tests using rented or abandoned vehicles that I had designed to sharpen her skills. Renita caught on fast. Above all else, Renita was a serious and focused student the entire time. She didn't play around, as she had so often done in the past when I was attempting to school her. Renita and I walked over, snapping on our latex gloves. Instead of shaking hands with the detectives, Renita and I nodded at them and voiced simple greetings.

"Any luck?" I asked after our welcome.

"None," Angel said with cold disappointment.

McCaskill confirmed Angel's assessment with a defeated, "Nothing."

Angel let us have a look at the contents inside the trademark manila envelope they had found with the four packages. Just as before, there was a laser-printed discovery letter along with the personal effects of the presumed deceased. We saw nothing out of the ordinary in any of the items, we told Angel and McCaskill as I returned the envelope to Angel. Angel turned the envelope over to a forensics officer standing by, who carefully slipped it into an evidence bag.

"You're up," Angel said. "Maybe you two can find something we missed."

"We'll give it a try," I said.

Angel and McCaskill removed their gloves as they stepped away, giving us room to operate. Forensics had finished their jobs and moved away, as well.

Renita and I went to it. We were as careful during our survey as Angel and McCaskill were during theirs. Renita did everything I taught her. She was conscientious and methodical, keeping her eyes and nose peeled for anything out of the ordinary. Renita conducted herself as if she had been doing crime scene investigation for years. When in doubt, she asked. That's the hardest lesson to teach any rookie in law enforcement. I was proud of my partner. Neither of us found anything—aside from the packages—that was unusual. We were just as stumped as Angel and McCaskill. I waved for the detectives to join us back near the Escalade.

"Anything?" Angel asked as she stepped to face me.

"Nothing," I said, ripping off my gloves.

"Not even a hair." Renita slipped off her gloves in front of McCaskill, who was facing her.

"This perp is as good as he is dangerous," McCaskill said.

"Thanks for lending us your fresh eyes," Angel added.

I expected McCaskill to sarcastically rebut, "A lot of good they did us." Instead, McCaskill extended her hand. "Thanks for your help." I shook McCaskill's hand, wondering about her sincerity, followed by a handshake with Angel.

"You're welcome," I said to both detectives.

"Sorry we couldn't have been of more help." Renita shook the detectives' hands, as well.

I asked, "Any witnesses to who was driving the vehicle?"

"None," McCaskill said. "A uniform is getting a copy of recent security tapes to see if anyone jumps out at us."

"You two want in on the tape viewing?" Angel asked.

"Sure," I said, "give us a call when you're ready."

"Maybe the lab will turn up something on this guy." Angel signaled the ME team to pick up the mundane-looking packages.

"If there's something to be found, Blake will find it," I said.

"That's for sure," Angel said.

"Any idea of who the victim is?" I asked.

"The Escalade is registered to a Mitchell Baker," McCaskill answered.

"The multimillionaire developer," I said.

"The same Mitchell Baker who was responsible for the gentrification of a number of Multnomah County communities," Renita added.

"And beyond," I said.

Angel and McCaskill stared at us, impressed by our wealth of knowledge on the possible victim.

"One and the same," McCaskill said. "And how do you two know so much about Baker?"

"I took some non-credit courses in modern Northwest history at PSU," I said.

"C. J. told me about some of the fascinating things he'd learned. Those were some of the facts that stuck."

"And you took those history courses why?" McCaskill asked.

"Why not?" McCaskill gave me an acquiescent nod.

"How much do you want to bet that what's left of Baker is inside those packages," Angel said.

Renita swallowed so hard it was audible. I looked at Renita and could tell the conversation was making her nauseous. Angel and McCaskill noticed it, too. No doubt, fresh visions of the butchered body of Brian Dixon were running through Renita's mind. I changed the subject.

"You want us to hang back until you've finished interviewing anyone involved with the victim?"

"That would be best," Angel said. "We'll get you a copy of our report ASAP. The report will, of course, contain who we interviewed and what they had to say."

"Thanks," I said. "We'll let you know if we come up with any breakthroughs."

"We could use one," McCaskill said. Renita and I nodded before we walked away.

"How are you feeling?" I asked Renita when were out of earshot of the detectives.

"A little nauseous, but I'll live. I can taste that seafood salad I had for lunch."

"Try to put it out of your mind. Think good thoughts."

"Does it ever get easier?"

"What?"

I looked over my shoulder in time to see the last of the packages loaded into the meat wagon. Angel signaled for the tow truck to haul the Escalade away.

"I've seen dead people before, but nothing like what we saw of Brian Dixon in the morgue." Renita shivered.

"You've seen dead people in funeral homes or during wakes."

"That's true."

"After the mortician has worked their magic to clean up the callous disregard nature has for the decaying appearance of death."

"I suppose so."

All entrances to the Lloyd Center Mall parking garage had been closed by PPB. Renita and I had parked on the street. Being the gentleman that I am, I escorted Renita to her car.

"What you saw in the morgue was a murder in its most vile and repulsive form," I said as we strolled from the parking garage out into the sunshine, "the mutilation of a human being."

"Is the feeling always this bad? I know most murder victims don't wind up mutilated, but..." Renita could not find the words to finish.

"Most murder victims don't wind up mutilated, but death is death, and the living care a lot more about how it looks than the dead."

Renita took a couple of deep breaths.

"Feeling better?" I said.

"A little."

"If it's any consolation, we all go through what you're going through."

"Was your first time as bad for you?"

"Upon seeing my first homicide, I puked at the crime scene; and this coming from a man who had seen combat."

"I would have paid to see that."

"Me in combat, or me puking?" I said with amusement.

"You puking," Renita said, enjoying my embarrassing confession.

"It wasn't pretty. I was a green recruit on my first street-level enforcement case. We were working surveillance on a drug gang in Baltimore. We had a confidential informant on the inside. He was a kid we flipped after we busted him dealing in a neighborhood across town. It turned out the kid was a sergeant in the gang we were watching. He was doing a little side business. If his gang found out that he was making extra income, he was toast. We used that information to our advantage to add fuel to our fire of persuasion. It worked.

"The kid didn't show up at our scheduled rendezvous spot to update us on the target's latest activities and plans. We went looking for him. Found him dead in a back alley of an apparent OD. We knew our snitch was clean. The kid was a dealer, not a user. The gang somehow found out he was a snitch and tried to set up his murder to look like a drug overdose. His name was Eldon Wilson. He was fifteen years old."

"That's awful."

"More like tragic."

"Were you sent home after you vomited?"

"Nope, I was consoled by other agents, given a quick pep talk by my Task Force Officer, and sent back at it. I had constant nightmares about Eldon for a while afterwards."

"I've been having nightmares about Kylie Preston. The last one was a couple of nights ago. I woke up in a cold sweat, crying."

I found it odd Renita was having nightmares about Kylie Preston rather than the mutilated corpse of Brian Dixon. The memory of his remains will likely be forever seared into her brain, but I remained silent on that observation. "Renita, I'm sorry. Why didn't you say anything?"

"I didn't want you to think I couldn't handle doing homicide investigations. I'm always badgering you about putting me on tougher assignments. How could I tell you I wasn't sure I was up to it?"

"That's nonsense, you're doing great. You're doing what you need to, and that's focusing on the investigation. That's what we can do for the murder victims. Finding their killer is the best medicine we can give ourselves."

"Did you catch Eldon Wilson's murderer?"

"We did. We brought down the gang's operation, as well."

"Did it stop the nightmares?"

"It helped."

"Will catching The Butcher stop my nightmares?"

"I can't promise you that, but I believe it'll help ease your subconscious. That, in turn, may dilute the trauma you experienced. Time may be the only cure."

"That's a big help," Renita said with an uneasy smile. Some of her old fight had climbed back into her eyes.

"Glad I could not be of service." Renita let out a short burst of laughter.

"If you ever need to talk," I said in all seriousness, "don't hesitate to come to me. You're more than my investigation partner. You're my friend. I will always be there for you when you need me."

Renita hugged me. I could feel her body trembling as I hugged her back. The sobbing and the tears came as an almost natural progression. We stood there on the street hugging each other. To passersby, we must have appeared strange: a woman sobbing into a man's chest with their arms wrapped around each other. We were that way until the sobbing and tears subsided and the trembling ceased. Renita pulled away from me, looking embarrassed.

"Where did that come from?" There was a sound of relief in her voice.

"From your humanity."

Renita took my arm as we finished our walk to her car. Ordinarily, I would have admonished her for such unprofessional behavior. I threw the practiced playbook out of the window for the moment. My friend needed me.

"What do you think?" Renita asked as we stood by the driver's door of her tomato-red Audi R8.

"About what?"

"About our chances of capturing The Butcher?"

"We've got to go back to the drawing board. There's something we've missed."

"I'll see you back at the office." Renita gave me a peck on the cheek before she got into her car and drove away.

CHAPTER FIFTY-FOUR

The next day Angel telephoned the office to inform us of the identity of the third murder victim. Blake had confirmed the deceased as Mitchell Donovan Baker, the retired multimillionaire developer. All early indications were that the M.O. was identical to the two previous Butcher murders.

My decision to wait for Angel and McCaskill's report before conducting our independent investigation was a trying one. Once we had read the detectives' report, then Renita and I could refine our approach. That could give us forward momentum. We wouldn't have to retread ground already covered by the detectives unless we saw good reason to do so. That aspect of my reasoning was sound. It did go against my preferred unsullied, fresh eyes and ears approach to hammering out an investigation. In an effort at bipartisanship with my PPB comrades, I felt it was the best way to proceed. The bulldog investigator in Renita and me disagreed.

"Can't we at least do a little snooping around?" Renita had taken a seat in my office in the visitor's chair. I had been sitting in my office chair churning over in my head the first two murders; trying to discern if there was anything we had missed. Renita was frustrated. Waiting around with nothing concrete to occupy our time did not help. We had taken an even closer look at the short list of people we had derived from the information Carl Wheaton had provided us, hoping to discover some kernel of enlightenment that we missed. Nothing jumped out at us that seemed worthy of reexamination. We were right back where we started before the third body popped up.

"I told Angel we would lay low until she gave us their report," I said in answer to Renita's frustration.

"What about taking on another case in the interim?"

"We promised Carl we would work exclusively on the Kylie Preston case."

"So what do we do in the meantime? Wait until The Butcher kills again?"

I thought about Renita's question. My radio was playing low and was tuned to smooth jazz. The DJ had given the daily weather forecast as clear with an expected high in the low eighties. I turned to peer out through the open vertical blinds. The sun was smiling from a clear blue sky.

"It's a beautiful day," I said.

"Yes, it is."

"Let's go." I jumped up to leave. Renita followed.

"Where are we going?"

"You'll see."

***

I drove Renita to Washington Park in the scenic west hills of Portland to one of the most authentic Japanese gardens outside of Japan. A tranquil retreat nestled high above the hectic Rose City, the Japanese Garden was an idyllic haven for contemplation and meditation.

"How long has it been since you've been here?" I asked Renita as we walked through the lower entrance.

"Years." I could hear the tension receding in her voice. The Japanese Garden had that intended effect on people.

"Me too," I said, letting Renita know she was not alone in her spiritual neglect. "How much do you know about the Japanese Garden?"

"Besides it being amazing, not much."

My photographic memory kicked in. I recalled almost everything I had read about Portland's Japanese Garden. Even the correct Japanese pronunciations came back to me, as if being whispered into my ear by Atsuko Murakami, a Multnomah County Central Librarian who was kind enough to walk me through them. Even though I could have gone into a fair amount of detail about the Japanese gardens, I gave Renita the abbreviated pamphlet version.

I began with a brief history of the Japanese Garden, mentioning that, in many ways, a Japanese garden echoes the enduring traditional culture and history of Japan. I told Renita that Japanese gardens were influenced by Taoist, Shinto and Buddhist values; gardeners attempted to convey in their designs that there was always more than meets the eyes in these creations of stone, water, and plants.

"Recognized as one of the most authentic Japanese gardens outside of Japan," I said, "the Portland Japanese Garden stretches out over nearly 5.5 acres. Following the traditional Japanese way, the Portland Japanese Garden contains five separate gardens orchestrated along major and minor themes: The Flat Garden (Hira-niwa), Stroll Garden (Chisen kaiyu shiki teien), Tea Garden (Cha-niwa or Roji), Natural Garden (Zoki no niwa), and Sand and Stone Garden (Kareasansui). Additional elements such as pagodas, bridges, stone lanterns, arbors, and water basins are also involved in the designs. Even the tool sheds are part of the landscape, crafted as functioning works of art. The five gardens are woven together as cohesive entities with the express intention of creating a sense of harmony, peace, and tranquility. Japanese gardens are of an unbalanced design to reflect nature in perfect form. Human scale is preserved throughout to promote a connection with the environment, instead of being overwhelmed by it."

"You sound like a tour guide," Renita said, both impressed and dismayed.

"Thank you."

"And how do you know all of this?"

"I don't apologize for my unquenchable thirst for knowledge and understanding. They're important to me. Here was this amazing gift, altruistically offering that opportunity. How could I not accept?"

Renita could only smile. "There was a time I was a regular here," I said in a whisper. The atmosphere was conducive to hushed tones, if not complete silence.

"I wouldn't describe myself as a regular," Renita replied in a whisper, "but I used to pass through a couple of times a year during the summer."

"Why'd you stop?"

Renita reflected for a moment. "I don't know." Then, after a brief instant of thought, she asked, "Why'd you stop?"

"I suppose even paradise can become mundane after a while." Renita nodded.

"Did you remember to turn off your cell phone?" I asked.

"Smartphone; and yes, I did. Did you?"

"I have to remember to turn mine on."

Renita took my arm as we continued to stroll.

"Let's enjoy some of the best this world has to offer," I said, "and disregard the rest."

"I'll try," Renita said with a sheepish grin.

Time is contrary to our desires. When we want it to speed up, it slows down. When we want it to slow down, it speeds up. In Portland's Japanese Garden, that basic rule did not apply. We strolled through paradise for the entire afternoon without realizing it. Time seemed irrelevant. We allowed ourselves a welcomed plunge into peace and tranquility. A westerner's fast food helping of Zen, I suppose. That was how I felt. From the look in Renita's eyes, I could tell she was in the same place. It was a space neither of us ever wanted to vacate. Purged of thoughts of murder, it turned out to be a beautiful day.

CHAPTER FIFTY-FIVE

It had been two days since the discovery of the black Escalade in the Lloyd Center parking garage. We were all hoping that either forensics or the ME's office, or both, would have more success than we did at the dumpsite. Renita and I were going over our financial records for the last quarter when Shawn Calloway burst into Cavanaugh Investigation Agency, slamming the door in his wake. Calloway spied Renita and me in my office and rushed in. We greeted him with glares.

"I want to help you nail that bastard," Shawn growled. Shawn looked as if he were referring to the bully who had just taken his lunch money. His face was flushed with rage. Our stares softened.

"Which bastard is that, Shawn?" I calmly queried.

"I just spent five hours being grilled by Alvarez and McCaskill as the prime suspect in Mitchell Baker's murder." Shawn was agitated.

"What?" Renita said.

"That asshole—"

"Asshole," Renita said to Shawn.

"Aka The Butcher," Shawn said. "He disguised himself as *me* to get close enough to Baker to whack him."

"Did the detectives tell you that?" I asked.

"More like their questions did. A couple of Baker's neighbors saw someone who looks like me enter and exit his house on the day he went missing. I never even met the man!"

"What else did the detectives say?" I asked.

"I thought you were investigating The Butcher," Shawn said.

"We're investigating Kylie Preston's murder," Renita said.

"The other murders are important to us because they fit the same M.O. So what else did the detectives' questions reveal?"

"On no, you don't," Shawn said, regaining his guile. "I'm the one asking the questions."

"Good luck on getting any answers," I said.

Shawn fired off a string of questions that rendered him no new information from us on The Butcher while confirming some of what Renita and I had conjectured about the third victim–minus the Shawn Calloway masquerade.

"They honestly believed I was capable of killing someone—and then cutting them up like they were a side of beef." Irritation resonated in his voice with a genuine touch of nausea.

"The Butcher is a lot more precise than that, as I'm certain you know by now," Renita said.

"That's not the point."

"What is the point?" I asked.

"The point is that I had nothing to do with Baker's murder." Shawn was upset at being considered a murder suspect.

"Shawn, calm down," I said. "I'm sure Alvarez and McCaskill were simply going through the motions. They had to press you to make certain you weren't somehow involved."

"The detectives also wanted to alleviate any doubts that you received special treatment," Renita added.

"Why would I receive special treatment?"

"You are somewhat of a local celebrity," Renita said.

"If PPB simply wrote you off as a suspect," I added, "then it might appear to the general public and your press colleagues that you received special treatment."

"You know how that goes?" Renita said.

"Then why did Angel and McCaskill warn me not to leave town?"

"Standard procedure," I said. "I'm sure they eliminated you as a prime suspect the moment you were released."

"They know like we know. You're much more likely to write a killer story than murder anyone."

"I do believe in Mark Twain's philosophy of 'Don't pick a fight with someone who buys ink by the barrel.'"

"There you go," Renita said.

"Although being a murder suspect would provide an interesting angle to cover this story: Shawn Calloway, Prime Suspect, a gruesome tale from both perspectives."

"You may be too late on that angle," I said.

"Why?"

"By now every local news outlet has picked up the fact that you've been questioned by police as the prime suspect in The Butcher murder investigation. How long do you think that's going to take before it spreads like a national news brush fire?"

"You are the story this time, Shawn," Renita said.

"*Damn it.* Maybe if I hurry, I can get ahead of the wave."

"Good luck," I said.

"You two will keep me posted on any new developments?"

"We report to our client and the police," Renita said.

"And, considering you're a suspect in a serial murder investigation, that wouldn't be ethical," I quipped.

"How does it feel to be a prime suspect?" Renita chimed in.

"Ha-ha, funny. Who's your client again?"

"Confidential," I said.

"I don't believe I know him. Is that his first or last name?"

"Neither," Renita said.

"I've gotta run. I'll see you for dinner later," Shawn said to Renita.

"In your dreams," Renita said.

"How did you know I was dreaming about you?"

"I thought you said you had to run," I said.

"Right, that story's not going to write itself." Shawn rushed off.

"Wow," Renita said. "Our chameleon struck as Shawn Calloway. That took some guts to disguise himself as someone who is a minor celebrity in this town."

"This guy is good. I can't wait to get my hands on Angel's report."

"I can't wait until we're back in the field doing our own research."

"Patience; let's add this last bold stroke to our criminal profile and wait to see what else pops up."

CHAPTER FIFTY-SIX

It had been four days since the confirmed murder of Mitchell Baker. Renita and I were getting antsy to dive into the fray. True to our word, we stood fast, awaiting the official investigation report from Angel. Since we had also kept our plates clean of other cases, as promised, we searched for ways to keep ourselves occupied. Card, computer, and board games helped us fill the void.

Renita was having lunch with Ernest again, which had become a regular event. I was meeting Destini for lunch, which had also become a regular event. I was enjoying a red-hot noon concert by The Music Makers in Pioneer Courthouse Square. The day was bright and clear; a fact trumpeted by the golden leaf sun emerging from the silver-colored weather orb, cresting a tall metal column that reminded me of a mercury thermometer. The Square was packed with wall-to-wall listeners emanating a positive vibe of their own. Winston was playing the electric piano, this time. Smoky switched between an electric and a stand-up bass. Winston and Smoky often played different instruments during their jam sessions. It made it fun for them and gave their music a different flavor.

I had come early to stake out seats for Destini and me on the brick steps in Portland's living room. Destini was a no show due to a last minute homicide assignment. I gave up my seat. I decided instead to stand near one of the decorated stone columns, a place that gave me a great view of the band.

"*Detective Cavanaugh.*" A baritone voice came through over the music. I turned to see Richard Weston, the family and relationship counselor I'd met at the rec center. Weston wore a floral Hawaiian shirt, extra-long baggy khaki cargo shorts, and Birkenstock leather sandals with white sweat socks that did nothing for his pale hairy legs. He looked like a laid-back tourist. His brown hair was longer than I remembered, but the rest of him appeared much the same. "I thought that was you," Weston said.

"How are you, Richard?" I asked, matching Weston's volume.

"Good, and you?"

"Not bad."

I looked Richard Weston over. "Nice outfit," I said, not masking my humor. Weston chuckled. He looked himself over as if seeing what he was wearing for the first time. "I know it's rather hackneyed, but to me, it says summer."

To me, it says 'sucker' is what I thought. "Ah," is what I said.

"And just for the record, everyone calls me Wes, remember?"

"My mistake, I'll remember from here on. Call me C. J."

"Alright, C. J."

"And by the way, I'm a private investigator not a detective."

"What's the difference?"

"Detectives work for law enforcement agencies. Private investigators are just that: they investigate on behalf of private individuals, organizations, or businesses."

"Aren't you working for the Portland Police?"

"Cavanaugh Investigation Agency is working *with* PPB. We're *working* for a private party on that matter."

"My apologies."

"No need."

"These guys are great," Wes said with admiration.

"Yes, they are."

"What are they doing here?"

"You mean, giving a free noon concert; or here at The Square in general?"

"Both."

"They enjoy it."

"They could make the big time, no problem."

"I'm sure you're right." I opted not to share Winston and Smoky's professional musical history with Wes. "What brings you to the neighborhood?"

"I was doing a little shopping." Wes raised a reusable linen tote bag with an illustration of the Golden Gate Bridge to show me.

"Getting ready for a big date?" I kidded.

"More like bare necessities," Wes said, taking the jab in stride.

"How's that murder investigation going, anyway?"

"You mean the one involving The Butcher?"

"Are you working any other murder investigations besides that one?"

"Not at the moment. The investigation's not going well. We're no closer to catching The Butcher than we are Jack the Ripper."

"Sorry to hear that. I've been following the case in the newspaper. I suppose most people are. It doesn't sound like the police are having any more luck than you are."

"I'm afraid that's true. How would you profile someone like The Butcher?" I asked in an attempt to take advantage of the Wes' expertise in human behavior.

"That's way out of my league. I wouldn't know where to start my analysis without interviewing the man. Even then, I doubt that I'd be of much good. This is a job for criminal profilers. I'm nowhere near qualified to analyze someone predisposed to that level of violence. I'm much more effective diagnosing people who are not that far off the normal path."

"I understand."

"Although I must say, I have been batting around one theory."

"Let's hear it."

"It's based on the issue of the killer preserving so much of his victims," Wes said. "My father was a hunter. He had a creed that if you killed an animal, you used as much of your game as you could."

"Waste not, want not."

"Exactly."

"So you don't think it's the work of some angry sadistic person lashing out?"

"That could be at the root of it, along with a host of other issues. If it were simply that, then why would he go through all of that trouble?"

"I see your point."

"My father believed that in some way, that animal forfeited its life so that you could carry on. The least one could do was respect its noble gesture by making the most of its sacrifice."

"A number of indigenous people believe the same."

"Really?"

"Was your father Native American?"

"As far as I could tell, he was 100% European."

"You were saying."

"I have a feeling this person is operating under the same principle as my father."

"That could very well be," I said, giving Wes' theory serious thought. "Are you a hunter?"

"Heavens no. I never developed the stomach for killing. I'm a grocery store carnivore."

"I'm with you there."

"Anyway, that's my theory, for what it's worth. I'd better get going. I have an appointment in an hour."

"Good to see you, Wes; don't be a stranger."

"I won't." Wes and I shook hands before he left. He still had that viselike grip. I agreed with Wes' logic. His honorable hunter's theory made sense. Now, how was I going to shake loose this conscientious killer from the masses? I gave more thought on how to proceed as The Music Makers played "Mercy, Mercy, Mercy."

CHAPTER FIFTY-SEVEN

My doorbell rang. I answered it. Blake Saba was right on time. Away from the office, Blake preferred to dress casual. For Blake, that meant a pair of cowboy jeans, a denim shirt, a Schonchin bolo tie, and leather zippered boots. Sometimes he wore a black fur felt hat with a four inch brim and a cattleman's crown. Tonight was not one of those occasions. Blake still wore his hair back in a ponytail. This time the ponytail holder was sterling silver. I asked Blake about the tie and holder. Blake said they were handmade. A Navajo friend who lived in Arizona sent them to him.

Our informal get-together gave us a chance to catch up on our personal lives and discuss our shared passion for Native and African American history, all while enjoying a good meal. We alternated where we had our impromptu dinners between Blake's home and mine. This time Blake was a welcomed guest at mine. The next time I would delight in the same treatment at his.

As much as I enjoyed hosting Blake in my home, having supper at Blake's house was much more invigorating. Blake's entire family enjoyed the topic of history and participated with great enthusiasm. Blake's teenage son and daughter were almost as knowledgeable about Klamath history as their parents, grandparents, aunts, and uncles. The whole lot knew more about the history of indigenous people than I could ever dream. It made for lively debates and interesting discussions as history and generational points-of-views clashed. I chimed in when I had something I felt was relevant to the topic. Otherwise, I remained quiet, listened, and learned. A silence that was easy to maintain by filling my mouth with excellent homemade food.

For Blake, it was a win-win situation in the food category because he never cooked. Not because he couldn't; it simply wasn't required. When

Blake came to my home, I did all of the cooking. At his house, the women did all of the cooking.

Blake's family sent along their best wishes. I asked him to do the same on my behalf. Although Blake's family was just as welcome in my home as I felt in theirs, they rarely joined Blake when he came to my place. One day I would have to find the courage to ask Blake why. I certainly hoped it wasn't my cooking.

Blake arrived bearing gifts. In one hand, he had a German chocolate cake he bought from Rose's Restaurant and Bakery. In the other, he held two books. One was a book he had found at a library sale that dealt with American Indian mythology. The other was an encyclopedia of Native American tribes. Blake had read both and vouched for their contents. He believed I would find nourishment in and enjoy them. I thanked him. I had an earlier edition of the encyclopedia. It was not worth mentioning. I did not want to insult my friend for his generosity. They both would be fruitful additions to my library.

Blake asked about the twins. I told him that Destini was babysitting Booker and Andrew and that Destini said hello. Blake appeared disappointed by the absence of my Scottish terriers but said nothing. I believed he looked forward to seeing Andrew and Booker as much as he did me. I told Blake I'd bring Booker and Andrew by his office to say hello sometime soon. He smiled and nodded his approval. Blake made his rounds to say hello to my singing finches Toussaint, Coretta, Claude, and Truth, and my aquarium of tropical goldfish, as I checked on dinner.

I had prepared a three-meat stew of lamb, veal and beef with a blend of vegetables, wild rice, fresh mushrooms, garlic, onions, and white pearl onions all seasoned in a herb bouquet broth that made the stew a bit spicy. The stew filled the house with a mouth-watering aroma, as Blake noted when he joined me in the kitchen. Within minutes we were enjoying the stew with sweet yellow corn bread and a tossed spinach salad.

Our initial conversation circled around the latest exploits of Blake's two teenagers. After Blake grilled me on when I was going to marry Destini, we moved into the cerebral and intriguing topics of American Indian and African American history; topics that for us did not mean the espousing of dates, events, and individuals; but an exploration of social, cultural, philosophical and spiritual significance. Blake and I both shared the vision that history without such content was vacant of any true facts.

Destini had joined us for our first couple of get-togethers. She found our history discussions so boring that they nearly put her to sleep. Needless to say, Destini stopped coming. Had she been present, she would have probably taken a nap.

We were in the throes of a discussion involving the role of the Trickster type-character in Cherokee culture when Blake switched gears on me.

"I've been giving some thought to The Butcher," Blake said. We rarely talked shop during our dinners. To be quite frank, we considered it beneath our desired topics of conversation.

"I thought you were able to turn work off when you left the office."

"I can, but this guy has my mind turning."

"About what?"

"Not mortality, if that's what you're getting at." I nodded to affirm that I was thinking along those lines.

"To do what he did to his victims takes discipline and patience. Some of those procedures are quick; others require a more delicate touch. Whoever did this is capable of maintaining and rapidly shifting their focus."

"Like an experienced combat medic or trauma surgeon," I said, leaning back in my chair.

"Precisely."

"You're certain the same killer butchered Baker, Preston, and Dixon?"

"All of the evidence points that way. The same surgical style was used in each murder. The same meat cleaver was used to chop off the head and limbs. Most of a healthy human body can be recycled. The organs, tissue, and bone can be transplanted to a compatible human being."

"Hence the lucrative black market for organs and tissue," I said, leaning forward.

"Supply and demand."

"The blunt economic credo that justifies any means to make a buck. Without ethics and morality, business itself can be a crime."

"I agree. Without principles, business can be reprehensible. That's why we have laws to try to control that sort of wanton behavior."

"How's that working out for us?"

Blake shrugged. "Like most things, as well as its citizens allow."

The conversation I had earlier that day with Wes crossed my mind. I asked Blake about the conscientious hunter theory Wes had mentioned. Blake said it was feasible, but he couldn't make that determination from what he had seen. Our minds were churning. Our eyes fixed. We had entered full investigative mode.

"Do you believe the killer's reason for preserving his victims to be noble?"

"You mean, because his handiwork can be used to help others?"

"Yes."

"The way he preserved them suggests that was his intention. All I can say for certain is that his handling of his victims permitted the opportunity for others to be helped. Someone needs to stop him, in any event."

"We've talked about his skill level, but what kind of equipment would The Butcher need to pull off what he's doing?"

"A lot of the same equipment you would find in a regular hospital surgery or a morgue like ours." Blake expounded on what instruments and equipment The Butcher would need to accomplish his tasks. I listened intently, attempting to get a fix on the scope of what was required. I had given a great deal more consideration to what training and education the killer must have possessed to achieve his goals. I hadn't given much thought to what else was required. "And judging by the condition of his victims, I'd say our killer had a number, if not all, of those items at his disposal," Blake concluded.

"Would morticians be capable of doing that type of surgery?"

"Not customarily, but they could equipment their prep rooms to do so without much trouble. Do you have anyone particular in mind?"

Blake had come to know all of the morticians in the area from his line of work.

"Just fishing," I said. "Where can you find the items you would need to do surgery like The Butcher's been doing?"

"At any hospital supply store."

"Do you need any special clearance or license to get them?"

"Goodness no, all you need is the ability to pay. You can even order what you need online."

"You would also need a space big enough to accommodate your operation."

"That's where you were going with that mortician question."

"Correct."

"It would require a fair amount of space to be able to house the equipment and allow enough room to operate."

"Would you need an assistant to do what he's been doing?"

"It would make it easier, but it's not necessary. Operating on a corpse doesn't require the same requirements as operating on a live human being."

Blake and I ate in silence for a few moments, chewing over our thoughts as much as our meal. "Do you think harvesting is his primary motivation?" I asked.

"I couldn't say. You'll have to ask him when you catch him."

"You mean, if I catch him."

"I have faith in you." His confidence was appreciated, but it didn't dismiss the facts. Renita and I didn't have a clue who the killer was, or where to look for him.

"Angel and McCaskill might get to him first," I said.

"Angel's top notch and McCaskill's no slouch, but my money's on you. This stew is amazing," Blake said, switching gears on me again. "May I have the recipe?"

"So you can pass it along to your wife?" I quipped.

"I cook." Blake looked incredulous.

"Right," I said, escalating the joke.

"I do. I cook all of the time."

"Microwaving yours wife's leftovers does not constitute cooking."

"Very funny."

"More like amusing, but I'll accept your take on it." Blake laughed and then asked for seconds on the stew.

For dessert, I served a spicy desert tea along with organic vanilla soy ice cream for my lactose-challenged friend as a compliment to his rich German chocolate cake. If his wife were with us, I'm certain she would have admonished me regarding my contribution to the expanse of her husband's waistline. We had turned our conversation back to our way of encapsulating history by dessert. Before my friend left, I packed him some stew to go and wished him a safe trip home. We hugged. He made me promise to bring Andrew and Booker by for a visit. It was a promise that would be easy to keep.

CHAPTER FIFTY-EIGHT

The finches were singing when Destini dropped off Andrew and Booker bright and early the next morning. While the twins were happy to be home, I could tell they'd had a great time with Destini, evidenced by the fact they didn't want her to leave. They were not alone in their sentiment.

"Did they give you a hard time?"

"They were perfect angels."

"That doesn't sound like the Booker and Andrew I know. What's your secret?"

"We played a lot and we watched a movie."

"What movie?"

"Babe."

"Did they bark every time there was a talking dog?"

"Every time."

"I should have warned you about that. They have a tendency to talk to the screen when they see a talking dog."

"No stereotype there."

"They didn't get it from me."

"I didn't mind. They were such sweethearts."

"You must have some magic spell over them." I wrapped my arms around Destini's torso.

Destini was wearing a dark blue pants suit with a powder blue cotton blouse and black flats. Her jacket was open, exposing her shoulder-holstered service weapon. Her gold shield clipped to her black leather belt. Her hair was unbraided. As was usually the case for Destini, when she unraveled her braids, her hair lay flat. Her long satiny black ponytail reached to the small of her back. It was looped through a generic elastic aqua-colored ponytail holder. *I will have to talk to Blake about getting Destini some of his handmade ponytail holders,* I thought. *They would look great on her.*

Like the gold Nefertiti necklace I gave Destini for her last birthday, that appeared at home against her mocha skin. I gazed into Destini's hazel eyes. Her dimpled smile still had the power to disarm me.

"Are they the only ones?" Destini wrapped her arms around my neck in response to my comment.

"Not by a long shot." We kissed. The twins circled us, jockeying for attention. Destini and I managed to resist their charms. Destini asked about dinner with Blake. I told her it went well. Destini half-jokingly inquired about what we discussed. I told her the usual. Destini jibed about how sorry she was that she had missed it. I invited Destini to stay for breakfast.

"I would love to stay, but I have to get to the office. I have some paperwork to catch up on. I barely have time for a good morning and a quick kiss."

Destini asked for a rain check. I gave her one. She gave me a quick kiss, said goodbye to the twins, then me, and rushed off. The twins and I hated to see her go.

Since Destini declined breakfast, I decided to meditate and then go for my morning run, two things I was willing to forego until the afternoon in order to spend quality time with my baby. I asked the twins if they would like to join me. They gave me their answer by running away, a response they were more likely to give when Destini was around. Apparently, the time they had spent with Destini had a carryover effect.

***

I arrived to an empty office. I was early. Renita wasn't expected for at least another half-hour. I got everything from the office lights to coffee up to speed. Then I settled in to do some investigative work. I was excited about the prospect of developing a solid lead. From my conversations with Blake and Wes, I was able to piecemeal a basic blueprint of what to look for in The Butcher. What was still lacking was a firm personality or motivational workup. I still did not know what made this guy tick. Any investigator worth his salt knows that you find out what makes a person tick and you're three quarters of the way to catching them.

The physical evidence had left us with nothing in that area. My instincts were telling me the answer was somewhere in the files that Carl Wheaton had given us. I had been poring over a file from our short list for a couple of minutes when Renita arrived. Renita rolled her top-of-the-line Peugeot racing bike across the carpeted outer office. She was wearing skintight black Lycra cycling shorts, a snug-fitting lime-colored short-sleeve jersey, a blue and white road helmet that resembled an upside down bird's nest, high performance amber-tinted bicycle glasses, and black high-end road shoes and cycling gloves.

"What's up?" Renita asked, parked in the doorway of my office and appearing as if she were ready for the Tour de France.

"Da Capo al Fine," I said.

"*What?*"

"It's a musical term. It means 'from the beginning to the end.' I'll explain once you've settled in." Renita shrugged and left.

My ears became my eyes even as I scanned the case files of one of the people on the short list. I could hear Renita as she went through her routine. The clicking of her bicycle and faint thumping of her bike shoes on the carpet as she made her way to the exercise room. The mild grunt Renita made as she lifted her bike onto the wall mount in the exercise room. The coarse separation of Velcro ripping apart signaled she was removing her helmet and gloves. I heard her walk on the carpet to her office and gather what she needed. I shut down my sound pictures when Renita entered the bathroom to wash up and change.

Renita returned within twenty minutes wearing a white pleated skirt, a short-sleeve floral knit top, a pair of white low-cut tennis shoes, and sports ankle socks. The modest outfit did nothing to camouflage her athletic body. Her latté skin had deepened to dark caramel from the summer sun. Renita had stopped dyeing her shoulder-length hair light brown at Ernest's request. Her natural hair color suited her well. I never understood why Renita dyed her beautiful black hair in the first place. When I asked her about it, Renita nonchalantly answered, "Because it was different."

First, I gave Renita the back-story on what I was doing. I told her about my conversations with Wes and Blake. I explained to Renita that the clues we needed might still be within the files Carl had given us.

"We're looking for someone connected to a hunting accident death whose life insurance settlement was not honored," I said. "If they had children or close child relatives, all the better. Let's begin with the short list and then work our way backwards."

Renita listened carefully to what I had to say. She told me she wasn't convinced we needed to retrace our steps based on my Wes and Blake's assessments. Renita did agree with my rationale of doing so based on my new criteria.

"So you're committed to this line of thinking?" I asked.

"Count me in."

CHAPTER FIFTY-NINE

Fresh possibilities breathed new life into our investigation. Renita and I spent the next few days revisiting the insurance records that Carl had given us with a renewed vitality. We followed a similar procedure as before, only this time we were looking for any deaths linked to a hunting accident. Since we knew what we were searching for, it took us less time to scour the mountain of information to find the right claims.

During the process of retracing our steps, Angel and McCaskill dropped off their preliminary report on the Baker murder.

"It's crazy out there." Angel handed me the Baker report across my desk. I had stood to greet them when they entered my office. They turned down my offer to have a seat, so I continued to stand. The detectives looked as though they hadn't had much sleep.

"More than usual?" My snide remark put a brief smile on the detective's' sober faces.

"We've set up tip lines to handle the hundreds of calls we're receiving regarding The Butcher."

"Bogus leads and sightings," McCaskill added.

"One person even described the perp in question as an actual butcher wearing a bloody white apron and wielding a meat cleaver." Angel chuckled. McCaskill smirked.

"Did you check it out?" I wasn't kidding. On rare occasions, what may seem to be a loco tip could contain a kernel of truth.

"Of course we did," Angel snapped. "Because we're good detectives and that's what good detectives do."

"She was a real nut job." McCaskill shook her head.

"There's more where she came from," I said.

"The woman believed she was receiving messages from beyond about The Butcher."

"We turned her over to County," Angel said matter-of-factly. "Maybe they can help clear her head."

"It's bad enough we can't get anything on this guy." McCaskill sounded frustrated. "But we've got all sorts of people swearing they've seen him."

"Tensions are running high." Renita walked in on the tail end of McCaskill's declaration. She had been absorbed in her office, reviewing her portion of the claims. The detectives nodded their greeting. Renita settled in beside me. Everyone had on their game faces. I imagined we appeared as much the professional investigative team as McCaskill and Angel.

"We've interviewed over a hundred people with nothing to show for it," Angel remarked, her tone a hint of the mounting frustration of her partner.

"There are armed patrols roaming some of our neighborhoods on the lookout for this maniac." McCaskill's frustration was ratcheting up to irritation. Her eyes lit up like torches. Angel placed a calming hand on her shoulder. The gesture appeared to have the desired effect.

"You're doing all you can," I said, reassuring McCaskill, for what it was worth. Angel dropped her hand to her side. "Times like this bring out the vigilantes looking for any reason to act upon their aggressive impulses."

"Some people will use any excuse to hurt someone," Renita chimed in.

"There's been a few aggravated assault charges brought against people who *claimed* the vic they battered was The Butcher." McCaskill appeared soothed by her own statement, as if the news brought with it some small piece of justice thus far avoided in their major efforts to apprehend a serial killer.

"Those people were wrong and now they're going to pay for their mistakes," Angel said. There was a silent consensus.

By the time the detectives left, they appeared calmer than when they arrived. Venting about The Butcher investigations gave them an opportunity to air their frustrations in a safe, non-judgmental environment. Therapy comes in many shapes and forms. Most of us have to take it where we can find it.

As expected, there were no new leads in the Baker report. For the most part, the report provided us with a few more people to interview.

They were the same people Angel and McCaskill had crossed off their list as viable suspects devoid of any pertinent information that could lead them to Baker's killer.

We didn't share what we were working on with the detectives. We led them to believe that we were going over the insurance records in the desperate hope we might find something that could help. I didn't see any reason to reveal our unsubstantiated theory. I felt it best to let the detectives pursue their course of investigation and we pursue ours. Renita agreed. Angel and McCaskill would know the whole story when the time was right.

Beginning with our previous short list, we found one lethal hunting accident that resulted in death. A surprising sixteen Lunsford life insurance policyholders were killed by hunting accidents under Kylie Preston's watch. Of the sixteen, ten were accidentally shot by other hunters, two accidentally discharged their own weapons, killing themselves, three were inadvertently killed by their drunken hunting companions fooling around, and the last slipped and broke his neck. Based on Kylie Preston's strong recommendations, Lunsford honored none of the claims. In each case, Kylie Preston managed to prove the victims were negligent in some way that resulted in them contributing to their own demise. Half the cases went to court. All claimants lost.

From our list of sixteen, we compiled from their files an inventory of names associated with the deceased. This list became our preliminary suspect pool. We narrowed the suspect pool to twelve, based upon living relatives who would be of adult age. Gathering as much intelligence as we could without alerting our suspect pool, Renita and I were able to build compressed backgrounds on each of them. That was the information we would take to the field.

There was a disturbing matter that we needed to address before proceeding to the field. Based upon what Renita and I had learned about the hunting accidents from the insurance files, there was some distressing conduct we could not ignore. We were apprehensive about how complicit Carl was with Kylie Preston in ripping off those policyholders. We were also troubled with the sanctity of our number one client. Did the top brass at Lunsford know that these types of cutthroat tactics were being employed? If so, did they condone the actions, or choose to look the other way? Our ethics and morality would not allow us to continue working for anyone who instituted such tactics. We needed answers. My partner and I decided to go to the one person who could give us some.

***

I gave Carl Wheaton a call. Carl was very busy, but he agreed to carve out an hour for lunch to meet with us to discuss the Kylie Preston investigation. I didn't mention over the phone our concerns regarding the legitimacy of some of his former mentor's work. That kind of discussion was best had face to face.

Carl's office was in the Lewis and Clark building on the west side of Portland, where Lunsford's main headquarters were housed on the top floors. The Lunsford family owned the building, but they did not exercise the typical corporate vanity of naming it after themselves. Trébol, the restaurant Carl wanted us to meet at, was just around the corner from the Lewis and Clark building. I happened to know it was one of Carl's favorite lunchtime haunts.

Trébol was clean, bright, and festive, with good service and great Mexican food. TV personalities, politicians, entertainment, and business executives frequented Trébol. For that reason, the press core was known to be sniffing around for news. It was not the kind of place you would want to have the sort of conversation we were going to have with Carl. I persuaded Carl to meet us at The Lair. The Lair would provide us with privacy in a controlled atmosphere. An important consideration regarding the sensitive issues we would be discussing surrounding the Preston case.

Renita and I arrived a few minutes early. Renita waited for Carl with Ernest, downstairs at Fullman's Restaurant. I met with Monty Halbrook upstairs in The Lair to ask for his aid in making certain we would not be disturbed or overheard. Monty was cooperative. All was in order by the time Renita came upstairs with Carl.

Monty showed Renita, Carl and I to a reserved dining table. Carl and I had shaken hands and exchanged a few pleasantries before we all sat. Carl looked no different from when we last saw him. The menacing beard had given way to his baby face. This time he was wearing a charcoal three-piece woolen suit.

Monty had given us a table near the back of the dining area far away from the bar. He put "Reserved" signs on the tables surrounding us to prohibit people from being within earshot of our conversation. Monty also turned up the jazz music loud enough to drown out our voices, but not so loud as to become annoying.

Elma Washington was our waitress. Elma was the manager of Fullman's Restaurant. Elma had been with Monty and Ernest for years. She was one of their most valued employees. Being our waitress was a temporary post Elma must have agreed to as a special favor to Monty. Elma could be trusted to honor our privacy and keep her mouth shut if she happened to overhear anything. The sole drawback with having Elma as our server was that the brown-eyed, feisty, five-five, bronze-skinned body builder was in love with Ernest. That meant that she despised Renita for—in her view —stealing her man. It didn't matter that Ernest was never interested in Elma. Once Elma took our food orders and cleared out, we got down to business.

"What have you got for me on Kylie's murder?" Carl asked.

"Before we get to that, Carl," I said. "We need to ask you about the business practices of your former boss."

"What do you mean?"

"During our second round of combing through her list of clients, we found that Kylie Preston employed some questionable tactics."

"That's a very serious charge, C. J." Carl sounded indignant.

Renita jumped in, "It would seem Kylie denied claims that appeared to us to be legit."

"You'd better have evidence to back up dire accusations like that against a stalwart, respected member of the Lunsford Insurance family, not to mention a dear friend." Carl allowed his anger to show.

"Have you ever known us not to have the goods before we presented our case?" I observed Carl for any telltale signs that his ire over the purposed smearing of his beloved company colleague was false. Carl licked his lips and dropped deep into thought for a moment. It appeared to me that Carl was steeling himself for what was to come.

"Present your case," Carl said with the resolve of an accused about to hear charges leveled against him. Renita and I rattled off the names of suspicious unpaid life insurance claims for hunting accidents. Carl said he remembered several of the claims, particularly the ones that went to court. A few of the cases, he handled. With each case we mentioned, Carl's anger dissipated until the near boil became cool, still water.

"I did as I was told in those days," he said, his voice weighted with remorse. "I did whatever it took to win the approval of my superior."

"In this case, you're referring to Kylie Preston," I said.

"Yes. I knew it was wrong to deny those claims. Kylie was obsessed with climbing the executive ladder. She knew that one of the fastest ways to ascend the promotion ladder was by keeping her payouts low while maintaining a high profit margin. Life insurance is typically your biggest payout. Kylie targeted certain high-risk activity life insurance claims to minimize her "kickback to the client" as Kylie called it. Hunting was regarded as one of those high-risk activities."

Renita shook her head with disappointment. "So you admit Kylie Preston defrauded those people."

"Yes," Carl said with shame, his descent from indignant outrage complete. "Kylie could be a cruel and vindictive person to anyone who stood in her way."

"Do you believe anyone in the Lunsford family was aware of what Kylie Preston was doing?" I asked.

"You mean, defrauding customers?"

"Yes," Renita said.

"I doubt it. The Lunsfords rarely concern themselves with details. They kept their eyes on the bottom line."

"What about customer satisfaction? Lunsford has a great reputation for that." Renita knew from where she spoke. Lunsford insured us for that very reason.

"And it's well deserved. We have an independent internal department dedicated to assuring customer satisfaction. It wasn't always that way. Back in mine and Kylie's day, the Lunsford family took the word of their managers and supervisors."

I asked what we were all thinking. "Do you believe the Lunsford family had anything to do with Kylie Preston's murder?"

"At first I held out the slight possibility they might have had something to do with Kylie's death, but not for the reasons you're thinking. If the Lunsfords discovered Kylie had cheated any of their clients, they would have fired her and sought to make restitution to the wronged parties."

Renita and I eyed Carl with curiosity. Carl looked around then leaned forward and lowered his voice. We did the same.

"I was investigating Kylie Preston under orders from the Lunsford family."

"Why?" I asked.

"The Lunsford family had their suspicions that Kylie was in league with the insurance cartels."

"Insurance cartels?" Renita quizzed.

"They're groups of insurance companies that dominate the private insurance market. They're strictly profit driven. The Lunsford family despises them. They believe they give insurance a bad name because the cartels will do anything to fatten their bottom line, frequently at the expense of inadequate support for their most vulnerable carriers. Lunsford is one of the few private independent insurance companies that can still compete with the insurance cartels while still offering their clients the best in financial protection. Lunsford dominates the northwest market and has made strong headway into Idaho, Nevada and Northern California. If the insurance cartel were to gain control of Lunsford, they would control those territories and could bilk Lunsford clients in the same way they do their own."

I nodded in agreement with the Lunsford family thinking. "Did you find their suspicions warranted?" I asked.

"They were much more than suspicions. The insurance cartels had been after Lunsford to join them for years. When that didn't work, they tried buying Lunsford out, which turned out to be another dead end. As can be typical in big business, if you can't buy or run your competitors out of business, seek to destroy them from the inside. Kylie was that weak link. As President of Acquisitions, Kylie had a great deal of power to do serious damage to Lunsford's financial standing. A few bad investments could put Lunsford in the red in a hurry."

"Why not just fire her?" Renita asked. "Or at least move her into a position where she couldn't do any harm?"

"Without probable cause, that would make for a very ugly public lawsuit. That means bad press and everything that goes along with it. We needed to catch Kylie with her hand in the cookie jar, so to speak." Renita nodded that she understood. Carl continued. "Kylie always had green fever. She had been clandestinely meeting with heads of the three largest health care insurance providers in the nation. I reported to the Lunsfords about what I had uncovered. They ordered me to maintain heavy surveillance on her."

"Did that include bugging her home and office?" I said, knowing that to be standard procedure.

Carl nodded. "I also had a couple of office insiders keeping a close eye on Kylie; one of which was her personal assistant."

"What did you find?" Renita asked.

"Kylie was planning to set Lunsford up for a hostile takeover by one of the major insurance cartels." Carl sounded disappointed.

Renita asked, "Which one?"

"The highest bidder. From what we discovered, the bidding war for Kylie's services was still in progress. We already knew Kylie had a secret meeting scheduled the day after her death with an agent representing one of the cartels. I had one of my people keeping an eye on Kylie at the restaurant that night to make certain the meeting didn't happen sooner. Once she confirmed that Kylie was simply having a girl's night out, I called her off."

Carl dropped his eyes toward the table. I knew what he was thinking. If he had kept his agent on Kylie Preston, she might still be alive. While I could sympathize with Carl, I was more upset about the shafting of people who trusted him and Kylie Preston to do right by them.

"I feel bad about what happened to those people whose claims were wrongfully denied," Carl said, as if reading my mind. From the look in his eyes and his pitiful expression, Carl's apology seemed honest and sincere.

"I can't believe you were one of those greedy bastards," Renita blurted out. Carl looked away in shame. Although I felt the same as Renita about Carl at that moment, I managed to keep a handle on my emotions. Remaining focused on what would be best for our ongoing investigation was what was necessary.

"I was supposed to deliver the bad news of denying a life insurance claim to Allison Kern, the widow of Gary Kern, at his wake," Carl said, still looking away as if watching the memory play out before him. "I suggested to Kylie that I should wait for a more appropriate time. Kylie said the sooner the better. 'What better time to drop the bomb than when the widow is most vulnerable to accept our decision,' Kylie said. I knew refusing her claim was bogus."

"How could you be certain?" I asked.

"I looked into the circumstances of Gary Kern's death." Carl returned his gaze to us. "Back then, it was common for insurance people to be jacks of all trades when it came to their clients. From everything I found, the claim was legit."

Renita and I nodded our affirmation. Carl continued.

"When I said I wouldn't do it, Kylie threatened to reassign my case to someone who was more dedicated. Kylie salted the threat by assuring me she would note my insubordination in my personnel file. I was still trying to get my footing in the company. Kylie had been my biggest supporter. I caved.

"When I arrived at the wake and saw the grieving family, I was somehow able to maintain a callous attitude to follow through on what Kylie had convinced me was necessary. When I look back on that moment, I ask myself: How could I add to their suffering?" Carl shook his head as a baseball pitcher shaking off his catcher's pitch sign.

"I almost lost my soul that day," Carl said, as much to himself as he did to us. "I was just about to deliver the terrible news to the widow when her little boy interrupted us. He needed to use the bathroom. Allison asked if I would take him for her. I, of course, was glad to do so. By the time I returned her son to his mom, there was no way I could be a part of ripping Allison Kern off."

"How old was Allison's son?" I asked.

"Six," Carl said. "I remember because I asked him."

There was an uneasy silence. None of us wanted to voice what we were thinking. Dixieland jazz filled the void.

"What was his name?" I asked.

"You don't think that child...?" Carl could not finish his thought.

"He's a man now, Carl," I said. "What's his name?"

"Reginald, but he said everyone called him Reggie."

"Reginald Kern," I said, nodding.

"He's on our list of people to interview," Renita added.

"If he's doing these horrible killings, then it's all my fault."

"Whoever's doing this is disturbed and needs help," I said. "His actions are his own."

"I planted the seed."

"What you did, didn't help, that's for sure." I gave Renita a stern glance to let her know her comment was cruel and unnecessary. Renita stared back at me as if to say 'tough.' Carl stared toward the bar. His face and eyes shared his shame. That moment in profile was the most humble I had ever seen Carl. His unflappable self-assurance appeared a thing of the past.

"There's more," Carl said.

"You mean it gets worse?" Renita said.

"A few days after the funeral, Allison Kern came to me, pleading for my help in an effort to obtain the settlement her family deserved. By that time, Gary Kern's policy had been taken from me and given to a shark in our office whose lone concern was profit."

"A precursor to the cartel mentality," I said.

"Yes. There was nothing I could do."

"Doing nothing," Renita said, "is not the same as being incapable of doing something."

"If anyone planted the seed, as you said, it was Kylie Preston and not you," I said to Carl. "In any event, the person responsible for murdering and butchering those people is the killer; no one else."

"When I returned with her son from the bathroom," Carl leveled his eyes on us, "the widow asked me when she could expect to receive her husband's life insurance settlement. I had sold Gary Kern his life insurance policy with the promise it would give his family financial security in the event of his death. Like a coward, I told Allison that someone would be in touch soon, and then I hightailed it out of there like a bat out of hell. That moment changed me. It made me realize what kind of man I am. After my experience with the Kern family, I got on the straight and narrow and have never, *ever*, swindled another client since."

"How noble," Renita scoffed.

"What do you want from me? There's not a day that goes by that I don't regret what I did."

"You had a choice. You could have said no to Kylie Preston and done the right thing by the Kerns."

"Weren't you listening? I did say no. I told Kylie as soon as I returned to the office that I wasn't going to do it. Kylie shrugged me off, told me 'suit yourself,' and handed the Kern case off to another representative. That person did what Kylie wanted. There wasn't a person in that office that didn't do what Kylie wanted, including me. In the end, the Kerns got screwed."

"Was there a trial?" Renita asked.

"Yes." Carl whispered.

"Did you testify on behalf of the Kerns about what you knew?" Carl looked away. "In a way, you still did what Kylie Preston wanted by standing by and watching her rake another client over the coals." Renita paused for a heated moment. Neither Carl nor I knew what to say.

"I can't tell you how disappointed I am in you, Carl." Her anger dissipated to discontent.

"When I look back on that time, I can't tell you how disappointed I am in myself."

"Through your sins, you found redemption."

"Something like that, C. J."

"Better late than never, I guess," Renita said.

"Better late than not at all," I said. I had to confess that while I was disappointed with Carl, I wasn't shocked. People make mistakes. Even the ones you consider friends. I knew I would forgive Carl a lot sooner than Renita. Renita still hadn't made enough major mistakes in her life to culture pools of absolution.

"There was another issue regarding Kylie and myself," Carl said. "Kylie was not only my boss...she was my lover. I believed we were going to get married someday. The better I got to know Kylie, let's just say, the less desirable that life became." Renita and I nodded in both compliance to Carl and in confirmation of what we had already suspected. "The truth is, I never stopped loving Kylie."

There was a nagging question Renita and I had about the Kylie Preston files information that we had received from Carl on this case, that had to be asked. "Did you plant the information we found about the Lunsford and Kylie Preston situation?" I said.

"Any information of that sort that found its way into your hands was an oversight by me and my staff," Carl said, as if testifying from a witness stand. That was an off-the-record yes; one inherent with plausible deniability.

"You had an ongoing affair with Kylie Preston?" Renita stated, changing gears.

"Yes."

"That your wife knows about?"

"Yes, she's known for some time."

"And Kylie's husband?" I asked, in an attempt to get the questioning back on proper footing.

"Unless Kylie told him, I don't know how he could have known, although he suspected as much. You don't think Nick had anything to do with Kylie's murder?"

"No. He doesn't have the skill, education or training to do what has been done to those murder victims. According to the ME, there was no evidence that the killer had any ill will toward the victims while he operated. It was all done in a very neat, clinical, and rather detached manner."

"None of those qualities define Nick," Carl said.

"And that's part of what makes these cases so troubling—besides the obvious," Renita said.

"I don't follow," Carl said.

"Are these cases related, or random?" I speculated. "If they are related, how; if they're not related, then how is the killer choosing his victims?"

"How far along are you on these murder investigations?"

"Investigations," Renita said. "You mean investigation."

"C'mon, Renita, I'm not a fool," Carl responded, his confidence returning. "I know my hiring you to find Kylie's murderer may have been your initial reason for becoming entangled in this mess, but I also know your lumping them together will accomplish the same goal."

I eyed Renita. Renita eyed me. We both looked back at Carl, who was eyeing the both of us, waiting for a response. He had us, and Renita and I knew it.

"We have a couple of theories not worth discussing that we're pursuing," I said.

"I get the feeling this meeting was more about me than Kylie's murder investigation."

I said, "It was both. Is there anything specific you remember about the cheated people involved in those hunting accident cases that still stands out in your mind?"

"You mean, besides what I've told you already about the Kerns?"

"Yes, but anything more about the Kerns, as well," I said.

Our food arrived as Carl pondered my question. Carl shared some details about each of the cases that did not amount to much. I mentally added what little new information Carl gave us to what we already had amassed. Renita and I decided to share our theories with Carl regarding the person of interest. The three of us speculated about the killer's motives as we ate.

I thanked Monty for his help with a generous payment that I gave to him behind closed doors in his office. Monty would settle with Elma in due course. The payment assured me that Monty and Elma would remain silent on the matter. By the time Carl, Renita and I parted company,

Renita and I believed we had discovered a possible motivation and person connected to Kylie Preston's murder.

There was another element to be factored into our analysis that we touched upon during our lunch. What was the connection between the three victims? From what we had learned, there was none. They didn't even know each other, from what we could tell. Did that make the murders random? Did they have some sort of connection with the killer? Due to the specific nature of each murder, I was leaning toward the idea that they had a connection with the killer. Revenge was at the top of my list of reasons. On that point, I was with the majority of people involved in The Butcher murder investigations. Like everyone else, nailing down the motivation had eluded us. Renita and I were hoping our conversations with Allison and Reginald Kern would prove fruitful in that area.

CHAPTER SIXTY

Renita and I wasted no time following up on our best lead since The Butcher murders had begun. Allison Hawkins, formerly the widow Allison Kern, had been easy to track down. We found street parking about half a block from her North Buffalo Street home in North Portland. Renita had asked to take the lead on Allison's interview because Renita felt she needed the practice. I understood. The Butcher investigation was all we had been working on for some time. Renita had been tagging along with me for all of our interviews as a part of her grooming process on how to conduct a proper murder investigation. Renita felt she was ready to take the reins for a change. I saw no reason why she couldn't.

Renita and I recapped what we had discussed about interviewing Allison Hawkins as we approached her white stucco house in her working-class, clean, quiet neighborhood on a clear, warm, sunny day.

"Remember what I said. Lock in on her telltale signs as quickly as possible. Try to get a feel for when she's lying or telling the truth. Gauge what makes her uncomfortable and then steer the conversation in that direction."

"Got it," Renita said.

"Always look to stay on point. We're here to uncover facts, not for a social call."

"I understand."

"Just relax and you'll be fine."

"I *am* relaxed; enough already."

Renita was right. I was the one who was nervous. Renita had done a number of personal interviews for a variety of non-lethal cases we had worked. For some reason, her going toe-to-toe with a possible murderer put me on edge. Not because I didn't believe Renita couldn't do it. My concern revolved around the possibility of Allison Hawkins getting out of control. That sort of episode could turn on a dime. Renita could defend herself just fine. It's a lot easier defending yourself against an irate insurance fraud than it is a deranged killer or their possible accomplice. I was confident that I could stop Allison Hawkins or anyone else, if it came to that. I didn't want to see my friend injured in the process.

We walked up onto the shaded front porch. The front door was open. The screen door closed. We weren't surprised to find Allison at home, since she worked the hospital night shift. I stood behind the right shoulder of my partner as she rang the doorbell. Being more than a head taller, I loomed over Renita like a protective shadow. We positioned ourselves to be both visible and as non-threatening as possible. A portly woman of average height sauntered to the door. Her face was pleasant and her clear blue eyes were serene. She was wearing a red and white striped V-neck Tee shirt that revealed a Jesus of Nazarene cross tattoo on her upper right arm and praying hands with a rosary tattoo on her upper left arm. Judging by the quality of the work, it appeared to have been inked in the free world.

"Hello," she said, "may I help you?"

"Allison Hawkins?" Renita said.

"I'm Allison Hawkins." Allison ran her manicured fingers through her short, grayish-blonde hair. Allison had the character lines of a fifty-something woman who had gone a few rounds with life.

"I'm Private Investigator Renita Harris and this is my partner, C. J. Cavanaugh."

"How are you?" I said. Allison responded with a curt nod. We showed Allison our IDs. She took a moment to examine them before she spoke.

"What are you investigating?"

"Your first husband's death," Renita said. The pleasantness drained from Allison's face. She appeared as if a weight had dragged her soul back down into the depths of despair.

"What about it?"

"We're looking into the life insurance policy your husband had with Lunsford Insurance," Renita said. "We believe that you and a group of other Lunsford life insurance policy holders were wrongly denied monetary settlements."

"Are you saying you're after Gary's life insurance money?" Allison said, reclaiming her peace.

"Yes, ma'am." Renita was telling Allison Hawkins the truth. After our meeting with Carl, Renita and I had already decided to do what we could to help those hunting accident victims get what they deserved from Lunsford Insurance.

"I no longer have the policy. I threw it away some time ago."

"That's not necessary. We were able to find a copy."

"Well, I'll be. The Lord does work in mysterious ways."

"May we come in? There are a few questions we need to ask you about your late husband."

"*Come in, come in.*" Allison unlocked her screen door and allowed us inside. The curtains were open, filling the house with the golden glow of sunshine. Her home was tidy and comfortable. There was nothing extravagant, but nothing appeared cheap. Family photos abounded, along with a framed color print of an Anglo Christ that hung above the living room mantel.

"Won't you have a seat?" Allison offered us seats in the living room. We sat on a couch at a right angle to a pair of matching reading chairs separated by a dainty table.

"Can I get you anything to drink?" Allison asked with a warm smile.

"No, thank you," Renita said.

"I'm fine, thanks."

Allison took a seat in the reading chair closest to us. "How can I help?"

"We need some details surrounding the death of your husband, for starters," Renita said. "The insurance report said he died from a hunting accident."

"That's right, Gary went hunting with friends. They were out tracking deer when Gary was accidentally shot and killed by another hunter who was shooting at a deer and missed."

"Lunsford disagreed with that assessment."

"Not as much disagreed as they redirected culpability. They blamed Gary for getting shot."

"How so?" I asked, even though I already knew the answer. It was important for me to interject something every now and then. Otherwise, Allison could become uncomfortable with someone sitting there just staring at her.

"They said Gary wasn't wearing the proper safety gear. Lundsford claimed it was due to Gary's own neglect that the other hunter didn't see him, and that resulted in Gary being shot."

"You took Lunsford to court over the matter?" Renita asked.

"I did, and lost. The hunter who shot Gary agreed with their story. He testified on behalf of Lunsford to that effect."

The man who shot Gary Kern sounded like a real coward. He had probably cut some kind of deal with Kylie Preston to lighten the charges against him. "Do you recall what sentence the man received who killed your husband?" I asked.

"He had one of the best defense attorneys in town," Allison said with dismay. "I found that odd for an out-of-work electrician. Add to that, Kylie Preston testified on his behalf. He was convicted of involuntary manslaughter and sentenced to three to five years. The last I heard, he got out in three, for good behavior, with a job waiting for him to boot."

That clinched it. The man who killed Gary Kern should have been convicted of no less than ten years for what he had done. He had obviously cut a deal. I was tempted to ask Allison more questions on the matter, but thought better of it. We had peeled back that scab far enough.

"We've reviewed the case and found the ruling against you unfair, in our opinion," Renita said.

"It came down to who the jury believed," Allison said. "Kylie Preston was a better liar than I was a truth-teller."

Here was the tricky part: transitioning from the death of her husband to what Allison and her son had been up to since. Renita and I had come bearing a lot of information from her background check. We were looking for both confirmations from Allison and clues that might lead us to The Butcher.

"Did you resent Kylie Preston for what she had done?" Renita asked.

"Of course. Are you sure this is about my husband's life insurance policy and not the horrible death of that woman?"

Renita had asked the Kylie Preston question too soon. Renita was losing her edge. Her candor was inappropriate and Allison was reacting badly to it. This situation required finesse. Renita was not utilizing her instincts. She wasn't picking up on the telltale clues of human behavior. I needed to step in before we lost her.

"What did you do after the unfortunate outcome of your lawsuit?" I asked.

Allison sighed. "I went into a funk for a while. I loved Gary. I loved Gary a lot. With him gone and me becoming a single mom with no other skills other than being a homemaker, I was pressed on how to take care of my family. Thank goodness for my mom."

"Your mom helped out?" I said.

"Yes, God bless her. She's gone now, but when she saw how upset I was, she insisted that me and Reggie move in with her."

"Reggie?" I knew to whom Allison was referring.

"My eldest son," Allison said with pride. "His name is Reginald, but everyone calls him Reggie."

"He was young when it happened?" I said.

"He was just a boy, but he was a trooper. If it hadn't been for him and my mom, I doubt I would have made it."

Allison slipped into a state of remembrance. With little prodding from us, she confirmed a great deal of what we already knew about her personal history, adding insightful information regarding her severe bouts of depression and multiple contemplations of suicide. After her unsuccessful bid to win her husband's rightful life insurance claim from Lunsford Insurance, Allison and Reggie moved in with her mother, who lived in Santa Rosa, California. Allison fell in with the wrong crowd in Santa Rosa. Three years after Allison moved in with her mom, she was busted for selling marijuana.

Her mom and Reggie never lost faith in Allison. They stayed in constant contact, doing whatever they could to keep Allison's spirits high and to make certain she was reminded of how much they loved her. In prison, Allison found religion. Christianity gave her life purpose. Allison abandoned that which had caused her incarceration and vowed to change her life for the better, once released; a promise she had maintained.

After her short stint in a California state prison, Allison got her life on track. She went to school to become a nurse's aide. Allison found related work at a community hospital in Santa Rosa. She loved the work and the people. Everything was going well until her mom died.

Gary's family never liked Allison; not even enough to care about his son. They blamed Allison for ruining Gary's life with an unwanted pregnancy that somehow led to his sudden death. Allison was left with one living relative who still cared about her, a maternal cousin who lived in Salem, Oregon. Upon urging from her cousin, Allison sold her mom's house and moved in with them.

"How's Reggie doing?" I asked. Reginald Kern was our person of interest. If we were fortunate, we could gain some knowledge into his current state of mind from his mother.

"He's doing quite well," Allison said with pride. "He's a funeral director. While I admit it's not something I would have wished for him, it seems to fit him to a tee."

"It must have been difficult for a boy without his father?" Renita said, catching on.

"There were some rough patches along the way, but we managed. Cecil has been as much a father to Reggie as Gary was."

"You had to be angry about what Kylie Preston did," Renita said. I internally winced. That question was too direct. I could see suspicion creeping back into Allison's eyes.

"I know I would have," I said, trying to lighten the mood. It seemed to allay Allison's suspicions for the moment.

"Of course I was angry, at first. Once I found Jesus Christ, all was forgiven."

"Is your entire family born again?" I asked.

"Just me and Reggie, at the moment. I'm working on the rest. My husband, Cecil, is hanging on to his Catholic roots. My two teenagers, Jenny and Walter, are undecided about what faith to follow, if any at all. My daughter's given name is Jennifer, after my mom, but everyone calls her Jenny."

The mere thought of her teenagers made Allison perk up.

"Jenny's turned into a wonderful young lady," Allison said with pride. "She wants to be a doctor so she can help people. Walter is my youngest, but everyone calls him Walt because he prefers it. He's still finding his way in life. There's no rush. He has time. We don't believe in forcing our children to follow in our religious footsteps. Give them the information and let them decide, I always say. I can't deny I keep praying that someday they will allow Jesus Christ into their hearts."

"I'm sure one day your prayers will be answered," I said.

"From your lips to God's ears," Allison smiled.

"I have to say," I said. "If I was screwed over—forgive my language."

"No problem," Allison said with a forgiving wave of her hand. "I've heard a lot worse."

"If my dad died and someone hurt my mom by lying, I would be very upset."

"When Reggie was a teenager, he was bitter about the whole thing," Allison said, as if by agreeing with me she was justifying her son's love for her. "It didn't help that my second marriage was to an abusive man. The only good thing that came out of that marriage was my daughter Jenny."

"That had to be rough," Renita said.

"At times it was brutal. My second husband, Joe, was a janitor at the hospital where I worked. We hit it off pretty well, dated for a while, and got married. I didn't know Joe was an alcoholic before we were married. His drinking wasn't something I paid much attention to, to be honest."

"Most people wouldn't," I said. "When you're dating, it's all a part of the fun and games."

"*Exactly*. About a year after I had Jenny, I learned the hard way. That was when the hitting started. My second husband was a mean alcoholic. Mostly he was verbally abusive. In public, he was a fun-loving guy who got along with everyone. At home, he started wanting to hit something. Most times, that something was me."

"Why didn't you leave him?" Renita asked.

"I was trying to keep our family together. To give my daughter a chance that Reggie didn't have, to have her father around as she grew up. I wanted to try and make it work for Jenny's sake."

"Did Joe ever hit Reggie?" I asked.

"*Heavens, no*. He knew that if he ever touched Reggie, I'd kill him."

Renita and I nodded our understanding.

"I stopped Reggie from shooting Joe when that sick man was hitting me one time for having made his dinner too hot."

"*Oh no*," I said with emphasis, to let Allison know I was sympathetic to her and Reggie's plight.

"Oh yes," Allison said, nodding.

"Where did Reggie get the gun?" I asked.

"From Joe's gun collection. Reggie was trying to protect his mom. I convinced him to pray with me instead. That was when I knew it was time to leave Joe for the sake of my son."

My compassion for Allison was genuine. I could only imagine how she must have suffered, trying to make an abusive marriage work while looking out for the welfare of her children. It's been my experience that most people aren't good at heart. They're good when it's convenient. Allison Hawkins was an exception to that rule.

"Reggie's all better now?" I asked.

"Much. Once I divorced Joe, our lives settled down."

"Thank goodness," Renita said. Judging by my partner's expression and body language, she was caught up in the drama and had—at least momentarily—lost focus on why we were there.

"Amen," Allison said. "My Reggie can have a temper, on occasion, but all in all he's a good man."

"After what the two of you have been through, who could blame him?" Renita said.

"Exactly," Allison said.

"We've taken up enough of your time," I said before Renita could ask another question.

"Oh!" Allison appeared startled by my sudden termination of our conversation.

"We'll let you know as soon as we have something regarding Gary Kern's life insurance settlement," I said. Renita and I gave Allison one of our business cards.

"If you think of anything else that might be helpful to Gary's case," I said, "please don't hesitate to give us a call."

"I will."

Allison Hawkins escorted us out of her charming home. She had braved tempests in the high seas of life and discovered serenity in a world peppered with pain. I would hate to have to destroy that tranquility by bringing her Reggie up on murder charges.

"How'd I do?" Renita asked as we walked back to my car.

"Not bad." The lecture on how Renita could improve her interviewing methods could wait for another time.

CHAPTER SIXTY-ONE

Holland's Chapel in southeast Portland was a two-story Flemish brick building that may have once been part of a modest estate. The inviting portico entrance and unique combination of casement and church windows gave the place a homey, almost spiritual, feel, lending no portents of what occurred inside. The closer you looked, the less your initial impression held up. Thick black drapes obstructed every window. Near the south side of the building, you could catch the sallow glint of headstones propped against the wall. The brass plaque mounted to the right of the front entrance and embossed with the chapel name could have belonged to a museum or a historic monument.

I had asked Renita about how she felt about funeral homes. Renita said they didn't bother her. If Renita had told me she wasn't up to it, I would have understood. I checked her reaction as I opened the door and allowed Renita to enter before me. There was no sign that Renita wasn't telling the truth. I suppose that after seeing the remains of Brian Dixon, visiting a funeral home had become a walk in the park.

We stepped into the entrance hall. A visitor's book was open on a console table off to our right. Next to it stood a barrel-chested, debonair-looking man dressed in a black suit.

"May I help you?" the man asked in a bass voice scarcely above a whisper.

"Yes," I said. "We're here to see the director."

"Do you have an appointment?"

"No, we don't. But he's expecting us."

I had telephoned ahead to see if Reginald Kern would have time to speak with us regarding a matter involving his father's life insurance. He said that he would. The man eyed us for a moment. "Mr. Kern is in the embalming room. He doesn't like to be disturbed during the cleansing process. Can this wait for another time?"

"I'm afraid not. It may be a matter of life and death." The man eyed us as if he didn't believe me.

"Wait right here. I'll check to see if the director's available. Your name is?"

"I'm Cavanaugh and this is my associate, Renita Harris." The man nodded and left.

We waited in silence as we looked around from where we stood. To move from the place the barrel-chested man had ordered would have seemed sacrilegious. Much of the interior was standard for a funeral home. There were velvet drapes, dark wood, muted lighting, and soft melodic hymns wafting in the background. Serenity was its theme, and it played out well. Off to the left was an open casket on a waist-high bier. A few rows of wooden folding chairs were set before it. The lid's shiny underbelly was upholstered in white satin. I could just make out the ill-fated occupant. He was an elderly man made to look as though he were asleep. I looked at Renita. She looked at me. The sight of the deceased made her sad.

In a few minutes Reginald Kern appeared, although it seemed as though it took longer. The debonair man accompanied him. Even as they walked toward us in lockstep, two abreast, there was no doubt Reggie was in charge. Reggie was taller than his counterpart, with broad shoulders and short dark blond hair. He, too, was well groomed and dressed in a black suit that appeared to be crafted by the same tailor.

"Mr. Cavanaugh," Reginald Kern said as we shook hands. "And you must be Ms. Harris."

"I am," Renita said as she and Reggie shook hands. He had his mother's eyes. Reggie addressed us in the hushed tone of someone who was accustomed to dealing with bereaved. He had the gasoline smell of embalming fluid drifting off his person, an occupational hazard for some, I'm told.

"Do you mind if we conduct this meeting in my office?"

"Not at all," I said.

Reggie led the way. The barrel-chested man returned to his post beside the console table.

Reggie's office was a study in order. Everything was in its place and everything had a place. On his desk were framed photographs of Gary and Allison Kern, his mother and Cecil, his maternal grandmother, his sister Jenny and brother, Walt, his wife (who we knew to be Stephanie), and their girls Kayla and Denise. Reggie offered us a chair. We accepted.

"You said you wanted to talk to me about my father."

"Yes," I said. "What do you remember about his passing?"

"Not much. I was only five years old when it happened."

"Do you recall how your mother reacted to your dad's death?" Renita asked.

"Hard; very hard. Mom believed she and Dad were soulmates. When he died, a big part of her died with him. I don't understand why you're asking me these questions about my mother if this is about Dad's insurance?"

"To tell the truth, we're looking into some cold Lunsford Insurance cases where we believe the clients didn't get a fair shake," I said. "Your family, we feel, was one of them."

"And you're doing this why?"

"As part of our pro bono work. It's one of our ways of giving back to the community."

I was winging it. Reggie shrugged off my explanation. Whether he believed us or not didn't seem to matter.

"Lunsford; now there's a name that still gets my dander up. It was bad enough my mother had her heart ripped from her chest when my father died. But to compound it by not paying what they owed us from his life insurance policy; that was cruel."

"I can imagine," Renita said, spurring Reggie on.

"How could they, in all good conscience, do something like that?"

"That's what we're trying to find out," I said. "How did your mom take it?"

"At first she was angry. We took them to court, as you probably already know."

Renita and I nodded.

"That didn't work out. The court ruled in favor of the insurance company that my father was at fault for accidentally dying," Reggie sarcastically said. "After Mom lost the court case, she became a zombie. She'd go through the motions of living, but her spirit was gone. Thank God for my grandma."

"What makes you say that?" I said.

"She made my mom move back home with her. It took some time, but my grandmother was able to breathe life back into my mother."

"So your mom was okay after that?" I asked, preferring Reggie to corroborate what we believed we knew.

"Yes and no. Mom started running with people who were not looking out for her best interest, let's just say. She became involved in drugs. My grandmother tried to stop her, but she couldn't. One day my mom was busted dealing pot. While she did her time, my grandmother took care of me."

"When your mom got out of prison," I said, "did she seem changed, to you?"

"Of course. Mom told me, when we visited or she wrote, that she was going to have to become hard, to survive. Not long after she got out, she went back to being the sweet, caring mom I knew and loved."

"She's doing alright for herself, these days," Renita said with a smile.

"Yeah," Reggie said, smiling back. "Mom said prison taught her a lot about life. She found religion and a purpose. When she got out, she knew she wanted to do something to help people. Since she was a felon, being a nurse or a doctor seemed out of the question. Being a nurse's aide was still within reach, so she went for it."

"Does your mom harbor any sort of resentment for Lunsford Insurance for what they did?" I asked.

"None that I know of. Mom has moved on."

"What about you, Reggie?" I asked. "How do you feel about how your family was treated?"

"We got a raw deal, no doubt about it. As long as my mom is okay, then I'm okay."

I had kept a close eye on Reggie during our conversation. At no time did I get a sense he wasn't being forthright and sincere. I believed Reggie in the same way I believed his mother.

"Thank you for your time, Mr. Kern," I said as I stood and Renita followed.

"We're sorry to have bothered you," Renita said. I could tell that Renita's compassion had welled up inside of her for Reggie's fate. She felt what I felt: that he and his mom had done a great job of moving past events that would have ruined lesser people.

"Not a problem." Reggie handed us each a business card. "You never know when you might need our services. I pray it's a long time before you do."

"Thank you," Renita and I said as we handed Reggie one of our business cards. Reggie Kern courteously escorted us from his office to the front entrance. The family and friends of the deceased on view had arrived. There was whimpering and soft words amongst the solemn gathering. The debonair man stood nearby, unobtrusively observing the affair; ready to serve whatever needs might arise. We shook hands with Reggie at the front entrance.

"Go in peace," Reggie said with his hands in the prayer position at his chest. Reggie joined the grieved. Renita and I watched the gathering for a moment longer before we silently exited.

When we left Reggie Kern, I had cooled on the possibility that he was The Butcher. I was convinced Reggie was a man who was at peace with himself and the circumstances of his life. I knew Carl would be relieved to hear that. As for Renita and me, we were left fishing in our shallow suspect pool.

CHAPTER SIXTY-TWO

The Butcher opened a sliding mirrored glass door to his walk-in bedroom closet. He stepped inside. To his immediate right was a tier of five L-bracketed red birch ply shelves mounted into the white plaster wall, which he had installed himself. On the shelves was his unimpressive collection of shoes, caps, and hats. Throughout the rest of his bedroom closet hung his equally-unimpressive wardrobe. The Butcher removed a small skeleton key from beneath his Portland Winter Hawks cap and pocketed it. He firmly pressed the left side of the top shelf. There was a dull click made from the release of a magnetic lock. The Butcher swung open the blindly-hinged wall like a door. Behind the wall was a crawlspace of equal height and width of the shelves. The Butcher removed a wooden chest from inside. He carried the chest over to his queen-size bed. He placed the chest in the ribbon of sunlight that cut across the crisply made floral bedspread.

The Butcher sat next to the wooden chest and eyed it. The chest had been handmade by his father. His father did so in response to his wife's complaints about their son leaving his toys, books, and such scattered around, making the house a mess. His dad made a deal with his son. If he were to make him a chest, would he pick up his things and keep them in it? The Butcher agreed to do so. His father kept his end of the bargain.

He remembered watching as his dad explained to him each step in the process of assembling the wooden chest, in the cramped space of a small workshop that was not much bigger than a tool shed out behind the house. His father made the chest out of cedar stained with black walnut. In answer to his son's wishes, he made it to resemble a pirate treasure chest complete with a domed lid, brass-buckled black leather straps, black leather handles, and a black iron hasp. His father held onto the steel padlock and key he had purchased for the chest. His dad told him he would give him the lock and key when his son proved himself responsible enough not to lose the key. His dad didn't live long enough for his son to demonstrate himself worthy.

The Butcher ran his hands over the handmade chest as if it were the body of a desirable woman. He fingered the brass plate engraved with his first and last name on the crest of the lid of the chest. With a heavy sigh, The Butcher unlocked the chest and opened it for what must have been the hundredth time. Inside was a variety of precious mementoes, meticulously arranged in the red felt-lined chest. He reminisced over color and black-and-white photos of him as a child, his mom, and his dad. He reread letters that he had memorized sent to him by his parents when he was away at summer camps. There was no evidence of any other family in his life because there had been none. His mom grew up in an orphanage. His dad lost his father in the coal mines when he was seven and his mother from cancer when he was fourteen. His father never made mention of any grandparents, aunts, uncles or cousins. His dad's philosophy was they had each other, and that was all they needed.

Along with the treasures of the chest lurked a few dark memories. One was an old life insurance policy for his father. Another was a letter addressed to his mother from Lunsford Insurance. The letter opened by offering his mother their sincere condolences for her loss. The letter went on to say that based upon careful, unbiased consideration, it was determined that his father was responsible for his own death. An in-depth investigation had revealed that his father was not wearing proper safety clothing at the time of his shooting. That constituted negligence on his father's part, according to Lunsford. For that reason, they said, "Our life insurance policy states that if the insured is deemed at fault for their own demise, then the company is released from any liability. We therefore cannot, in all good conscience, honor your claim. We regret having to give you this news. If we can be of any service, please do not hesitate to contact us."

It was distressing enough that his mother had lost the love of her life. To take away dire financial support during their time of crisis was inexcusable. Even though his mom fought back as best she could, in the end even the justice system did not deliver on its promise. The letter closed with "Deepest Regrets, Carl Wheaton."

The Butcher went on to read the court's decision that had sided with Lunsford insurance. Carl Wheaton had been a lucky man. During the trail, it was disclosed that Kylie Preston had sent the letter to his mom. She had "mistakenly" (as Kylie Preston put it during her testimony) used Carl Wheaton's name in the closing. Had that not been the case, the police would have discovered Carl Wheaton's remains wrapped in brown butcher's paper; not Kylie Preston's.

Viewing the contents of the chest renewed his purpose. His family had suffered a great deal. It was not often that someone could point to specific individuals in their life and determine they were the cause of most of their troubles. Three of those people had been made to pay. When all were eliminated, then he would stop. Redemption was near. The Butcher had given a great deal of thought about his next quarry. All of his previous plans had worked to perfection. He expected no less from the next. It was time to hunt and trap his subsequent deserving prey.

The Butcher completed his stroll down memory lane and reverently returned all of his mementoes to the pirate chest. He locked the chest, then solemnly returned the chest to its hidden cubbyhole and secured the secret door. The Butcher returned the key beneath the Portland Winter Hawks cap, closed the mirrored closet door, and set out to put his next plan in motion.

CHAPTER SIXTY-THREE

Renita and I dragged ourselves back into the office after interviewing Reggie Kern. Our prime suspect was a bust. After having met Reggie, I could honestly say I was pleased about that. Renita and I were in my office, deciding in what order we would interview our evaporating suspect pool, when my phone rang.

"*Guess what?*" Destini said before I could finish identifying myself. Destini sounded elated. Renita left to give me some privacy once she knew I was speaking to Destini, a new courtesy Renita had developed since the Brian Dixon incident.

"The Charles River isn't named after Charles," I sarcastically answered.

"Then who is it named for?"

"Bernie."

"Ha, ha. We're going out to dinner tonight."

"Thanks for asking; I love it when you go all cave woman on me."

"We're having dinner with Dave and his new girlfriend."

"Yippee, I'll make sure to wear my good suit."

"Wear that white Versace cotton blazer I got for you with your lavender and white striped shirt and a faded pair of relaxed, straight leg, medium-blue jeans. It'll match what I'm going to wear—no tie. This'll be an informal affair."

"Yes, dear." I was impressed with how well Destini knew my wardrobe.

"I love it when you get all whipped man-friend on me."

"Does that mean you'll marry me?" It was a slip that made for silence in our otherwise-jaunty conversation.

"Are you ready to accept what I do for a living?" Again, silence.

"You can't tell me you're not as excited as I am about this development," Destini said, allowing the awkward moment to pass and getting the conversation back on course.

"Yes, I can. I'm not as excited about this as you are."

"Aw, c'mon: this is our chance to meet the mystery woman."

"That's nice."

"You know you're as curious about her as I am."

"No, I'm not. I assumed Dave would introduce us when he was ready."

"Well, he's ready."

"Why do I get the feeling you pressured him into this?"

"Whatever do you mean?" Destini said sarcastically. "I would never do such a thing."

"Yeah, you would," I said, playing along. "When and where do we meet this mystery woman?"

"Jimmy Mak's, seven o'clock; pick me up at six-thirty."

"So much for liberation."

"You didn't think I was going to pick you up, did you? I reserve the right to call upon old-fashioned chivalrous behavior when it suits me."

"When do I get to exercise some old-fashioned male dominance?"

"When I deem it's appropriate. See you at six-thirty sharp."

"I'll be there."

"Love you." For Destini to say that during working hours meant she was out of earshot of anyone from her department, including Dave.

"You say that because I let you take advantage of me."

"You do, and I love that about you."

"I love you, too."

"I know," Destini said before she terminated the call.

***

The Butcher watched the summer-dressed joggers run through Tom McCall Waterfront Park on the west bank of the Willamette River. The waterfront park ran the length of downtown Portland and paralleled the sensuous curve of the Willamette River that runs north, separating east from west in the most populated city in the state of Oregon. It was a clear Northwest sunny day; albeit a bit warm for an evening run in the Willamette Valley. The cherry blossoms lining the park were in full bloom. Mount Taber could be seen to the east along the city's breathtaking skyline. Snowcapped Mount Saint Helens to its right and snowcapped Mount Hood to its left were visible, as well. The Butcher had completed his run and cool down about ten minutes prior to camping out on a park bench to partake of the summer feast. People were everywhere, enjoying the day in a laid-back state of mind. The Willamette River glistened like sparkling diamonds from the beaming northwest sun. A gentle kiss of blue sky yawned across the landscape like a billowing blanket before coming to rest on the scenic Portland landscape.

After his mother died of a drug overdose, he became a young orphan of an already homeless family. The Butcher did what he needed to do to survive, including some things that would make the average person nauseous. He learned to ride the rails. He found odd jobs here and there, but most of the time his survival depended on the kindness of strangers. He was panhandling in Denver, Colorado when a kind gentleman asked if he could buy him lunch. The Butcher accepted his offer with a fierce warning to his potential benefactor that if he tried anything creepy, he would break the stranger's nose. The man laughed at him and promised that he wouldn't.

They talked over lunch. It turned out the man had been watching him for a couple of days. He explained to The Butcher that he and his wife couldn't have children, and they had been thinking about adopting. They had also talked about helping homeless children find a home. The more he and his wife discussed the possibilities, the more they realized: why not start with their own home. The man asked The Butcher if he would be interested in coming to live with them.

The Butcher couldn't believe his ears. He kept questioning the man to try to determine if there were some dark ulterior motives that he might be missing. He took the gamble and it paid off.

The Butcher made the most of his opportunity. After a year of living with his new family, they officially adopted him, giving him a hyphenated version of their surname. After a while, he no longer felt like the child of his birth parents but more like the son his stepparents always wanted. One day, he asked them: if they had given birth to him, what would they have named him? They told him. He asked to have his name legally changed to their wishes. They did so. He felt reborn. He has been known by the name ever since.

He did some acting while in high school to impress a girl he liked. He found he enjoyed it. What it amounted to in his mind was becoming an accomplished liar. He had mastered the art of lying during his homeless period, as a survival instinct. He would practice on any and everyone from a complete stranger to his stepparents as an extension of exercising his craft, as he saw it. He once talked a Nevada State Trooper out of giving him a speeding ticket by convincing him that he was the governor's son. How foolish the trooper must have felt when he discovered the governor only had two daughters. Why suffer the consequences of an inconvenient truth when a credible lie could sweep it all clean? That was his flexible philosophy; one that had served him well.

The Butcher did well in school, excelling in the sciences. He graduated from medical school. Instead of going into the private sector, he felt the call to join the armed forces. There, he excelled, as well. He served admirably during combat as a medic in both Afghanistan and Iraq. When the time came for him to re-up for a third tour, he opted out. It wasn't until his stepparents died in a tragic boating accident during one of their out-of-the-way fishing trips that he realized he had some unfinished business.

He had contemplated, off and on, the plight of his birth parents. Sometimes the memories made his anger boil over to physical violence. That anger stood in the way of him ever maintaining a romantic relationship. In time, he had learned to channel his anger through exercise and sports; but not enough that he could trust himself to invite anyone special into his life. After the death of his stepparents, that process was no longer enough. He came to believe that his stepparents' deaths served a greater purpose. There was something he needed to do in order to put those demons to rest.

The Butcher zeroed in on one particular jogger. He glared from behind dark sunglasses at the man he was convinced was responsible for the descent of his mother from a respectable woman to the whore, prostitute, and drug addict she became. The jogger was a lean man with wiry white hairs that covered his bare, pale chest. The man did warm-up stretches, leaning into his lean, six-two legs which stuck out of his extra-long black jogging shorts. A colorful do rag that covered most of his more-salt-than-pepper hair had already started to stain with sweat. The Butcher didn't need to get closer to know the man's face. He remembered him from his childhood; but, more recently, from following him around to determine his routines. The man in his sights had steely gray eyes that seemed to burn right through you when he looked at you.

His face was hairless and lean and sharp and was poised for serious debate.

Nicholas Burnhouse was the Northwest Senior Executive President of The Private Financial Group for one of the nation's largest banks. The Butcher knew him from another time. He knew Burnhouse from when he was a loan officer at a community bank in Portland. Burnhouse was in charge of his birthparent's' home loan. The loan officer had a lustful interest in his mom that even as a child The Butcher noticed, even if he wasn't clear on what it meant; an interest that wasn't quelled by the fact that Burnhouse was married with two children. After his father died, Burnhouse wasted no time exploiting his mother's inability to keep up her house mortgage payments. Burnhouse agreed to defer those payments in exchange for sexual favors from his mother, The Butcher later learned.

After a quarter of a year, Burnhouse tired of his mother and discarded her like a disposable diaper. Burnhouse also decided to force his mom to make good on her deferred home loan payments. His mom, of course, could not. Burnhouse threatened to foreclose if she didn't. His mom threatened to tell Burnhouse's wife. Burnhouse laughed at his mom. He told her to tell her, if she wanted. Burnhouse told his mom that she wasn't the first and that she wouldn't be the last. Burnhouse also said that if his wife wanted to leave him, he could care less, as long as she took those two brats with her.

Burnhouse's wife did divorce him and took with her their two children. The Butcher's research revealed that his ex accepted a very healthy divorce settlement rather than child support and alimony on the condition that Burnhouse stay away from her and their children. From all reports, Burnhouse heartily agreed with the provision. Burnhouse never remarried. He seemed content being a bachelor who had no trouble finding much younger female companionship.

Burnhouse began his run. The Butcher would give him a couple of minutes to make certain Burnhouse didn't bail for some reason, such as an injury or lack of will. Once The Butcher was confident Burnhouse would complete his run, he rushed to a nearby motel room he had rented. There he would prepare himself to execute the next stage of his plan.

***

I paid our cover just before seven and Destini and I walked in holding hands. Destini looked exquisite, wearing a pleated, strapless lavender taffeta dress that matched my shirt. It was a weekday and Jimmy Mak's was filled with lively patrons. Dave would later mention that he was glad he had the forethought to reserve a table. Otherwise, we would have been out of luck.

We spotted Dave Liederman and his presumed mystery girlfriend waiting for us at a dining table near center stage. When we made our way to their table, we came face-to-face with something that was both amusing and unnerving to every man. Dave was wearing a twilight navy cotton poplin blazer with very fine pinstripes, a cotton pink and purple check button-down collar shirt, and relaxed straight-leg dark indigo jeans—no tie. His girlfriend was wearing a bright fuchsia floral-printed pleated satin dress that (Destini and Renita had taught me) had a paper bag waist. Even the casual observer could tell their clothes matched. It stood to reason that Dave's girlfriend had dressed him in the same way Destini had dressed me. Dave was not the kind of man who would normally go along with the whole dress-alike scenario. That may have been all of the evidence we needed to be convinced of how serious Dave was about this woman with long, straight brown hair, olive skin, high cheekbones, dark brown eyes, and a pleasant smile.

"Glad you made it," Dave said as he stood with his apparent date.

"We wouldn't have missed it," Destini said.

"Allow me to introduce you to Nora Doucette. Nora, this is my partner, first-rate Homicide Detective Destini Pendleton."

"Nice to meet you," Nora said. "Dave has told me so much about you."

"And this guy is…what's your name again, fellow?" Dave said in jest.

"C. J., the ex-college boyfriend you didn't want Dave to know about," I said to Nora. Nora laughed.

"If you were ever my boyfriend, I wouldn't have forgotten you," Nora said, displaying her pleasant smile.

"I like her," I said.

"He's easy," Destini said about me. "Trust me, I know."

Everyone laughed. I smiled. Destini and I have great instincts when it comes to people. I could tell by the way that Destini was smiling back at Nora that Destini had taken to her. I was certain Dave noticed that about Destini, too. Having Destini's approval meant a lot to him. He wouldn't have been embarrassed to admit it. They were more than professional partners. They were dear friends. I always believed that if I weren't in the picture, Destini and Dave would be the couple I would be having dinner with.

"Please, let's sit down," I said. After we sat, the ladies ordered wine and Dave and I ordered sodas. We were driving. I draped my arm around the back of Destini's chair. Dave did the same with Nora.

"I guess you're dying to know how we met," Dave said.

"I'm not, but she is," I said, giving a quick jerk of my head in Destini's direction.

"How did you two meet?" Destini asked, ignoring my dig.

"I was in town visiting some old friends," Nora said.

"Were any these old friends male?" I interrupted.

"C. J." Destini had that 'behave yourself' tone in her voice; or was it 'don't be an asshole'? Sometimes I get the two confused.

"I'm just trying to get specifics, honey."

"A couple of them were," Nora confessed.

"We've already been down that road. There's no one in her past for me to worry about. Not even you."

"Forget those two," Destini said. "They'll be going at each other all night."

"Not *all* night," Dave said.

"An hour or two, tops."

"As you were saying," Destini said to Nora, dismissing Dave and me with a wave of her hand.

"Since I was in the area, I popped into our downtown store to see how things were going."

"Doucette Imports," Dave filled in.

"You own Doucette Imports?" Destini more reiterated than asked.

"Our family maintains controlling interest in Doucette Imports. I'm an active member of the board of directors. We've been in the import/export business for four generations."

"You're beautiful, successful, and obviously brilliant; so explain to me, Nora: why are you with this guy?"

Nora laughed before answering me. "Because he's charming, witty, handsome, and just plain adorable."

"Do you hear that, C. J.? Adorable. Now there's a word I'll bet no one's ever used to describe you."

"Not since I was a kid."

"C. J. can be adorable." Destini playfully pinched me on the cheek. "Now doesn't happen to be one of those times. If you two don't mind, I would like to hear the rest of the story of how Dave and Nora met."

"In other words," Dave said, "Nora dropped in for a surprise inspection." I nodded in agreement with Dave.

"It was no such thing," Nora mildly protested. "I've known the manager since I was a teenager, and I simply stopped by to say hello."

"That's her story and she's sticking to it," I said. Dave agreed with a smile.

"Are you two going to shut up, or am I going to have to give you a time out?" Dave and I put our hands up in mock surrender to Destini.

"So that's how you get them to behave," Nora said.

"Children sometimes need a firm hand. As you were saying?" Destini returned her full attention to Nora.

"I was in the store when in walked this tall, dashing man. I took one look at him and I knew he was the one."

"I thought this was a story about how you and Dave met," I said. Nora laughed. "As flattering as that was for you to say, you and I can never be."

Dave chuckled. "I'll agree with that."

"Will you two shut up already?" Destini said.

"Yes, dear," I said.

"Yes, Lieutenant," Dave said.

"Please continue," Destini said.

"I walked up to this tall, dashing man I now know as Dave," Nora said. Dave stuck out his tongue at me. I chuckled. "And I asked if there was anything I could help him find. And he said—"

"I believe I've found it," Dave said. "The question is, are you married?"

Dave and Nora gazed into each other's eyes.

"And I said no, I'm not," Nora said.

"Are you seeing anyone?" Dave said.

"At the moment, you."

"It was then that I asked her out on our first date. Fortunately for me, she said yes."

"And we've been seeing each other ever since."

There was a lull in the conversation. I knew Dave was seeing Nora in the same light that I saw Destini. It was at that moment I decided to put away my playful gibes.

"He really said that 'I believe I've found it' line?" Destini said.

"It wasn't *what* he said. It was *how* he said it that made him irresistible." Nora was still gazing into Dave's eyes. When they kissed, Destini looked at me and smiled. I gave Destini an approving nod and smiled back. We were bearing witness to the kind of love most people want, but few discover. It felt good to be in such company.

Nora and Dave went on to tell us about their first meeting and a lot more with a passionate excitement that only true love can bring. Nora was forthcoming about herself during our casual conversation. She had grown up between Europe and the United States, having been educated in both places. Nora elaborated on the proud history of Doucette Imports, begun by her great-grandfather back in a small shop in London to become a premier international import/export business with offices all over the world. Regaling us with wonderful stories about her exploits abroad and a few right here at home, Nora Doucette proved to be worldly, personable, and intelligent and just right for Dave (as Destini later put it to me when I was driving her home).

At one point, the conversation excluded Dave and me. Nora and Destini had become instant girlfriends and were behaving as such by ignoring us men. Dave and I interjected something into the conversation every now and then. For the most part, we listened and spoke when we were spoken to.

We were enjoying our meals and comfortable four-way conversation when the digital version of Wynton Marsalis "New Orleans" was halted. A dapper Master of Ceremonies took the stage as the house lights dimmed and the stage lights brightened. The instruments had been set up while we were there, but there was no sign of the performers. When the MC announced that the scheduled band could not make it due to health reasons, there was a collective moan. The MC sympathized before he began his buildup of their replacement. By the time the MC introduced The Music Makers featuring Holland "Smoky" Jenkins and Winston Davis, the crowd was ecstatic.

Dave was as much a jazz aficionado as I was. Dave used the appearance of The Music Makers as an opportunity to educate Nora on the world of jazz. I had done the same thing with Destini during our early courtship. We were witnessing musical history and neither of us could contain our excitement. Nora and Destini soaked up our enthusiasm, enjoying the moment as much as we were. On this night, Winston switched between the saxophone and stand-up bass. Smoky played the electric piano. We were not disappointed. The Music Makers received more than one well-deserved standing ovation during their performance.

At the night's end, we parted company with the spring couple under a velvety, royal blue, starlit summer sky. Destini and Nora agreed to call each other and make plans for when all of us could get together again. The ladies concluded that if it were left to Dave and me, it would never happen. They were almost right. Closer to the truth is that it would rarely happen if things were left up to their men. I drove Destini home, accepting a gracious invitation from her to spend the night.

***

As The Butcher removed Burnhouse's heart, he recapped in his mind how well his plan had worked. The Butcher had parked his car a few stalls down from Burnhouse's Jaguar XKR convertible. He waited for Burnhouse with an unfolded Portland city map sprawled out over his dashboard. The moment The Butcher saw Burnhouse exit the elevator, he stepped out of his car, folding his map. The Butcher was the picture of a frustrated tourist who couldn't find his way around. He walked by Burnhouse as he opened the trunk of his car to grab a spare towel. There were no surveillance cameras in the parking garage to be concerned about.

"Can you help me?" The Butcher said, sounding flustered in an excellent but fake Midwestern accent. Burnhouse eyed him. The Butcher could see in his eyes that Burnhouse had no recognition as to who was addressing him.

"Yes," Burnhouse said, annoyed, as he closed the trunk, toweling himself off.

"Can you tell me where this place is that they call 'Portland's Living Room'?" The Butcher said, keeping up the act. Burnhouse gave him a derisive smile. He could tell that Burnhouse saw him as some out-of-town bumpkin who couldn't find his way to the Rose Garden if he were standing in front of it.

"You take the elevator—" The Butcher aimed the tranquilizer pistol he had been holding behind his back and shot Burnhouse below the clavicle with a tranquilizer dart before Burnhouse could finish his sentence. Burnhouse was too stunned to move or speak. He groggily reached his hand up to extract the dart. The Ketamine was already at work. The Butcher had used enough to drop a horse.

Burnhouse teetered forward. The Butcher caught him in his arms. He grabbed the keyless entry remote from Burnhouse's hand and dragged his prey around to the passenger side of the vehicle as if he were a drunken friend. The Butcher opened the passenger door and shoved Burnhouse inside. He positioned Burnhouse in an upright-seated position and slammed the door.

The Butcher returned to his car to grab a gym bag from his passenger seat. As he grabbed the gym bag, a couple of loud-talking teens entered the garage from a stairwell nearest Burnhouse's car. The teenagers headed his way. The Butcher remained calm and got into his car. He pretended to be rooting around for something in his glove compartment. The teenagers walked past him without appearing to notice him. More importantly, they didn't seem to notice Burnhouse slumped over in the passenger seat of his car. The teenagers disappeared around a corner of parked cars. The Butcher listened and waited. He heard their car start up. They drove past him with rap music blaring, heading for the exit still not noticing him or his anesthetized victim.

Once he was certain the coast was clear, The Butcher wasted no time. He locked up his car and jumped into Burnhouse's. He removed a pair of dark sunglasses and a Portland Beaver's baseball cap from his gym bag. He put them on Burnhouse. From the same gym bag, he removed and put on a pair of dark sunglasses and a Portland Trailblazer's baseball cap. Then he started up the Jaguar. The safety belts locked in place. It helped keep Burnhouse upright. He reclined the passenger seat enough to help prevent Burnhouse's limp body from flopping about. The Butcher drove home without a hitch.

Once Burnhouse's car was stored in his garage, The Butcher reviewed the final part of his plan as he removed Burnhouse's liver. He would text for pickup of the transplantable organs, expecting everything to go as smoothly as usual. He would load the vehicle and abandon it at an inconspicuous dumpsite. Then, as before, he would make an anonymous call to the Portland Police Homicide Department to let them know where to find Burnhouse's remains. The Butcher would make certain to speak to Detective Vasquez this time. He believed there was an unspoken rapport between them that he trusted. He wasn't delusional in thinking that they had a romantic connection or that she had some sympathetic understanding of his motivation to kill. Vasquez was pleasant to talk to and excellent at her job. Not like the time he spoke to Detective Whimple, whom he did not like or trust. Whimple reminded him of the type of people he was killing.

The Butcher could not foresee any immediate obstacles to his plans. There were rumors the FBI had been called in to help capture him. He found no evidence to that effect, although he was surprised that they hadn't been. If the FBI were involved, he was confident that America's most elite domestic crime fighting organization would have no more success finding him than local authorities. However, he did discover that C. J. Cavanaugh had become part of the home team trying to catch him. The Butcher had discreetly asked around about Cavanaugh. What he discovered more intrigued than concerned him. Cavanaugh was a great bloodhound. The problem, even for a good bloodhound, is when there is no scent, there is no trail. So far, he hadn't even left a whiff of himself behind for anyone to follow.

It was almost over. A long-awaited self-imposed justice was almost complete for the undue suffering caused his beloved birthparents. Soon he would be able to retire The Butcher forever and get on with a normal life.

CHAPTER SIXTY-FOUR

The Butcher checked his inexpensive watch, which held a glow in the dark face that he didn't currently need. 8:06, it read. Detective Vasquez was due in at eight. He knew about Vasquez's start time because he had phoned the PPB front desk earlier, pretending to be the distraught spouse of a murder victim in dire need of a case update from the detective.

After returning the Jaguar to a parking space near where he had abducted Nicholas Burnhouse, The Butcher was able to get into his car unnoticed and drove away. The Butcher had left his car in the garage overnight. He relocated to a parking garage with no security cameras at the opposite end of downtown Portland of where the Jaguar was parked. The Butcher turned on his fourth disposable cell phone and telephoned Detective Vasquez. Angel picked up after the third ring.

"We're going to have to stop meeting like this, Detective, or people are going to talk," The Butcher said after Angel identified herself.

"Why don't we meet face-to-face. I'll buy you a beer. That'll give them something to talk about."

"I'm sure you'd like that."

"I look forward to it."

The Butcher had to give Detective Alvarez credit. She was doing a good job of sounding chummy. He knew she was attempting to keep him on the line long enough to trace his call.

"Let's get down to it, shall we?"

"Sure; mind if I ask a couple of questions first?"

The Butcher ignored Angel's ploy. "You'll find a frost-blue Jaguar XKR convertible in the parking garage on 3rd and Alder near Waterfront Park. The car is parked on the fourth level. You can't miss it."

"Hold on."

"Included with the remains are the usual amenities."

"I'll need to get a pen to write this down."

"Let's hope your memory is good enough." The Butcher hung up, turned off the cell phone, and tossed it into the glove compartment.

After a weighty sigh, he started his car and headed for home. The Butcher had to admit he was tired. Between preparing Burnhouse's remains and cleaning up his facilities afterwards, it had taken him all night.

To help him stay awake, he turned on his car radio. It was tuned to a station that he liked that played music from the sixties to the eighties. The song "Make It With You" by Bread came on. His mother loved that song. The first time he heard it was when his mom played the 45 while tidying up after him. When he asked her about the music, his mom explained that it was the song she and his father had their first dance to at their wedding. After he expressed his displeasure at dancing as "Yuck," his mom swept him up in her arms and waltzed him around the room singing "Make It With You" to him. He could still see the glow of joy in his mother's eyes, and the bright light of her smile. He could still feel the tenderness of her body pressed against his, and her warm breath on his face as she blissfully sang in her marginal singing voice, concluding her version of the song by giving him a raspberry on his cheek. The memory brought tears to his eyes. The Butcher couldn't stop the flow of tears even after he pulled over to toss the disposable cell phone down a nearby storm sewer.

***

I dropped Destini off at work the morning after we met Nora Doucette. My terrier twins were excited to see me when I got home. So much so, that they joined me on my morning run without any coaxing. I attended to my pets after my cooldown, showered, shaved, and had a light breakfast. The Butcher was the farthest thing from my mind as I fed my tropical fish after dressing for work. The telephone rang. It was Angel. They had found another body.

***

The Jaguar was discovered where The Butcher had said it would be, according to Angel. Renita and I again waited until Angel and McCaskill and all official crime scene investigative personnel were finished gathering information. Once again, not one immediate clue became available to any of us. We all came up empty, on our criminal. We walked away knowing only the victim's identity; the same result as the three previous murders. Our thin hopes of discovering any criminal leads rested upon the hopeful findings of the crime lab and the ME's office.

The mood at the crime scene was gloomy, to say the least. There wasn't even any gallows humor to lighten the mood. Always the eternal optimist, even Angel was feeling frustrated and irritable at the lack of progress. I couldn't blame her. I was beginning to lose hope of capturing the killer, myself.

CHAPTER SIXTY-FIVE

It had been a couple of days since the discovery of Nicholas Burnhouse's remains. We were waiting on the official police report from Angel and McCaskill. Our own investigation had netted us nothing. Our shallow pool of potential suspects dried up all but for one person. John Bell was nowhere to be found. According to our research, the son of Richard and Anne Bell had dropped off the face of the earth.

Richard Bell had been one of the Lunsford unfortunates to die in a hunting-related accident during the gluttonous reign of Kylie Preston. I had asked for help from a buddy in the FBI. He worked out of the D.C. office and specialized in locating missing persons. It had been a few days and still no word from him. I knew that these things took time. Since he was doing it as a favor for me off the clock, who was I to complain. With nothing else to go on, I felt like a lovesick teenager awaiting a call from that special girl.

Renita and I had made ourselves comfortable in my office to consider what our next move might be in trying to unmask the killer. We were having hot tea and pumpkin muffins to help sweeten the session. We had done all we could in regards to weeding out people closest to the victims. We were discussing widening our net to interview people who may have had a fleeting acquaintance with any of the deceased.

The office door opened and in walked Shawn Calloway. I was surprised it had taken him this long to pay us a visit. I was in the mood for something to break the monotony of our discussion. One glance at Renita proved that she was feeling the same.

"Muffins," Shawn said, stepping into my office as if it were his own. Shawn reached for a muffin. Renita slapped his hand away.

"Judging by your upbeat disposition, I take it you're off the hook for the Baker murder?" I said.

"Not even a person of interest any longer." Shawn sounded disappointed.

"How'd it feel being the prime suspect in a murder investigation?"

"C. J., the man in me was terrified. The reporter in me was intrigued."

I nodded my understanding.

"That must have blown a hole in your dual prospective angle."

"That ship sailed before I could even untie the moorings, Renita. I've been in the hard news business for a while, and even I'm surprised at how fast a hot story can cool."

"That's good for you," I said. "I mean, in terms of your reputation."

"Yeah, it is. Enough about me; what's the deal with The Butcher?"

"Could you be more specific?"

"Let's not play games, C. J. He killed Nicholas Burnhouse, a bigshot President of a major bank, not to mention one of our most prominent citizens."

"Just because Burnhouse was wealthy and powerful didn't mean he was a prominent citizen."

"In today's world it does, Renita," Shawn said.

"The Butcher hasn't been confirmed as the killer," I said.

"Sounds like someone's a little slow on the uptake; my sources at PPB tell me different."

"We couldn't even tell you for certain that a man's doing the killings," I said.

Shawn noticed both the sincerity and frustration in my statement. "Seriously?"

"Dead serious," Renita said. "No pun intended."

"None taken. Has the FBI been called in?"

I reflected on my call to my FBI connection. "Not that we're aware of. If this keeps up, I don't see how it can be avoided."

"Can I quote you on that?"

"Sure. It'll probably carry more weight with your readers if you get the same quote from the mayor or Chief of Police."

"Good point. You don't have any leads on The Butcher?"

I grabbed the Portland white pages out of my lower left drawer and handed it to Shawn. "Take your pick. That's as close as we've come to pinning down a suspect."

Shawn let out a low whistle as he laid the telephone directory on my desk. "Are Angel and McCaskill as far off the green as you two?"

"You'll have to ask them," Renita said. "Or maybe you could check with your inside sources at the PPB."

"Is that a yes?" Shawn was trying to coerce a damning statement from us regarding the homicide detectives.

"It means," I said, "that we cannot speak for Detectives Vasquez and McCaskill on the state of their investigation."

Shawn smiled. "It was worth a shot."

"No, it wasn't." Renita flashed a counterfeit grin at Shawn.

"I've got to run if I'm going to get anything worth writing about on The Butcher. Dinner tonight?" Shawn said to Renita. "Six o'clock at the restaurant of your choice."

"No," Renita said, not sounding the least bit interested.

Shawn handed Renita one of his business cards. "Call me anytime, day or night. My personal number's on the back."

Renita tossed the business card into my trashcan.

"I know. You need time to think about us."

"No, I don't."

"I'm sure you do."

"No, I don't."

"Do you like roses?"

"Get out."

"Until next time, my sweet." With that, Shawn left. I smiled at Renita.

"What are you smiling about?"

"Calloway's not going to give up. He likes you."

"The feeling is not mutual—at least, not in a romantic way."

"I know that and you know that. He doesn't."

"That's his problem."

"You're enjoying the attention."

"I am not."

"Yes you are."

"You're being ridiculous, and I get plenty of attention from men a lot hotter than Shawn."

"You need to muzzle Calloway or he's not going to stop coming on to you."

"And how do you suppose I do that? Shoot him?"

"Nothing that drastic."

"Why don't you have a talk with him on my behalf, since you're so concerned."

"I'd gladly do so if I thought it'd do any good. Anything I'd have to say to Shawn about his waste of time trying to date you goes in one ear and out the other."

"You're making way too much out of this. Shawn will eventually meet somebody and move on."

"Eventually is the key word. In the meantime, to him, you are that somebody."

"Whatever."

"When you're serious about poisoning his well of affection for you, let me know. I have a few tricks that'll send him packing."

"I'm serious now."

"I've seen you more forceful when you've wanted Booker and Andrew to leave you alone than you were with Calloway just now. And you love my dogs."

"What are you trying to say, C. J.?"

"I've already said it. You're flattered by his infatuation."

"I am not. How many times do I have to tell you that?"

I could see in her eyes that her denial was false. "Yes, you are. And why shouldn't you be? Shawn is a decent-looking, smart, talented, successful guy who's enamored with you."

"He's not my type."

"He doesn't see it that way."

"If you have a point, please get to it, because you're making me question your sanity right now." Renita grinned. I smiled.

"Persistency is in Calloway's nature. It's part of what makes him a good reporter. You're enjoying his attention now, but there'll come a time when Shawn is going to become a real nuisance if you don't slam the door on his romantic notions."

"You mean like you've done with me."

I didn't see that coming. I looked away from Renita, ashamed that I had made her feel that way. I didn't know what to do or say about it. There was no apologizing for my short-circuiting Renita's advances in what must have been, from her perspective, at times callous rejection. It was necessary for the preservation of my relationship with Destini. Without intending to, I had already put into practice (on her) my unsolicited advice about what Renita should do about Shawn.

"And I thought my girlfriends watched too many advice and counseling shows." Renita gave a half-hearted chuckle. Her comment burned away enough of my embarrassment that I could look Renita in the eyes. "Do you mind if we drop this ridiculous conversation and get back to doing some investigative work on finding a serial killer?"

"As you wish," I said, relieved at the welcome change of subject.

"And whatever you do, Renita, don't tell Ernest about Shawn."

Renita and I both knew that if Ernest discovered that Shawn was pursuing Renita, Ernest would kill him. Neither of us wanted to see Calloway dead or Ernest go to prison.

"My lips are sealed."

CHAPTER SIXTY-SIX

McCaskill delivered to our office a complete copy of the Nicholas Burnhouse police report just four days after his murder.

"That was quick," I said to McCaskill as she handed me the inch-thick folder.

"Everyone worked round the clock on this one," McCaskill said.

"And?"

"Nothing: no prints, no DNA, no fibers; nothing." McCaskill sounded disheartened. "This guy might as well be a ghost, from what we've got on him."

"I hear you."

While McCaskill still wasn't happy about Renita and me working her murder cases, she had mellowed on the open hostility. I didn't kid myself into believing for one second that McCaskill had come to accept us. I knew the Captain had a conversation with her regarding his expected cooperation. I wouldn't be surprised if Angel hadn't reinforced that mindset with a brief lecture on collaborative professionalism before she asked McCaskill to hand deliver their report; a report that could have been emailed. If McCaskill was going along with the program, it wasn't due to some goodwill gesture on her part. It most likely was for the sake of her career.

"Where's Angel?" I asked.

"Grabbing our lunch."

"Is she buying?"

"Not today," McCaskill said with a genuine smile that vanished no sooner than it appeared. "Any messages you want me to deliver?"

"Keep the faith."

"Yeah," McCaskill said with a smirk. "I was thinking more along the lines of a lead."

"No."

McCaskill stared at me. I could tell she was biting her tongue, holding back on some gibe remark about my overrated investigative prowess. At the moment, I wasn't certain that I wouldn't agree with her.

"If we don't come up with something real soon, the Captain is going to be forced to call in the FBI," McCaskill said, as if she'd rather have her wisdom teeth extracted. I nodded in acknowledgment of how doing such a thing could damage a law enforcement officer's pride. Since I left the DEA, I no longer felt territorial about any of my investigations. I didn't care who got credit for it. Capturing this criminal was my only concern.

"Can I offer you some coffee?"

"No thanks," McCaskill said with a slight smile. "I'd better get back. Believe it or not, Angel and I have other cases we have to work. Cases we're making headway on."

"I'm surprised the Captain didn't have you pass those off to other detectives so that you could concentrate on The Butcher."

"He would have if we had any leads." McCaskill seemed almost embarrassed to admit it.

"We'll catch him. Maybe not today or tomorrow, but somewhere down the road, we'll catch him."

McCaskill nodded. "Let us know if you come up with anything."

"Will do."

McCaskill left. I watched her go. For the first time, McCaskill looked vulnerable to me. Her posture was that of someone who appeared defeated. The bravado was gone. A large dose of crime-solving limitations will do that to anyone. The Butcher was humbling us all.

I leafed through the Burnhouse file. As in previous police reports, it not only contained Angel and McCaskill's work, but forensics and the ME's as well. Renita walked in about fifteen minutes after McCaskill had left. Renita had been shopping and had a variety of store bags to prove it. I had read McCaskill's report and started reading Angel's.

"Is that the police report?" Renita popped into my office holding her shopping bags. Judging by her glow, a shopping spree had lifted her spirits.

"Yep."

"Anything interesting?"

"Not as far as I can see. Which report do you want first?" I had already separated the reports in categories of detective, forensic, and ME.

"I'll take the ME's report; might as well get the worst of it out of the way."

I attempted to hand Renita the copy of the ME's report. Renita went to grab it before realizing her hands were full. She rushed to her office and dropped off her bags. I was still holding the report aloft when Renita returned to retrieve it.

"You're not going to believe what happened," Renita was bubbling with enthusiasm. "I found the perfect pair of shoes to go with this new dress I've been dying to wear."

I stared blankly at my partner.

"You're not interested in my shoes discovery, are you?" Renita dialed it down.

"No, although I am happy for you."

"I'll get going on the ME file."

"Thank you." No sooner had my partner cleared my doorway than I was back at reading through Angel's report.

CHAPTER SIXTY-SEVEN

We did on the Burnhouse investigation what we had done on the three previous murders. We interviewed everyone connected to the victim, spoke to and viewed forensic and ME's evidence, and searched for a connection with Lunsford Insurance, specifically regarding the hunting accident cases. Our results gave credence to McCaskill's flippant theory that The Butcher was a ghost. In the end, we still had nothing to go on.

***

The Butcher remembered watching their hopes and expectations ripped from them as a child. He had witnessed his mom's spirit torn from her like skin from flesh. His mother seemed to descend deeper into distress at each downward spiral their lives took. At the time, his mother needed money to pay the mortgage. Tino Gallo was the biggest and most ruthless loan shark in the city. His mother had nowhere else to turn. She had tried every legitimate means to obtain a loan or extension on her mortgage. Gallo agreed to loan his mother the money at thirty cents on the dollar. If she didn't pay up within a week, the rate would climb five cents on the dollar for every week she was late. When the inevitable occurred and his mom could not keep up the payments, Gallo made arrangements so that his mom could work it off in trade.

Prostitution was something his mother could not do without a way to numb the humiliation. At first, she used alcohol as her anesthesia. When that stopped working on its own, she added marijuana to the mix. A short step later found her shooting up heroin. Whatever money his mom could make as a prostitute went more and more into her veins and less for loan payments and their necessities. Her drug addiction robbed his mother of her good looks and attractive body. By the time she plummeted to the point of being undesirable, she had become a liability to Gallo. He wasted no time discarding her like trash, as did most of her johns.

They lost their home. They lost their possessions. Above all else, they lost their dignity and self-esteem. They were living on the street when he and his mom managed to hustle enough money to get them a motel room for a couple of days. The Butcher had gone out to buy them something to eat. He returned to find his mother dead from a heroin overdose. The hypodermic syringe was still stuck in her arm, hanging from one of her few remaining good veins like an unquenchable manmade mosquito. For the longest time, The Butcher could only stare at the pale, withered corpse of his mother, sobbing and praying that his tear-filled eyes were deceiving him.

The Butcher shook his head to clear away the agonizing memory. He wiped the warm tears (which the recollection could still evoke) from his cheeks. From his Toyota Camry, he could see the entrance to the Red Dog Lounge from where he was parked across the street. Tino Gallo frequented the Red Dog Lounge. It was once a beehive for illegal activity. Today it served as a dimly-lit dive for over-the-hill criminals to regale each other with redundant tales of the bad old days.

He had entered the bar once to get a feel for his prey. With his thinning blond-gray ponytail wig, fake scruffy beard, false paunch, sandals, faded jeans, and tie-dyed T-shirt, he looked the part of a middle-aged hippie who had just stepped out of the hemp-filled haze of his hippie van. The old-timers eyeballed him as if he were part monkey. A few hurled insults his way that drew laughter from the snarling crowd. Gallo was one of the instigators. The Butcher gave them an easy nod, a chilled-out smile, and a peace sign. He stepped up to the bar and ordered a cool draft. After they had their fun, the regulars went back to talking about their glory days and forgot he existed.

The Butcher was grateful he was wearing dark granny shades. It hid the incendiary rage he felt for Tino Gallo. He could mask how he felt with a false grin or a timid gesture. At times like those, when he was that close to someone he loathed as much as Gallo, his eyes could disclose his true feelings.

From what he observed, Tino Gallo had fallen into the bottle so far, he was drowning. In his prime, he was a solid-bodied, decent-looking fellow with slick black hair and a wicked sneer for a smile. Hard times, hard living, and age had combined to rob him of any physical virtues that would have made him remotely appealing. The Butcher considered allowing him to live. Allowing him to wallow in the pathetic life he had wrought for himself might have proven punishment enough. He rejected the notion that karma had already exacted his revenge. To make the circle complete, it had to be done. If a note of compassion were warranted, then he could view Tino Gallo as a mercy killing.

Ordinarily The Butcher would wait a few weeks to allow things to cool down a little from his previous kill before committing his next. He knew that everyone, including the authorities, hoped that if they couldn't catch him, then he would simply disappear. The Butcher had become anxious to conclude his revenge spree. It hadn't been as gratifying as he had expected. Taking those lives, while not leaving him with any feelings of remorse, did not give him a great sense of satisfaction. Tonight would be his final feasting from the dish best served cold.

***

The abduction went like clockwork. The Butcher had studied Gallo's routine for a couple of weeks. He waited for Gallo in a stolen van parked in the parking lot across the street from the Red Dog Lounge. While it wasn't a hippie van, it would still serve his purposes. Gallo left the Red Dog at about ten-thirty, as he did every night except for Sunday, when the bar was closed.

The Butcher stepped out of the van and waited for Gallo to come his way. The Butcher wore the hippy disguise he had worn the sole time he had patronized the Red Dog. He knew the disguise would give Gallo a false sense of familiarity and comfort. Gallo staggered by the parking lot on his way to his low-rent apartment, just as The Butcher knew he would. The Butcher asked Gallo for a light for his joint. Gallo gave The Butcher a smirk. "Fucking hippie," Gallo said to him as he offered The Butcher a light from his silver lighter with its diamond-studded horseshoe. The Butcher jabbed a hypodermic syringe filled with Ketamine into Gallo's fat neck. Gallo was too stunned and drunk to put up a fight. The Butcher loaded Gallo into the van and hauled him home.

When The Butcher cut open Tino Gallo, he discovered his body was a medical minefield. His kidneys and liver were shot. His lungs and intestines were riddled with cancer. He had so much cholesterol built up in his arteries that a heart attack was imminent. On top of that, he had a weak heart that was near failure. His abuse of alcohol and cigarettes had so damaged his internal organs that they would be of no use to anyone. It was a wonder that Tino Gallo was still alive. From the looks of things, The Butcher estimated he might have been dead within a year; two, tops.

Nothing was worthy of donation from Gallo's decimated body. That was a reflection of his soul. The surgeon did not take the same meticulous care as he had done with his previous victims. He became more of an actual butcher rather than a surgeon, completing his procedures with less concern than if he were slaughtering a diseased animal. The more he dissected, the more The Butcher felt that his time would have been better spent whacking Tino Gallo and abandoning him in an alley for the police to find. He knew for a fact that Gallo had killed and ordered killings of people who were unceremoniously dumped in unholy places. Discarding Tino Gallo would have been poetic justice. No part of Gallo would perpetuate in another human being. He would package this vermin and deposit all of him, including his internal organs, to be disposed of by the police.

CHAPTER SIXTY-EIGHT

Renita and I were playing chess in my office. We were still solely committed to capturing The Butcher, but were fresh out of suspects, leads, and ideas. I was contemplating my next move in a well-played game when my office phone rang. I answered it, not taking my eyes off the board.

"C. J., I've got that information you requested," FBI Agent Hagibis Abutin said. I mouthed who it was to Renita. Renita left to get herself a cup of coffee.

"Great, at least one of us is making progress."

"I take it that means you haven't made any headway on The Butcher?"

"You've got it. It's been like running into a brick wall."

"I hope this helps."

Hagibis gave me a quick overview on what he'd uncovered about John Bell. When he got to the part about a family adopting him and John Bell changing his name, I was shocked. I asked Hagibis to send me all he had on Bell. He said he would e-mail the information to me right away. I thanked Hagibis and hung up. I yelled for Renita. Renita dashed in.

"*What's wrong?*"

"Lock and load." Renita stood frozen, staring at me.

"Are you serious?" Renita finally said.

"Very." Renita left, looking puzzled.

"Hey, C. J.," Shelly Morton said, sounding upbeat when he answered his office phone. "Did you call to tell me you'll be volunteering to help out at the annual picnic next Saturday?"

"Gladly. In the meantime, I need some information, and I need it fast."

"How can I help?" Shelly asked, changing his tune as he recognized the sense of urgency in my voice. Renita returned to my office with her shoulder-holstered Browning BDA .38 that she kept locked in her desk drawer.

"Do you have Weston's office and home address?" I asked Shelly.

"Wes? Yes, of course."

"Give them to me."

I heard Shelly punching keys on his computer keyboard. "What's this all about?"

"I'll explain later." Renita watched me. She was chomping at the bit to know what set me off. Shelly gave me the information. I committed it to memory and rang off. Renita and I could go through Agent Abutin's findings later. We would have plenty of time, once we had the prime suspect in custody.

"What's going on?" Renita asked as I armed myself. For me, that meant my 380 Glock and my calf-holstered Colt 32 as my backup weapon.

"We've gotta move. I'll explain everything on the way."

Renita and I bolted out of the office.

***

I explained to Renita about John Bell and Richard Allan Weston being the same person, on our way to my car.

"He's been right under our noses all along," Renita said in disbelief on the drive over to Weston's practice on SW Barbur Blvd.

"Looks that way."

"I liked that guy," Renita said. "You know, as a person."

"What's not to like? He seemed like a nice guy, and he did a fair amount of good at the community center."

"*Hello*, he's a murderer."

"We didn't know he had that character flaw, then."

"I can't believe you're so nonchalant about a serial killer," Renita said.

"Sorry, gallows mindset; it helps keep me from getting emotionally involved."

"Maybe I'll develop a sense of humor like that one day."

"I hope not."

I had Renita call Angel to let her know what we'd uncovered. Angel wasn't in. Angel had been called away on a family emergency, the detective who answered Angel's phone told Renita. When Renita asked to speak to McCaskill, the same detective told Renita that McCaskill was out to lunch. Renita thanked the detective, hung up, and called McCaskill to leave a brief message on her voicemail.

Hagibis had mentioned to me that Weston had been a medic in the Army and a butcher in civilian life. From what Hagibis had told me about Weston, he had the medical training, education, and experience to do what The Butcher had been doing to his victims. Hagibis also enlightened me about the fate of Richard Bell and the plight of Anne Bell and their only child. The fact that Richard Allan Weston was their biological son spoke to revenge as a strong motive.

***

We checked with the concierge at the Bannock Building where Weston's practice was located. The concierge hadn't seen Dr. Weston all day. We went up to Weston's suite. The door was unlocked. We walked in. There was no sign of Weston in the sparsely furnished, bare-necessities office. Renita and I rushed out, hoping we weren't too late.

***

When we arrived at Weston's house, my knuckles were tingling.

"This is it," I said.

"How can you be sure?" Renita said.

"I just know it in my gut."

"Be careful," I said to Renita as we got out of the car. "We already know this man's a killer."

"Don't forget to take your own advice."

We approached the residence with caution, keeping sharp eyes out for anything suspicious. As I walked up onto the front porch, I couldn't help but notice that the house had a morbid feel, with its blackout drapes and deep shadows. I rang the doorbell twice. There was no answer. I knocked on the door a couple of times. There was still no answer. We tried to peek inside. The drapes wouldn't allow it. Entering without permission from the owner would constitute trespassing. We weren't law enforcement. Reasonable suspicion might not save us from prosecution even if the end resulted in capturing a serial killer.

"Let's have a look around," I said to Renita. Had a trained law enforcement individual accompanied me, I would have ordered us to fan out. That not being the case with Renita, I ordered her to stay close.

We looked around the sides and the back of the house. Like the front of the house, all windows had blackout drapes. We noticed a green Toyota Camry parked in the garage that we assumed belonged to Weston. That gave us hope that our prime suspect was still around. There were no signs of life inside the house, from what we saw and heard. I decided we should go to the precinct to see if we could catch up to McCaskill. If McCaskill wasn't around, then we would tell Captain Williamsen what we knew about Richard Allan Weston aka John Bell.

***

John Bell had watched his unwelcome visitors leave. He was confident Cavanaugh and Harris hadn't noticed him when he peeked around one of the living room drapes to verify their departure. The Butcher expected Cavanaugh and Harris would return with the police. Cavanaugh leading the police right to his doorstep was a possibility he'd foreseen. What had tipped Cavanaugh off was a question to ponder another day.

John opened his secret crawlspace in his bedroom closet. The wooden chest was no longer there. He had shipped it to Milan, Italy using one of his two fake European identities a week prior to killing Tino Gallo, in anticipation of his new life in Europe. In place of the chest was a cardboard shoebox. Inside the shoebox was what he called his 'fresh life kit.' It consisted of a forged passport and a leather wallet. Inside the wallet was a variety of items, including a debit card, credit card, and driver's license, along with two thousand dollars cash.

His new passport and wallet information said he was George Clark from Bangor, Maine. He would remain George Clark until he could make it to the Cayman Islands to empty out his safe deposit box. Inside of his safe deposit box were two-hundred-thousand euros; money he would have wired to a secured account he had already opened in Milan. That would be enough money to tide over a frugal-living man for quite some time. There were also two forged European passports and two leather wallets inside the safe deposit box. The leather wallets contained all of the same counterfeit items as his American wallet, only for European identities and euros instead of dollars.

From the Caymans, John Bell would fly to Europe as George Clark, returning to a modest flat he had leased in Milan. While his Italian was decent for someone who had studied for three years, John was not gullible enough to believe that he wouldn't be identified as an American. Milan was a stopover for him to have plastic surgery that included altering his fingerprints. From Milan, he would make his way to a modest farmhouse he had purchased a couple of years earlier in rural northern Finland, to begin his life anew. Who knows? Maybe he would even get married and start a family.

John put on a pair of sharp-pressed blue jeans, a crisp white button-down dress shirt, shined black leather shoes, and a two-button, blue chambray, cotton sport coat. He checked his look in the closet door mirror. With his clean-shaven face and shaved head, he looked like a business professional in casual wear. That was the look he was going for. He put on a short brunette wig and a matching false mustache and then scrutinized his appearance again. Nothing changed. A few minor adjustments to his wig and mustache and he was ready. Years of planning was about to pay off. After pocketing a pair of dark sunglasses, John was set to leave.

***

McCaskill was at lunch, picking up her car from a garage on West Burnside. The garage was a few minutes from downtown. She had hopped on a bus to get there. Laurie had stopped at a Subway to pick up a chicken teriyaki sub on the way. She devoured the sub while she waited for the mechanic to finish with her car. The sandwich had hit the spot. Thankfully, her car only needed to have its cooling system flushed, to pass inspection. With Angel away, McCaskill hadn't bothered to mention her errand to anyone, since she was doing it during her lunch break.

Laurie called in to check her office voicemail on her way to her car. She heard Renita's urgent message about Weston and decided to check things out for herself. Rather than waste time going back to the precinct to grab an unmarked vehicle, McCaskill decided to use her own car. Laurie would have called it in, had she remembered to bring along a radio. She would phone it in using her personal cell if the lead turned out to be legitimate.

***

McCaskill went to Weston's office. He wasn't there. Laurie asked the concierge about Weston. The concierge told McCaskill the same thing he had told C. J. and Renita: that he hadn't seen Dr. Weston all day. McCaskill raced over to Weston's home. McCaskill arrived at Weston's residence about ten minutes after C. J. and Renita had left.

***

On the drive to the station, I had Renita call Shelly and ask him if he had any face pics of Weston. Shelly said that he did, on his computer. Renita had Shelly send a couple of Weston's best face shots to her cell. My guess was that Weston would be wearing a disguise if he suspected anyone was onto him. The snapshots would at least give law enforcement something to work with.

McCaskill wasn't there when we got to the downtown precinct. We informed Captain Williamsen about John Bell. The captain tried contacting McCaskill. Dispatch couldn't raise her. Dispatch informed the captain that McCaskill was not assigned a vehicle or a radio. Captain Williamsen checked the sign-out board. McCaskill was signed out for lunch. The captain asked the detectives present in the squad room if any of them knew where McCaskill went for lunch. No one had any idea. The captain decided he would fill in his young detective when she returned. I had a feeling Kelby was going to give McCaskill a dressing-down on proper procedure for an on-duty detective, as well.

"Where's Angel?" I asked.

"Her youngest had to go in for an emergency appendicitis operation," Captain Williamsen said. "Angel wanted to be with her every step of the way. I wouldn't bother her under those circumstances, even with something this important."

Renita and I nodded our accord. Captain Williamsen loaded the digital photographs we had of Weston onto his computer. Within a few minutes, he had an APB out on Richard Allan Weston, complete with a digital likeness. I asked the captain about acquiring a search warrant to scour Weston's premises. The captain said there would be time for that once they had Weston in custody, or if he discovered Weston had slipped their noose.

While I respected Kelby's judgment, in my opinion, that was a bad decision. The more time you gave Weston, the more chances he had to cover his tracks; or, worse yet, disappear. I kept my mouth shut because it wasn't my call to make. Renita and I had done all that we could. We left homicide to do what needed to be done.

***

The doorbell rang. John Bell hadn't heard any police sirens. He wondered if Cavanaugh or Harris had returned without him noticing. There was no more time to waste. He opened his nightstand drawer. From inside, he grabbed his 9 mm M9 pistol that was next to two Ketamine hypodermics. He had readied the hypos for Cavanaugh and Harris. He slipped the pistol into the back of his pants at the small of his back and covered it with his sport coat.

The doorbell rang again. John placed the hypos in his coat pocket.

"Who is it?" Bell queried from behind the door after the doorbell rang a third time.

"Detective McCaskill from the Portland Police."

John looked through the peephole. The detective was alone. "How can I help you, Detective?"

"I'd like to ask you a few questions, sir, about some suspicious happenings in the neighborhood."

John knew she was lying. She was there to arrest him. He needed to get a move on if he was going to make his escape. John cracked open the door.

"What sort of suspicious happenings?"

"May I come in?"

"May I see your ID?"

McCaskill showed John Bell her badge and ID.

"Come in."

"Thank you," McCaskill said, looking around as she stepped inside. John closed the door behind her.

"Can I offer you any refreshment, Detective?"

"No, thank you. Are you Richard Allan Weston?"

"I am."

"Mr. Weston, I have it from a reliable source that you were once John Bell."

"*John who?*"

"You know, John Bell," McCaskill said, feeling smug. "The serial killer everyone's looking for. The man they're calling The Butcher."

"You must have me confused with someone else," John said as he drew his weapon. "Hands behind your head."

"Let's not do anything rash," McCaskill said, irritated she had lost her advantage.

"Shut up! Turn around."

McCaskill turned. John disarmed McCaskill.

"Down on your knees."

"You don't want to do anything foolish." McCaskill was beginning to lose her composure.

"Shut up."

"I'm a police officer."

"I said, shut up!" John jammed the hypo into McCaskill's neck. Out of reflex, McCaskill grabbed at the hypo, trying to extract it. John pressed his weapon to the back of McCaskill's head.

"Let go," John snarled. McCaskill did as ordered, with shaking hands. John finished injecting the Ketamine into her system. It didn't take long for it to take effect. McCaskill was lying on the floor in a fetal position within minutes.

***

My knuckles tingling at Weston's house was bothering me. I suggested to my partner that we swing by Weston's house again to have another look around. Renita was game.

When we arrived, I was surprised there wasn't a patrol car staking out Weston's place. Perhaps the captain hadn't gotten around to ordering one. That was something the lead detective was responsible for, in those situations. During one of our rare moments of small talk, McCaskill had mentioned to me she was thinking about getting a new car. She felt that she had outgrown her Honda Accord. Upon further discussion on the matter, McCaskill mentioned that it was a new red Honda Civic hatchback. By coincidence, a car fitting that description was parked near Weston's home; a car that wasn't parked there before. If that was McCaskill's car, then where was McCaskill? My hope was that McCaskill hadn't gone gung ho and tried to capture Weston on her own. My knuckles were tingling again, along with a souring in the pit of my stomach.

As we approached the house from the sidewalk, I bore in mind that there was a serious possibility of an officer in trouble. Some things required one to throw out the rulebook and make things happen, damn the consequences.

I rang the doorbell twice. There was no answer. I knocked on the door twice; still no answer. I tried the doorknob. It was unlocked. An odd thought crossed my mind: didn't this guy ever lock anything? Once again, I ordered Renita to stay behind me. We entered with our weapons drawn.

The house was as quiet as an empty church. We checked all of the downstairs rooms first. It was in the downstairs bedroom that we discovered Detective Laurie McCaskill. She was flat on her back with her arms relaxed by her side. McCaskill appeared to be sound asleep. I checked her vitals. She was stable, but we couldn't wake her. I had Renita call for an ambulance while I checked the remainder of the house.

There was no one else in the house besides the three of us. I called Chief Williamsen and filled him in on the latest developments. The captain said he had already made finding Weston priority one. Every available officer was working on locating him. Security, from the airport to light rail, had been notified to be on the lookout for Weston, as well. What went unsaid was that if Weston were wearing a disguise, as we both expected, then picking him out of a crowd might require more luck than skill.

I didn't feel good about our chances of catching Weston when I hung up from talking to Kelby. It seemed as though Weston had been miles ahead of us every step of the way. Each premeditated murder had been calculated right down to the smallest detail. I had a sinking feeling his escape had been just as strategically planned.

***

John Bell had gotten what he wanted. The five people he held responsible for the disgrace of his mother and dishonoring of his father were dead. He had paid visits to the gravesites of both his biological and stepparents to say his final goodbyes. He would never set foot on American soil again. It would be too dangerous. He knew that international law enforcement would be searching for him because of what he had done. John Bell harbored no remorse. Whatever happened from here on out, he would accept. If the consequences of his actions landed him in prison for life or resulted in a death sentence, so be it. He stood by his deeds. He was not going to apologize to anyone. He certainly wasn't going to make bringing him to their so-called justice easy. Good luck in finding him. They were going to need it.

John had hopped a business-class direct flight from PDX to Atlanta with no problem, since he had made a reservation under George Clark well in advance. From Atlanta, he grabbed a shuttle flight to Miami. He caught his connecting flight from Miami to the Caymans with minimal delay. His nonstop flight to Owens Roberts International Airport in the Grand Cayman was scheduled to touch down in less than an hour. John relaxed as the plane soared above the clouds. The sky was crystal blue and the sun beamed down on an azure ocean. The seat next to him was not empty by chance. He had paid to keep it that way, in order to be left alone. Flying first class was a luxury John had never availed himself. He had opted to splurge for this special occasion.

Having a backup dissimilar escape disguise, forged passport, and false ID packed wallet-ready at a rented storage unit under the same false name turned out to be a godsend. He had intended to destroy them if his initial escape plan worked.

By now, he expected the police had found Detective Laurie McCaskill. John sincerely hoped that the PDX baggage handler he had cloned for his initial disguise would not get into any trouble on his account.

John expected the police would uncover his surgery. They may even have found out about his secret storage unit. The only secret that might survive their scrutiny was his clandestine crawlspace in his downstairs bedroom closet. Even if they found every portion of his secret life, none of it mattered. He had left nothing behind that would lead them to him, just as he had left no clues for them to find The Butcher.

"Would you like a cocktail, sir?" the flight attendant asked in a sensuous voice.

"Water, please, with a twist of lemon."

"Coming right up, sir," the attendant said with a smile before she left to serve him.

No champagne yet, Bell thought. There were still miles to go before he slept. He did have a few regrets. As Richard Allan Weston, he had made friends and a positive difference in a number of lives. He wished them well and hoped they remembered him as Wes and not as John Bell the serial killer. As John Bell, he had wanted to say goodbye to Detective Alvarez. He liked her. He had followed her tracking him in the newspapers. Because he had intimate knowledge of the crimes, he could read between the lines of her scripted statements to the press. They made him realize that Detective Alvarez was very good at her job. He respected that about anyone.

John stared out of the window, humbled by the majesty of what he saw. Richard Bell stood behind John in the cramped tool shed, instructing his son on how to make something. Anne Bell danced John around the room, singing out of key to her favorite song. John laughed with his stepparents around the dinner table at jokes only his adopted family found funny.

John reclined his seat back enough to elevate his feet. The flight attendant returned with his lemon water. He kindly thanked her before resuming his recollections. They were memories that filled him with joy instead of sorrow. In them, he found tranquility. The purging of evil from his life had worked. He already felt like a new man.

CHAPTER SIXTY-NINE

Laurie McCaskill awakened in a hospital bed. Bell had only injected Laurie with enough Ketamine to knock her out for a few hours. McCaskill thanked Renita and I for saving her. She gave a good description of the man who had accosted her. By that time, Richard Allan Weston had vanished.

The FBI was called in the next day. The mayor took the heat for doing what some described as too little, too late. That, of course, had a thunderstorm effect of drenching the police commissioner, who wasted no time taking it out on his homicide captain. Kelby accepted all blame and offered his resignation. The mayor and the police commissioner refused to accept it.

To Kelby's credit, the buck stopped with him. Aside for reaming McCaskill out for not following proper procedure while on duty, Kelby never publicly scapegoated anyone in his department for what he termed as critical mistakes on his part. After it was determined by everyone involved in the manhunt that Richard Allan Weston was no longer on U.S. soil, an international alert was put out for the man also known as John Bell. The whole scenario played out in two weeks.

Laurie McCaskill was ashamed that she had allowed Bell to escape. Had Laurie followed protocol, it probably wouldn't have happened. That part of Bell's escape did not find its way into the public record. Not even Calloway's inside sources leaked that information. McCaskill bore her shame in private, with only a trusted few privy to the truth.

The nasty business of The Butcher was in the side view mirror of our law enforcement lives; an event still closer than it appeared. The police uncovered Bell's secret underground surgical wing. A few days later, they found a rented storage unit where Bell had changed before doing a Houdini. The poor PDX baggage handler who fit McCaskill's description was released after a few hours of questioning determined he had nothing to do with The Butcher. John Bell had made good his escape. While the result was not what criminal justice required, there was a consensus that The Butcher would remain radio-silent. It was also my opinion that The Butcher was John Bell. The person who'd helped people and was liked by many was Richard Allan Weston.

In reflecting on the plight of John Bell, I couldn't help but think of the Pawnee saying that misfortunes do not flourish on one path; they grow everywhere. John Bell could not dismiss the dreadful voyage he had taken before becoming Richard Allan Weston. Had he viewed his transformation as a deliverance from a dark place instead of a calling for revenge, perhaps he could have been a vessel for life instead of death.

The disappearance of The Butcher had pricked the balloon of tension that had gripped Portland for some time. Calm settled over the city like mist on a lake. I handed over copies of the information that Hagibis had sent me to Detective Alvarez, along with my written report as to The Butcher's motives and rationale as to why Bell chose to preserve as much of his victims as possible. I left out of my report any determination regarding John Bell's state of mind. Besides it not being my job to do so, I couldn't render an opinion as to whether I believed John Bell was insane. His actions spoke to that mindset. His cold and calculating reasoning made him cognizant of what he was doing. Killing is killing; the powerful in society decide which are just or not, and who is executioner or murderer. I had killed in the line of duty. I had done so in some cases with as little sympathy as one would have for an annoying fly. Did that make me insane? Was I any different in my motivation to take a human life than John Bell?

Autumn arrived on the backs of dried leaves and shorter days. Things had returned to normal at our office; or at least as normal as they could be, considering the extenuating circumstances of The Butcher murders. Renita and I had done what we told Allison Hawkins we would. We investigated the rejected, hunting-related life insurance claims that involved Kylie Preston with the full support of Carl Wheaton. All but two of the claims had been wrongly denied. With Carl by our side, we presented our compelling evidence to the Lunsford Insurance board which consisted exclusively of the Lunsford family. They agreed with our findings and promised to do all that they could to rectify the situation for any surviving members of their maltreated policyholders. I left the meeting confident that the Lunsford family would make good on their word.

I stared out at my rectangular backyard with a cup of hot green tea in hand, wearing my ivory Egyptian cotton terry bathrobe and chocolate hard sole wool slippers. I had mowed the grass and pruned the Canadian hemlock and white Japanese wisteria yesterday; something I had felt compelled to do myself for a change, rather than assign to the gardening service I employed. The yard looked good, if I did say so myself. The combined natural fragrances were aromatically soothing. I watched the terriers play what amounted to It-tag, in my mind. I had gone for a Sunday run, earlier. Andrew and Booker had joined me in the cool morning light.

When I returned home after my cool-down, I attended to Andrew and Booker, my tropical fish, and the zebra finches. Toussaint, Coretta, Claude, and Truth were in great voices. Having set my house in order, I showered, shaved, and had a banana and peach soy yogurt.

Destini had spent the night and slept soundly in my bed. Destini was called in on a Saturday evening to a double homicide that kept her out until well past two a.m. That summons put a cramp in our movie night plans. We were going to see a special showing of Alfred Hitchcock's classic Rear Window at the independently-owned Laurelhurst Theater and Pub.

My backyard was, at times, my Zen garden. Today I would attend to my Coxswain roses and my garden of pink astilbes, red orchids, white narcissuses, and leopard's bane. As I looked out at my frolicking twins, I experienced a complete sense of harmony. It was one of those rare times when I felt at one with the universe. I would get a real breakfast started in a few minutes; the aroma of which would beckon Destini out of bed and into the kitchen. For the time being, I was going to embrace the moment.

www.ingramcontent.com/pod-product-compliance
Lightning Source LLC
Chambersburg PA
CBHW020253120726
47904CB00001B/186